NEW YORK REVIEW BOOKS
CLASSICS

THE HUMAN COMEDY

HONORÉ DE BALZAC (1799–1850), one of the greatest and most influential of novelists, was born in Tours and educated at the Collège de Vendôme and the Sorbonne. He began his career as a pseudonymous writer of sensational potboilers before achieving success with a historical novel, *The Chouans*. Balzac then conceived his great work, *La Comédie humaine*, an ongoing series of novels in which he set out to offer a complete picture of contemporary society and manners. Always working under an extraordinary burden of debt, Balzac wrote some eighty-five novels in the course of his last twenty years, including such masterpieces as *Père Goriot*, *Eugénie Grandet*, *Lost Illusions*, and *Cousin Bette*. In 1850, he married Eveline Hanska, a rich Polish woman with whom he had long conducted an intimate correspondence. Three months later he died. In addition to the present collection, NYRB Classics publishes a translation of Balzac's *The Unknown Masterpiece* and *Gambara*.

PETER BROOKS taught for many years at Yale, where he was Sterling Professor of Comparative Literature. He has written about Balzac in a number of books, including *The Melodramatic Imagination*, *Reading for the Plot*, *Henry James Goes to Paris*, and *Enigmas of Identity*. He is currently Andrew W. Mellon Scholar at Princeton and is at work on *Flaubert in the Ruins of Paris*.

LINDA ASHER has translated works by Milan Kundera, Georges Simenon, Victor Hugo, Jean-Pierre Vernant, Restif de la Bretonne, and many others. A former fiction editor at *The New Yorker*, she has been awarded the French-American Foundation, Scott Moncrieff, and ASCAP Deems Taylor translation prizes and is a Chevalier of the Order of Arts and Letters of the French Republic.

CAROL COSMAN is a translator of French literature and letters. Her work includes *Exile and the Kingdom* by Albert Camus, *Colonel Chabert* by Honoré de Balzac, *America Day by Day* by Simone de Beauvoir, *The Elementary Forms of Religious Life* by Emile Durkheim, and *The Family Idiot* (a study of Flaubert) by Jean-Paul Sartre.

JORDAN STUMP is a professor of French at the University of Nebraska–Lincoln; the author, most recently, of *The Other Book: Bewilderments of Fiction*; and the translator of some twenty works of (mostly) contemporary French prose by authors such as Marie NDiaye, Eric Chevillard, Antoine Volodine, and Jean-Philippe Toussaint. His translation of Claude Simon's *The Jardin des Plantes* won the French-American Foundation's annual translation prize in 2001.

THE HUMAN COMEDY
Selected Stories

HONORÉ DE BALZAC

Edited and with an introduction by
PETER BROOKS

Translated from the French by
LINDA ASHER
CAROL COSMAN *and*
JORDAN STUMP

NEW YORK REVIEW BOOKS

New York

THIS IS A NEW YORK REVIEW BOOK
PUBLISHED BY THE NEW YORK REVIEW OF BOOKS
435 Hudson Street, New York, NY 10014
www.nyrb.com

Library of Congress Cataloging-in-Publication Data
Balzac, Honoré de, 1799–1850.
[Comédie humaine. Selections. English]
 The human comedy : selected stories / By Honoré de Balzac ; edited and with an
Introduction by Peter Brooks ; [translated by] Linda Asher, Carol Cosman, Jordan
Stump.
    pages cm. — (New York Review Books Classics)
 ISBN 978-1-59017-664-1 (pbk.)
 I. Brooks, Peter, 1938- editor of compilation. II. Asher, Linda, translator. III. Title.
 PQ2161.W813 2014
 843'.7—dc23

                        2013026922

ISBN 978-1-59017-664-1
Available as an electronic book; ISBN 978-1-59017-698-6

Printed in the United States of America on acid-free paper.
10 9 8 7 6 5 4 3 2 1

CONTENTS

INTRODUCTION

HONORÉ DE BALZAC is known for immensity, excess, all-night writing sessions in his monk's robe sustained by countless cups of coffee, producing more than ninety novels and tales in the space of some twenty years. Rodin's great, looming sculpture suggests a visionary who wanted to capture the whole of French society of his time, and more: the forces that animated it, the principles that made its wheels spin.

It may seem a paradox, then, to link Balzac's vast *Human Comedy* to the adjective "short." We think of Balzac as long, often too long—descriptions, explanations that correspond to the leisure associated with reading nineteenth-century novels, of a length for evenings without television or smartphones. His novels are often freighted with extended presentations of things and people, and weighty excurses on every imaginable subject. He was one of the first generation of writers to make a living from his work, and the need to generate ever more of it—since he was usually in debt—drove his pen. He produced masterpieces nonetheless, though not of the chiseled, perfect sort sought by Flaubert, for instance. Balzac's claim lies rather in his capacity to invent, to imagine, to create literally hundreds of characters capable of playing out their dramas with convincing power. He stands as the first true realist in his ambition to see society as an organic system. Oscar Wilde came close to the heart of the matter when he declared: "The nineteenth century, as we know it, is largely an invention of Balzac's." Balzac "invents" the new century by being the first writer to represent its emerging urban agglomerations, its nascent capitalist dynamics, its rampant cult of the individual personality. By seeing and dramatizing changes that he mainly deplored, he initiated his readers into understanding the shape of the century. "Balzac's great glory is that he pretended hardest," declared his faithful disciple Henry James: In the art of make-believe, Balzac was the master.

Yet interspersed among the ninety-odd titles that make up *The Human Comedy* are a number of short stories and novellas that are among the best work Balzac did. Here he produces his striking effects, his thunderous climaxes, his acute psychological twists with greater economy than in the full-length novels. And he uses short fiction to try out some of his boldest imaginative flights. Here is the place to dramatize extremes of emotion: the loss of self in madness, artistic creation, and passion; the inventive forms taken by vengeance; the monomania of the artist; and, especially, the wilder shores of love, whether of a duchess, a castrato, or a panther. Somehow the short form works to liberate Balzac's imagination from the need to be "the secretary of society," as he put it. Not that society is missing here but rather that it, too, is given in its essence: as the conversation and interaction of social beings. In fact, Balzac's short fiction tends to be extraordinarily fixed on the moment of oral exchange, on the telling of and the listening to stories. In this manner he renews an age-old tradition of oral storytelling, now given a new and knowing form. These stories, which often show us humanity in extreme situations, are also about the power of storytelling—and about the effect of that power on those listening.

Take for instance "Another Study of Womankind," which opens at two o'clock in the morning. Félicité des Touches, herself a novelist, has asked the finest minds in her already select group of friends to linger after one of her large evening gatherings. The narrator, one of these chosen few, describes the scene:

Secrets artfully betrayed, exchanges both light and deep, everything undulates, spins, changes luster and color with each passing sentence. Keen judgments and breathless narrations follow one upon the next. Every eye listens, every gesture is a question, every glance an answer. There, in a word, all is perspicuity and reflection. Never did the phenomenon of speech, to which, when carefully studied and skillfully wielded, an actor or storyteller owes his glory, cast so overpowering a spell on me.

The phenomenon of speech stands at the very center of fictional creation, in the capacity to spin stories and to tell them to others. If, as Walter Benjamin tells us in "The Storyteller," the novel is the form of the solitary modern individual—and a genre that one generally reads in solitude—Balzac's many conversational tales take us back to an imagined golden age of storytelling where the living voice of the narrator is part of the story, and the reactions of listeners indicate the force of the story told and suggest also that there is a further story to be told about the relations of the tellers and the listeners. His characters evoke the spirit of an earlier age of sociability, all the while conscious that it is doomed by a world of commerce, journalism, and the devaluation of leisure. In "Another Study of Womankind," the final episode is recounted by Horace Bianchon, the medical doctor who shows up repeatedly in *The Human Comedy* (we know several other guests as well from prior appearances in other novels and tales), and its effect is briefly registered: "The tale at an end, all the women rose from the table, and with this the spell Bianchon had cast on them was broken. Nevertheless, some had felt almost cold on hearing those final words." This final tale of honor, vengeance, agony, and slow death casts a chill and breaks up the circle. Stories enchant but then leave us to meditate, alone, on their often sinister meanings.

Not only the tellers of stories but also the listeners to them are crucial here, and the scene of narrative exchange is itself dramatic. As Benjamin declared in his essay extolling the vanishing art of the oral tale, storytelling is about the transmission of wisdom. Something passes from teller to listener. It is this very process of transmission that matters to Balzac as much as the content of the tale. The act of narration can be dangerous, as the man who is about to begin telling the story of the origin of the Lanty family fortune warns the Marquise de Rochefide in "Sarrasine." But she is impatient to hear. For his part, the narrator seems to believe that the intimacy of a late-night storytelling session alone with the marquise will bring an erotic reward. But the very subject of the story he has to tell proves difficult to manage, its effects uncontrollable. You can't always get what you want by telling a story. You may be punished instead for what you have told.

A formalist critic would note that Balzac very often makes use of the "framed tale," or the "embedded tale," using an outer frame to establish the narrative situation and then turning the narration over to one of the characters. Sometimes, as in "Sarrasine," the character who listens to the tale reemerges at the end to comment on it. In "Another Study of Womankind" there are multiple tellers and listeners, members of a privileged Parisian group that for Balzac retains the conversational art of prerevolutionary aristocratic society. In contrast, "The Red Inn" gives a Gothic twist to the embedded tale. Its recital of gore, guilt, and responsibility is chilling enough, but the main drama may come in its effect on one of its listeners. The tale is proto-Dostoyevsky, adumbrating elements of *Crime and Punishment*. Dostoyevsky was an admiring disciple of Balzac, and we often feel the French novelist giving a first sketch of those damned questions at the center of the Russian's work.

Maybe it's because these short stories often speak directly to the very process of creation itself that Balzac appears to enjoy himself and to let himself go here more than anywhere else. Nowhere is this more evident than in the short sketch entitled "Facino Cane," where the embedded tale concerns an old blind musician—he lives in the Paris hospice for the blind—who claims to be a Venetian nobleman with secret knowledge of how to break into the hidden treasury of the doges, which is piled high with gold and diamonds. The reward for listening to his story—for believing in it—could be an immense fortune. The impoverished young writer to whom this story is confided, and who tells it to us, is dazzled by the possible payoff from what he's heard. Living in a working-class district of Paris, he has so far been content with the riches found in his imaginative life. He uses his imagination to enter into the lives of those he meets or, simply, those he follows in his urban rambles. He makes the claim that "observation had already become an intuitive habit; it could penetrate into the soul without neglecting the body, or rather, so thoroughly did it grasp the external details that it moved immediately beyond: It allowed me to live a person's life, let me put myself in his place, the way a dervish in *The Thousand and One Nights* would take over a person's body and soul by pronouncing certain words over him." Here the grim realities of the Parisian poor—and the narrator himself is living on only a few sous a day—are displaced or transformed by a movement of the imagination into another person, allowing the creative thinker to live vicariously. That's not quite right: The imaginative leap here goes beyond what we normally think of as vicarious existence to a kind of identity theft. You can be yourself and another through your capacity to enter into others' stories. "Listening to these people, I could join in their lives: I would feel their rags on my back, I would be walking in their tattered shoes; their longings, their needs would all move through my soul, or my soul through theirs." The narrator wonders at the sources of his gift, fears it may carry a certain curse: "To what do I owe this gift? Is it some second sight? One of those talents whose overuse could lead to madness? I have never looked into the sources of this capacity—I have it and I use it, that's all."

This could of course be Balzac talking about his own extraordinary gift for getting under the skin of others, espousing their vision of the world, creating a contemporary *Thousand and One Nights* wrought from the apparently ungrateful material of contemporary Paris, which turns out to be as full of stories as any sultan could wish. Balzac was in fact haunted by the belief that he might be creating too much—overreaching, usurping a power that should only be wielded by God the Father. The fear of madness—which afflicts Facino Cane as it threatens the narrator who discovers him and listens to his tale—lurks throughout *The Human Comedy*. It may lie in wait for those who attempt to know and to create too much. The work is full of mad inventors—such as Balthazar Claës in *The Search for the Absolute*; or the composer in "Gambara," whose invented "panharmonicon" produces a cacophony, though he can sing beautifully when drunk; or the painter Frenhofer of "The Unknown Masterpiece," who appears to destroy his masterpiece in searching to perfect it. Again and again Balzac makes us privy to a fear that his teeming imagination may lead him over the brink. And in fact the ultimate wise man of *The Human Comedy*, the philosopher Louis Lambert, ends in madness and aphasia after an attempt at self-castration on the eve of his marriage. There seems to be a haunting fear that self-expression will meet with an insurmountable obstacle: with sterility, madness, the inability to speak.

But madness may be something more than the loss of reason: a state of the ecstatic, of a beyond reason—the place you end up when you have pushed beyond the permitted limits of human thought, creation, experience. It is the most extreme version of the many extreme psychological conditions that interest Balzac. "Adieu," the story of a woman who goes mad following the crossing of the Berezina River during the retreat of the French army after Napoleon's disastrous invasion of Russia, offers one of the most extraordinary probes into the psyche in a period that was already intuiting the Freudian revolution to come. Balzac was always interested in the latest scientific (or pseudoscientific) lore. In this tale he seems to have picked up some of the premises of the *traitement moral* developed by Dr. Philippe Pinel, who took over the directorship of the Salpêtrière hospital for insane and incurable women at the time of the French Revolution. His "psychological treatment" (*moral* in French can mean psychological as well as moral) often involved inducing patients to relive the moment of trauma that severed them from normal functioning. Pinel understood that a return to the initial scene of suffering that caused the flight from reality into illness could be the starting point of a cure. Despairing of any other form of therapy for his beloved Stéphanie de Vandières, Philippe de Sucy in "Adieu" attempts the reconstruction, more nearly the reproduction of the moment of trauma and loss. It reminds me of the final scene of

Shakespeare's *The Winter's Tale*, where the falsely suspected Hermione after a gap of many years is ransomed from seeming death: "Oh, she's warm! / If this be magic, let it be an art / Lawful as eating." So in that case white magic, not black. Balzac's result is less certainly on the lawful side. The attempt to cure insanity may itself be a kind of overreaching, something for which a high price will be exacted.

Madness and the erotic are also closely allied in Balzac. In "A Passion in the Desert," surely one of the strangest tales ever published, a French soldier taking part in Napoleon's Egyptian campaign gets lost in the Maghreb desert, finds a small oasis with palm trees and a cave, and takes shelter—only to discover that it is inhabited by a panther. The soldier's developing relations with the panther, which is constantly compared to an alluring and dangerous woman, result in one of Balzac's most telling explorations of erotic passion. The panther allows him to talk about female sexuality (as understood by a male: those teeth!) in a way that wasn't possible when talking about "respectable" women of society. As the French soldier caresses the beast he calls "Mignonne" with his dagger, he finds in himself emotions he has never known before. The extreme situation seems to cut through social repression. In the extended analogy of panther to woman, Balzac is remarkably explicit in describing a kind of sexual foreplay leading to what the soldier later describes as a "misunderstanding." There are other kinds of extreme situations of love and sexuality: Balzac stages moments of near-incest, same-sex relations among both women and men, fetishism, borderline S/M, as well as intoxicating self-immolations in chastity. Proust, an avid reader of Balzac, was especially alert to such moments. He noted that "under the apparent and outward action of the drama circulate the mysterious laws of flesh and passion": among other things, an acknowledgment of Balzac as precursor in the exploration of sexualities that did not quite dare speak their name.

Again in "A Passion in the Desert" we are given a framed tale of some complexity: The story opens at Monsieur Martin's menagerie (an actual Parisian attraction of Balzac's time). The narrator's woman companion expresses surprise that Martin's beasts have been so thoroughly tamed that he can enter their cage with impunity. To which the narrator responds that he, too, was surprised on his first visit to the menagerie, but that he encountered there a one-legged soldier who claimed it could be easily explained. It is from this soldier that the narrator heard the tale of the panther met in the desert, which he now writes down for his woman friend—but withholding the end, which he will have to deliver as a spoken coda to the tale. The links between the tale told and the situation of its telling are by no means obvious here. What, if anything, does the soldier's amputated leg have to do with his adventure with the panther? Are her teeth responsible? And if we learn from contemporary accounts that Monsieur Martin was reputed to master his wild beasts by satisfying them sexually before a performance, what further connections do we want to tease out among the various forms of passion? Freud began his momentous *Three Essays on the Theory of Sexuality* with a discussion of "the perversions," in order to go on to show that "normal" sexuality was simply what was most widely accepted on a spectrum of "psychosexuality," that is to say, sex in the mind.

There are passions other than the erotic at play in these tales: those aroused by politics and money, for instance. In "Z. Marcas," the ups and downs of the title character's political career during a turbulent period in French history are told episodically, partially, obliquely by the two students who share a landing with him in a cheap lodging house. It's as if Balzac were writing a political biography but refusing to do it straight, understanding that the story of a disillusioned political veteran can be more effectively told through its effects on two ambitious young men with their futures before them. If Marxist critics, starting with Karl Marx and Friedrich Engels, have been among the most appreciative of Balzac's readers, it's because Balzac —who loudly declared himself a monarchist and Catholic—had no use for the compromise regimes of his lifetime, and denounced their incoherence and corruption. Born in 1799, in the year following Napoleon's coup d'état, Balzac lived as a child through the epic of the Napoleonic Wars and the Empire, then the collapse of Waterloo and the subsequent Restoration monarchy, which in turn collapsed in the Revolution of 1830, which brought the rule of the "Citizen King," Louis Philippe d'Orléans (from the younger branch of the royal family), along with the exile of the last of the Bourbon monarchs. The Restoration ought to have pleased Balzac—but it was in his judgment not a true, vigorous reinstatement of monarchy but a simulacrum, where the aged rulers of France were out of touch with the real dynamics of the time, and the restored aristocracy was far more concerned with its privileges and petty class distinctions than with the responsibilities of power and leadership. It ended, as it deserved, in revolution, in 1830, and the "bourgeois monarchy" of Louis Philippe, no longer king of France but "King of the French." Marcas suffers through these regimes, with the reward of ingratitude.

Balzac's quarrel with the Restoration returns in "The Duchesse de Langeais," the four-part novella in which the opening of the second chapter is devoted to a disquisition about the place of the Faubourg Saint-Germain in French politics and history. Named for the quarter of Paris where the aristocracy began settling in large town houses in the late seventeenth century—many of them still stand in the seventh arrondissement of Paris—the "noble Faubourg" was a place, a class, and a concept. But according to Balzac, it never took on the role that it should have for the Restoration to be a success. The nobility, concerned with its own privileges and prerogatives, didn't recruit aspiring young men of talent—like Balzac—who were only too eager to join its ranks. It failed to act on the model of the Tory Party in England, which reached into the middle class to renew its forces and anchor itself more firmly in the affections of the citizenry. The French Restoration was a gerontocracy—the two kings of the era, Louis XVIII and Charles X, were both brothers of Louis XVI, guillotined in 1793, and old men by the time they ascended the throne—out of touch with the youth of the country. It was, in Balzac's judgment, a cold, mean, selfish time. The result was a more and more vigorous and vocal political opposition. Journalists were in the vanguard during the three "glorious days" of the Revolution of 1830: New rules tightening censorship of newspapers helped to spark the insurrection.

The Revolution was no more to Balzac's liking than the Restoration. The rule of a king who dressed in the bourgeois black frock coat and top hat only confirmed his cynical view of the forces in control of his country. France entered an era of capitalist and industrial expansion. "*Enrichissez-vous*": get rich, the prime minister François Guizot said (perhaps apocryphally) to his countrymen. And so the French did—at least those who had the means to invest in factories, railroads, and various manipulative stock market schemes. The workers—witness the revolts of the Lyons silk workers and various short-lived uprisings of the Paris proletariat—were largely excluded from this newfound prosperity. Balzac, writing most of his *Human Comedy* in the 1830s and 1840s, after the July Revolution but setting the majority of his tales under the Restoration, has the benefit of a historian's hindsight on a regime and a cultural moment that failed. That lends depth to his analysis. But hindsight also increased his anxiety about the future of French society. If social historians continue to find Balzac a great source text, it's because he delved into most of the forces that were transforming his country and saw what the Marxists call the contradictions of a nascent capitalist society.

"Capitalist" is what Balzac calls the usurer Gobseck in the long short story, or short novella, that bears his name. It's possibly a misuse of the term, yet Gobseck's loans, often at exorbitant rates of interest, do oil the capitalist machinery. At a time when loans between individuals most often took the form of the kind of IOU known as a *lettre de change*—an exchangeable and discountable promissory note—the moneylender was a key figure. Gobseck sits at the still center of the turning earth in *The Human Comedy*. He probably appears in more of the novels and tales than any other character, with the possible exception of the lawyer Derville, who is the narrator of Gobseck's story here. Sooner or later, it seems, everyone must come to Gobseck for cash. In this manner, as he tells the young Derville, he gets to see the spectacle of human emotion in its rawest and most stripped-down condition. Gobseck lives without wearing himself out through the ravages of passion, including sex, that he sees devouring his compatriots. He has learned the superior pleasures of the observer. "Well, I tell you," he says to Derville, "every human passion, writ larger by the play of social interests, they all come and parade before me in my life of calm. Furthermore, that scientific curiosity of yours, a kind of struggle with man always getting the worst of it—I replace it with insight into the springs that set mankind moving. In a word, I possess the world with no effort at all, and the world has no grip on me."

Money offers possession of the world without an expenditure of life's vital forces—which Balzac believed to be limited, expendable in a brief flaming existence, or else to be hoarded over the long life of the miser and the observer. The elegant young men and women of Paris parade through Gobseck's life—as well as the honest seamstress Fanny Malvaut, whom he will bring to Derville's attention. In the process, we as readers get to see the stuff of other dramas recorded elsewhere in *The Human Comedy* in a new perspective. In particular, "Gobseck" casts a new light on the final chapter of Balzac's most famous novel, *Le Père Goriot*. In *Old Goriot* we saw Anastasie de Restaud, one of Goriot's daughters, as a tragic figure exploited by her husband; here we are given the husband's point of view, as he struggles to rescue the family fortune that Anastasie is squandering on her unscrupulous lover, Maxime de Trailles.

Derville tells the story of Gobseck late one evening in the noble house of the Vicomtesse de Grandlieu, in the Faubourg Saint-Germain. The Vicomtesse is concerned that her daughter, Camille, is paying too much attention to the suit of young Comte Ernest de Restaud. She believes him to be without fortune, and though his father is of impeccable nobility, his mother (née Goriot) she can scarcely tolerate. Ostensibly, then, Derville tell his story of Gobseck in order to reassure the Vicomtesse and Camille that Ernest will soon come into a handsome fortune (though the story becomes racy enough along the way that the Vicomtesse feels obliged to pack

Camille off to bed). It's a long detour through Gobseck's affairs—including the loan at fifteen percent that allows Derville to set up his law office—before we reach the story of how the old Comte de Restaud set up a transfer of funds into Gobseck's name in order to save them from his wife—but then on his deathbed was so closely guarded by her (since she is afraid he will disinherit her two adulterine children in favor of Ernest) that he could not sign the codicil that would have returned the money to his son. Anastasie, Ernest, and the rest of the family are reduced to penury—which proves character-building. And now that Gobseck has died, at age eighty-nine, Ernest will have a tidy sum.

A kind of cautionary tale, then, to assuage the fears of the Vicomtesse about a future son-in-law, but far more than that: the story of money itself in its accumulation. Money is indeed one of Balzac's chief protagonists throughout *The Human Comedy*, and here we are at the heart of its acquisition and growth. It is telling that at the end of the tale, Gobseck has acquired more than he can disburse: Bankrupt creditors have filled his apartment with things, with goods, many of them spoiling and useless, a kind of accumulation of surplus capital that the system cannot handle. Though it is only alluded to in this story, the future of Gobseck's cash legacy is instructive. He leaves it to his one descendant, his niece Esther. She has had an extraordinary existence, from bit player at the Opéra to fashionable prostitute, then redemption through her passionate love for the young poet and novelist Lucien de Rubempré—but then a forced return to prostitution willed by Jacques Collin, alias Vautrin, the former convict and mastermind of Lucien's career who knows Lucien must raise one million francs in order to buy back his mother's entailed properties, proving his right to carry the name of landed gentry and enabling his marriage to Clotilde de Grandlieu of the noble Faubourg. The plot goes awry. Esther is sold to the Baron de Nucingen, an Alsatian banker and the husband of Goriot's other daughter, Delphine—but after one night spent honoring "the debt of dishonor," as she calls it, Esther commits suicide. She leaves Nucingen's payment in an envelope for Lucien under her pillow—

but it's stolen by the household servants, which will lead to Lucien's arrest. When Derville tracks her down with the news of her immense legacy, it's too late. Too late for everyone: Esther is dead, and Lucien has hanged himself in prison. The money is parceled out to Lucien's provincial relatives. The trajectory of Gobseck's fortune suggests Balzac's thoroughly ironic view of the new moneyed classes coming to power in France.

"The Duchesse de Langeais," the final tale of the volume, clearly cannot be classified as a short story or tale but rather as what Henry James called "the blessed *nouvelle*," indicating by his word choice that he thought it a French form little used by English novelists. Its advantage for Balzac seems evident, and here it yields one of his most perfect works. "The Duchesse de Langeais" shows, once again, how short forms both stimulate and discipline Balzac's extraordinary imaginative powers. Rather than bursting the seams of novelistic form—as some of his longer works do—the short stories and novellas seem packed to the stretching point but nonetheless intact, with a palpable form to them. Here Balzac's mastery becomes evident in his concentration of force within form.

The story of the duchess and her admirer General Armand de Montriveau opens with a notable and enigmatic abruptness on a rocky island in the Mediterranean, site of a convent of the Barefoot Carmelites where the music of the choir of nuns reveals to the interested, passionate listener—the general who has lost her and has been seeking her everywhere—the hidden presence of a Frenchwoman. Then we flash back some years, to the games of love and seduction as they are played in the Faubourg Saint-Germain. As we read into the third chapter, though, these will take on a sinister kind of seriousness, leading to a scene that might figure in *The Story of O* and seems to result in an erotic conversion but one that the other party can't understand. And then the fourth chapter, returning to the Mediterranean isle, plays out the dramatic denouement. The presentation of the story is highly cinematic: It is full of strikingly rendered settings and moments of intense confrontation and fraught dialogue—and it has been made into a film several times, most recently by Jacques

Rivette (in a version that to me loses much of the dynamic of the story). The novella shows Balzac's ability to manipulate different time strata with perfect ease, to reveal the deep nature of the central enigmas of love and passion parsimoniously, so that when we think we have understood it's only in part, and perhaps most notably his ability to sustain a kind of erotic tension throughout: Games of love become almost unbearably intense. Desire rules over the organization of life, and of story. "The Duchesse de Langeais" is one of the most perfect of Balzac's works—everything, even the very baroque excursus on organ music as a go-between bringing together the divine and the human, even the scene of incipient S/M, fits perfectly and ministers to the overall effect.

Balzac has repeatedly, from the beginning of his career, been accused of writing badly. It is true that he often reaches for a kind of sublime that seems tasteless and over the top. We may sometimes wonder at Henry James's unstinting admiration for someone who had little of his own delicacy of touch. Yet once we have accepted the premises of Balzac's kind of expressionism—his recourse to melodramatic plots, hyperbolic speech, and dramatic confrontations where all the moral stakes are laid on the table—we can see that when he is writing at highest intensity he is incomparable. The goal of his melodramatic imagination is to find the latent intensities of life, to make dramatic action tell us about the ethical stakes of our engagements with ambition, love, and one another. That this takes him beyond the bounds of the "realism" for which he became famous into something else, some more occult realm where the real is trumped by the nearly surreal, has bothered those who want to confine the novel to more behavioristic premises. Balzac refuses to be confined in any manner—for him, fiction has a permit to go anywhere and explore anything. His short fiction may give him the greatest freedom of all; it allows the exploratory probe onto ground that not only is forbidden to politer, more repressed forms of expression but also is only partly grasped. Some of its mystery can never quite be known. To open up what society and the novel of manners repress, to stage a kind of explosive upthrust of that which is ordinarily kept down, under control, is Balzac's delight and his passion. He asks to be read in a spirit of adventure and daring.

—Peter Brooks

THE HUMAN COMEDY

FACINO CANE

To Louise, in witness of fond gratitude

AT THE time, I was living on a little street you probably do not know, rue de Lesdiguières: It starts at rue Saint-Antoine across from a fountain near place de la Bastille, and ends at rue de la Cérisaie. A passion for knowledge had flung me into a garret room where I worked nights, and I would spend the day in a nearby library established by Monsieur, the king's brother. I lived frugally; I had accepted all the conditions of monastic life so necessary to serious workers. In fine weather I would at most take a brief stroll on boulevard Bourdon. There was only one activity that could draw me away from my studious routine, although this was virtually part of the same passion: I would walk about observing the customs of the neighborhood, its inhabitants and their character. As poorly dressed as the workmen myself, careless about decorum, I never put them on their guard—I could mingle in their groups, watch them closing deals and arguing as they ended the day. In my own work, observation had already become an intuitive habit; it could penetrate into the soul without neglecting the body, or rather, so thoroughly did it grasp the external details that it moved immediately beyond: It allowed me to live a person's life, let me put myself in his place, the way a dervish in *The Thousand and One Nights* would take over a person's body and soul by pronouncing certain words over him.

Occasionally, on some nights between eleven and midnight, I would come across a workman and his wife on their way home from the Ambigu-Comique music hall, and I would spend some time following them from boulevard du Pont-aux-Choux to boulevard Beaumarchais. These good folk would be chatting about the show they had just seen; eventually they would get around to talking about their work; the woman tugged her child by the hand, ignoring his whining or questions; the parents calculated the money they expected to collect the next day, the twenty different ways they'd spend it. Then they would move on to the household details: laments over the high price of potatoes or the long winter and the rising cost of peat; vehement remarks on the baker's bill; then on to more venomous spats with each displaying his feelings in picturesque terms. Listening to these people, I could join in their lives: I would feel their rags on my back, I would be walking in their tattered shoes; their longings, their needs would all move through my soul, or my soul through theirs. It was a waking man's dream. I would rage with them against the tyranny of the shop foremen or the bad clients who made them come back time and again without giving them their pay.

Dropping my own habits, becoming another person through a kind of intoxication of my imaginative faculties, and playing the game at will—that was my delight. To what do I owe this gift? Is it some second sight? One of those talents whose overuse could lead to madness? I have never looked into the sources of this capacity—I have it and I use it, that's all. I will say, though, that from that time on, I have gone on teasing apart the elements of the heterogeneous mass we call "the people," analyzing and evaluating its good or bad features.

Already back then I understood how useful this neighborhood could be, this seedbed of revolution, seething with heroes, inventors, skilled workmen, with rascals and scoundrels, with virtues and vices, all exacerbated by poverty, strangled by need, drowned in wine, ravaged by strong liquor. You cannot imagine how many ruined hopes, how many unknown dramas in that city of sorrow! How many horrible and beautiful things! Imagination could never touch the reality hidden there, a reality no one could ever uncover—one would have to burrow too deep to find these amazing scenes, tragic and comic, masterpieces born of chance. I don't know how I've gone so long without telling this story: It is one of those strange tales left behind in the sack that memory randomly draws from, like lottery numbers. I have plenty more of them, all as singular as this one, just as thoroughly buried, though they will have their moment, believe me.

One day my housekeeper, a workman's wife, asked for the honor of my presence at the wedding of one of her sisters. To give you an idea of what such a wedding would be like, I will tell you that I paid forty sous a month to this poor creature, who came in every morning to make my bed, clean my shoes, brush my clothes, sweep the room, and prepare my lunch; the rest of the day she spent turning the lever of some machine, and for that hard labor she earned another ten sous a day. Her husband, a cabinetmaker, earned four francs a day. But as the household also included three children, they could barely manage to put an honest loaf of bread on the table. I've never come across more earnest decency than I saw in this man and woman. When I moved away from the neighborhood, for the next five years this Mother Vaillant would visit me with birthday greetings, bearing a bouquet and oranges—this woman who never had ten sous to spare. Poverty had brought us close. I was never able to pay her more than ten francs, often borrowed for the occasion. This may explain why I promised to attend the wedding; I meant to nestle into the happiness of these poor folks.

Both the ceremony and the festivities took place at the warehouse of a wine merchant on rue Charenton, one floor up in a large hall lit by tin reflector lamps; the walls were hung with filthy paper at table level and lined with wooden benches. Inside the room some eighty people gathered in their Sunday best, with flowers and ribbons all around, everyone soaring with the nightlife spirit of the dance halls at La Courtille; their faces flaming, they danced as if the world was about to end. The bride and groom hugged and kissed to the general satisfaction of the guests, cheered on by lewd teasing of "Hey hey, thataway! Haha!"—actually, less indecent than the bashful glances of well-bred young ladies. The whole crowd gave off an animal good humor that was somehow contagious.

But neither the faces of this bunch, nor the wedding feast, nor anything of that world matters to my story. Just keep in mind the oddness of the setting, picture the cheap red-painted warehouse, smell the pungent odor of wine, listen to the shouts of hilarity, stay firmly in that neighborhood, among those workmen, those old-timers, those poor women throwing themselves into a night's pleasure!

The musical ensemble consisted of three blind men from the hospice for the blind—the Quinze-Vingts. One played violin, the second clarinet, the third the flageolet. The three together were paid seven francs for the night. At that price, of course, they offered no Rossini or Beethoven, they played what they wanted and what they could, and no one complained—sweet tact! Their music was such an assault on the eardrum that once I had scanned the crowd, I turned my attention to this trio of blind men and was immediately disposed to indulgence as I recognized their shelter hospice uniforms. The players were seated in a recess before a casement window; to make out their faces, one had to come in close. I didn't approach right away, but when I did, that was it: The party and its music fell away. My curiosity was roused to the highest pitch, my soul crossed over into the body of the clarinetist. The violin and the flageolet players both had commonplace faces, the familiar face of the blind—wary, attentive, unsmiling—but the clarinetist's was one of those phenomena that stop the artist and the philosopher in his tracks.

Imagine Dante's plaster death mask, lit by the red glow of the oil lamp and topped by a thicket of silver-white hair. The bitter, sorrowful expression of that magnificent face was heightened by blindness, for the dead eyes were alive with the mind's energy; it shone through like a burning beam of light, generated by some unique unceasing desire, writ firmly on the domed brow crossed by deep creases like the brick courses in an old wall.

The old fellow was blowing randomly into his clarinet without the slightest concern for rhythm or melody; his fingers lifted and lowered, pressed the ancient keys with mechanical habit. He was not at all disturbed at producing what musicians call "sour notes," the dancers noticed them no more than did the two colleagues of my Italian fellow—for I had been hoping he was an Italian, and he *was* Italian. There was something grand and despotic in this old Homer, who harbored within himself an Odyssey consigned to oblivion. It was a greatness so authentic that it even triumphed over his abject condition, a despotism so lively that it prevailed over poverty. Not one of the violent passions that lead a man to good or to evil, that make a convict or a hero, was lacking in that nobly carved face, lividly Italian, hooded by graying eyebrows that threw their shadow over deep hollows where one feared to see reappear the glow of thought, as one fears to see emerge from a cave's mouth some bandits armed with torches and daggers. There lived a lion within that fleshly cage, a lion whose rage had been vainly spent against the iron of the bars. The flame of despair had guttered out in the cinders, the lava had gone cold, but the gullies, the crags, a wisp of smoke, still bore witness to the violence of the eruption, the ravages of the fire. These ideas, awakened by the sight of that man, were as hot in my soul as they were cold on his face.

Between contra dances, the violin and the flute players, utterly intent on their glass and bottle, would hook their instruments to the buttons of their reddish redingotes, stretch a hand to a small table set within the window recess where their refreshment stood, and regularly offer the Italian a full glass. He could not reach it himself, for the table was set behind his chair, and each time the clarinetist would thank them with a friendly nod of the head. Their actions were executed with the precision always amazing in blind men from the Quinze-Vingts, which seems to imply they can see.

I drew closer to the three blind men to listen to their conversation, but when I neared they must have recognized a non-laborer type and fell silent.

"What country are you from, you playing the clarinet?"

"From Venice," the blind man answered with a faint Italian accent.

"Were you born blind, or are you blind from—"

"Blind from an accident," he answered brusquely, "from a case of the damned *gutta serena*."

"Venice is a beautiful city, I have always dreamed of going there."

The old man's face brightened, his creases shifted, he grew violently excited. "If I went there with you, it would be worth your time," he told me.

"Don't talk to him about Venice," said the violinist, "or this doge of ours will start up his rant, on top of the fact that he's already got two bottles' worth in his belly, the prince does!"

"All right now, let's begin, Papa Canard," said the flutist.

The three of them set to playing again, but all the while they performed the four contra dances, the Venetian sniffed me out, sensing my unusual interest in him. His face dropped its chilly expression of sorrow; some sort of hopefulness flushed his features and flowed like a blue flame along his wrinkles; he smiled, and he mopped his brow, that bold formidable brow; in time he became jolly like a man climbing onto his hobbyhorse.

"How old are you?" I asked him.

"Eighty-two!"

"How long have you been blind?"

"Fifty years now," he answered, with a tone that implied that his regrets had to do not only with the loss of his sight but with some great power that had been stripped from him.

"Why do they call you the doge?" I asked him.

"Ah, it's a joke," he said. "I am a patrician of Venice, and I might have become doge as readily as anyone else."

"What is your name, then?"

"Here, I'm called Old Man Canet. My name can never be registered any other way on the public records, but in Italian it is Marco Facino Cane, Prince of Varese."

"What! You're descended from the famous condottiere Facino Cane, whose conquests were inherited by the dukes of Milan?"

"*È vero*," he said. "Back then, to avoid being killed by the Viscontis, Cane's son fled to Venice and got himself registered in the

Golden Book. But now there are no more Canes and no more book."
He made a frightening gesture—of patriotism long dead and of disgust for human affairs.

"But if you were a senator of Venice, you must have been rich. How did you lose your wealth?"

At my question he lifted his head toward me, as if to consider me with a movement that was truly tragic, and he replied, "Through a number of misfortunes..."

He had no further interest in drinking; with a gesture he waved away the wineglass the old flageolet player held out to him, and then he lowered his head. These details were not likely to quench my curiosity. During the contra dance the three fellows played next, I contemplated the old Venetian nobleman with feelings that devour a man of twenty. I could see Venice and the Adriatic, I could see its ruins on that withered face. I walked that city so cherished by its inhabitants, I went from the Rialto to the Grand Canal, from the Schiavoni wharf to the Lido, I returned to the San Marco Basilica, so outlandishly sublime; I gazed at the Cà d'Oro's windows, each with its different ornamentation; I contemplated those richly marbled old palaces—in short, all those marvels a scholar loves, and loves all the more for coloring them himself as he wishes, refusing to allow the spectacle of reality to de-poeticize them.

I thought back along the life course of this scion of the greatest condottiere, seeking the traces of his troubles and the causes of his profound physical and moral degradation—a degradation that rendered all the lovelier the glints of grandeur and nobility now reawakened. Our thoughts might have been alike, for I believe that blindness makes mental communications swifter by keeping attention from scattering over external objects. Evidence of our common thinking was quick to arrive. Facino Cane quit playing, rose, came to me, and said, "Let's leave!" which hit me like an electric shower. I gave him my arm and we left the place.

When we reached the street, he said, "Will you take me to Venice? Will you lead me there? Will you put your faith in me? You will be richer than the ten richest houses in Amsterdam or London, richer than the Rothschilds, yes, rich as *The Thousand and One Nights.*"

I thought the man was mad, but there was in his tone a power that I obeyed. I let myself be directed and he led me to the moat around the Bastille as if he had eyes. He sat down on a stone in a very isolated spot where they have since built a bridge that connects the Canal Saint-Martin to the Seine. I took a seat on another stone facing the old man, whose white hair shone in the moonlight like silver threads. The silence, barely disturbed by the stormy noise from the distant boulevards, the purity of the night—everything contributed to make this scene truly fantastic.

"You mention millions to a young man, and you think he would hesitate to brave a thousand obstacles to collect them! Are you making fun of me?"

"May I die unconfessed," he answered violently, "if what I am about to tell you is untrue.

"I was twenty, like you are now; I was rich, I was handsome, I was a nobleman, I started out with the greatest folly of all—with love. I loved as no one loves any longer these days—to the point of closing myself into a chest and taking the risk of being stabbed in it for just the promise of a kiss. To die for her seemed to me worth life itself. In 1760, I fell in love with a woman of the Vendramin family, eighteen years old, married to a Sagredo, one of the richest senators, thirty years old and mad about his wife. My mistress and I were innocent as a couple of cherubs when one day the husband caught us talking of love. I was unarmed. He aimed and missed me. I leapt on him. I strangled him with my bare hands, twisting his neck like a hen's. I was ready to run off with Bianca but she refused to come. That's women for you! I left by myself. I was convicted, my wealth was impounded for my heirs. But I did carry off my diamonds, five Titian canvases rolled up, and all my gold. I went to Milan, where no one bothered me; my adventure held no interest for that state . . .

"One small remark before I continue," he said after a pause, "is whether or not a woman's fantasies during pregnancy or conception might affect her child. It is a known fact that while she was pregnant my mother had a craving for gold. Gold is for me an obsession; satisfying it is so necessary to my life that, no matter what my situation, I am never without gold on my person. I am constantly handling gold—as a youth I always wore jewels and always carried two or three hundred gold ducats."

As he spoke these words, he drew two ducats from his pocket and showed them to me.

"I smell gold. Blind as I am, I pull up short when I pass a jeweler's shop. This passion ruined me; I became a gambler to gamble for gold. I was not a swindler, I was swindled, I drove myself to ruin. When I no longer had any fortune left, I was gripped by a frenzy to see Bianca. I returned secretly to Venice and found her again. I was happy for six months, hidden in her house and fed by her; I expected delightedly to live out my life that way. She was being courted by the *provveditore*; the man sensed there was a rival, in Italy they have a feel for that sort of thing; he spied on us, caught us in bed, the coward! Imagine our terrific struggle! I didn't kill him, but I wounded him seriously. The adventure put an end to my happy life.

"From that day on I have never found another Bianca. I have had great pleasures, I have lived at Louis XV's court among the most renowned ladies, but never, anywhere, have I found the qualities, the charms, the love I knew with my darling Venetian.

"The provveditore called out his men and the palace was surrounded, invaded; I defended myself, hoping to die before the eyes of Bianca, who was helping me kill the provveditore. In earlier days the woman had refused to flee with me, but now, after those six months of happiness together, now she wanted to die along with me, and she suffered several wounds herself. Someone threw a greatcoat over me; I was caught in it, rolled up, and carried off in a gondola to a dungeon cell, one of the *pozzi* beneath the Doge's Palace. I was twenty-two years old.

"I was still gripping the pommel of my sword so hard that to take it from me would have required cutting off my fist. By a curious chance—or rather, inspired by some idea of precaution—I hid that iron stub in a corner of my cell, as if it might someday be useful. I was treated; my wounds were not fatal. At twenty-two, a person gets over everything. I was sentenced to be decapitated; I played the invalid to gain time. I calculated that my dungeon cell lay alongside the canal, and my plan was to escape by digging through the wall and swimming across the canal, at the risk of drowning. You see the kind of reasoning on which my hopes depended. Whenever the jailer brought me food, I would study the words that had been scratched onto the walls, such as 'palace side,' 'canal side,' 'basement side,' and I eventually worked out a map whose orientation was a bit puzzling but which could be explained by the still-unfinished state of the ducal palace.

"With the ingenuity that arises from the appetite for freedom, by fingering the surface of a stone I managed to decipher an inscription in Arabic. An early prisoner had alerted those who followed to stones he had loosened along the bottom edge of the wall, with eleven feet of tunnel behind it. To continue the man's work would mean depositing the rubble of excavated stone and mortar on the cell floor. But even if the guards and the Inquisitors had not been confident that the building's construction demanded only exterior surveillance, the dungeon floor lay a few steps below grade, which would allow any gradual rise in level to go unnoticed by the jailers.

"This enormous labor had been useless, at least to the man who had begun it—its unfinished state meant that the unknown prisoner must have died. In order that his devoted labors should not be forever wasted, some later prisoner must know Arabic—but I had studied Eastern languages at the Armenian convent! A line inscribed into the rear of the stone told the fate of this unfortunate fellow: He died a victim of his immense wealth, which the state of Venice had coveted and seized.

"It took me a month to achieve visible results. As I worked, and especially in those moments when I was undone by fatigue, I heard the chink of gold, I saw gold before me, I was dazzled by diamonds. Oh, but wait: One night, my blunted steel hit wood; I sharpened the sword butt and bored a hole into the wood.

"To manage the work, I squirmed on my belly like a serpent. I stripped bare and advanced like a mole, thrusting my hands ahead of me and pressing against the stone itself to force my way forward. Two nights before I was to appear before my judges, I determined to make a last effort—I pierced the wood, and my steel tool encountered nothing beyond it. Imagine my amazement when I set my eyes to the hole! I was in the wall panel of a cellar where by a faint light I could make out a mound of gold. The doge and one of the Council of Ten were there in the vault, I could hear their voices. From their talk I understood that this was the republic's secret treasury, the repository of gifts to the doges and stores of booty, known as the '*denier de Venise*'—taxes levied on the plunder from expeditions. I was saved! When the jailer entered my cell, I proposed that he should facilitate my escape and leave with me, carrying all we could manage. With no reason to hesitate, he accepted.

"A ship was leaving for the Levant, and all the arrangements were made. Bianca aided in the preparations I dictated to my accomplice. To avoid suspicion, Bianca was to join us at Smyrna. In a single night, the hole was cut larger, and we descended into the secret treasury of Venice. What a night! I saw four full bins of gold; in the anteroom, silver was stacked in two great piles with a pathway between for crossing the room, and the coins stood five feet high against the walls. I thought the jailer would go mad, he was singing, leaping about, laughing, frolicking in the gold; I threatened to strangle him if he wasted time or made any more noise. In his joy, he failed at first to notice a table piled with diamonds. I threw myself on them nimbly enough to load up my sailor's smock and my trouser pockets. Good Lord! And I didn't take even a third of what was there. Beneath the table were gold ingots. I persuaded my companion to load gold into as many sacks as we could carry, pointing out that this was the only way to avoid detection abroad. 'The pearls, the jewelry, the diamonds would mark us,' I told him. Avid as we were, still we couldn't take away more than two thousand pounds in gold, which already required six trips through the prison to load the gondola. The sentinel at the canal gate had been bribed with a sack holding ten pounds in gold. As for the two gondoliers, they believed they were simply doing a job for the republic.

"We left at daybreak. When we were in the open sea, and I recalled the events of the night—when I remembered the sensations I had experienced, saw again that enormous treasury where, by my calculations, I had left behind thirty million in silver and twenty million in gold, several millions more in diamonds, pearls, and rubies—I was struck by a fit of madness. I had gold fever.

"We disembarked at Smyrna and immediately set sail again for France. As we boarded the French ship, by God's grace I was rid of my accomplice. At the time I didn't grasp the full effect of this mishap, which delighted me. We had been so agitated, pressing on in a daze with barely a word between us, waiting until we should be safely far away to relax. It is not surprising that the strange fellow should have lost his head. But you will see how God eventually punished me. I did not rest easy until I had sold off two-thirds of my diamonds in London and Amsterdam, and converted my gold into commercial tender.

"For five years, I hid out in Madrid; then, in 1770, I returned to Paris under a Spanish name and led a dazzling life. Bianca had died. Then, in the midst of my dissipations, and with a fortune of six million, I was stricken blind. I am convinced that the affliction is the consequence of my time in the dungeon, my work digging the tunnel—unless my capacity to see gold somehow was an abuse of the visual faculty that predestined me to lose my sight.

"At the time, I was in love with a woman to whom I expected to bind my own destiny. I had told her the secret of my identity—she belonged to a powerful family—and I had great hopes for Louis XV's evident favor toward me. I put my trust in that young woman, who was a friend of Madame du Barry. She urged me to consult a renowned oculist in London, but after several months' stay in that city, she abandoned me in Hyde Park; she stripped me of my whole fortune and left me without resources—for, as I was obliged to hide my name, lest it deliver me to the vengeance of Venice, I could not call on anyone for help; I feared Venice.

"My disability was exploited by spies that woman had set upon me. I'll spare you tales of adventures worthy of Gil Blas. Your Revolution occurred. I was forced into the Quinze-Vingts shelter, where that woman had me committed after holding me for two years in the Bicêtre asylum as insane. I was never able to kill her as I couldn't see and as I was too poor to pay someone to do it. If, before losing Benedetto Carpi, my Venetian jailer, I had asked him to set down the exact location of my dungeon cell, I could have recognized the treasury, acknowledged my crime, and returned to Venice when Napoleon abolished the republic there.

"But now, never mind my blindness, let's be off to Venice! I will find the prison door, I will see the gold through the walls, I will sense it beneath the waters that flow above it. The events that have overthrown Venice's powers are such that the secret of the treasure trove must have died with Vendramino, Bianca's brother, a doge who I had hoped would arrange my peace with the Council of Ten. I sent missives to the First Consul, I proposed a treaty with the Austrian emperor—they all dismissed me as a madman! Come now, let us leave for Venice: We leave as beggars and we'll return as princes! We'll buy back my properties and you will be my heir, the Prince of Varese!"

Dazzled by this pronouncement, which in my imagination expanded into the dimensions of a poem, I gazed at the sight of his white head, and there before the dark water of the Bastille moats, water as still as that in the Venice canals, I made no answer. Facino Cane must surely have felt that I was judging him, as everyone else had done, with disdainful pity, for he waved his hand in a gesture that evoked all the philosophy of despair. The tale must have carried him back to his happy times in Venice; he seized his clarinet and dolefully played a Venetian song, a barcarolle for which he drew once more on his first talent, the talent of a patrician in love. It was something like the psalm "Super flumina Babylonis." My eyes filled with tears. If a few late-night strollers happened along boulevard Bourdon just then, they probably stopped to listen to that ultimate prayer of the exile, the last longing for a lost name, touched with the memory of Bianca. But soon gold took the upper hand again, and that fateful passion stamped out the youthful gleam.

"That treasure-house," he whispered, "I can still see it, bright as a dream. I'm strolling through it, the diamonds sparkle, I am not so blind as you think: Gold and diamonds light my night, the night of the last Facino Cane—for my title will pass to the Memmi clan. Ah, Lord! The murderer's punishment has begun so very early! Ave Maria..."

He recited a few prayers that I did not hear.

"We'll go to Venice!" I cried when he stood up.

"So I have found myself the right man!" he exclaimed, his face aflame.

I gave him my arm and took him home. He shook my hand at the door of the Quinze-Vingts, just as several people from the wedding party passed by on their way home, shouting and carousing their heads off.

"Shall we leave tomorrow?" asked the old man.

"As soon as we've put together some money."

"But we can go on foot, I'll beg alms along the way... I'm sturdy, and a person is young when he sees gold ahead."

Facino Cane died during the winter, after a two-month illness. The poor man had suffered a bad cold.

Paris, March 1836
Translated by Linda Asher

ANOTHER STUDY OF WOMANKIND

To Léon Gozlan, in sincere literary fellowship

THERE are two very different parties to be found at nearly every Parisian ball or rout. First the official party, peopled by its invitees, a fine crowd of very bored people. Everyone poses for his neighbor. Most of the young women have come solely for the sake of one person. Once each is satisfied that for this person she is the most beautiful woman of all, and that a few others have formed the same opinion, then—after exchanging a few trivial sentences ("Will you be leaving soon for La Crampade?" "Didn't Madame de Portenduère sing beautifully!" "Who is that little woman with so many diamonds?") or tossing out a handful of epigrammatic remarks of the sort that cause fleeting pleasure and lasting wounds—the crowd thins, the indifferent guests go on their way, the candles burn down into their rings. But with this the mistress of the house holds back a few artists, people of good cheer, friends, saying, "Stay, we're having a late supper among ourselves." They gather in the little drawing room. Here the second, true party begins, a party in which, as under the ancien régime, everyone hears what is said, in which the conversation is shared in by all, in which each is obliged to display his wit and contribute to the public amusement. All is in high relief; openhearted laughter replaces the starchy airs that, in society, dull the prettiest faces. In short, where the rout ends, pleasure begins. The rout, that dreary review of fashionable fineries, that parade of well-dressed self-infatuations, is one of those English inventions currently *mechanifying* the other nations. England seems determined to see the entire world bored just as she is, and just as bored as she. This second party is thus, in France, in a few houses, a welcome affirmation of the spirit that was once ours in this ebullient land. But alas, few houses thus affirm, and for a very simple reason: If people rarely take part in these suppers today, it is because there have never been, under any regime, fewer people settled, established, and secure than under the reign of Louis Philippe, in which the Revolution has begun a second time, legally. Everyone strives toward some goal or scurries after fortune. Time has become the dearest commodity on the market, and so no one can indulge in the prodigious prodigality of returning home a day after leaving, with no plans save to sleep late. Thus, that second party is found today only in the homes of women endowed with the means to open their salons; and since July 1830, such women can be counted on the fingers of one hand in Paris. Braving the mute opposition of the Faubourg Saint-Germain, two or three women, among them Madame la Marquise d'Espard and Mademoiselle des Touches, have declined to abandon the influence they once held over Paris and have not closed their doors.

The salon of Mademoiselle des Touches, celebrated in Paris, is the last refuge for the lost art of French conversation, with its hidden profundity, its thousand digressions, its exquisite politesse. There you will still find manners of genuine grace, despite all the conventions of etiquette; you will find talk enjoyed with abandon, despite the innate reserve of the comme il faut set; above all, you will find noble and magnanimous ideas. There no one thinks of keeping his thoughts to himself with a mind to penning a drama, and in an anecdote no one sees a book to be written. In short, the hideous skeleton of a desperate, moribund literature never walks through the door when a felicitous jape is made or an interesting subject raised. The memory of one such evening has remained with me particularly, less for a tale told in confidence, by which the illustrious de Marsay laid bare one of the deepest recesses of the female heart, than for the observations his account inspired concerning the changes wrought in French womankind since the fateful July revolution.

That evening, chance had assembled a small crowd whose indisputable talents have earned them reputations all across Europe. This is not an appeal to French national pride, for there were more than a few foreigners among us. But it was not in fact the most famous who shone brightest that evening. Ingenious repartee, subtle observations, sparkling gibes, pictures painted with brilliant clarity came thick and fast in a spontaneous, effervescent rush, offered up without arrogance or artifice, spoken with sincerity, and savored with delight. Above all, the guests shone by their refinement and their inventiveness, which were nothing short of artistic. You will find elegant manners elsewhere in Europe—you will find cordiality, bonhomie, sophistication—but only in Paris, in this salon, and in those of whom I've just spoken, does there flourish the special wit that gives all these social virtues a pleasing, multifaceted unity, a sort of fluvial momentum by which that profusion of musings, aphorisms, tales, and pages from history wend their way in an easy and untrammeled flow. Paris alone, the capital of taste, possesses the secret that makes of conversation a joust, in which every temperament is encapsulated in a quip, in which each has his say, all his experience condensed in a word, in which all find amusement, refreshment, and exercise. And only there, too, will you truly exchange your ideas; there you will not, like the dolphin in the fable, carry a monkey on your shoulders; there you will be understood, with no danger of wagering gold against pot metal. Secrets artfully betrayed, exchanges both light and deep, everything undulates, spins, changes luster and color with each passing sentence. Keen judgments and breathless narrations follow one upon the next. Every eye listens, every gesture is a question, every glance an answer. There, in a word, all is perspicuity and reflection. Never did the phenomenon of speech, to which, when carefully studied and skillfully wielded, an actor or storyteller owes his glory, cast so overpowering a spell on me. I was not the only one bewitched by this magic; it was a delicious evening for all of us. The conversation soon fell into an anecdotal mood, its precipitous course ferrying some curious confidences, several portraits, a thousand follies, making that delightful improvisation utterly untranslatable.

But if these things are told with all their candor intact, all their natural forthrightness, all their illusory aimlessness, perhaps you will fully grasp the charm of a true French party, captured at the moment when the sweetest companionship makes everyone forget his own interests, his exclusive self-love, or, if you like, his pretensions.

Toward two in the morning, our supper winding down, no one was left at the table but intimate friends, tempered by fifteen years' frequentation, or people of great taste, well bred and worldly. By an unspoken, unquestioned convention, everyone renounced his importance at supper. Absolute equality was the order of the night, though there was no one who was not entirely proud to be who he was. Mademoiselle des Touches keeps her guests at the table until they go on their way, having often observed the great mental change that takes place when one is forced to move. Between the dining room and the drawing room, the spell is broken. According to Sterne, the ideas of a freshly shaved author are not what they were just a few minutes before. If Sterne is right, could we not make so bold as to claim that the mood of a crowd of tablemates is no longer their mood when they have returned to the drawing room? Gone is the headiness of the atmosphere; no more does the eye gaze over the gleaming disarray of dessert, bathed in the benevolence, the salutary idleness of mind that settles over a man with a nicely filled belly, comfortably ensconced in one of those well-cushioned chairs that can be had nowadays. Perhaps people speak more freely over dessert, in the company of fine wines, come that delicious moment when each can rest his elbow on the table and his head on his hand—and not only speak but listen as well. Digestion nearly always sharpens the mind, but it can be silent or voluble, depending on the temperament. Everyone finds his own pleasure. Let us take this preamble as necessary to prepare you for the charms of a story told by a famous man, now deceased, portraying the innocent Jesuitism of womankind with the finesse peculiar to those who have seen much of life, and which makes of statesmen such captivating raconteurs, when, like the Princes de Talleyrand and von Metternich, they consent to recount their experiences.

De Marsay, named prime minister six months before, had already given evidence of superior abilities. Although his longtime acquaintances were not surprised to see him display all the varied talents and aptitudes of a statesman, one might well wonder if he knew himself to be a great politician from the start or if he evolved in the heat of circumstances. This very question had just been put to him, in a philosophical frame of mind, by a man of intelligence and discernment whom he had named as prefect, a veteran journalist whose admiration for de Marsay was untainted by that vinegary dash of disparagement by which, in Paris, one superior man exculpates himself for admiring another.

"Was there, in your earlier existence, some deed, some thought, some desire that taught you the nature of your vocation?" asked Émile Blondet. "For surely, like Newton, we all have our apple, revealing our true calling as it falls."

"There was," answered de Marsay. "I'll tell you the story."

Pretty women, political dandies, artists, old men—de Marsay's private circle—everyone then sat back, each in his own pose, and fixed their eyes on the prime minister. Need it be said that the servants had all withdrawn, that the doors had been shut and the portieres pulled? So deep was the silence that the coachmen's muted conversation could be heard from the courtyard, and the stamping and snorting of the horses, impatient to be back in their stables.

"One quality alone makes a statesman, my friends," said the minister, playing with his gold- and mother-of-pearl knife, "an unfailing self-mastery, a talent for grasping the full import of an event, however fortuitous it may seem—in short, the possession of a coolheaded, disinterested self deep inside, who observes, as if from without, all the movements of our life, our passions, our emotions, and who in all things whispers to us the decree of a sort of moral multiplication table."

"Which explains why there are so few statesmen in France," said old Lord Dudley.

"Where the sentiments are concerned, this is a dreadful thing," the minister resumed. "And so, when that phenomenon appears in a young man—think of Richelieu: a letter informs him that his bene-factor Concini will be murdered the next morning at ten, and he sleeps until noon!—when that phenomenon occurs in a young man, say Pitt or Napoleon, then he is a monster. I myself became that monstrosity at a very early age, and all thanks to a woman."

"I would have thought," said Madame de Montcornet, with a smile, "that we women unmade many more politicians than we made."

"The monster of which I speak is a monster only because he re-sists you," replied de Marsay, archly bowing his head.

"If this is to be a tale of amorous adventure," said the Baronne de Nucingen, "may I ask that it not be interrupted by incidental reflections?"

"Reflection has no place in such things!" cried Joseph Bridau.

"I was seventeen years old," de Marsay resumed. "The Restoration was beginning in earnest, and my old friends will remember the im-petuous young hothead I was in those days. I was in love for the first time, and, I can say this today, I was one of the prettiest young men in Paris. I had youth, beauty, two advantages conferred by chance, and of which we are as proud as if they were hard-won. I will hold my tongue concerning the others. Like all young men, I loved a woman six years older than I. None of you," he said, glancing around the table, "can guess her name nor recognize her. Only Ronquerolles, at the time, saw through my secret; he kept it well. I would have feared his smile, but he has left us," said the minister, looking around him.

"He declined the invitation to supper," said Madame de Sérizy.

"For six months, possessed by my love, unable to grasp that my passion was becoming my master, I gave myself over to those charm-ing idolatries that are both the triumph and the fragile joy of youth. I kept *her* old gloves, I drank an infusion of the flowers *she* had worn, I rose at night to go and gaze up at *her* windows. My head grew light on inhaling the perfume *she* had adopted. I was a thousand leagues from the realization that every woman is a stove with a marble top."

"Oh! Spare us your horrible judgments, won't you?" said Ma-dame de Camps with a smile.

"I believe I would have poured withering scorn on any philosopher who published that terrible, profoundly true thought," de Marsay went on. "You all know too well what's what for me to say anything more of it. Those few words will remind you of your own follies. A grande dame if ever there was one, and a childless widow—oh! nothing was missing!—my idol closeted herself away to stitch a mark into my linens with her hair; in short, she answered my follies with follies of her own. And how not to believe in passion, when it is vouchsafed by folly? We devoted our every thought to concealing so perfect and so beautiful a love from the eyes of the world, and we succeeded. Oh, what charms did our escapades not possess? Of her I will tell you nothing: Perfect back then, still today she is considered one of the most beautiful women of Paris, but in those days people would have signed their own death warrant for one glance from her. Her fortune was still quite sufficient for a woman worshipped and in love, but scarcely suited to her name, now that the Restoration had granted it a new luster. Things being as they were, I was too full of myself to think of being wary. Although my jealousy had the strength of a hundred and twenty Othellos, that redoubtable sentiment slumbered inside me, like the gold in a nugget. I would have ordered my servant to beat me with a stick had I been so ignoble as to doubt the purity of that angel, so frail and so strong, so blond and so naïve, pure, artless, whose adorably docile blue eyes let my gaze plunge straight into them, all the way to her heart. Not one iota of reticence in her manner, in her eyes or her words; always white, fresh, and open to her lover, like the Oriental lily in the Song of Songs! . . . Ah! my friends!" the minister cried despondently, a young man once more. "One has to crack one's head very hard against the marble top to drive out that poetry!"

This heartfelt lament struck a chord among the tablemates and goaded their curiosity, already so ably aroused.

"Every morning, mounted on that fine Sultan you'd sent me from England," he said to Lord Dudley. "I used to ride past her calèche, the horses deliberately slowed to a walk, and read the daily message written in the flowers of her bouquet, in case the opportunity for a quick exchange of words was denied us. Although we saw each other nearly every evening in society, and although she wrote me every day, we had adopted a certain code of conduct to deceive inquisitive eyes and thwart untoward remarks. Never looking at each other, avoiding each other's company, speaking ill of each other, preening and boasting of oneself, or posing as a spurned suitor, none of those old ruses can match this: each lover openly admitting a false passion for an indifferent person and an air of indifference for the genuine idol. If two lovers choose to play that game, the world will always be duped, but they must have absolute faith in each other. Her chosen surrogate was a man then in favor, a man of the court, austere and devout, whom she never received at home. That comedy was performed for the benefit of fools and drawing rooms, and they duly laughed. Never did the question of marriage arise between us: A difference of six years might well have given her pause; she knew nothing of my fortune, which, as a matter of principle, I have always kept to myself. For my part, charmed by her wit, her ways, the breadth of her acquaintances, her worldliness, I would have married her without a second thought. Nevertheless, I liked her reserve. Had she been the first to raise the subject of marriage, I might well have found something vulgar about that ineffable soul. Six full months, a diamond of the finest water! Six good months: There is my allotted share of love in this world. One morning, laid low by the fever that accompanies an oncoming cold, I wrote her a note to postpone one of those secret sessions of merrymaking that take place beneath the roofs of Paris, invisible as pearls in the sea. No sooner had the letter been dispatched than I found myself beset by remorse. 'She won't believe I'm genuinely ill!' I reflected. She often played at jealousy and suspicion. When jealousy is real," said de Marsay, interrupting himself, "it is the unmistakable sign of an exclusive love."

"Why is that?" Princess de Cadignan briskly asked.

"True, exclusive love," said de Marsay, "produces a sort of bodily inertia, in harmony with our meditative mood. The mind then complicates everything, it tortures itself, it conceives wild fancies, it transforms them into realities and torments, and such a jealousy is as delightful as it is distressing."

A foreign minister smiled, glimpsing the truth of this observation by the light of a memory.

"Besides, I asked myself, how could I say no to a moment of bliss?" said de Marsay, returning to his tale. "Was it not better to go with a raging fever? Besides, on learning I was ill she might have come running to my side and compromised herself. I summoned my strength, wrote a second letter, and carried it myself, for my valet had gone off. We were separated by the river, I had all of Paris to cross, but finally, at a suitable distance from her home, I spied an errand boy and enjoined him to have the letter brought up to her straightaway, and I had the fine idea of passing by her front door in a fiacre to see if she might not by chance receive the two messages at once. Just as I pulled up, at two o'clock, the main door is being opened for a carriage, and whose carriage is it, do you suppose? The surrogate's!" Fifteen years have gone by... and yet, as he tells it to you now, the world-weary orator, the minister hardened by long experience with matters of state, still feels a tumult in his heart and a fire in his diaphragm. "An hour later, I passed by again: The carriage was still in the courtyard! My note must have stayed with the porter. Finally, at half past three, the carriage set off, affording me an opportunity to study my rival's expression: He was somber, not a trace of a smile on his face; but he was in love, and no doubt it was some private concern that was troubling him. I went to our meeting place, and the queen of my heart comes as well, and I find her calm, pure, serene. Here I must confess that I've always thought Othello not only a fool but also a man without taste. Only a half Negro could do such a thing. Indeed, Shakespeare sensed this quite clearly, since he titled his play *The Moor of Venice*. The sight of a woman we adore comes as such a balm for the heart that it can only dispel all our sorrow, our doubts, and our grievances. My anger subsided, my smile returned. At my present age, such a demeanor would be a vile dissimulation, but at that time, it simply reflected my youth and my love. All jealousy stilled, I found the strength to observe her. My ill health was plain to see, and the dreadful doubts tormenting me had aggravated it still further. At last I found an opportune moment to slip in these words: 'So you had no callers this morning?'—justifying the question by my fear that she might have made other plans for her day on reading my first note.

"'Ah!' she said, 'only a man could have such ideas! Do you really believe I could think of anything but your misery? Until that second word came, I did nothing but try to find some way of coming to see you.'

"'And you were alone?'

"'Alone,' she said, looking at me with an air of the most perfect innocence. It must have been just such a look that drove the Moor to do in Desdemona. As she was the sole resident of her *hôtel particulier*, that word was clearly an ignoble lie. One single falsehood shatters the perfect confidence that is, for some at least, the very foundation of love. In order to grasp what was taking place within me at that moment, let us imagine that we each have an inner self of which the visible *us* is the sheath, and that this self, brilliant as light, is also as delicate as a shadow…well, that fine *me* was then garbed in crepe for all eternity. Yes, I felt a cold, fleshless hand drape the shroud of experience over me, sentence me to the eternal mourning that a first betrayal injects into our soul. Lowering my eyes lest she note my distress, I steadied myself with this prideful thought: 'If she is untrue to you, she is unworthy of you!' I blamed the sudden redness of my face and the tears in my eyes on an abrupt aggravation of my symptoms, and that sweet creature insisted on accompanying me home, with the coach shades carefully drawn. On the way, her tenderness and solicitude would have deceived that same Moor of Venice I've been using as a point of comparison. Indeed, as any intelligent spectator can see, if that overgrown child hesitates two seconds longer, he will be begging Desdemona's forgiveness. From which we may conclude that killing a woman is truly the act of a child! She wept as we parted, distraught that she couldn't minister to me herself. She wished she were my valet, whose happiness was for her a subject of undying jealousy—and all this said with such turns of phrase, oh!

precisely like what a happy Clarissa would have written. Even in the prettiest and most angelic of women, there is always an ape!"

Here the women lowered their eyes, as if wounded by that cruel truth, so cruelly put.

"I will say nothing to you of the night that ensued, nor the week," de Marsay resumed. "It was then that I realized I was a politician."

This quip was so neatly said that a gesture of admiration escaped us all.

"Reviewing, in a diabolical mood, all the cruel vengeances one can exact on a woman," de Marsay continued, "and, since we were in love, some of them were terrible indeed, and irreparable, I felt only contempt for myself, I felt vulgar, little by little I was drawing up a horrible code, the code of indulgence. When we seek vengeance for the sake of a woman, are we not acknowledging that there is only one woman for us, that we cannot do without her? And in that case, is vengeance the way to win her back? If one does not think her indispensable, if there are others, then why not allow her the same right to change that we claim for ourselves? This, let me be clear, applies only to extramarital passion; otherwise it would do harm to society, and nothing better proves the necessity of an unbreakable marriage bond than the instability of passion. The two sexes must be chained, like the fierce beasts they are, by unyielding laws, deaf and mute. Take away vengeance, and betrayal is of no import in love. Those who believe there is only one woman in all the world for them must choose vengeance, and in that case there is only one, Othello's. Here is mine."

These last words provoked in us all that slight stirring in our seats that journalists represent in parliamentary speeches with the word *commotion*.

"Cured of my cold and of absolute, pure, divine love, I inaugurated an adventure with a most charming heroine, her beauty of a sort perfectly counter to that of my fickle angel. I was careful not to break it off with that woman, that brilliant, unflappable actress, for I'm not sure that true love holds any pleasure so sweet as those afforded by faithlessness. Such duplicity is as good as virtue. I do not speak for you Englishwomen, milady." This last comment the minister interjected sotto voce to Lady Barimore, Lord Dudley's daughter. "In short, I tried to remain the same lover as before. My new angel required a keepsake fashioned from my locks. I thus called on a skilled artist who lived, at the time, on rue Boucher. This man had the monopoly on capillary souvenirs, and I provide his address for those who have little hair of their own: He has it in all colors and of every sort. Once he had heard me describe what I wished, he showed me his wares, among which I saw works of patience surpassing anything folktales attribute to fairies, any prisoner's pastime. He told me of the caprices and fashions that governed the hair-worker's trade. 'For the past year,' he said, 'the rage has been to mark linens with a stitching of hair. Happily, I have a fine collection of hair and some excellent seamstresses.' Suspicion takes hold of me on hearing these words. I pull out my handkerchief and say, 'Then this was done in your establishment and with false hair?' He looked at the handkerchief and said, 'Oh! She was a most difficult customer, she insisted that the match with her own hair be perfect. My wife stitched those handkerchiefs herself. You have here, monsieur, one of the finest pieces ever produced.' Before this last ray of light, I might still have believed in something, I might still have paid heed to a lady's word. I left that place still believing in pleasure, but where love was concerned, I had become as atheistic as a mathematician. Two months later, I was sitting alongside that exquisite woman, in her boudoir, on her divan. I held one of her hands clasped in my own, and such lovely hands they were; we were scaling the Alps of emotion, picking the prettiest flowers, pulling the petals from daisies (one always ends up pulling the petals from daisies, even in a drawing room, without a daisy in sight). At the peak of tenderness, when one is most in love, love is so aware of its fleetingness that each lover feels an imperious need to ask, 'Do you love me? Will you love me forever?' I seized that elegiac moment, so warm, so florid, so radiant, to make her tell her most wonderful lies, in that glittering language of exquisite poetry and purple prose peculiar to love. Charlotte laid out all her prettiest falsehoods: She couldn't live without me; I was the only man for her in all the world; she feared she might bore me, as my presence stripped her of her wit; when I was beside her, her every faculty turned solely to love; she was too full of tenderness not to be frightened; for six months she'd been seeking the manner to bind me to her eternally, and for that, the good Lord above alone knew the way—in short, she made of me her god!"

The women listening to de Marsay seemed put out to see themselves so skillfully mimicked, for he accompanied these words with expressions, simperings, and sidelong glances that created the perfect illusion.

"Just when I was on the point of believing those adorable untruths, still holding her moist hand in mine, I asked, 'And when do you marry the duke?' That stab was so point-blank, my eyes staring so straight into hers, and her hand so gently laid in my own, that the start she then gave, however slight, could not be entirely concealed; her gaze faltered, and a faint blush tinged her cheeks. 'The duke! Why, what do you mean?' she answered, feigning astonishment. 'I know all,' I told her, 'and my advice is to delay no longer. He's a rich man, a duke, but he's not merely devout, he's religious! Thanks to his scruples, I've no doubt you've been faithful to me. I can't tell you how urgent it is that you compromise him before himself and before God, otherwise you'll never be done with it.' 'Am I dreaming?' she said, clapping her hand against her brow—La Malibran's celebrated gesture, fifteen years before La Malibran. 'Come now, my angel, don't be childish,' I said, attempting to take her hands in mine. But she crossed her arms over her waist with an air of offended virtue. 'Marry him, I have no objection,' I went on, answering her gesture with a polite *vous*. 'You can do better than me, and I urge you to do so.' 'But,' she said, falling to her knees, 'there's been some terrible misunderstanding: You're all I love in this world; you may ask me to prove it however you like.' 'Stand up, my dear, and do me the honor of speaking the truth.' 'As if before God.' 'Do you doubt my love?' 'No.' 'My fidelity?' 'No.' 'Well, I have committed the gravest of all crimes,' I answered. 'I have doubted your love and fidelity. Between two moments of bliss, I began to look around me dispassionately.' 'Dispassionately!' she cried, with a mournful sigh. 'That's all I need to know. Henri, you don't love me anymore.' As you see, she'd already found a way out. In these sorts of scenes, an adverb is a most dangerous thing. But fortunately curiosity compelled her to ask, 'And what did you see? Have I ever spoken to the duke other than in society? Did you once glimpse, in my eye—' 'No,' I said, 'in his. And eight times you took me to Saint-Thomas-d'Aquin to see you hearing the same mass as he.' 'Ah!' she cried at last, 'so I've made you jealous.' 'Oh! I'd be happy to be jealous,' I said, admiring the agility of her intelligence, those acrobatics that succeed in dazzling only the blind. 'But all those hours in church made me skeptical. The day of my first cold and your first deception, when you thought me in bed, the duke called on you here, and you told me you'd seen no one.' 'Do you realize your behavior is abominable?' 'In what way? I consider your marriage with the duke an excellent bargain: It gives you a very fine name, and the only place in society worthy of you, a glorious and eminent rank. You'll be one of the queens of Paris. I would be doing you wrong if I stood in the way of that arrangement, that honorable existence, that excellent alliance. Ah! One day you'll thank me, Charlotte, when you realize how different my character is from other young men's . . . You would have had no choice but to deceive me . . . He keeps a close watch on you: You would have been hardpressed for a chance to break it off with me. It's time we went our separate ways, for the duke is a man of severe virtue. If you want my advice, you shall have to become a proper lady. The duke is vain, he'll be proud of his wife.' 'Ah!' she said to me, tears flowing. 'Henri, if only you'd said something! Yes, if you'd wanted it'—it was all my fault, do you see?—'we could have run away to some quiet spot and lived out our lives, married and happy, for all the world to see.' 'Ah well, it's too late for that now,' I answered, kissing her hands and striking an afflicted pose. 'My God! But I can call it all off,' she said. 'No, you've come too far with the duke. I must leave on a journey to seal our separation. Otherwise we would both have to fear the force of our love.' 'Do you believe the duke suspects, Henri?' I was still Henri, but no longer *tu*. 'I think not,' I answered, adopting the manner and tone of a *friend*, 'but you must be perfectly devout, you must recommit yourself to God, for the duke is looking for signs, he's wavering, and you must make up his mind for him.' She rose, paced two or three times around the boudoir in real or feigned distress; then she found a pose and a gaze to suit this new state of affairs, for she stopped before me, held out her hand, and in a voice thick with emotion, said, 'Well, Henri, you're a loyal, noble, and charming man: I shall never forget you.' An admirable bit of strategy! The position she wanted to occupy with respect to me required a change on her part, and she was ravishing in that new guise. I adopted the posture, the expression, and the gaze of a man so deeply tormented that I saw a weakening in her newfound rectitude; she looked at me, took me by the hand, led me to the divan, almost threw me down, but gently, and after a moment of silence said, 'I am profoundly sad, my child. You love me?' 'Oh yes!' 'But what will become of you?'"

Here all the women exchanged a glance.

"While the memory of her betrayal pained me for some time to come, I still laugh today at the absolute certainty and quiet satisfaction with which she foresaw, if not my imminent demise, then at least a life of undying sorrow," de Marsay went on. "Oh! don't laugh yet," he told his audience, "the best is yet to come. After a pause, I gave her a long, reverent look and said, 'Yes, I have asked myself that very question.' 'Well, what will you do?' 'So I wondered, the day after my cold.' 'And?' she said, visibly anxious. 'And I made my arrangements with that little creature I was supposedly courting.' Charlotte leapt up from the divan like a startled doe, trembled like a leaf, shot me one of those looks in which women forget all their dignity, all their discretion, their finesse, even their beauty, the gleaming stare of a cornered viper, and answered, 'And to think that I loved this man! That I struggled! To think that I . . .' She followed that third thought, which I will allow you to guess for yourselves, with the most majestically ringing silence I have ever heard. 'My God!' she cried. 'Poor women! We can never be loved. In the purest sentiments, you men see nothing serious. But, you realize, even when you deceive us, you remain our dupes.' 'I can see that all too clearly,' I said, with a chastened air. 'Your rage is too neatly phrased for your heart to be suffering in earnest.' This modest epigram redoubled her fury; she found tears of spite to shed. 'You're tarnishing all existence in my eyes, the whole world,' she said, 'you're shattering my illusions, you're poisoning my heart.' Everything I had a right to say to her, she was saying to me with a guileless effrontery, an innocent audacity that would certainly have left any other man wholly disarmed. 'What will become of us, we poor women, in this society Louis XVIII's new Charter is creating!' (See the lengths to which her eloquence led her.) 'Yes, we women are born to suffer. In matters of passion, we're always above mere loyalty, and you always beneath it. You haven't a shred of sincerity in your hearts. For you love is a game, and you always cheat.' 'My dear,' I said to her, 'to take anything seriously in contemporary society would be to swear eternal devotion to an actress.' 'What abominable treachery! It was all reasoned out.' 'No, it was simply reasonable.' 'Adieu, Monsieur de Marsay,' she said. 'You've wronged me atrociously.' Adopting a submissive attitude, I asked her, 'Will madame la duchesse remember Charlotte's insults?' 'Surely,' she said, in a bitter voice. 'Then you despise me?' She bowed her head, and I told myself, 'Nothing is lost!' I left her feeling that she had something to avenge. Now, my friends, I have carefully studied the lives of men who had some success with women, but I do not believe that even Marshal de Richelieu could have pulled off such an expert disengagement on his first attempt, nor Lauzun, nor Louis de Valois. As for my mind and my heart, they were tempered there forever, and the mastery I thereby gained over the thoughtless impulses that lead us into so many foolish acts granted me the perfect coolheadedness you know me for."

"How I pity the second woman!" said the Baroness de Nucingen.

An imperceptible smile on de Marsay's pale lips made Delphine de Nucingen blush.

"Zo qvickly ve forget!" cried the Baron de Nucingen.

The illustrious banker's ingenuous remark met with such success that his wife, who was that *second woman* of de Marsay's, could not help joining in the laughter.

"You're all so quick to condemn this woman," said Lady Dudley.

"Well, I can perfectly understand her not seeing that marriage as an act of inconstancy! Men never want to distinguish between constancy and fidelity. I knew the woman whose story Monsieur de Marsay has told us, and she's one of your last grandes dames!"

"Alas, milady, you're right," de Marsay answered. "For what will soon be fifty years, we've been seeing the steady collapse of all social distinctions. We should have rescued women from that wreckage, but the civil code has tamped them down with its great leveling stick. However terrible the words, let us say it: Duchesses are disappearing, and marquises along with them! As for baronesses, begging the pardon of Madame de Nucingen, who will find herself a countess as soon as her husband becomes a peer of France, baronesses have never managed to be taken seriously."

"The aristocracy begins with the viscountess," said Blondet, smiling.

"Countesses will remain," de Marsay went on. "An elegant woman will be more or less a countess, a countess of the Empire or of yesteryear, a countess of time-honored tradition or, as they say in Italy, a countess by courtesy. But as for the grande dame, she died with the opulent entourages of the last century, along with powder, beauty spots, high-heeled slippers, whalebone corsets adorned with a delta of bows. Today duchesses stride through doorways that have no need to be widened to accommodate their panniers. In short, the Empire has seen the last of gowns with trains! I am still at a loss to understand how the sovereign who wanted his court swept clean by the satin or velvet of ducal robes could have failed to establish an inalienable right of succession, for certain families at least. Napoleon did not foresee the effects of his cherished code. When he created his duchesses, he gave birth to today's creature of fashion, the indirect product of his legislation."

"Wielded like a hammer by both the obscure journalist and the child just out of school, ideas have shattered the glories of the social state," said the Comte de Vandenesse. "Today any oaf who can decently hold his head up atop a collar, who can cover his mighty breast with two feet of satin in the guise of a cuirass, who can advertise his putative genius on a brow surmounted by a crown of curled locks, who can totter on two varnished pumps set off by six-franc silk stockings, today any such man can squint his monocle into place and, whether law clerk or entrepreneur's offspring or banker's bastard, insolently ogle the prettiest duchess, appraising her as she descends the staircase of a theater, and say to his friend, dressed by Buisson like the rest of us, and mounted on patent leather like any duke: 'There, my dear fellow, is a true creature of fashion.'"

"You failed," said Lord Dudley, "to become a party, so you will have no political force for a long time to come. You French talk a great deal about organizing labor, and you have not yet organized property. And here is the result: Once any duke—and there were still some to be found under Louis XVIII or Charles X, with an annual revenue of two hundred thousand pounds, a magnificent *hôtel particulier*, a full staff of domestics—could lead a truly lordly life. The last of those great French lords was the Prince de Talleyrand. Now that same duke leaves four children, two of them girls. Even if he marries them off advantageously, each of his heirs will collect only sixty or eighty thousand pounds per annum; each is the father or mother of several children, and so must live in an apartment, on the first or second floor of a house, with the strictest economy; perhaps, who knows, they will be reduced to seeking their own fortune! And so the wife of the eldest son, who is a duchess only in name, has neither her own coach, nor her own domestics, nor her own box at the theater, nor time to herself; she has neither her private rooms in her *hôtel particulier*, nor her fortune, nor her baubles; she is swallowed up in her marriage like a woman of the rue Saint-Denis in her trade; she buys her dear little children stockings, she feeds them, she looks after her daughters, whom she no longer puts in the convent. Your most noble women have become nothing more than estimable brood hens."

"Alas! It's true," said Joseph Bridau. "Gone from our age are those wonderful feminine flowers that ornamented the great centuries of the French monarchy. The fan of the grande dame is broken. Woman no longer has any call to blush, to gossip, to whisper, to conceal herself, to display herself. The fan is now used only for fanning. Once a thing is nothing more than what it is, it's too useful to serve the cause of luxury."

"Everything in France has abetted the creature of fashion," said Daniel d'Arthez. "The aristocracy gave their consent by retreating to their ancestral lands, going off to die in hiding, emigrating into the depths of France hounded by modern ideas, as people once emigrated abroad hounded by the masses. Those women who could found European salons, who could command public opinion, who could turn it inside out like a glove, who could dominate the world by dominating the men of art or thought who would dominate it, they have committed the misstep of abandoning the terrain, ashamed at having to vie with a power-drunk bourgeoisie now stumbling onto the world stage only to be chopped to bits, perhaps, by the barbarians at their heels. And so where the bourgeoisie would see princesses, we find only fashionable young ladies. Princes today can find no more grandes dames to compromise, nor even raise a woman chosen by chance to an illustrious rank. The Duc de Bourbon is the last prince to have availed himself of that privilege."

"And God alone knows at what a cost!" said Lord Dudley.

"The wives of today's princes are mere creatures of fashion, obliged to share the expense of a box at the theater with their girlfriends, a box that not even the favor of the king could enlarge by a quarter inch, confined to the murky waters between the bourgeoisie and the nobility, neither entirely noble nor wholly bourgeois," said the Marquise de Rochefide in disgust.

"Woman's role has been inherited by the press," cried Rastignac. "Once every woman was a living gazette, a font of delicious slanders cast in beautiful language. Today all our gazettes are written, and written in a jargon that changes every three years, little journals amusing as undertakers, light as the lead in their souls. French conversations are couched in revolutionary babble from one end of France to the other, in long columns printed in *hôtels particulier* where the grind of a printing press has replaced the elegant circles that once scintillated there."

"The death knell of high society is sounding, do you hear?" said a Russian prince. "And the first toll is that modern expression of yours, 'the creature of fashion'!"

"Quite right, prince," said de Marsay. "This woman, fallen from the ranks of the nobility or hoisted up from the bourgeoisie, this woman who comes from anywhere at all, even the provinces, is the very image of our times, one final exemplum of good taste, wit, grace, and distinction, all bound up together but shrunken. We will see no more grandes dames in France, but for a long time to come there will be creatures of fashion, elected by public opinion to a feminine high chamber, and who will be for the fair sex what the *gentleman* is in England."

"And they call that progressing!" said Mademoiselle des Touches. "Where is the progress, I'd like to know."

"Ah! Here it is," said Madame de Nucingen. "In times past a woman could have the voice of a fishmonger, the walk of a grenadier, the brow of a brazen courtesan, cowlicks in her hair, an oversize foot, a fleshy hand, and she was still a grande dame, but today, even if she were a Montmorency, assuming the demoiselles de Montmorency could ever be thus, she would not be a creature of fashion."

"But what do you mean by *creature of fashion*?" Count Adam Laginski asked, ingenuously.

"She is a modern creation, a deplorable triumph of the electoral system applied to the fair sex," said the minister. "Every revolution has its word, a word that summarizes and portrays it."

"It's true," said the Russian prince, who had come to Paris in hopes of making his name in the literary world. "An explanation of certain words that have been added to your beautiful language over the centuries would be a magnificent history in itself. *Organization*, for instance, is a word of the Empire and contains all of Napoleon within it."

"But none of this tells me what a creature of fashion might be," cried the young Pole.

"Well, let me explain," Émile Blondet said to Count Adam. "You're out strolling the streets of Paris on a fine afternoon. It's past two o'clock but not yet five. You see a woman approaching, and your first glimpse of her is like the preface of a wonderful book, it hints at a whole world of fine and elegant things. Like a botanist combing hill and dale for exceptional specimens, you have finally chanced onto a rare flower in the midst of the Parisian vulgarities. She may be accompanied by two very distinguished men, at least one of them decorated; if not, some domestic in town clothes is following ten steps behind her. She wears neither bright colors nor openwork stockings, nor too finely wrought a belt buckle, nor pantaloons with embroidered cuffs ruffling about her ankles. You will observe on her feet either prunella flats with laces crisscrossed over a stocking of exceedingly fine cotton or solid gray silk, or perhaps lace-up boots of the most exquisite simplicity. A rather pretty fabric of moderate price will draw your eye to her gown, whose cut surprises more than one woman of the bourgeoisie: It's nearly always a fitted coat closed by knots and prettily edged with a braid or a discreet cord. This stranger has her own particular way with a shawl or a mantle; she can envelop herself from her neck to the small of her back, devising a sort of shell that would make a turtle of any bourgeoise, but beneath which this woman shows you the shapeliest curves, even as she veils them. How does she do it? This secret she keeps to herself, unprotected though it be by any patent. Her walk creates a certain concentric and harmonious movement that sets her innocent or dangerous forms wriggling under the fabric, like the noontime garter snake beneath the green netting of the quivering grass. Is it to an angel or a demon that she owes the graceful undulation that plays beneath the long cloak of black silk, that stirs the lace at its hem, that fills the air with an ethereal balm I might call the breeze of the Parisienne? About her arms, around her waist and throat, you will see the work of a science of drapery that bends even the most resistant cloth to its will and find yourself thinking of the ancient Mnemosyne. Ah! How perfectly she understands, if you will allow me this expression, *the cut of the walk*! See how she thrusts out her foot, molding the dress with such chaste precision that she excites in the passing stranger a wonderment spiked with desire but restrained by a profound respect! When an Englishwoman attempts that gait, she resembles a grenadier charging on a redoubt. None but the Parisienne knows the fine art of walking—hence the asphalt on our sidewalks, the least the city could do for her. This beautiful stranger does not jostle or shove: when she wishes to pass someone by, she waits with proud modesty for room to be made. The distinction peculiar to women of breeding is most clearly displayed by her way of holding the shawl or mantle crossed over her breast. Even as she walks, her air is tranquil and dignified, like the Madonnas of Raphael in their frames. Her manner, at once serene and aloof, compels even the most insolent dandy to step aside for her. Her hat is remarkably simple and adorned with crisp ribbons. There may be flowers, but the most expert of these women will have only bows. Feathers require a carriage, flowers too insistently attract the eye. Beneath that hat you will see the fresh, rested face of a woman who is confident but not smug, who looks at nothing and sees everything, whose vanity, jaded by ceaseless gratification, imbues her face with an indifference that arouses the interest of all who behold her. She knows she is being studied, she knows that nearly everyone, even the ladies, will turn around for a second look when she passes. Thus does she drift through Paris like gossamer, white and pure. This magnificent species prefers to keep to the warmest latitudes, the cleanest longitudes of Paris; you will find her between the 10th and 110th arcades on rue de Rivoli; along the equator of the Grands Boulevards, from the parallel of the Passage des Panoramas, where the products of the Indies abound, where industry's freshest creations flourish, to the cape of the Madeleine; in those lands least sullied by the bourgeoisie, between the 30th and 150th house on rue du Faubourg Saint-Honoré. In the winter, she sojourns on the Terrasse des Feuillants, in the Jardin des Tuileries, and not on the asphalt sidewalk that adjoins it. When the weather is fine, she glides along the allée des Champs-Élysées, within the bounds of place Louis XV on the east, avenue de Marigny on the west, the roadway on the south, and the gardens of the Faubourg Saint-Honoré on the north. Never will you encounter such a fine feminine specimen in the hyperborean regions of rue

Saint-Denis, nor in the Kamchatkas of muddy, small, or commercial streets; never anywhere at all in bad weather. These flowers of Paris bloom when the weather is Oriental; they perfume the promenades, and then, after five o'clock, close up like morning glories. Those you will see later in the evening, vaguely similar in their air, doing their best to mimic them, are mere creatures of passion; only the beautiful stranger, your Beatrice for a day, is the true creature of fashion. A foreigner, my dear count, may well find it difficult to spot the details by which seasoned observers distinguish the one from the other, for women are gifted actresses indeed. To a Parisian, however, those differences fairly cry out aloud: ill-concealed clasps, dingy laces showing through a gaping slit, frayed shoes, re-dyed hat ribbons, a billowing gown, an over-starched bustle. You will observe a sort of effort in the calculated droop of her eyelid. There is something conventional in her manner. A bourgeoise, on the other hand, could never be confused with a creature of fashion: She sets her off wonderfully, she explains the spell that your stranger has cast on you. The bourgeoise has things to do, goes out in all weather, scurries, comes, goes, looks, wonders whether to enter a shop or go on. Where the creature of fashion knows precisely what she wants and what she is doing, the bourgeoise dithers, hitches up her skirts to step over a gutter, drags a child beside her, keeping a vigilant eye out for oncoming coaches; she is a mother in public and chats with her daughter; she has money in her shopping bag and openwork stockings on her legs; in the winter she wears a boa over a fur cape, in the summer a shawl and a scarf; the bourgeoise has a remarkable talent for vestimentary redundancy. As for your beautiful stranger, you will see her again at the Théâtre des Italiens, at the Opéra, at a ball, where she will show herself in such a different form that you will swear the two incarnations have nothing in common. She has emerged from her mysterious garments, as the butterfly from its silken cocoon. Like some delicacy, she serves up before your enchanted eyes the forms that her bodice only hinted at that morning. At the theater she is never encountered beyond the mezzanine, save at the Italiens. Here you will have the leisure to study the trained indolence of her movements. That adorable tricksteress exploits all of womankind's little ploys with an innocence that forbids any suspicion of guile or premeditation. If she has a regally beautiful hand, even the shrewdest observer will believe it was vitally important that she twirl, plump, or push back the ringlet or curl she is caressing. If she has something splendid in her profile, you will feel sure she is offering her neighbor remarks full of irony or grace as she turns her head to produce that magical three-quarters-profile effect, so dear to the great painters, which lets the light fall over the cheek, clearly delineates the nose, illuminates the pink of the nostrils, cuts cleanly across the forehead, preserves the gaze's bright spark while directing it into space, and dots the white roundness of the chin with a point of light. If she has a pretty foot, she will throw herself down on a divan with all the coquetry of a cat in the sun, her legs outstretched before her, and in her pose you will see nothing other than the most delicious model of weariness ever offered up to the art of statuary. No one is at ease in fine clothes like the creature of fashion; nothing troubles her poise. Never will you catch her, as you will a bourgeoise, tugging up a recalcitrant shoulder strap, tugging down an insubordinate whalebone, verifying that the fichu is discharging its mission as the faithless guardian of two dazzling white treasures, nor glancing at herself in mirrors to be sure that her coiffure is obeying its confinement to quarters. Her appearance is ever in harmony with her character; she's had the time to examine herself, to choose only what best becomes her, having long since determined what does not become her at all. You will not see her later in the throngs pouring out of the theater; she vanishes before the curtain comes down. If by chance she appears, calm and noble, on the red steps of the staircase, she is then in the throes of the deepest emotion. She is there on command, she has a furtive glance to give, a promise to receive. It may well be to flatter the vanity of a slave whom she sometimes obeys that she is slowly making her way down those stairs. Should you encounter her at a ball or a party, you will drink in the honey, artificial or natural, of her lilting voice; you will be delighted by her empty words—empty but endowed with the force of deep thought by an inimitable artifice."

"Does a creature of fashion not need a fine mind?" asked the Polish count.

"More than anything else, she must have very fine taste," answered Madame d'Espard.

"And in France, to have taste is to have something more than a fine mind," said the Russian.

"This woman's conversation is the triumph of a very plastic art," Blondet went on. "You won't know what she said, but you will be enchanted. She will have nodded her head, or sweetly raised her white shoulders, she will have gilded an insignificant sentence with the smile of a charming little pout, or she will have expressed an entire Voltairean epigram in one *ah!*, one *hmm?*, one *well!* A cock of the head will be her most vigorous interrogation; she will impart meaning to the movement by which she tosses a vinaigrette attached to her finger by a ring. With her all is artificial grandeur, wrought by magnificent trifles; she nobly lets her hand droop, hanging over the arm of a chair, like dewdrops on the rim of a flower, and with this everything has been said, she has pronounced an unappealable judgment, eloquent enough for the most insensitive soul. She has heard you out, she has afforded you the opportunity to sparkle, and—I appeal to your modesty—such moments are all too rare."

The young Pole's wide-eyed stare sent all the tablemates into gales of laughter.

"With a bourgeoise, you haven't been chatting half an hour before she ushers in her husband, in one form or another," Blondet went on, grave as ever. "But even if you know your creature of fashion to be married, she will have the delicacy to conceal her husband so utterly that it will require a labor worthy of Columbus to discover him. Often you can't manage it single-handed. If you've found no one to question, at the end of the evening you'll see her staring significantly at a bemedalled middle-aged man, who will nod and go out. She's asked for her coach, and now she goes on her way. You're not her one and only, but you've been near her, and you go to bed beneath the gilded paneling of a delicious dream that will perhaps continue when Sleep, with her mighty finger, opens the ivory gates to the temple of fantasies. At home, no creature of fashion can be seen before four o'clock, when she receives visitors. She is no fool: She will always keep you waiting. You will find the signs of good taste all around you; luxury is her constant companion, replaced as necessary. You will see nothing under glass domes, nor the shapeless mass of a wrap hung on the wall like a feedbag. The stairway will be warm. Everywhere flowers will gladden your gaze—flowers, the only gift she accepts, and from only a few people. Bouquets live for just a day, give pleasure, and must then be changed; for her they are, as in the Orient, a symbol, a promise. You will see a display of costly and fashionable bagatelles, but nothing of the museum or the curiosity shop. You will discover her by the fireside, on her love seat, and she will greet you without rising. Her conversation will no longer be that of the ball. There she was your creditor; at home, her wit owes you a debt of pleasure. Creatures of fashion master these nuances wonderfully. She loves in you a man who will broaden her social circle, the sole object of care and concern that creatures of fashion permit themselves today. Thus, to keep you in her drawing room, she will prove a delightful flirt. In this, above all else, you sense the terrible isolation of women today, you understand why they want a little world of their own, for which they serve as a constellation. Without generalities, no conversation is possible."

"Yes," said de Marsay. "There you have put your finger on the great flaw of our age. The epigram, that book in one word, no longer centers on people or things, as it did in the eighteenth century, but on trivial events, and it dies at day's end."

"And so the wit of the creature of fashion, when she has any," Blondet continued, "consists in doubting all things, just as that of the bourgeoise serves to affirm them for her. Here lies the great difference between the two: The bourgeoise's virtue is a thing beyond question, the creature of fashion is not certain she hasn't lost hers nor that she never will; she hesitates and resists, where the other simply refuses to succumb. This hesitancy in all things is one of the last touches of elegance that our horrible age has allowed her. She is rarely in church, but will talk of religion and attempt to convert you should you have the good taste to play the freethinker, for you will thereby have opened the floodgates for well-worn pronouncements, for soulful gazes, for all the conventional gestures that every woman knows: 'Ah! Come now! I thought you far too deep a man to attack religion! Society is crumbling, and you would rob it of its one under-pinning. But religion today is nothing but you and me, it's property, it's our children's future. Ah! It is time we stopped thinking always of ourselves. Individualism is the malady of our age, and religion its only cure, it unites the families that your laws drive apart,' and so on. She then launches into a neo-Christian oration, generously laced with political concerns, something neither Catholic nor Protestant, but moralistic—oh, moralistic as can be!—in which you will recognize a patch of every fabric woven by our many competing modern doctrines."

The women could not repress a laugh at the simpers by which Émile illustrated his caricature.

"From that oration, my dear Count Adam," said Blondet to the Pole, "you will see that the creature of fashion is an embodiment of intellectual no less than political confusion, just as the glittering, flimsy objects around her are produced by an industry forever bent on destroying its own creations, so as to replace them. You will leave her house thinking, 'A woman of superior mind, no doubt about it!' You will believe this all the more firmly because she will have sounded your heart and your mind with a delicate hand, she will have sought out your secrets, for the creature of fashion gives the impression of knowing nothing in order to learn everything; there are some things that she never knows, even when she does. But you will be uneasy, for you will know nothing of the state of her heart. The grande dame of old loved with banners and broadsheets; today the creature of fashion's ardors are as orderly as a page of sheet music: half note, quarter note, eighth note, rest. She is but a vulnerable woman, and careful not to compromise her love, nor her husband, nor her children's future. The flags of name, rank, and fortune no longer command respect enough to ensure safe passage for the goods on board. No more does the entire aristocracy step forward to act as a screen for a fallen woman. And so unlike the late, lamented grande dame, the creature of fashion never goes too far, she can trample nothing underfoot, it is she who would be broken and crushed. She is thus the woman of the Jesuitical *mezzo termine*, of dubious compromises, respect for the niceties, anonymous passions conducted between two treacherous shorelines. She's afraid of her servants, like some Englishwoman who might at any moment find herself hauled up for *criminal conversation*. So free at the ball, so pretty as she strolls the streets, this woman is a slave in her own home; she enjoys her independence only behind closed doors or in her thoughts. She wants to remain a woman of fashion. That's her watchword. And today a woman abandoned by her husband, reduced to a meager pension, no carriage, no luxuries, no box at the theater, with none of the divine accessories that make up her raiment, today such a woman is no longer a woman at all, or a girl, or a bourgeoise: She is dissolved and becomes simply a thing. The Carmelites will have nothing to do with a married woman; that would be bigamy. Will her lover still want her? That is the question. The creature of fashion can perhaps be a subject of slander but never of gossip."

"All that is horribly true," said the Princess de Cadignan.

"And so," Blondet resumed, "the creature of fashion lives between British hypocrisy and the elegant brazenness of the eighteenth century; a bastard system all too typical of an age when nothing that comes along resembles what is lost, in which transitions lead to nothing, in which there are only shades of gray, in which all greatness pales, in which all distinctions are purely personal. I am convinced that no woman, even born near the throne, can hope to acquire before age twenty-five the encyclopedic knowledge of trifles, the gift for machinations, the great little things, the music of the voice and the harmonies of color, the angelic deviltries and innocent impostures, the language and the silence, the seriousness and the mockery, the wit and witlessness, the diplomacy and ignorance, that make up the creature of fashion."

"And where, in this system you've just laid out for us," said Mademoiselle des Touches to Émile Blondet, "would you place the woman writer? Is she a creature of fashion?"

"Save the occasional genius, she is a creature to be shunned," answered Émile Blondet, accompanying his response with an urbane glance that may just as well have been overt flattery for Camille Maupin. "That's not my opinion but Napoleon's," he added.

"Oh, don't blame Napoleon," said Canalis, with a sententious gesture. "It was one of his pettinesses to be jealous of literary genius, for pettinesses he had. Who will ever succeed in explaining, portraying, understanding Napoleon? A man always depicted in idleness, and who did all there is to do! Who was the finest power ever known, the most concentrated power, the most mordant, the most acid of all powers; a singular genius who led armed civilization everywhere and established it nowhere; a man who could do everything because he wanted everything; a prodigious phenomenon of will, taming an illness by a battle, and who would nonetheless die of an illness in his bed after a life lived amid shot and shell; a man who had in his head a code and a sword, word and deed; a visionary who foresaw everything but his own fall; an eccentric statesman who wasted men without number for the sake of economy, and who spared at all costs the heads of Talleyrand, of Pozzo di Borgo, and of Metternich, diplomats whose deaths would have saved the French Empire, and who in his mind outweighed thousands of soldiers; a man to whom, by a rare favor, Nature had left a heart in his body of bronze; a jovial, gentle man at midnight among women, and who the next morning toyed with Europe like a young girl amusing herself by splashing her bathwater! Perfidious and honorable, fond of flash and simplicity, devoid of taste and protective of the arts; and for all these antitheses, great in all things, by instinct or by conformation; Caesar at age twenty-five, Cromwell at thirty; and all the while, like a shopkeeper buried at Père Lachaise, 'a devoted father and a loving husband.' In short, he improvised monuments, empires, kings, codes, verses, a novel, his reach ever exceeding his grasp. Did he not seek to make all of Europe France? And then, once he had given us a weight on this earth that altered the laws of gravity, he left us poorer than the day he first laid hands on us. And he, who had acquired an empire along with his name, lost his name at the very edge of his empire in a sea of blood and soldiers. A man of pure thought and pure action, Desaix and Fouché rolled into one!"

"Purely arbitrary and purely just, every inch a king!" said de Marsay.

"Ach! Vaht a bleasure to zit hier tichesting vile you talk!" said the Baron de Nucingen.

"And you do realize, this is no common fare we're serving you?" said Joseph Bridau. "If you had to pay for the pleasures of conversation as you pay for the pleasures of music or dance, your fortune would never suffice! There's no repeat performance for a tour de force of wit."

"Are we women really so diminished as these gentlemen believe?" said the Princess de Cadignan, addressing the others of her sex with a smile both dubious and mocking. "Today, under a regime that reduces all things, you like little dishes, little apartments, little paintings, little articles, little newspapers, little books, but does that mean women must be small as well? Why should the human heart change, simply because you've changed your dress? The passions are the same in every age. I know of magnificent devotions, sublime sufferings; they're simply not public knowledge, they lack the celebrity, if you like, that ennobled the missteps of some of our women of old. But even without saving a king of France, a woman can still be Agnès Sorel! Do you believe that our beloved Marquise d'Espard is not in every way the equal of Madame Doublet or Madame du Deffand, in whose salons so many wicked things were said and done? Is Marie Taglioni not just as fine a dancer as La Camargo? Is Malibran not a soprano to rival La Saint-Huberti? Are our poets not superior to those of the eighteenth century? If, at this moment, by the fault of the shopkeepers who govern our land, we have no style all our own, did the Empire not have its special cachet, no less than the century of Louis XV, and was its splendor not as grand? Have the sciences lost ground?"

"I share your opinion, madame; the women of this age are truly great," answered General de Montriveau. "When posterity has put us all behind it, will Madame Recamier not shine as brightly as the loveliest women of times past? We have made so much history that the historians will never see! The century of Louis XIV had only one Madame de Sévigné; today we have thousands in Paris alone, who surely write better than she and do not publish their letters. Whether we call her a creature of fashion or a grande dame, the woman of France will always be the woman par excellence. Émile Blondet has painted us a portrait of the charms of a woman of today, but should the need arise, this woman who simpers and struts and chatters the ideas of Messieurs X, Y, and Z could be a heroine! And, let us say, your missteps, mesdames, are all the more poetic in that they will always and forever be surrounded by the greatest perils. I've seen much of society, perhaps I've observed it too late, but in those circumstances where the illicitness of your sentiments might be excused, I have always found that some sort of chance, something you might call Providence, inevitably undoes those we call faithless women."

"I hope," said Madame de Vandenesse, "that we can be great in some other way."

"Oh! Let the Marquis de Montriveau preach to us," cried Madame d'Espard.

"Especially because he has so often practiced what he preaches," added the Baronne de Nucingen.

"Indeed," the general resumed, "among all the dramas, since you're so fond of that word," he said, looking at Blondet, "in which I have seen the finger of God at work, the most terrible was almost my own doing."

"Oh, tell us!" cried Lady Barimore. "I so like a good shiver."

"A fitting fondness for a virtuous woman," replied de Marsay, looking at Lord Dudley's charming daughter.

"In the course of the campaign of 1812," said General de Montriveau, "I was the unwitting cause of a terrible misfortune that might help you, Dr. Bianchon," he said, looking at me, "you who study the human mind even as you study the body, to resolve a few of your lingering questions on the subject of the will. This was my second campaign; I was in love with danger and took nothing seriously, like the green young artillery lieutenant I was! By the time we arrived at the Berezina, the army had lost all its discipline, as you know, and had no sense of military obedience. It was a rabble of men from all manner of nations, all instinctively heading southward. The soldiers did not hesitate to chase a barefooted general in rags away from their bonfires if he had no food or fuel to contribute. This disorder in no way improved once we crossed that notorious river. I had made my way out of the swamps of Zembin all alone, with nothing to eat, and I went looking for a house where I might be taken in. Finding none, or driven away from those I did find, I had the good fortune to spy, just as night was falling, a shabby little Polish farm, a place of which no description can give you an idea unless you have seen the wooden houses of lower Normandy or the poorest smallholdings of the Beauce. These abodes consist of one single room, walled off with planks at one end, the smaller half being a storeroom for forage. Through the dusk I spotted a plume of smoke rising from that distant house, and I walked boldly toward it, hoping to find comrades more compassionate than those I had so far met up with. I entered to find the table set for dinner. Several officers, with a woman among them—not an uncommon thing—were eating a meal of potatoes, horse meat grilled over embers, and frozen beets. Among the tablemates I spied two or three artillery captains from the First Regiment, in which I had served. I was greeted by a hearty 'Hurrah!' that would have greatly surprised me on the other bank of the Berezina; but now the cold was less fierce, my comrades were idle, they were warm, they were eating, and the room, strewn with hay bales, promised them a most delightful night. We weren't so demanding back then. My fellow soldiers could be philanthropists without cost, one of the most common ways of being a philanthropist. I took my place on a hay bale and began eating. At the end of the table, beside the door to the little room full of straw and hay, sat my former colonel, one of the most extraordinary men I have ever

encountered in all the motley crowd it has been my lot to meet. He
was Italian. Now, when mankind is beautiful in the southern lands,
it is sublime. I don't know if you've ever noted the curious fairness of
Italians, when their skin is fair...it's magnificent, particularly by
lamplight. I was reminded of this man on reading Charles Nodier's
fantastical portrait of Colonel Oudet; I rediscovered my own impressions in each of his elegant sentences. An Italian, like most of
the officers who made up his regiment—borrowed by the emperor
from Eugène's army—my colonel cut an imposing figure; he was
easily five foot eight or nine inches tall, admirably proportioned,
perhaps a little fat, but prodigiously vigorous and agile too, graceful
as a greyhound. His abundant black curls set off his complexion,
which was as pale as a woman's; he had small hands, a nicely shaped
foot, a graceful mouth, and a slender aquiline nose with nostrils that
automatically clenched and paled when he was angry, as he often
was. His irascibility was a phenomenon beyond all belief, and so I
will tell you nothing of it; in any case, you'll have a sense of it soon
enough. No one could feel at ease in his presence. I alone, perhaps,
did not fear him; he had conceived for me, it is true, so singular a
friendship that everything I did he found right and proper. When
anger took hold of him, his brow tensed and his muscles sketched
out a delta in the middle of his forehead—something like Redgaunt-
let's horseshoe, to put it more plainly. That sign terrified you perhaps
even more than the mesmerizing fire of his blue eyes. His entire
body trembled, and his strength, already so great in his normal state,
became almost unbounded. He had a habit of gargling his *r*'s. His
voice, easily as mighty as that of Charles Nodier's Oudet, gave a
powerful resonance to the syllable or consonant on which that gar-
gle landed. If at times this mispronunciation was a most elegant
thing, it was quite different when he was commanding maneuvers or
in the grip of emotion: Never can you imagine the potency expressed
by that intonation, however vulgar it may be considered in Paris.
You would have had to hear him. When the colonel felt at peace,
his blue eyes painted a portrait of angelic mildness, and his noble
brow bore an expression full of charm. At a review, no man in all the

Italian army could rival him. D'Orsay himself, the magnificent d'Orsay, was bested by our colonel during Napoleon's final review of the troops before entering Russia. All was opposition in this extraordinary man. Now, contrast is the lifeblood of passion; no need to ask, then, if he exerted on women that irresistible influence to which your nature"—the general was looking at the Princess de Cadignan—"bends like molten glass beneath the glassblower's pipe. But by a curious caprice of fate, as any observer could see for himself, the colonel had very little luck with the ladies, or perhaps he neglected to try. To give you an idea of his tempers, let me recount in two words what I once saw him do in a fit of rage. We were climbing a very narrow path with our cannon, a rather high embankment on one side of the road and woods on the other. Halfway up, we met with another artillery regiment, headed by a colonel, coming the other way. This colonel ordered our regiment's captain, who was leading the first battery, to reverse course. Naturally our captain refuses, but the colonel waves his first battery forward, and despite the quick-thinking driver's attempt to steer into the woods, the wheel of the first cannon caught our captain's right leg and broke it at one go, tossing him over his horse. All this in the blink of an eye. From some distance away, our colonel spies the quarrel in progress and comes galloping forward, weaving his way between cannon and trees, at the risk of finding himself knocked flat on his back at any moment. He reaches the other colonel just as our captain is falling from his horse and crying for help. No, our Italian colonel was no longer a man! ... A foam like frothing champagne bubbled from his lips, and he growled like a lion. Unable to speak a word, unable even to shout, he made his fearsome meaning clear to his antagonist simply by drawing his saber and pointing toward the woods. The two colonels strode off into the trees. Two seconds later we saw our colonel's adversary sprawled on the ground, his head split in two. The other soldiers backed away, oh by God they did, and double-quick! Now, this captain who'd nearly been killed, still howling in the mud puddle where the cannon had deposited him, was married to a stunning Italian woman from Messina, who was not indifferent to our colonel's charms. This had only heightened his fury. The husband had been placed in his charge; he had to defend him, just as he would the woman herself. As it happens, in that hospitable hut just past Zembin, this same captain sat facing me at the table, and his wife at the other end, across from the colonel. She was a small woman by the name of Rosina, very dark, but all the heat of the Sicilian sun could be seen in her almond-shaped black eyes. She had grown frightfully thin; her cheeks were speckled with dirt, like a piece of fruit on a tree by a well-traveled road. Clad—and just barely!—in rags, weary from too much walking, her hair matted and uncombed beneath a torn marmot-fur shawl, she had nevertheless retained a certain womanliness: Her gestures were pretty to see, her mouth pink and puckered; her white teeth, the contours of her face and her bust—charms that privation, cold, and neglect had not entirely blighted—still spoke of love to anyone able to think of such things. Rosina offered a fine example of a nature frail in appearance but spirited and full of force all the same. The husband, a gentleman of the Piedmont, had a face made to express mocking camaraderie, if those two words may indeed be joined. Brave, educated, he seemed blissfully unaware of the liaison his wife and the colonel had kept up for some three years. I attributed this laxity to Italian mores or some private marital understanding, but there was in this man's physiognomy one feature that had always inspired in me an involuntary unease. His thin, mobile lower lip drooped at the corners rather than turning up, betraying, I thought, a deep-seated cruelty in what seemed a phlegmatic and indolent character. As you may well imagine, the conversation I'd walked in on was none too brilliant. My weary comrades ate in silence, though naturally they had a number of questions for me, and we recounted our misfortunes, mingling them with reflections on the campaign, on the generals, on their failings, on the Russians, on the cold. A moment after my arrival, the colonel, having finished his meager repast, wipes his mustaches, wishes us all a good night, turns his dark gaze toward the Italian woman, and says, 'Rosina?' Then, not troubling to await a reply, he goes off to bed in the little storeroom. The sense of the colonel's question was quite clear to us all, so clear that an indescribable gesture escaped the young woman, expressing at once her evident irritation at seeing her dependence so openly displayed, with no trace of respect for her autonomy, and the offense done to her womanly dignity or to her husband. But there was also, in her clenched features, in her darkened brow, a sort of foreboding: Perhaps she had foreseen her fate. Rosina sat silently at the table. A moment later, very likely after the colonel had lain down on his bed of hay or straw, he called out again: 'Rosina?' The tone of this second summons was even more brutally insistent than the first. The guttural *r*, the peculiar resonance the Italian tongue gives a word's vowels and ending, all this eloquently expressed the man's tyranny, his impatience, his willfulness. Rosina blanched, but she rose from the table and brushed past us to go and join the colonel. My tablemates sat in deep silence, but I, alas, looked around at them all and let out a laugh, and my laughter spread from one mouth to the next. '*Tu ridi?*' asked the husband. 'Oh, but my dear comrade,' I answered, serious again, 'I confess, I was wrong, I beg of you a thousand pardons, and if these apologies seem to you insufficient, I can only agree.' 'The fault lies with me, not with you!' he answered, grimly. With this we all settled down for the night in the main room, and soon we were sound asleep. The next day we each set off anew without waking the others, without seeking a traveling companion, in whatever direction we thought best, concerned only with ourselves, displaying the egoism that made of our disorderly retreat one of the most terrible dramas of human nature, of sorrow, and of horror that was ever played out beneath the heavens. Nevertheless, some seven or eight hundred paces from our quarters for the night, we nearly all met up again, and we walked on together, like a flock of geese driven along by the blind despotism of a child. One single, common need urged us ever forward. Arriving at a small hill within sight of the farmhouse, we heard cries like lions roaring in the desert, like bellowing bulls; but no, that clamor cannot be likened to anything known to man. Nevertheless, amid that horrible howl, we heard the faint shriek of a woman. We turned around, struck by some unnamable dread; there was nothing to be seen of the house, only a towering pyre. The building was wholly engulfed in flames and every doorway barricaded. Billows of windblown smoke carried those strident sounds our way, along with an overpowering odor. The captain was walking close by, having calmly come and joined our caravan. We gazed at him in silence, no one daring to question him, but suspecting our curiosity, he put his right index finger to his breast and, gesturing toward the blaze with his other hand, said, '*Son'io!*' We walked on without a word."

"There's nothing so fearsome as the revolt of a sheep," said de Marsay.

"It would be too awful to let us go with that horrible image in our memories," said Madame de Portenduère. "It will be in my dreams."

"And how will Monsieur de Marsay's first love be punished?" asked Lord Dudley, with a smile.

"An Englishman gibes with velveted claws," said Blondet.

"I'll let Monsieur Bianchon tell us," de Marsay answered, looking at me. "He was witness to her final moments."

"I was," I said, "and her death is one of the most beautiful I know. The duke and I had spent the night at her bedside, for her lung fever had attained its final stages and no hope was left. She'd been given last rites the day before. The duke soon fell asleep. Waking toward four in the morning, the duchess gave me a friendly gesture of the most touching sort, with a smile, enjoining me not to disturb him— and this when she was about to take her last breath! She'd grown extraordinarily thin, but her face and her features were, as always, truly sublime. In her pallor, her skin was like porcelain with a light glowing behind it. Her bright eyes and flushed cheeks stood out against that languidly elegant cast and an imposing tranquillity radiated from her face. She seemed full of pity for the duke, her emotion unbounded as her final moments approached. The silence was total. Softly lit by a lamp, the room looked precisely like every patient's bedchamber at the moment of death. Just then the clock struck. The duke awoke, distraught at having drifted off. I did not see the infuriated gesture by which he expressed his regret at closing his eyes on his wife in one of the last moments granted her on this earth, but surely anyone other than she would have misread it. A man of state, preoccupied with the interests of France, the duke had a thousand of those unguarded eccentricities for which a genius is often thought mad, but whose explanation is to be found in his mind's exquisite nature and the labors required of it. He sat down in an armchair beside his wife's bed and stared into her eyes. She reached out weakly, gave her husband's arm a faint squeeze, and in a voice at once quiet and full of emotion, said, 'My poor friend, who will understand you now?' Then she died, her eyes still looking into his."

"The doctor's tales always move us so deeply," said the Duc de Rhétoré.

"But so sweetly," added Mademoiselle des Touches.

"Ah! Madame," the doctor replied, "I have some truly terrible stories in my repertoire, but every tale has its own appointed time in a conversation, as Chamfort so neatly admonished the Duc de Fronsac: 'Ten bottles of champagne stand between this moment and that little jest of yours.'"

"But it's two in the morning, and the story of Rosina has prepared us," said the mistress of the house.

"Go on, Monsieur Bianchon! . . ." he was urged from all sides.

The doctor made a conciliatory gesture, and silence fell once again.

"Some hundred paces from the town of Vendôme, on the banks of the Loir," he said, "stands an aged brown house with high pointed roofs, perfectly isolated, neighbored by no squalid tannery or shabby inn of the sort that you see outside nearly any small city. Before that house lies a riverside garden whose boxwood shrubs, once cut short to border the walkways, now grow however they please. Born in the Loir, a row of quick-growing willows stands like a hedge, half concealing the house. Those plants we call weeds grace the riverbank's slope with their beautiful green. After ten years of neglect, the fruit trees offer no harvest, and their offshoots have grown into dense thickets. The overgrown espaliers make a canopy, as in an ornamental bower. The sand of the walkways is now thick with portulaca, but in truth no sign of a walkway remains. Standing atop the great hill that offers a perch to the ruined château of the Dukes of Vendôme, the only spot from which to see into that enclosure, one muses that in some indistinct past this patch of land was the joy of some gentleman with a passion for roses, for tulip trees, for horticulture in short, but above all for fine fruit. One spies an arbor, or what remains of an arbor; beneath it there still sits a table, not yet entirely obliterated by time. In that garden that is no longer a garden one can glimpse, as if in negative, the joys of the peaceable existence the provinces offer, just as one glimpses the life led by a good merchant from the epitaph on his grave. To cap off all the sad and beguiling ideas that deluge the onlooker's soul, one of the walls displays a sundial ornamented with this bourgeois Christian inscription: ULTIMAM COGITA! The roofs are in terrible disrepair, the shutters are always closed, the balconies are covered with swallows' nests, the doors never open. Tall grasses highlight the steps' cracks in green; the hinges have rusted. The moon, the sun, the winter's cold, the summer's heat have worn down the wood, warped the boards, scoured the paint. The desolate silence is troubled only by the birds, cats, ferrets, rats, and mice that dart unhindered this way and that, doing battle, devouring one another. Everywhere an invisible hand has written this word: *Mystery*. If, your curiosity piqued, you went to study this house from the street, you would see the broad outer door with its rounded top, liberally staved through by the local children. I later learned that this door had been sealed shut ten years before. Through those irregular breaches, you would note how perfectly the courtyard side of the house harmonizes with the garden side: The same disarray reigns over both. Sprays of tall grass outline the paving stones. Enormous cracks snake over the walls, whose blackened tops are enlaced by the thousand festoons of a wild pellitory. The front steps are askew, the rope on the bell has rotted away, the gutters are broken. What fire fallen from the sky has ravaged this place? What tribunal ordered that these grounds be sown with salt? Was God insulted here? Was France betrayed? one wonders. The lizards make no reply but merely crawl on their way. This empty, abandoned house is an enormous riddle whose answer is known to none. Formerly a small feudal estate, it bears the name La Grande Bretèche. The sight of that singular dwelling became one of the keenest pleasures of my sojourn in Vendôme, where Desplein had left me to look after a well-to-do patient. Was it not better than a ruin? A ruin is bound up with memories of an irrefutable reality, but this house—still standing, if suffering a slow demolition by a vengeful hand—this house held a secret, an unknown idea; at the very least, it bore witness to a caprice. More than once, after nightfall, I squeezed through the overgrown hedge that protected the grounds. Braving scratches and scrapes, I made my way into that garden with no master, that land now neither public nor private, and there I stayed for hours on end, contemplating its disarray. I would never have dreamt of consulting some talkative citizen of Vendôme in hopes of learning the story behind that strange sight. There I composed delicious novels in my head; I abandoned myself to little orgies of melancholy that filled me with delight. Had I known the perhaps perfectly ordinary cause of the house's desolation, I would have been robbed of the unspoken poems that so intoxicated me. For me, this asylum embodied the most varied images of human existence, darkened by its sorrows: now a cloister, without the monks; now a silent cemetery, without the dead speaking to you in their epitaphic language; today the house of the leper, tomorrow that of Atreus; but it was above all the provinces, with their meditative ideas, their hourglass lives. Often I wept there; I never laughed. More than once I felt a surge of terror on hearing the rustle of a ringdove's wings as it fled overhead. The ground there is damp; you must look out for lizards, vipers, and frogs, which wander with all the wild freedom of nature; above all you must have no fear of cold, for within a few moments you feel a chill mantle falling over your shoulders, like the hand of the commendatore on Don Giovanni's neck. One evening I shuddered there: The wind had set a rusted old weathervane spinning, and its creak was like the plaint of the house itself, all this just as I was concluding a rather grim drama in my mind, an explanation for this sort of monumentalized sorrow. I returned to my inn, consumed by somber ideas. After my supper, the landlady came to me with a mysterious air and announced, 'Monsieur Regnault is here, monsieur.' 'And who is Monsieur Regnault?' 'What, monsieur, you do not know Monsieur Regnault? Ah! How strange!' she said, walking out. I found myself facing a tall, thin man, all in black, hat in hand, with a stance like a bull about to charge, presenting to me a sloping brow, a small pointed head, and a pallid face rather like a glass of murky water. He seemed the very model of some government minister's private secretary. His suit was old and badly worn at the seams, but he had a diamond stickpin in his jabot and rings in his earlobes. 'Monsieur, to whom do I have the honor?' I asked. He sat down on a chair, warmed himself by my fire, set his hat on my table, and replied, rubbing his hands, 'Oh, isn't it cold! Monsieur, I am Monsieur Regnault.' I nodded, saying to myself, '*Il bondo cani!* What is he after?' 'I am,' he went on, 'a *notaire* in Vendôme.' 'Delighted, monsieur,' I cried, 'but I am not in a position to draw up my will, for reasons known only to me.' 'Beg pardon,' he answered, raising his hand as if to still my tongue. 'If I may, monsieur, if I may! I have learned that you are in the habit of stepping out for a stroll in the garden of La Grande Bretèche.' 'Yes, monsieur.' 'Beg pardon!' he said, repeating his gesture. 'That is a flagrant infraction. Monsieur, in the name of and as executor of the estate of the late Madame la Comtesse de Merret, I come to ask that you discontinue your visits. Beg pardon! I am not a Turk and do not wish to make too much of this. Besides, you have every right to know nothing of the circumstances that oblige me to let the finest house in Vendôme go to ruin. Nonetheless, monsieur, you seem a man of some learning, and must know that the law forbids incursions onto fenced property, under penalty of grave sanctions. A hedge is as good as a wall. But the current state of the house might justifiably serve to excuse your curiosity. I would like nothing better than to allow you to come and go freely in that house, but charged as I am with executing the wishes of the late countess, I have the honor, monsieur, of requesting that you never enter the garden again. I myself, monsieur, since the unsealing of the will, have not set foot in that house, which belongs, as I have had the honor of informing you, to the estate of Madame de Merret. We simply recorded the number of doors and windows to calculate the taxes, which I pay annually from a fund set up for that purpose by the late countess. Ah! My dear monsieur, her will caused quite a stir in Vendôme!' Here the distinguished gentleman paused to blow his nose. I made no attempt to quell his loquacity, understanding full well that Madame de Merret's legacy was the most significant event of his life, the source of his standing in this world, his glory, his Restoration. Farewell to my beautiful daydreams, my novels; I was thus in no way hostile to the pleasure of learning the truth from an official source. 'Monsieur,' I said, 'would it be indiscreet to ask you the reasons for this strange whim?' On hearing those words, the *notaire*'s face beamed with the deep delight of a man who loves nothing so much as straddling his hobbyhorse. He turned up his shirt collar with a satisfied air, pulled out his snuffbox, opened it, held it out to me; when I declined, he took a healthy pinch for himself. He was happy! A man with no hobbyhorse has no notion of all that life has to offer. A hobbyhorse is the precise middle ground between passion and monomania. At that moment, I understood the full sense of Sterne's eloquent term, and I grasped with what joy Uncle Toby mounted his steed, aided by Corporal Trim. 'Monsieur,' said Monsieur Regnault, 'I was once head clerk in the offices of Maître Roguin, in Paris. An excellent practice—perhaps you've heard of it? No? And yet the name has become widely known, owing to a most unfortunate bankruptcy. Lacking the wherewithal to open my own practice in Paris, the fees having been raised in 1816, I came here to purchase my predecessor's. I had relatives in Vendôme, among them a very well-to-do aunt, who gave me her daughter in marriage...' After a brief pause, he continued: 'Monsieur, three months after obtaining my license from the Ministry of Justice, I was summoned one evening, just as I was about to retire (I was not yet married), by Madame la Comtesse de Merret, from her Château de Merret. Her chambermaid, a fine girl who today serves in this very hostelry, was waiting at my door with the countess's coach. Ah! Beg pardon! I must tell you, monsieur, that the Comte de Merret had gone off to die in Paris two months before I came to this place. He died a sordid death, after indulging in all manner of excesses. You understand? The day of his departure, the countess had vacated La Grande Bretèche, taking everything with her. Some even claim that she burned the furniture, the tapestries, in short everything, for the most part of no very great value, that filled the premises currently rented by the aforementioned... (Wait, what am I saying? Forgive me, for a moment I thought I was dictating a lease.) That she burned them,' he resumed, 'on the grounds of the Château de Merret. Have you ever been to Merret, monsieur? No,' he said, answering for me. 'Ah! It's a beautiful place! For some three months,' he went on after a quick shake of the head, 'the count and countess had lived a curious life; they no longer received visitors, madame had her rooms on the ground floor, monsieur on the second. When the countess was alone, she went out only for church. Later, at home in her château, she refused to see the friends of both sexes who came calling. She was already very changed when she left La Grande Bretèche for Merret. That dear woman... (I say "dear" because this diamond comes to me from her, and yet I saw her only once in my life!) The good woman was very ill; no doubt she had abandoned all hope of recovery, for she died without allowing a doctor to be summoned. Many of our ladies believed she was not in full possession of her faculties. My curiosity was thus singularly aroused, monsieur, by the news that Madame de Merret desired my assistance. I was not the only one to take an interest in this matter. That very evening, late though it was, all the city knew I was bound for Merret. The chambermaid offered only evasive replies to the questions I posed on the way; nonetheless, she informed me that her mistress had that day been given last rites by the curé of Merret and seemed unlikely to live through the night. I arrived at the château toward eleven o'clock. I climbed the great staircase. I walked through several large salons, high-ceilinged and dark, devilishly cold and damp, and finally came to the master bedroom, where the countess lay. From the rumors I'd heard of this woman (monsieur, I would never be done with it if I set out to repeat all the tales people told of her!), I pictured her as a coquette. Just imagine, I had great difficulty even finding her in that enormous bed! It is true that to light that vast room, with molded friezes straight out of the ancien régime, so liberally coated with dust that the mere sight of them made you sneeze, she had only an old Argand lamp. Ah! But you've never been to Merret! Well, monsieur, the bed is one of those beds of days gone by, with a high canopy covered in floral calico. A small nightstand sat near the bed, and on it I saw *The Imitation of Christ*, which, parenthetically, I bought for my wife, along with the lamp. There was also a large bergère for the chambermaid and two straight-backed chairs. No fire, as it happens. No other furniture than that. It wouldn't have filled ten lines in an inventory. Ah! My dear monsieur, if you had seen, as I saw it then, that vast room, those brown tapestries on the walls, you would have thought yourself transported into a veritable novel. It was cold—and more than that, it was funereal,' he added, raising one arm in a theatrical gesture and marking a pause. 'I approached the bed, my eyes searching, and finally spied Madame de Merret, once again thanks to the lamp, which shone onto the pillows. Her face was yellow as wax and resembled two hands joined in prayer. Her lace bonnet revealed her hair, quite beautiful but white as cotton thread. She was sitting up with what seemed considerable difficulty. Her large black eyes, no doubt ravaged by fever, almost dead even now, scarcely moved beneath the bones under her eyebrows. This,' he said, pointing to his brow. 'Her forehead was damp. Her wizened hands were like bones wrapped in soft skin; her veins stood out clearly, her muscles. She must once have been very beautiful, but now her appearance filled me with an emotion without name. Never, according to those who buried her, had a living creature grown so emaciated and gone on living. Oh, it was terrible to see! The poor woman had been so cruelly withered by illness that she was nothing more than a ghost. Her pale purple lips seemed not to move when she spoke. My profession has accustomed me to such sights—I have been summoned to more than one deathbed, to record a patient's last wishes—but I will confess that all the agonies and lamentations I've witnessed pale to nothing beside that silent, solitary woman in that enormous château. I heard not the slightest sound, I saw no movement of the covers, as her breathing might cause; I stood riveted to the spot, lost in mute contemplation. I might almost still be there at this moment. Finally her large eyes moved; she tried to raise her right hand, then let it drop back to the bed, and these words emerged from her mouth, like a whisper, for her voice was already no longer a voice: "I've been waiting for you most impatiently." Her cheeks flushed bright red. Speaking, monsieur, was a great struggle for her. "Madame," I answered. She gestured me to be still. At that moment, her old housemaid stood and whispered in my ear, "Do not speak: The countess cannot hear a sound, and anything you say might upset her." I sat down again. A few moments later, Madame de Merret summoned all her remaining strength and moved her right arm, slipping it under the pillow with great effort; she stopped for a brief moment, then, expending the last of her forces, slowly extracted her hand. By the time she pulled out a sealed paper, drops of sweat were falling from her forehead. "I entrust to you my will," she said. "Ah! My God! Ah!" That was all. She took up a crucifix that was lying on her bed, pressed it quickly to her lips, and died. I still shiver when I think of the expression in her frozen gaze. How she must have suffered! There was joy in her final glance, an emotion that remained imprinted in those lifeless eyes. I took the will, and when it was opened I saw that Madame de Merret had named me her executor. Apart from a few individual legacies, she left all her assets to the Hospital of Vendôme. But here are her instructions concerning La Grande Bretèche. She ordered me to leave this house, for fifty full years, starting from the day of her death, just as it was at the moment of her demise, forbidding all entry into the rooms, forbidding even the most minor repair. She went so far as to set aside a pension to hire guards, should they be required for the perfect fulfillment of her intentions. At the end of that time, assuming her wishes have not been violated, the house will become the property of my heirs, for monsieur knows that a *notaire* can accept no bequeathal; otherwise, La Grande Bretèche will be passed on to her legal inheritors, but with it will come the obligation to fulfill the conditions of a codicil that can only be unsealed when those fifty years have elapsed.

No one has come forward to contest the will, and so ...' With this, and leaving his sentence there, the oblong *notaire* looked at me triumphantly, and I completed his delight with a few complimentary words. 'Monsieur,' I said in conclusion, 'your story has stirred me so deeply that even now I believe I can see that dying woman, paler than her sheets; her shining eyes frighten me, and I shall dream of her tonight. But you must surely have wondered at the instructions contained in that singular will.' 'Monsieur,' he answered, with comical dignity, 'I never permit myself to judge the conduct of those who have honored me with the gift of a diamond.' I soon loosened the tongue of the scrupulous *notaire* of Vendôme, who passed along, not without several lengthy digressions, the thoughts offered up by various local sages of both sexes, whose judgments are as holy writ in Vendôme. But so contradictory were those reflections, and so rambling, that I nearly drifted off, despite my great interest in this living history. My curiosity was no match for the grandiloquent delivery and monotonous tones of the *notaire*, no doubt long used to hearing himself speak and to commanding the rapt attention of his clients or compatriots. At long last, to my relief, he went on his way. 'Ah! Ah! Monsieur, many people,' he told me on the stairs, 'would like to live another forty-five years—but, beg pardon!' And slyly he laid his right index finger alongside his nostril, as if to say: Listen closely now! 'But if that is your goal,' he said, 'you'd best not be in your sixties.' I closed the door, roused from my apathy by this last quip, which the *notaire* thought very witty, and then I sat down in my armchair, propping my feet on the two andirons of my fireplace, my mind consumed by a living Ann Radcliffe novel built on the material offered by Monsieur Regnault. A few moments later, my door turned on its hinges, opened by a woman's adroit hand. My hostess came in, a fat, jolly sort, always in a sunny mood, who had missed her calling: She was a woman of Flanders, who should have been born into a canvas by Teniers. 'Well, monsieur?' she said. 'I imagine Monsieur Regnault regaled you with his beloved tale of La Grande Bretèche.' 'He did, Madame Lepas.' 'And what did he say?' In a few words I repeated the cold, dark story of Madame de Merret. With each sentence my hostess bent nearer, peering at me with an innkeeper's perspicacity, a sort of happy medium between the instinct of the gendarme, the cunning of the spy, and the guile of the shopkeeper. 'My dear lady Lepas!' I said as I concluded. 'You seem to know something more of all this. Am I wrong? Why else should you have come up to see me?' 'Ah! Word of an honest woman, and as true as my name is Lepas—' 'Swear no oaths, your eyes are heavy with secrets. You knew Monsieur de Merret. What manner of man was he?' 'Oh, Monsieur de Merret was a fine figure of a man, and he went on and on, he was so tall! An upstanding gentleman from Picardy, and a touch thin-skinned, as we say around here. He always paid cash, just so there'd never be trouble! He was hot-blooded, do you see? The local ladies all found him most amiable.' 'Because he was hot-blooded!' I answered. 'Quite likely,' she said. 'You understand, monsieur, he must have had something going for him, as they say, to marry Madame de Merret, who, no offense to the others, was the richest, most beautiful lady in all the area. She had an income of something like twenty thousand pounds. The whole town came to her wedding. She made an adorable bride, charming, a perfect jewel of a woman. Ah! They were a lovely couple back then!' 'Was their household a happy one?' 'Hmm hmm, yes and no, as best we can tell, for you can well imagine, they didn't cozen much with the likes of us! Madame de Merret was a wonderful woman, sweetness itself, perhaps a bit put-upon by her husband's hot temper, but we all liked him, even if he was a little proud. That's just how the man was, and it was nobody's business but his. When you're noble, you know...' 'And yet there must have been some sort of catastrophe, for Monsieur and Madame de Merret to part ways so abruptly?' 'I never said a word about any catastrophe, monsieur. I don't know the first thing about it.' 'I see. Now I know you know everything.' 'Well then, monsieur, I'll tell you the whole story. Seeing Monsieur Regnault heading up to your rooms, I had a feeling he was going to tell you about Madame de Merret, in connection with La Grande Bretèche. That gave me the idea of having a nice heart-to-heart with you, as you seem to me a man of good counsel, not at all the sort to betray a poor woman such as myself, who's never done any harm to anyone and who nevertheless now finds herself tormented by her conscience. I've never dared bare my soul to these people around here—they're a bunch of chattering parrots, with tongues hard as steel! And besides, monsieur, I've never had a traveler who stayed so long as you in my inn, someone I might tell the story of the fifteen thousand francs—' 'My dear Madame Lepas!' I answered, stanching that torrent of words. 'If your confession is of a nature to compromise me, I won't be burdened with it for anything in the world—' 'Have no fear,' she said, interrupting me. 'You'll see.' This insistence suggested that I was not the first she'd entrusted with this secret of which I was supposedly the sole repository, and I settled down to listen. 'Monsieur,' she said, 'years ago the emperor sent a number of Spaniards here to Vendôme, prisoners of war or what have you, and I was asked to provide lodging at government expense for a young Spaniard who'd been released on parole. Parole or no parole, he had to go and show his face to the subprefect every day. He was a Spanish grandee, no less! He had a name with an *os* and a *dia*, Bagos de Férédia or some such thing. I have his name written down in my register; you can go and see it, if you like. Oh! He was a most handsome young man, for a Spaniard—you know people say they're all homely. He can't have been more than five feet two or three inches tall, but nicely put together; he had small hands, and the way he looked after them! Ah! It was something to see. He had as many brushes for his hands as a woman has for all her primping put together! He had a big shock of black hair and an eye full of fire; his complexion was a touch coppery, but I liked it all the same. He wore linens like I've never seen on anyone, and remember, I've put up princesses, along with General Bertrand, the Duc and Duchesse d'Abrantès, Monsieur Decazes, the King of Spain, I could go on. He didn't eat much, but you couldn't hold that against him, he was always so polite and so amiable. Oh! I was very fond of him indeed, though he didn't speak four words in a day, and there was no way to have a conversation with him. You could talk all you liked, but he never answered. It was a quirk of his, though from what I've heard they're all just the same. He read his breviary like a priest; he went to Mass and all the services regularly. And where did he choose to sit? We only noticed it later: not two steps away from Madame de Merret's chapel. That was where he sat down on his first visit to our church, so no one ever imagined he had an ulterior motive. Besides, he never took his nose out of his prayer book, that poor young man! In the evening, he liked to walk on the big hill, in the ruins of the château. That was his one amusement, poor thing, it put him in mind of his homeland. They say it's all mountains in Spain! Almost right from the start, he loved to spend time up there. It worried me, not seeing him come back before midnight, but we soon got used to his little fancies. He took the front door key, and we stopped waiting up for him. He was staying in our house on rue des Casernes. And then one of our grooms told us a curious thing: He was taking the horses for a bath in the river one evening and thought he saw the Spanish grandee in the distance, swimming along like a regular fish. Next time I saw him, I told him to look out for the floating grasses, and he didn't seem happy to have been spotted in the water. Finally, monsieur, one day, or one morning, we didn't find him in his room; he hadn't come back. I gave the place a good going-over, and finally opened his table drawer, where I found a note, and then fifty of those Spanish gold coins they call portugaises, worth about five thousand francs, and then on top of that ten thousand francs' worth of diamonds in a little sealed box. The note said that if he didn't come back we were to use that money and those diamonds to fund Masses thanking God for his escape and safety. My husband was still with me in those days, and he ran off to hunt for him. And here's the queer thing! He came back with the Spaniard's clothes, which he'd found under a big rock, in a sort of pier on the bank of the river on the château side, more or less directly in front of La Grande Bretèche. No one would have seen my husband take them; it was too early in the morning. Once he'd read the letter, he burned all the clothes, and we reported that he'd escaped, just like Count Férédia wanted. The subprefect sent the whole gendarmerie out on his trail, but they never did catch him. Lepas thought the Spaniard had drowned. Myself, I'm not so sure. My idea is that he had something to do with that Madame de Merret business, because Rosalie told me her mistress had a silver-and-ebony crucifix she so loved that she wanted to be buried with it, and when he first came here Monsieur Férédia had a silver-and-ebony crucifix that I never saw with him again. Now, monsieur, is it not true that I should feel no remorse over the Spaniard's fifteen thousand francs, and that they truly are mine?' 'Certainly. But you never tried to question Rosalie?' I asked her. 'Oh! I did indeed, monsieur. But what can you do? The girl's like a wall. She knows something, but there's no way to wring it out of her.' After a few more moments' conversation, my hostess left me in the grips of vague, dark ideas, a yearning to understand, as any good novel inspires, a religious terror not unlike the profound sentiment that seizes us when we enter a dark church by night and spot a tremulous glimmer between the distant arches; a hesitant figure glides along, a rustling gown or cassock breaks the silence . . . a shiver runs through us. The image of La Grande Bretèche appeared fantastically before me, its tall grasses, its sealed windows, its rusted hinges, its locked doors, its empty rooms. I tried to find some way into that mysterious abode, seeking the key that would unlock this solemn story, this drama that had ended with three people dead. In my eyes, Rosalie was the most interesting creature in all of Vendôme. Examining her, I saw signs of unspoken thoughts, for all the simple good health that radiated from her dimpled face. She had in her some essence of remorse or anticipation; her manner bespoke a secret, like that of the devout women you see in church, rapt in over-fervent prayer, like the young infanticide with her child's last shriek still ringing in her ears. Outwardly, nonetheless, she was naïve and unpolished, there was no criminality in her dim-witted smile, and you would have thought her perfectly innocent based simply on the sight of the large red-and-blue-checked fichu that covered her generous bust, framed, squeezed, bound by a dress of red and violet stripes. 'No,' I thought, 'I will not leave Vendôme until I have learned the full story of La Grande Bretèche. And to that end I will become Rosalie's lover, if need be.' 'Rosalie!' I said to her one evening. 'May I help you, monsieur?' 'You're not married, are you?' She gave a small start. 'Oh! I'll have no lack of men, when the fancy to ruin my life strikes me!' she said with a laugh. She'd immediately recovered from her emotion, for all women have their own particular form of sangfroid, from the grande dame to the maidservant, inclusive. 'A fresh, appealing girl such as you should have no lack of suitors! But tell me, Rosalie, why go to work as a chambermaid when you've been in the employ of Madame de Merret? Did she not leave you some sort of pension?' 'Oh! She did indeed! But, monsieur, my place here is the best in all Vendôme.' This response was of the sort that judges and lawyers call dilatory. In this vast novel, Rosalie seemed to occupy the square at the very middle of a checkerboard; all the interest of the tale was centered on her, and all the truth; I thought her bound up in the tale's mainspring. This was no ordinary seduction to be undertaken; the girl held within her the last chapter of a novel, and so, from that moment on, Rosalie became the object of my every attention. After careful study, I found in her, as in all women of whom we make our principal preoccupation, a whole host of qualities: She was clean, conscientious; she was beautiful, that goes without saying; she soon took on all the allures that our desire lends to women, whatever their situation in life. Two weeks after the *notaire*'s visit, one evening, or rather one morning, for it was very early, I said to Rosalie, 'Tell me all you know about Madame de Merret, won't you?' 'Oh,' she answered, recoiling, 'don't ask that of me, Monsieur Horace!' Her lovely face dimmed, her bright, youthful colors faded, and her eyes lost their glistening, innocent glow. 'Well,' she went on, 'since you ask, I'll tell you, but you must keep my secret!' 'Come now, my poor girl, I'll keep all your secrets with the probity of a thief, the most loyal there is.' 'If it's all the same to you,' she said to me, 'I'd rather you keep it with yours.' With this, she put her fichu to rights and sat up in a storyteller's pose; for the body must be secure and at ease before we can tell a good tale. The best narratives are spun at a certain hour —look at all of us sitting here at this table! No one has ever told a good story on his feet nor with an empty stomach. Now, a whole volume would scarcely suffice to faithfully reproduce Rosalie's meandering eloquence, but since as it happens the event of which she offered me a tangled knowledge lies between Madame Lepas's chatter and the *notaire*'s, just as the middle terms of a mathematical ratio lie between the two extremes, I can recount it in just a few words. With some abridgement, then, here it is. The room occupied by Madame de Merret at La Bretèche lay on the ground floor. In one wall, a small closet, some four feet deep, served as her wardrobe. Three months before the evening in question, Madame de Merret had fallen ill, gravely enough that her husband had taken to sleeping upstairs, so as not to disturb her. By one of those unforeseeable strokes of fate, that evening he returned two hours later than usual from his club, where he often went to read the papers and talk politics with the locals. His wife thought him at home, in bed and asleep. But the invasion of France had sparked a most animated discussion; the billiard match had grown heated; he'd lost forty francs, an enormous sum in Vendôme, where everyone saves and where life is lived within the boundaries of an admirable modesty that may well be the source of a genuine happiness, for which no Parisian cares a whit. Monsieur de Merret had fallen into the habit, on his return from the club, of simply asking Rosalie if his wife had retired for the night; the answer was always affirmative, and so he went straight up to his rooms, with an amiability born of trust and routine. This particular night, he fancied he might pay a call on Madame de Merret, to tell her of his misadventure and perhaps seek some manner of consolation as well. He had found Madame de Merret most fetchingly dressed at dinner; now, on his way home from the club, he told himself that his wife's illness had passed, her beauty returning as she convalesced—and he noticed this, as husbands notice everything, a bit late. Rather than call for Rosalie, who was then occupied in the kitchen watching the coachman and the cook play a tense round of brisque, Monsieur de Merret made for his wife's bedroom, lit by the lantern he'd set down on the first step of the stairway. His distinctive footfalls echoed off the arched ceiling of the corridor. Turning the key to his wife's room, he thought he heard the closet door closing, but when he entered Madame de Merret was alone, standing before the fireplace. Naïvely, the husband thought it was Rosalie in the closet; nevertheless a burst of suspicion rang in his ear, like tolling bells, and put him on guard; he looked at his wife and found in her eyes something mysterious and wild. 'You're home very late,' she said. He thought he detected a faint agitation in that voice, ordinarily so mild and gracious. Monsieur de Merret made no reply, for just then Rosalie came in. He was dumbstruck. He paced through the room, from one window to the other, arms crossed over his chest. 'Have you had bad news? Are you ill?' his wife timidly asked, as Rosalie undressed her. He said nothing. 'Leave us,' said Madame de Merret to her chambermaid, 'I'll put my curlpapers in myself.' From the look on her husband's face, she foresaw some manner of trouble, and she wanted to be alone with him. When Rosalie was gone, or supposed to be gone, for she lingered a few moments in the corridor, Monsieur de Merret planted himself before his wife and said to her coldly, 'Madame, there is someone in your closet!' She looked at her husband, impassive, and answered simply, 'No, monsieur.' Monsieur de Merret was sorely aggrieved by that 'no'; he didn't believe it. And yet never had his wife seemed to him purer nor more pious than at that moment. He stalked off to open the closet; Madame de Merret grasped his hand, stopped him, looked at him dolefully, and told him, with singular urgency, 'If you find no one, understand that everything will be over between us!' The remarkable dignity of his wife's manner revived the gentleman's deep esteem for her and inspired him to one of those resolutions that need only a grand theater to become immortal. 'No,' he said, 'Joséphine, I won't look. Whatever I find, we would be parted forever. Listen, I know how pure is your soul and how saintly your life; you would never throw all that away by committing a mortal sin.' Madame de Merret looked at her husband, wild-eyed. 'Here, here is your crucifix,' the man added. 'Swear to me before God that no one is there. I will believe you, and I will never open that door.' Madame de Merret took the crucifix and said, 'I swear.' 'Louder,' said the husband, 'and repeat: I swear before God that there is no one in that closet.' She repeated the sentence without batting an eye. 'Very well,'

said Monsieur de Merret coolly. And then, after a moment of silence: 'This is a very fine thing you have here; I've not seen it before.'
He was studying that ebony crucifix, artistically carved and in-
crusted with silver. 'I found it at Duvivier's. He bought it from a
Spanish monk when those prisoners came through Vendôme last
year.' 'Ah!' said Monsieur de Merret, replacing the crucifix on its
nail; and he rang. A moment later Rosalie appeared. Monsieur de
Merret went briskly to meet her, led her to the window that looked
onto the garden, and said to her quietly, 'I know that Gorenflot is
eager to marry you, that poverty alone stands in your way, that
you've told him you won't be his wife until he establishes himself as
a mason. Well, go and fetch him; tell him to come out at once and
bring his trowel and tools. See to it that no one in his house is awakened but him; his reward will exceed your desires. Above all, leave
this place without one word to anyone, or...' He scowled. Rosalie
set off, but he called her back. 'Here, take my passkey,' he said. 'Jean,'
cried Monsieur de Merret in a thundering voice from the corridor.
Jean, who was both his coachman and his valet, abandoned his game
of brisque and came to him. 'Everyone to bed,' said his master, beck-
oning him nearer, and in a whisper he added, 'Once they're all
asleep—*asleep*, do you hear?—come downstairs and tell me.' Monsieur de Merret had kept one eye on his wife as he delivered these
orders; now he calmly joined her before the fire and began to recount the events of the billiard match and the discussions at the
club. Rosalie returned to find Monsieur and Madame de Merret
chatting most amicably. The gentleman had recently had new ceil-
ings made for his ground-floor reception rooms. Plaster is a rarity in
Vendôme, its cost increased by the need to transport it in; he had
thus ordered a generous quantity, knowing he would always find
buyers for the excess. It was this that inspired the plan he was now
setting in motion. 'Monsieur Gorenflot is here,' said Rosalie, quietly.
'Show him in!' her master answered. Madame de Merret paled a
little on seeing the mason. 'Gorenflot,' said the husband, 'go and
fetch some bricks from the shed, enough to wall up the closet; you
can use my leftover plaster to seal the door.' Then, drawing Rosalie

and the mason to him, he said in low tones, 'Listen, Gorenflot, you will sleep here tonight. But tomorrow morning, you will have a passport to go to a foreign country, and a city that I will name. I'll give you six thousand francs for the journey. You will live in that city for ten years; should it not be to your liking, you may move to another, so long as it's in the same country. You will go by way of Paris, where you will wait for me. There, I will guarantee you by contract a further six thousand francs, payable on your return, assuming you fulfill our bargain's conditions. That price should assure your most profound silence on all that you do here tonight. And for you, Rosalie: ten thousand francs, to be delivered only on your wedding day, so long as you marry Gorenflot, but in order for the marriage to take place, you must hold your tongue. Otherwise, no dowry.' 'Rosalie,' said Madame de Merret, 'come and do my hair.' The husband paced lazily around the room, watching over the door, the mason, and his wife, taking care to conceal all suspicion. Gorenflot could not help making some noise. Seizing on a moment when the worker was unloading bricks and her husband happened to be at the far end of the room, Madame de Merret whispered to Rosalie, 'A thousand francs annual pension for you, my dear child, if you can tell Gorenflot to leave a gap at the bottom.' Then, aloud, she offhandedly ordered her, 'Go and help him!' In all the time Gorenflot spent sealing the doorway, Monsieur and Madame de Merret did not speak a word. On the husband's part, this silence was a stratagem, not wanting to give his wife the occasion to speak coded words to the others; in the case of Madame de Merret, it was prudence or pride. When the bricks filled half the doorway, the quick-witted mason waited for the gentleman to turn his back, then struck one of the door's two windows with his pickax. This gave Madame de Merret to understand that Rosalie had spoken to Gorenflot. The three of them then saw the face of a man, dusky and tanned, black hair, eyes afire. Before her husband turned around, the poor woman had time to nod at the foreigner, for whom this sign signified, 'Do not lose hope!' At four o'clock, just as the sky was beginning to lighten, for it was the month of September, the wall was done. The mason remained under Jean's guard, and Monsieur de

Merret went to bed in his wife's room. The next morning, on rising, he said blithely, 'Ah! Hang it all, I've got to go to the mayor's for the passport.' He put on his hat, took three steps toward the door, turned back, took the crucifix. His wife was trembling with joy. 'He means to call at Duvivier's,' she thought. As soon as the gentleman was gone, Madame de Merret summoned Rosalie and cried out, in a desperate voice, 'The pickax, the pickax, and to work! I watched how Gorenflot went about it last night; we'll have time to make a hole and repair it again.' In the blink of an eye, Rosalie came back with a sort of ax, and with a vigor that cannot be described, the countess began to demolish the wall. She had already dislodged several bricks when, stepping back to strike a blow still more furious than the last, she saw Monsieur de Merret behind her and fainted away. 'Lay madame on her bed,' said the gentleman coldly. Foreseeing what would take place in his absence, he had set a trap for his wife; he had quite simply written the mayor and sent for Duvivier. The jeweler arrived after the room had been tidied up. 'Duvivier,' asked the gentleman, 'did you not buy several crucifixes from the Spaniards that passed through this town?' 'No, monsieur.' 'Very well, I thank you,' he said, shooting his wife a glance fierce as a tiger's. 'Jean,' he added, turning to his valet, 'I'll be taking my meals in Madame de Merret's bedchamber; she's not well, and I won't leave her side until she has fully recovered.' For twenty days that heartless man did not leave his wife's room. In the beginning, noises could sometimes be heard from the walled-up closet, and Joséphine stared imploringly at her husband in hopes that he might spare the dying stranger's life. He would not allow her to speak a word, and his answer was always the same: 'You swore on the cross that was no one was there.'"

The tale at an end, all the women rose from the table, and with this the spell Bianchon had cast on them was broken. Nevertheless, some had felt almost cold on hearing those final words.

Translated by Jordan Stump

THE RED INN

To M. Le Marquis de Custine

SOME TIME ago, a Paris banker with extensive commercial relations in Germany was giving a dinner party for a man who till then
was unknown to him, an acquaintance of the sort that businessmen
acquire here and there through their correspondence. This friend,
the head of a rather large firm in Nuremberg, was a good hefty German, a man of taste and erudition, above all a connoisseur of pipes,
with a broad handsome Nuremberger face, the wide smooth brow
crossed with a few sparse strands of blond hair. He looked the very
model of the sons of that pure noble Germania, so fertile in honorable characters, and whose peaceable ways have never failed even after seven invasions. The foreigner laughed readily, listened attentively,
and drank remarkably well; to all appearances he enjoyed our champagne wines perhaps as much as he would his own straw-toned Jo-
hannisbergers. His name was Hermann, like most Germans whom
authors write about. As a man who can do nothing lightly, he sat
solid at the banker's table, eating with that Teutonic appetite famous throughout Europe and bidding a conscientious farewell to
the cuisine of our great Carême. To do his guest honor, the master of
the house had gathered a few good friends, capitalists and merchants, and a number of pretty and pleasant ladies whose agreeable
banter and open manner harmonized with the cordial German
spirit. Truly, if you could have experienced, as I had the good fortune to do, this merry gathering of people who had retracted their

commercial claws to speculate instead on life's pleasures, you would have found it difficult to detest usurious loans or deplore bankruptcies. Man cannot spend all his time doing evil, and even in the company of pirates there must be some sweet moments on their sinister ship when you feel as if you were aboard a pleasure yacht.

"Before we part tonight, Monsieur Hermann is going to tell us another one of those chilling German stories." The announcement came from a pale, blond young woman who had doubtless read the stories of Hoffmann and Walter Scott. She was the banker's only child, a ravishing creature who was putting the final touches to her education at the Gymnase and adored the plays that theater presented.

The guests were in the contented state of languor and quiet that results from an exquisite meal, when we have demanded a little too much of our digestive capacities. Leaning back in their chairs, wrists and fingers resting lightly upon the table's edge, a few guests played lazily with the gilded blades of their knives. When a dinner reaches that lull some people will work over a pear seed, others roll a pinch of bread between thumb and index finger, lovers shape clumsy letters out of fruit scraps, the miserly count their fruit pits and line them up on their plates the way a theater director arranges his extras at the rear of the stage. These small gastronomic felicities go unremarked by Brillat-Savarin, an otherwise observant writer. The serving staff had disappeared. The dessert table looked like a squadron after the battle, all dismembered, plundered, wilted. Platters lay scattered over the table despite the hostess's determined efforts to set them back in order. A few people stared at some prints of Switzerland lined up on the gray walls of the dining room. No one was irritable; we have never known anyone to remain unhappy while digesting a good meal. We enjoy lingering in a becalmed state, a kind of midpoint between the reverie of a thinker and the contentment of a cud-chewing animal, a state that should be termed the physical melancholy of gastronomy.

Thus the guests turned happily toward the good German, all of them delighted to have a tale to listen to, even a dull one. For during that benign interval, a storyteller's voice always sounds delicious to our sated senses; it promotes their passive contentment. As an observer of scenes, I sat admiring these faces bright with smiles, lit by the candles and flushed dark by good food; their various expressions produced some piquant effects, seen through the candlesticks and porcelain baskets, the fruits and the crystal.

My imagination was suddenly caught by the appearance of the guest directly across the table from me. He was a man of average height, somewhat plump, cheerful, with the style and bearing of a stockbroker, and apparently endowed with only a very ordinary turn of mind. I had not noticed him before, but just then his face, probably shadowed by a flicker of the light, seemed to me to change character: It had gone dull, earthen, furrowed with purplish folds. You might have described it as the cadaverous head of a dying man. He was immobile like a figure painted into a diorama; his vacant eyes stayed fixed on the glittering facets of a crystal stopper on a bottle, but he was certainly not counting them and seemed lost in some strange contemplation of the future or the past. I studied that puzzling face at some length, and it made me wonder: "Is he ill? Has he drunk too much? Has the market collapsed? Is he considering how to swindle his creditors?"

"Look across there!" I murmured to the woman on my left, indicating the face of the unknown fellow. "Wouldn't you say that's the look of a bankruptcy about to happen?"

"Oh," she answered, "he'd be looking jollier if that were the case." With a graceful tilt of the head, she added: "If that man should ever lose his fortune, it would be world news. He has millions in real estate. He used to be a provisioner for the imperial armies—a good fellow and rather unusual. He married his second wife as a financial move, but he does make her extremely happy. He has a pretty daughter, whom he refused to acknowledge for a very long time, but his son died—unfortunately killed in a duel—and that forced him to take the girl back into the household as they could no longer have children. The poor girl has suddenly become one of the richest heiresses in Paris. The loss of his only son has plunged this dear man into a grief that surfaces from time to time."

At that moment, the provisioner lifted his eyes to mine; his gaze made me shiver, it was so somber and pensive! That glance must sum up a whole lifetime. But suddenly his face turned merry: He took up the crystal stopper, set it crisply onto a carafe full of water that stood before his plate, and turned his head toward Monsieur Hermann with a smile. The man was beatific with gastronomic pleasure; he probably hadn't a thought in his head, wasn't pondering a thing. I immediately felt rather ashamed of squandering my powers of divination *in anima vili*—on a mere thickheaded financier. While I was engaged in pointless phrenological observation, the good German had filled his nose with a dose of snuff and started on his story. It would be difficult to reproduce the tale in the same terms, what with the man's frequent interpolations and verbose digressions, so I have written it again here in my own way, leaving out the Nuremberger's mistakes and using any poetic and interesting elements it might contain, with the boldness of those writers who somehow neglect to state on the title page of their publications: "Translated from the German."

THE IDEA AND THE FACT

Late in the month of Vendémiaire in year VII of the republican era—or according to the style of our day, October 20, 1799—two young men left the city of Bonn in the morning and by day's end had reached the outskirts of Andernach, a small town on the left bank of the Rhine a few leagues from Koblenz.

At the time, the French army under General Augereau was holding maneuvers before the Austrian forces then occupying the right bank of the river. The republican division headquarters was Koblenz, and one of the demi-brigades from Augereau's corps was stationed at Andernach. The two young travelers were French. By their

uniforms (blue mixed with white and faced in red velvet), by their
sabers, and especially by the hats covered in green oilcloth and ornamented with a tricolor plume, even the German peasants could recognize that these were military surgeons, men of science and skill
who were generally well liked, not only by the army but also by the
people whose lands the French troops had invaded. At that time,
many youngsters of good family who were snatched from their medical training by General Jourdan's recent conscription law quite naturally chose to continue their studies on the battlefield rather than
be assigned to action as a soldier, a role so little suited to their previous training and their peaceable purpose. Men of science, pacific and
useful, such young men did some good amid so much misery, and
they got on well with the educated people in the various countries
through which the cruel civilization of the Republic drove its way.
Each carrying a travel warrant and credentials as assistant surgeon
signed by Coste and Bernadotte, the two were reporting to their assigned demi-brigade. Both came of bourgeois families in Beauvais
who were only moderately wealthy but in which the genteel manners and loyalties of the provinces were transmitted as part of their
legacy. Drawn by a curiosity quite natural in the young to see the
theater of war before they were actually obliged to begin their duties, they had traveled by coach as far as Strasbourg. Maternal prudence had provided them each with only a meager sum of money,
but they felt rich with their few louis in hand, a veritable treasure in
a period when the revolutionary banknotes had dropped to their
lowest value and gold was worth a great deal.

The two assistant surgeons, twenty years old at most, succumbed
to the poetry of their situation with all the enthusiasm of youth.
From Strasbourg to Bonn, they had toured the lands of the Electorate and the banks of the Rhine as artists, as philosophers, as observers. People of a scientific bent are at that age truly multifaceted
beings. Even when making love, or traveling, a medical intern should
be collecting the rudiments of his fortune or of his future renown.
So the two youths surrendered to that profound admiration that
seizes an educated person at the spectacle of the banks of the Rhine

and the Swabian countryside between Mayence and Cologne: powerful, rich, hugely various nature full of feudal traces, lush green but everywhere stamped with the scars of steel and fire. Louis XIV and Marshal Turenne have cauterized that gorgeous land. Here and there ruins attest to the pride, or perhaps the foresight, of the Versailles king, who ordered the destruction of the fine châteaus that once graced this part of Germany. Seeing this marvelous forested terrain abounding in the picturesque quality of the Middle Ages, however ruined, you sense the German spirit, its reveries and its mysticism.

The two friends' stay at Bonn had served the goals of both science and pleasure. The main hospital of the Gallo-Batavian Army and of Augereau's division was installed in the actual palace of the elector. The newly qualified surgeons thus went there to see old schoolmates, present their letters of recommendation, and become acquainted with some basic aspects of their profession. But also, there as elsewhere, they were stripped of some of the narrow prejudices we all retain for so long about the superiority of the monuments and beauties of our own homeland. Surprised by the spectacle of the marble columns decorating the electoral palace, they went on to admire the grandeur of German buildings, and at every turn found still more antique or modern treasures. Time and again, the roads the two friends wandered on their way to Andernach would take them onto the peak of some granite mountain higher than the rest. From there, through a gap in the forest, through some crevice in the rock, they would glimpse the Rhine framed in the sandstone or festooned with vigorous plant life. The valleys, the trails, the trees released an autumnal fragrance that transports one toward reverie; the treetops were starting to turn golden, to take on warm, brown tones that signal aging; the leaves were dropping but the sky was still a deep azure, and the dry roads traced yellow lines through the landscape lit now by the slanted beams of the setting sun. Half a league before Andernach, the two friends walked their horses through a deep silence, as if the war were not devastating this lovely land, and they followed a trail cut for goats across the high bluish granite walls with the Rhine roiling past below. Soon they descended a slope of the gorge at whose base lay the little town set charmingly at the river's edge, offering sailors a pretty port.

"Germany is truly a beautiful country!" exclaimed one of the two youths, the one called Prosper Magnan, as he caught sight of Andernach's colorful houses, nestled like eggs in a basket and separated by trees, gardens, and flowers. Then he stood for a moment admiring the pointed roofs with their projecting gables, the wooden staircases and galleries of a thousand tranquil houses, and the boats rocking to the waves in the harbor.

When Monsieur Hermann pronounced the name Prosper Magnan, the provisioner seized the carafe, dashed water into his glass, and swallowed it in a single gulp. The movement having drawn my attention, I thought I noticed a slight trembling in the capitalist's hands and a dampness on his brow.

"What's the provisioner's name?" I quietly asked my helpful neighbor.

"Taillefer," she replied.

"Are you feeling ill?" I asked him, seeing the curious fellow turn pale.

"No, no," he replied, thanking me with a polite wave. "I am listening," he added, and nodded toward the other guests, who had all turned at once to look at him.

Monsieur Hermann went on: "I've forgotten the name of the second young man, but from Prosper Magnan's account, I learned that his companion was dark-haired, rather thin, and good-humored. If I may, I'll call him Wilhelm, to make the storytelling easier to follow."

And so the good German took up the tale again, having—with no concern for the romantic or for local color—baptized the young French doctor with a Germanic name.

When the two young men arrived at Andernach, night had fallen. Assuming that they would lose a good deal of time seeking out their commanders, establishing their credentials, and arranging for military billets in a city already full of soldiers, they resolved to spend their last night of freedom at an inn situated a short distance outside Andernach, and which from the rocky cliffs above they had admired for its rich coloring, lovelier still in the flames of the setting sun. Painted entirely in red, the building stood out sharply from the rest of the landscape, separated as it was from the general mass of the town itself and setting its broad crimson swath against the greens of the varied foliage, its vivid walls against the grayish tones of the water. The place owed its name to its exterior paintwork, which had probably been laid on eons ago at the whim of its original owner. A marketing superstition quite natural to the successive owners of the inn, renowned as it was among Rhine boatmen, had assiduously preserved the traditional decor. Hearing horses approach, the proprietor of the Red Inn came to the doorway.

"Good lord," he exclaimed. "Gentlemen, a moment later and you would have had to bed down outdoors under the stars, like most of your countrymen bivouacking at the other end of Andernach. My place is full. If you must have a real bed, all I can offer you is my own room. As for your horses, I'll have hay put down for them in a corner of the courtyard. Today my stable is full of Christians … The gentlemen are arriving from France?" he went on after a slight pause.

"From Bonn," replied Prosper. "And we've had nothing to eat since morning."

"Oh well, as for food," said the innkeeper nodding his head, "people come from ten leagues around to feast at the Red Inn! You'll have a banquet fit for a prince—fish from the Rhine! That says it all."

Handing over their exhausted mounts to the host, who called rather uselessly for his grooms, the two young surgeons stepped into the inn's common room. At first a thick whitish cloud exhaled by a crowd of smokers prevented them from seeing much of the people they would be joining, but once they were seated at a table, with the practical patience of philosophical travelers who have come to understand complaints are useless, they made out through the tobacco fumes the obligatory furnishings of a German inn: potbelly stove, clock, tables, beer mugs, long pipes; here and there a face stood out, Jewish, German, the rough mugs of a few river men. The epaulettes of several French officers glittered within the fog, and spurs and sabers clattered constantly against the stone floor. Some men were playing cards, others bickering or silent, eating, drinking, walking about. A short heavy woman wearing a black velvet bonnet, a blue-and-silver stomacher, a pincushion, a bundle of keys, a silver clasp, with her hair in braids—the distinctive markers of all mistresses of German inns, an outfit so regularly pictured in a thousand popular prints that it is too commonplace to bother describing—well then, the innkeeper's wife did a skillful job of keeping the two youths alternately waiting and grumbling. Gradually the din lessened, the travelers retired, and the cloud of smoke cleared. By the time the doctors' plates arrived and the classic Rhine carp appeared on the table, it was eleven o'clock and the room was empty. Through the nighttime silence they could hear the horses chomping their fodder and stamping a hoof, the murmur of the Rhine, and those indefinable sounds of a full house when everyone is bedding down. Doors and windows open and close, voices mumble half-heard words, and a few queries echo from the bedchambers. In that moment of quiet bustle, the two Frenchmen and their host—who was busily extolling Andernach, the food, the Rhine wine, the French Republican army, his wife—all pricked up their ears at the hoarse cries of a few sailors and the scrape of a boat against the wharf. The innkeeper, doubtless familiar with the guttural talk of boatmen, abruptly left the room and soon returned. He brought with him a short stout man trailed by two sailors carrying a heavy valise and a few bundles. The sailors set down the packs, and the man picked up his valise himself and kept it close as he unceremoniously sat down at the table facing the two young doctors.

"Go sleep on your boat," he told the sailors, "as the inn is full. All things considered, that will be better."

"Monsieur," said the innkeeper to the new arrival, "this is all the food I have left." And he pointed to the supper he had served to the two Frenchmen. "I haven't one bread crust more, not a bone."

"No sauerkraut?"

"Not even enough to fill my wife's thimble! And as I had the honor of telling you, there's not a bed to be had but the chair you're sitting in, and no room but this one."

At these words, the short man cast upon the innkeeper, the room, and the two Frenchmen a gaze expressing equal measures of fear and caution.

Here Monsieur Hermann interrupted his tale. "At this point I must note," he said, "that we never learned either the actual name nor the story of this stranger. His papers showed that he had come from Aix-la-Chapelle; he went by the name Walhenfer, and he owned a rather sizable pin factory outside Neuwied. Like all the manufacturers in that area, he was wearing a plain fabric redingote, trousers, and a waistcoat of deep green velours, boots, and a wide leather belt. His face was quite round, his manner open and cordial, but throughout the evening he had difficulty fully masking some secret worries, or perhaps some racking trouble. The innkeeper has always thought that the German businessman was fleeing his country. I later learned that his factory had been burned down by one of those random events unfortunately so frequent in wartime. Despite his generally anxious look, his face showed a very comradely disposition. He had handsome features, in particular a thick neck whose whiteness was so nicely set off by a black cravat that Wilhelm jokingly remarked on it to Prosper..."

Here, Monsieur Taillefer drank down a glass of water.

Prosper politely offered to share their supper, and Walhenfer accepted easily, like a man sure he could return the courtesy. He laid his valise flat on the floor, set his feet upon it, took off his hat, pulled up to the table, and removed his gloves and two pistols that were tucked into his belt. The host quickly laid him a place and the three clients silently set about satisfying their appetites. The atmosphere in the room was so warm and the flies so numerous that Prosper asked the innkeeper to open the casement window onto the entryway to freshen the air. The window was barricaded by an iron bar whose two ends fit into holes carved into the two sides of the recess. For still greater security, a heavy screw fastened into a bolt on each shutter. Prosper idly watched the way the host went about opening the window.

Since I mention these details, I should describe the inn's interior arrangements; the interest of the story does depend on an exact understanding of its layout. The room where the three clients sat had two exit doors. One opened onto the Andernach road running along the Rhine; across the way in front of the inn, naturally, was a small wharf where the businessman's hired boat was tied up. The other door opened onto the courtyard of the inn. This courtyard was enclosed by very high walls and was filled, for the moment, with cattle and horses, the stables being full of people. The main gate out of the courtyard had just been so elaborately barred for the night that, to be quicker, the innkeeper had brought the businessman and the sailors indoors through the common-room door from the river road. After opening the window as Prosper Magnan had requested, the innkeeper went back to lock the door, slipping its crossbars into their recesses and turning the bolts. The host's own bedroom, where the two young surgeons were to sleep, adjoined the common room and was separated by a thin wall from the kitchen, where the innkeeper and his wife would presumably be spending the night. The serving girl had just left for a bunk, the corner of the hayloft, or some other place. It was plain that the common room, the innkeeper's bedroom, and the kitchen were somewhat isolated from the rest of the inn. In the courtyard were two large dogs, whose deep barking made clear they were vigilant and very irritable guardians.

"What silence, and what a beautiful night!" Wilhelm exclaimed, looking out at the sky while the host locked the door. The slap of the waves was now the only sound to be heard.

"Gentlemen," said the businessman to the two Frenchmen, "allow me to offer you a few bottles of wine to wash down your carp. We will relieve some of the day's fatigue by drinking. From your faces and the state of your clothing, I can see that, like me, you have traveled a long way today."

The two friends accepted, and the innkeeper left through the kitchen door to go down to the cellar. When the five fine old bottles he brought up were on the table, his wife served the rest of the meal. With her proprietor's eye she surveyed the room and the dishes; then, confident that she had seen to all the travelers' needs, she returned to the kitchen. The four companions—for the host had been invited to drink with the others—did not hear her retire, but later, during the quiet intervals in their conversation, some very loud snores, made more resonant by the hollow planks of the shed where she had settled, brought a smile to the faces of the friends, and especially to the host's.

Toward midnight, with nothing left on the table but biscuits, cheese, dried fruits, and good wine, the companions—mainly the two young Frenchmen—grew talkative. They spoke of their home country, of their studies, of the war. With time, the conversation grew livelier. Prosper Magnan brought a few tears to the eyes of the fleeing businessman when, with the openness of a boy from Picardy and the naïve manner of a good, tender nature, he pictured what his mother might be doing at that very moment as he sat here on the banks of the Rhine.

"I can just see her, reading her evening prayer before bed! She certainly hasn't forgotten me, and she must be wondering 'Where is he now, my poor Prosper?' But if she's won a few francs at cards from a neighbor—maybe from your mother," he added, nudging Wilhelm's elbow, "she'll go put them away in the big clay pot where she's collecting the money she needs to buy the thirty acres next to the little plot she owns in Lescheville. Those thirty acres will easily cost about sixty thousand francs. Really good meadowland ... Ah, if I can ever put that amount together, I would live my whole life in Lescheville and never want another thing! How often my father would talk about wanting those thirty acres and the pretty brook that winds through the fields! Well, in the end he died without ever managing to buy them. I used to play there so often!"

"Monsieur Walhenfer, haven't you got some secret wish of your own?" asked Wilhelm.

"Yes, young man, yes indeed! But it actually did come true, and now..." The good fellow fell silent without finishing his sentence.

"Me," said the innkeeper, his face slightly flushed, "last year I bought a field I'd been wanting to own for more than ten years."

They went on chatting that way, as men do when tongues are loosened by wine, and they conceived that passing affection for one another that we indulge more generously when we travel—so that, as they stood up to prepare for sleep, Wilhelm offered the businessman his bed.

"You can accept it the more easily," he told Walhenfer, "since I can bed down with Prosper. It certainly won't be the first time nor the last. You are our elder, and we must honor age!"

"Ah, no!" the innkeeper said. "My wife's bed in that room has several mattresses, you can put one of them on the floor." And he went to close the casement window, causing the noise the cautious operation entailed.

"I accept," said the businessman. Then, lowering his voice and looking at the two comrades, he added, "I confess I was hoping for this. My boatmen seem a little suspect... For tonight, I am not unhappy to be in the company of two decent, kind young men—two French soldiers! I have a hundred thousand francs' worth of gold and diamonds in my valise!"

The affectionate reserve with which the two young men received this reckless revelation reassured the German fellow. The innkeeper helped his visitors to take apart one of the beds. Then, when all was arranged for the best, he wished them good night and went off to sleep. The businessman and the two doctors joked about the difference in their headrests: Prosper put his instrument bag and Wilhelm's under his mattress to replace the missing pillow, while Walhenfer took special care to set his valise beneath the head of his bed.

"We'll both of us be sleeping on top of our fortunes—you on your gold and I on my medical bag. It remains to be seen whether my instruments will ever make me as much gold as you've already acquired."

"You certainly have every reason to hope so," said the businessman. "Hard work and honesty do win out, but it takes patience."

Walhenfer and Wilhelm soon fell asleep. Perhaps because his bed on the floor was too hard, perhaps because his extreme fatigue caused him insomnia, perhaps through some fateful state of mind, Prosper Magnan lay awake. His thoughts gradually took a bad turn. He could think of nothing else but the hundred thousand francs the businessman was sleeping on. For him, a hundred thousand francs was an enormous ready-made fortune. He began by putting it to a thousand different uses, building castles in Spain, as we all do so happily in those moments before sleep when images come alive confusedly in our minds, and when often, in the quiet of the night, ideas take on a magical force. He fulfilled his mother's wishes: He bought the thirty acres of meadowland; he married a girl from Beauvais whom he could never hope to court with the present disparity in their circumstances. With the money he bought himself a whole lifetime of delights, and he saw himself happy—a father, a rich man, a figure of consequence in his province, perhaps even mayor of Beauvais. His Picard imagination caught fire as he sought a way to turn these fictions into reality; he put enormous energy into working out a hypothetical crime. Dreaming the businessman's death, he distinctly saw visions of gold and diamonds. His eyes were dazzled. His heart pounded. This deliberation itself was certainly already a crime. Entranced by piles of gold, he grew drunk with murderous imaginings. He questioned whether that poor German fellow really needed to go on living, and posited that the man had never existed at all—in short, he conceived the crime in a way that gave it impunity. The other shore of the Rhine was occupied by the Austrians; beneath the window were a boat and boatmen; he could cut the sleeping man's throat, toss him into the Rhine, slip out through the casement window with the valise, give the sailors some gold, and cross over to Austria. He went so far as to calculate whether by now he had accrued enough skill with his surgical instruments to slice off his victim's head before the fellow could utter a single cry...

Here Monsieur Taillefer wiped his brow and took another sip of water.

Prosper rose from his mattress slowly and silently. Certain he had wakened no one, he dressed, walked into the common room; then, with that special intelligence a man can suddenly find in himself, with that power of skill and determination that never fails either prisoners or criminals in accomplishing their aims, he unscrewed the iron bars, slipped them from their holes without the faintest sound, set them against the wall, and opened the shutters, pressing on the hinges to muffle any creaking. The moon cast its pale brightness onto the scene and allowed him a faint view of the objects in the room where Wilhelm and Walhenfer lay sleeping. For a moment he paused, he told me. His heartbeat was so strong, so deep, so resonant that it frightened him. He feared he would not manage to act coolly; his hands were trembling and the soles of his feet felt as if they were pressing down on fiery coals. But the execution of his plan was accompanied by such elation that he saw a kind of predestination in Fate's approval. He opened the window, returned to the bedroom, picked up his instrument bag, and looked in it for the tool best suited to carry out his crime.

"When I came to the man's bed," he told me, "I automatically prayed for God's blessing." Just as he raised his arm and gathered all his strength, he heard a kind of voice within him and seemed to glimpse a light. He flung the instrument down onto his mattress, rushed into the common room, and went to the window. Standing there, he was struck with a profound horror at himself; and sensing nonetheless that his virtue was frail, still fearing he could succumb to the trance gripping him, he leapt quickly out onto the road and strode along the Rhine, pacing back and forth before the inn like a sentinel. Several times he got as far as Andernach in his headlong walk; and several times his steps took him all the way to the slope that led to the inn. But the silence of the night was so profound, and he had such trust in the guard dogs, that at times he failed to keep watch on the window he had left open. He wanted to exhaust himself and bring on sleep. However, as he paced beneath a cloudless sky, as he gazed in wonder at the lovely stars, also perhaps affected by the pure night air and the melancholy rustle of the waves, he fell into a reverie that gradually brought him back to a wholesome moral state. Eventually reason completely swept away his momentary madness. The teachings from his upbringing, religious principles, and above all, he told me, images from the modest life he had led till then beneath the parental roof all prevailed over his troubled thoughts. After a long meditation, whose spell overtook him on the riverbank as he leaned on a broad stone, he came back and felt, he said later, so far from seeking sleep that he could stand guard over millions in gold. As his righteous character rose up again proud and strong from that struggle, he dropped to his knees in a rush of ecstasy and bliss—he thanked God, he felt happy, light, content, as he had on the day of his First Communion, when he believed himself worthy of the angels because he had spent the whole day without sinning in word, action, or thought.

He slipped back into the inn, locked the window without concern for any noise, and dropped instantly into bed. His moral and physical weariness delivered him unresisting to sleep. Moments after laying his head on the mattress, he fell into that strange, primal somnolence that often precedes deep sleep. The senses grow heavy and life is gradually abolished; thoughts go unfinished, and the last few starts of our senses simulate a kind of dream state. The air is so very heavy in here, Prosper thought, I feel as if I'm breathing damp steam. Vaguely he told himself that the atmospheric effect must be due to the contrast between the room's muggy temperature and the fresh outdoor air. He became aware of a rhythmic sound, rather like water dripping from a spout. In a moment of panicky terror, he thought to rise and call to the innkeeper, wake the businessman or Wilhelm; but then to his misfortune, he remembered the big wooden clock and deciding that what he heard was the swing of the pendulum he fell asleep with that hazy, muddled idea.

"Would you like water, Monsieur Taillefer?" asked the host, seeing the provisioner reach mechanically for the carafe.

It was empty.

Monsieur Hermann went on with his tale after the short pause occasioned by the banker's query.

The next morning Prosper Magnan was awakened by a great uproar. He thought he heard piercing cries, and he felt that violent wrench of nerves we experience when, as we wake, a painful sensation begun during our sleep persists. A physiological event occurs in us, a jolt (to use a workman's term) that has never been sufficiently examined, even though it involves phenomena of some scientific interest. That awful anguish, possibly the effect of a too-abrupt rejoining of our two natures that are nearly always separated during sleep, is usually quick to pass, but now in the poor young doctor it persisted, even suddenly increased, and rose to a dreadful horripilation when he saw a pool of blood between his mattress and Walhenfer's bed. The poor German's head lay on the floor, his body sprawled on the bed. All the blood had poured out from the neck. Seeing the eyes still open wide and staring, seeing the blood that stained his own sheets and even his hands, recognizing his surgical instrument on the bed, Prosper Magnan fainted, and collapsed into Walhenfer's blood.

"It was a punishment for my thoughts," he told me later.

When he regained consciousness, he found himself in the common room. He was seated on a chair, surrounded by French soldiers before a watchful, curious throng. He stared in a stupor at a French Republican officer who was taking testimony from several witnesses and must have been compiling a report. He recognized the innkeeper and his wife, the two sailors, and the serving girl from the inn. The surgical instrument the murderer had used . . .

Here Monsieur Taillefer coughed, pulled a handkerchief from his pocket to wipe his nose, and mopped his brow. These rather ordinary actions were noticed by no one but myself; all the other guests were gazing at Monsieur Hermann and listening to him with a kind of avidity. The provisioner leaned his elbow on the table, put his head in his right hand, and stared fixedly at Monsieur Hermann. From then on he never betrayed a single sign of emotion or interest, but his face remained pensive and ashen, as it had been earlier when he was playing with the crystal stopper.

The surgical instrument the murderer had used lay on the table with Prosper's bag, wallet, and papers. The spectators gazed in turn at the material evidence and at the young man, who looked near to dying and whose dulled eyes seemed to see nothing. A hubbub from outdoors indicated the presence of the crowd drawn to the inn by news of the crime and perhaps also by the hope to glimpse the murderer. The pacing of the sentinels stationed beneath the windows of the room, the sound of their rifles, rose over the crowd's chatter; but the inn was closed, the courtyard empty and silent. Unable to bear the gaze of the examining officer, Prosper Magnan felt his hand being clasped by someone, and he raised his eyes to see who could be his protector among this enemy mob. From the uniform he recognized the surgeon general of the demi-brigade stationed at Andernach. The man's look was so piercing, so severe, that the poor young doctor shuddered from it, and let his head fall onto the back of his chair. A soldier put vinegar beneath his nostrils, and he quickly revived. Still, though, his haggard eyes seemed so empty of life and awareness that after taking his pulse the surgeon general told the examining officer, "Captain, it's impossible to question this man right now."

"Well, all right. Take him away," the captain responded, interrupting the surgeon to address a corporal standing behind the young doctor.

"Damned coward," the soldier muttered to Prosper. "At least try to walk strong in front of these German dogs and uphold the honor of the Republic." The words stirred Prosper Magnan—he stood up straight and took a few steps. But when the door opened and he felt the rush of the outside air, saw the crowds hurry forward, his strength failed him and he tottered, his knees buckling.

"This rotten little sawbones, he ought to die twice over! Step it up! March, you!" growled the two soldiers supporting him.

"Oh, the coward! The coward! That's him! There he is, look, here he comes!" The words seemed to chorus from a single voice, the clamoring voice of the mob running along beside him hurling insults, its numbers growing at every step. On the way from the inn to the prison, the uproar from the townsfolk and the soldiers as they walked, the jumble of a hundred different conversations, the sight of the sky and the coolness of the air, the scene of Andernach and the quivering of the Rhine waters—all these impressions at once assailed the doctor's soul, indistinct and tangled, dulled like all his sensations since he woke. There were times on that walk, he told me, when he felt he had ceased to exist.

I was in prison myself at the time. (M. Hermann said, interrupting his tale.) Ardent as we all are at twenty, I was determined to defend my country, and I commanded a band of freelance resistance troops I had mustered in the Andernach region. A few nights earlier, I had run into a detachment of French troops, eight hundred men. We were two hundred at the very most. My spies had sold me out. I was thrown into the Andernach prison. It was expected I would be shot as an example to intimidate the locals. The French were talking about reprisals as well, but the murder they planned to avenge through executing me had been committed somewhere else, not here within the Electorate. My father had obtained a three-day stay of execution to go and ask for a pardon from General Augereau, who granted it. So I saw Prosper Magnan as he was brought into the prison at Andernach, and I was struck by a profound pity. Pale as he was, disheveled, all bloody, still his face had a quality of candor, of innocence, that affected me powerfully. To my eyes, he looked like Germany itself, with his long blond hair, his blue eyes. A veritable picture of my poor faltering country, he seemed to me a victim, not a murderer. As he passed my window, he threw out—I don't know to where—the bitter, mournful smile of a madman recovering a fleeting glimmer of sanity. That smile was absolutely not the smile of a murderer. When I saw the jailer, I asked about his new prisoner. "He hasn't said a word since we put him into his cell. He sat down, he set his head in his hands, and now he's sleeping, or thinking about his troubles. From what the Frenchmen say he'll be tried tomorrow morning, and he'll be shot within twenty-four hours."

That evening, during the brief moment I was permitted to walk in the prison yard, I loitered under the young man's window. We spoke a little and he gave me a straightforward account of his awful adventure, answering quite precisely my various questions. After that first conversation, I never doubted his innocence. I asked and was granted permission to spend a few hours with him. So I saw him several times, and the poor child acquainted me openly with all he was thinking. He felt both guilty and innocent at once. Recalling the frightful temptation he had found the strength to resist, he feared he had committed—during his sleep, in a somnambulant trance—the crime he had dreamed while awake.

"But what about your companion?" I asked him.

"Oh," he exclaimed excitedly, "Wilhelm could never . . ." He didn't even finish the sentence. Hearing that warmhearted cry, full of youth and decency, I pressed his hand. "When Wilhelm woke up," he went on, "he must have been terrified, he must have panicked and run off."

"Without waking you?" I said. "But then your defense should be an easy matter, for Walhenfer's valise will not have been stolen."

Suddenly he burst into tears. "Oh yes! I am innocent!" he cried. "I never killed anyone . . . I remember what I dreamed that night—I was playing prisoner's base with my old schoolmates. I couldn't have cut off a man's head while I was dreaming about running!"

Despite the flashes of hope that occasionally afforded him a little peace, he still felt crushed by remorse. He had in fact raised his arm to slice off the man's head; he judged himself and could not see his heart as pure when in his mind he had committed the crime. "And yet, I am good!" he would cry. "Oh, my poor mother! At this very moment she could be happily playing a game of imperial with her neighbors in her little sewing parlor. If she knew I had even lifted my hand to murder someone—ah, she would die! And I am in prison, accused of committing a crime! I may not have killed that man, but I will certainly kill my mother!"

Now he was no longer weeping, but, stung by that sudden swift fury common among Picards, he flung himself against the wall, and if I had not held him back he would have cracked his skull.

"Wait for your trial," I told him. "You'll be acquitted; you're innocent! And your mother—"

"My mother," he cried wildly. "The first thing she will hear is the accusation! In those small towns that's how it is, the poor woman will die of pain from it. Besides, I am not innocent. Do you want to know the whole truth? I feel I have lost the virginity of my conscience."

After that terrible sentence he sat down, crossed his arms on his chest, bent his head, and gazed darkly at the floor. Just then the guard appeared and asked me to return to my own cell. Reluctant to abandon my companion at a moment of such profound disheartenment, I clasped him to me in friendship.

"Be patient," I told him. "It may turn out well. If a decent man's voice has any chance of stilling your doubts, know that I respect you and love you. Accept my friendship, and rest on my heart if you are not at peace with your own."

The next morning toward nine o'clock, a corporal and four riflemen came to take the young doctor away. Hearing the soldiers approach, I went to my window. As the young man crossed through the courtyard, he turned his eyes up at me. I will never forget that gaze full of thoughts, apprehensions, resignation, and a kind of sorrowful, melancholy grace. It was like a silent, intelligible final testament of a man bequeathing his lost life to a friend. The night must have been very hard, very lonely for him, but perhaps the pallor on his face testified to a stoicism drawn from a new sense of self-esteem. Perhaps he was cleansed by remorse, and felt he was washing his sin away with pain and shame. He walked with a firm step now, and had removed the bloodstains he had unwittingly acquired. "My hands must have trailed in the blood as I slept, for my nights are always very agitated," he had said the evening before, in a horrible tone of despair.

I learned he would appear before a court-martial. The division was to move out in another day, and the commander was unwilling to leave Andernach without having tried the crime where it was committed.

I paced my cell in terrific anxiety while the court-martial sat. Finally, toward noon, Prosper Magnan was brought back to the prison. I was having my usual walk outside just then; he saw me and rushed over to throw himself into my arms.

"Lost!" he said. "I am lost, no hope at all! For everyone here, I shall always be a murderer." He lifted his head proudly. "This injustice has completely restored my innocence. My life would have been always troubled; my death will be blameless. But is there a future?"

The whole eighteenth century was contained in that abrupt query. He turned pensive.

"Well," I said, "how did you answer? What did they ask you? Did you not tell the story, straight out, as you told it to me?"

He stared at me for a moment; then, after another frightening pause, he responded in a feverish rush of words. "First, they asked, 'Did you leave the inn during the night?' I said yes. 'By what exit?' I flushed and answered, 'By the window.'

"'So you had opened it?' 'Yes,' I said. 'You must have been very careful about it; the innkeeper heard nothing.' I was stupefied . . . The sailors had reported they saw me walking first toward Andernach, then back toward the forest, they said I'd made several trips, I'd buried the gold and diamonds. The valise never had been found! And besides, I was still battling my own feelings of remorse—whenever I started to speak, a pitiless voice would shout: 'You did mean to commit the crime!' Everything was against me, even myself! They questioned me about my comrade and I completely absolved him!

"They said, 'We must find somebody here guilty—you, your comrade, the innkeeper, or his wife. This morning all the windows and doors were found latched from the inside!'

"At that, I was left speechless—without voice, without strength, without soul. More confident in my friend than I was of my own self, I could not accuse him. I understood that the two of us were considered equally complicit in the murder, and that I seemed the clumsier one! I tried to explain the crime by claiming somnambulism, hoping to clear my friend; I began to babble and lost the thread. I could see my conviction in my judges' eyes. They could not suppress disbelieving smiles. It is over. No more uncertainty now. Tomorrow I'll be shot...I'm not thinking of myself any longer," he went on, "but my poor mother!" He stopped and looked up at the sky, no trace of tears, his eyes dry and blinking hard. "Frederic! He—"

"Ah, that's it—Frederic!" cried Monsieur Hermann in triumph. "Yes, Frederic—that was his name, the other fellow—Frederic!"

My neighbor nudged my foot, and she nodded toward Monsieur Taillefer. The provisioner had negligently let his hand fall over his eyes, but between his fingers we saw what seemed a dark flame to his gaze.

"Hmm?" the woman murmured in my ear. "Suppose our friend's first name is Frederic?"

I responded with a glance as if to say, "Quiet."

Monsieur Hermann took up his story again...

"Frederic!" the young soldier cried. "Frederic deserted me—it's vile, shameful! He must have been frightened. Maybe he hid somewhere in the inn, because that morning our two horses were still in the courtyard...What a mystery it is—incomprehensible." After a moment of silence, he added, "Somnambulism! I had it only once in my life, and that was back when I was six years old...

"Am I to leave this life," he went on, stamping his foot, "taking with me the last shred of friendship that existed in the world? Am I to die a double death, doubting a brotherly love begun at the age of five and carried on through school and university? Where is Frederic?"

He wept. It seems we cling harder to a sentiment than to life.

"Let's go inside," he said. "I'd rather be back in my cell. I don't want people to see me weeping. I will go to death bravely, but I cannot play the hero at a time when I feel the opposite, and I confess that I do mourn my young, wonderful life. All last night I couldn't sleep; I was recalling scenes from my childhood, and I saw myself running through those fields . . . the memory that may have brought about my undoing.

"I had a future," he said, interrupting himself. "Twelve men . . . an officer shouting, 'Ready arms! Aim! Fire!,' a drumroll, and then . . . infamy! That's my future now! Oh, there is a God, there must be, or else all this makes no sense."

Then he gripped me in his arms, a powerful embrace. "Ah, you will have been the last man I could pour out my soul to. You will be free, you! You will see your mother again! I don't know if you are rich or poor, but it doesn't matter! To me you are the whole world! These people won't be fighting forever! So when there is peace again, go to Beauvais. If my mother survives the terrible news of my death, you will find her there. Bring her these words of consolation: 'He was innocent!' She will believe you. I will write her now, but you will bring her the last sight of me, you'll tell her that you were the last man I embraced. Ah, how she will love you, the poor woman! You who will have been my last friend.

"Here," he continued after a moment of silence, during which he seemed to buckle beneath the weight of his memories, "here, officers and soldiers are all strangers to me, and I horrify them. Without you, my innocence would always remain a secret between me and heaven."

I swore I would faithfully carry out his last wishes. My words, my rush of feeling touched him. Shortly thereafter, the soldiers came and took him back to the court-martial. He was condemned to death. I do not know what formalities would accompany or follow that initial judgment; I do not know whether the young surgeon argued for his life in the course of the procedures; but he did expect to go to his ordeal the following morning, and he spent the night writing to his mother.

"We shall both be free," he smiled when I went to see him the next day. "I am told that the general has signed your pardon."

I stood silent, gazing at him to etch his features into my memory. Then his expression turned to disgust, and he said, "I have been a pitiful coward! All night long I begged these walls for deliverance." And he pointed to the walls of his cell. "Yes, yes," he went on, "I howled in despair, I rebelled, I went through the most terrible moral agonies. I was alone! Now, I consider what people will say... Courage is a costume worth putting on. I must go decently to my death. So..."

TWO KINDS OF JUSTICE

"Oh, don't finish!" cried the girl who had asked for the story, and who now broke in on the Nuremberg visitor. "I want to stay unsure and believe that he was spared. If I hear now that he was shot, I will not sleep tonight. Tell me the rest tomorrow."

We rose from the table. As she accepted Monsieur Hermann's arm, my neighbor said to him, "He was shot, was he not?"

"Yes, I was witness to the execution."

"What, monsieur! You were capable of—"

"He wished it, madame. There's something very terrible about following behind the cortege of a living man, a man one loves, an innocent man! The poor lad never took his eyes off me. He seemed to be living only through me! He wanted... he said he wanted me to report his last sigh to his mother."

"Ah! And did you ever see her?"

"When the Treaty of Amiens was signed, I traveled to France to bring his mother the beautiful news of his innocence. I undertook the journey as a sacred pilgrimage. But Madame Magnan had died of consumption. With deep emotion, I burned the letter I was carrying.

You may tease me for my German excessiveness, but for me there was a sublime, sad drama to the obscurity that would forever shroud those farewells calling between two graves, unheard by all the rest of creation, like a scream deep in the desert from a lone traveler set upon by a lion—"

I interrupted: "And suppose someone were to point out a man, right here in this drawing room, and tell you 'This is the murderer!' Would that not be drama too? And what would you do?"

Monsieur Hermann went to collect his hat and left the house.

"You're behaving like a child, and very thoughtlessly," my neighbor told me. "Look at Taillefer over there! Sitting in the easy chair by the fire, with Mademoiselle Fanny bringing him a cup of coffee. He's smiling. Could a murderer—for whom that storytelling ought to have been torture—could he display such calm? Doesn't he look the classic patriarchal figure!"

"Yes," I exclaimed, "but go ask him whether he was in Germany during the war."

"Why not?" she replied. And with that audacity women rarely lack when some project catches their fancy, or curiosity overtakes their imagination, my neighbor approached the provisioner.

"Have you ever been to Germany?"

Taillefer nearly dropped his saucer.

"I, madame? No, never."

"What's that you're saying, Taillefer?" the banker interposed. "Weren't you handling the provisions for the Wagram campaign?"

"Ah, yes!" Monsieur Taillefer replied. "I did go there then."

"You're mistaken, he seems a good fellow," my neighbor said as she returned to my side.

"Oh?" I exclaimed. "Well, before this night is out I'll flush the murderer out of his hiding place!"

Every day we come across some moral phenomenon that is astonishingly significant but yet is too simple to draw notice. If two men meet in a drawing room, one of them having reason to dislike or even hate the other, either from knowledge of some private and latent compromising information or over some undisclosed situation, or even over a revenge to come, the two will sense a chasm that separates them or could. They keep covert watch, preoccupied with each other; their glances, their gestures give off an indefinable emanation of their mutual awareness; there is a kind of magnet force between them. I do not know which exerts the stronger pull: vengeance or crime, hatred or insult. Like the priest who cannot consecrate the Host in the presence of an evil spirit, both men are uneasy, suspicious; the one may be polite, the other sullen, no telling which; the one blushes or blanches, the other quakes. Often the grudge-holder is as apprehensive as the victim; few people have the courage to commit an unpleasant act, even a necessary one; and many men keep silent or excuse a wrong out of reluctance to cause gossip, or from fear of some tragic outcome. Well, such an intussusception, such an intrusion of our souls and feelings caused a subtle struggle between the provisioner and myself. From the moment I first questioned him during Monsieur Hermann's narrative, he had avoided my glances. He may have been avoiding those of the other guests as well! And now he was chatting with the unsophisticated Fanny, the banker's daughter—probably, like all criminals, feeling the need to draw close to innocence, hoping to find some ease in its presence. Though I was some distance away, I was listening to him, and my piercing gaze held his own in a kind of fascination. When he thought he might examine me with impunity, our glances would meet, and his eyelids dropped instantly. Weary of the strain, Taillefer moved to end it by joining the card game. I went over to bet on his opponent, but hoping he would lose. My wish was granted: the fellow lost.

I took his seat, and came face-to-face with the murderer.

"Monsieur," I said as he was dealing me my cards, "would you be so kind as to begin again?"

He promptly moved his chips from left to right. My dinner partner came to stand beside me; I threw her a meaningful glance.

"Would you be Monsieur Frederic Taillefer," I asked him, "whose family I knew quite well in Beauvais?"

"Yes, monsieur," he answered.

He dropped his cards, turned white, put his head between his hands, asked one of his bettors to take over his game, and stood up. "It is too warm in here!" he exclaimed. "I fear—"

He did not finish. His face suddenly looked terribly ill, and he hastily left the room. The master of the house saw Taillefer out, quite concerned about his state. My neighbor and I looked at each other, a kind of bitter disapproval on her face.

"Do you think your behavior is very merciful?" she asked, drawing me into a window recess as I left the card table after losing the game. "Would you assume the power to see into every heart? Why not let human justice and divine justice take their course? We might possibly avoid the one but never the other. Does a judge's position strike you as enviable? You've practically played the executioner's role tonight."

"So, then . . . first you share and even stimulate my curiosity, and now you give me moral lessons?"

"You have made me reconsider," she said.

"In other words, it's peace to scoundrels, war to the miserable, and deify wealth! But let's drop the subject," I went on, laughing. "Please look at the young lady who's just entering the room."

"Yes, and . . . ?"

"I saw her three days ago at the Neapolitan ambassador's ball, and I've fallen passionately in love with her. I beg you, tell me her name. No one there was able to."

"That is Mademoiselle Victorine Taillefer!"

My head spun.

"Her stepmother," my companion said, and I could barely hear her voice, "has brought her home from the convent where she was late to finish her education. For a long time her father refused to acknowledge her. This is her first visit here. She's very beautiful and very rich."

Her words were accompanied by a sardonic smile. Just then we heard violent, muffled screams. They seemed to come from a nearby apartment, and they resounded faintly through the gardens.

"Isn't that Monsieur Taillefer's voice?" I cried.

We turned all our attention to the sound as fearsome groans reached our ears. The banker's wife ran hastily toward us and closed the window. "We must avoid any scenes," she said. "If Mademoiselle Taillefer were to hear her father, she could have a nervous attack!"

The banker returned to the salon, sought out Victorine, and spoke quietly to her. The young woman uttered a cry, rushed to the door, and disappeared. The occurrence caused a great sensation. The games stopped. People questioned one another. The murmur of voices rose and groups formed.

"Could Monsieur Taillefer have—" I asked.

"Killed himself?" my neighbor said, teasingly. "You'd be glad to wear mourning, I imagine!"

"But what has actually happened to him?"

The mistress of the house replied, "The poor man, he has some disorder—I never do remember the name, although Dr. Brousson has told me often enough—and he has just had another attack."

"What sort of trouble is it?" a magistrate asked suddenly.

"Oh, it's a terrible thing, monsieur," she replied. "The doctors have no remedy for it. I understand the pain is atrocious. One day poor Taillefer had an attack while he was staying with me in the country, and I had to go to a neighbor's house to get away from the sound. He screams horribly, he wants to kill himself: So his daughter had to have him lashed to his bed and put in a straitjacket. The poor man claims there are wild animals in his head, gnawing at his brain; it stabs and saws at him, this dreadful tugging inside every nerve. He has such pain in his head that he couldn't even feel those burning moxa sticks they used to apply in an effort to relieve him, but Dr. Brousson—he engaged him as his doctor—forbade that treatment, saying that this is a nervous disorder, an inflammation of the nerves, and what he needed was leeches to the neck and opium on his head...indeed, the attacks do come less often, only once a year now, in late autumn. When he recovers, Taillefer says he would rather be put to the wheel than experience such pain again."

"Well, he does seem to be suffering a great deal now," said a broker, a fellow considered the wit among the group.

"Oh," she continued, "last year he nearly died. He had gone out alone to his country property on some urgent business and had an attack; with no one there to help him, it seems he lay for twenty-two hours, stretched out stiff on the verge of death. Only a very hot bath brought him to."

"Then is it a kind of tetanus?" asked the broker.

"I don't know," she said. "He's suffered for thirty years now; he says it began in the army, when a shot on board ship sent a wooden splinter into his head. But Brousson hopes to cure him. They say the English have discovered a safe way to treat the condition with prussic acid."

Just then a scream more piercing than any before echoed through the house and sent a chill of horror through us.

"There, that's what I was hearing every few moments," the banker's wife resumed. "It would make me leap out of my seat, it was a terrible strain on my nerves. But the strange thing is—even suffering such unimaginable pain, poor Taillefer is never at risk of dying from it. He eats and drinks normally in the intervals when the dreadful torture lets up. (Nature is very bizarre!) A German doctor told him it is a kind of gout of the head, and Brousson believes something similar."

I left the group gathered around the mistress of the house and went to join Mademoiselle Taillefer, just as a valet came to fetch her.

"Ah, my God, my God!" she sobbed. "What did my father ever do against heaven to deserve to suffer this way? Such a good man!"

I went down the stairs with her, and as I helped her into her carriage I saw her father doubled over inside. Mademoiselle Taillefer tried to quiet her father's moans, covering his mouth with her kerchief; unfortunately he caught sight of me, his face seemed to tighten still more, and a convulsive cry split the air. He gave me a hideous look, and the carriage drove off.

The dinner that evening had a cruel influence on my life and feelings. I loved Mademoiselle Taillefer, perhaps precisely because honor and decency forbade me to marry into the family of a murderer, no matter how good a father and husband he might be. Some incomprehensible force drove me to arrange my introduction into houses where I knew I might encounter Victorine. Often, after swearing that I would never see her again, the same evening I would find myself at her side. My pleasure was immense: My legitimate love, burdened by that chimerical remorse, came to feel like a criminal passion. I detested myself for greeting Taillefer civilly when he chanced to be with his daughter, but greet him I did!

Unfortunately Victorine is not merely a pretty woman—she is cultivated, full of talents and grace, without the least pedantry or the faintest hint of pretention. She is reserved in conversation, her nature has a melancholy grace that no one can resist; she loves me, or at least she lets me think so; she has a certain smile she reveals to no one but myself; and when she speaks to me her voice grows gentler still. Oh, she does love me—but she adores her father; but she praises his goodness, his kindness, his exquisite qualities. These tributes become so many dagger thrusts into my heart.

One day I almost implicated myself in the crime of the Taillefer family's wealth: I nearly proposed to Victorine. So I fled. I traveled—I went to Germany, to Andernach...

But then I returned. I found Victorine pale, grown thin! If I had found her hearty and merry, I would have been spared. But now my passion flared anew with extraordinary force. Fearing that my scruples could degenerate into monomania, I decided to convoke a Sanhedrin, a council of unbiased minds, to cast some light onto this ethical and philosophical problem. The issue had become more complicated since my return.

Two days ago I gathered those of my friends whom I consider to possess the greatest degree of probity, delicacy, and honor. I invited two Englishmen (one a secretary at the embassy and one a Puritan), a former French government minister (now a mature political figure), a few young fellows still living in a rapture of innocence, an elderly priest, my old guardian (an unsophisticated man who handed in so fine a guardianship report on me that the Palace still remembers it), as well as a lawyer, a notary, a judge...That is, a range of social viewpoints, of practical capacities. We began with good food, good talk, a good boisterous racket; then, at dessert, I gave a straightforward account of my story and, without disclosing the name of my beloved, I asked for some solid counsel.

"Advise me, my friends," I said as I ended the tale. "Discuss the question seriously, as if it were a legislative proposal. The voting urn and the billiard balls will be brought in, and you will vote for or against my marrying, with all the confidentiality proper to an election."

Suddenly a deep silence fell. The notary recused himself: "I have a pressing contract to draw up."

The wine had reduced my old guardian to silence, and soon I put him into the hands of another guardian to see that no accident should befall him on his way home.

"I understand!" I exclaimed. "Not giving me an opinion tells me very emphatically what I must do."

The group stirred.

A landowner, who had donated funds for General Foy's children and his tomb, quoted Racine: "Like virtue, there are different degrees to a crime!"

"Babbler," the former minister muttered, nudging me with his elbow.

"What is the problem?" asked a duke, whose fortune consisted of property confiscated from the Protestants who resisted the revocation of the Edict of Nantes.

The attorney rose. "As a matter of law, the case before us would not pose the slightest difficulty. Monsieur the duke is correct!" declared the legal mouthpiece. "There is such a thing as a statute of limitations. Where would we all be if it were required to look into the source of every fortune! This is a matter of conscience. If you insist on seeking an answer from some tribunal, go to the one that deals with penitence—the confessional." That said, the code incarnate sat back down and swallowed a glass of champagne.

The man charged with explicating the Gospel, the good priest, rose to his feet. "God made us frail things," he declared firmly. "If you love the heiress to the crime, marry her, but take only the property she inherited from her mother's side and give the father's portion to the poor."

"But," exclaimed one of those merciless quibblers so commonly found in social circles, "the father himself may have married so well only because of his ill-gotten fortune. Thus, even the least of his privileges might be considered a fruit of his crime."

"This very discussion is itself a verdict. There are some matters a man does not puzzle over," declared my former tutor, who believed he was enlightening the group by this drunken sally.

"Yes!" said the embassy secretary.

"Yes!" cried the priest.

The two men meant different things.

A man of the Doctrinaire Party, who had missed election to the parliament by one hundred fifty votes out of one hundred fifty-five, rose to speak. "Messieurs, this phenomenal accident, intellectual in its nature, is the sort of event that stands out most vividly from the usual conditions ruling society," he intoned. "Thus, the decision should be reached through an extemporaneous act of consciousness, a sudden idea, an instructive judgment, an ephemeral nuance of our inmost apprehension, akin to the flashes that make up the sensation of taste. Let us vote."

"Let us vote!"

I had supplied each man with two balls, one white and one red. The white, symbol of virginity, would rule out the marriage; the red ball would favor it. Out of delicacy, I myself abstained from voting. My friends numbered seventeen, thus nine would make an absolute majority. Each person stepped up to drop a ball into a narrow-necked reed basket used to shake up the numbered marbles that tournament players draw to determine their order; we were spurred on by lively curiosity, for the idea of deciding a strictly ethical question by ballot was quite novel.

In the end I counted nine white balls! A result that didn't surprise me, though I did consider how many men my own age I had invited to join my tribunal. There were nine of these casuists, and they all felt the same.

"Ah!" I thought. "There is an unspoken unanimity here in favor of the marriage, and another unanimity against it! How shall I get out of this fix?

"Where does the father-in-law live?" blurted one of my classmates, who was less clever at dissembling than the others.

"There is no longer a father-in-law," I declared. "Until recently, my conscience spoke clearly enough to make it superfluous to ask your advice. That voice may be weaker now, and here is the reason for my uncertainty: Two months ago I received this enchanting letter."

I showed them the following invitation, drawn from my wallet:

YOU ARE INVITED TO ATTEND
THE FUNERAL PROCESSION, SERVICE, AND INTERMENT
OF MONSIEUR JEAN-FREDERIC TAILLEFER
OF THE MAISON TAILLEFER & COMPANY,

FORMER PROVISIONER OF MEATS TO THE
ARMY COMMISSARY,
IN HIS LIFETIME CHEVALIER OF THE LEGION OF HONOR
AND OF THE GOLDEN SPUR,
CAPTAIN OF THE FIRST COMPANY OF GRENADIERS
OF THE SECOND LEGION OF
THE NATIONAL GUARD OF PARIS

DIED MAY 1 IN HIS HOUSE ON RUE JOUBERT

WHICH WILL TAKE PLACE AT…
SENT BY…

"Now what do I do?" I went on. "I shall set you the question very broadly. There is certainly a pool of blood in Mademoiselle Taillefer's estate; the father's legacy is bloodstained ground, I know that. But Prosper Magnan left no heirs; I have been unable to locate the family of the pin manufacturer who was murdered at Andernach. To whom, then, should the fortune be 'restored'? And should it be the whole fortune that is restored? Have I the right to disclose a truth discovered by chance; the right to add a decapitated head to the dowry of an innocent girl, to cause her to dream bad dreams, to strip her of a cherished illusion, to kill off her father a second time by telling her, 'Your every sou is stained with blood'? I borrowed an old churchman's copy of the *Dictionary of Problems of Conscience*, and I found no solution to resolve my doubts. Set up a religious fund to pray for Prosper Magnan, or for Walhenfer, or for Taillefer? This is the middle of the nineteenth century! Build a hospice or establish some award for good works? The prize would go to rascals. As for most of our hospitals, they seem to have become havens for vice these days! And anyhow, such grants, which mainly benefit personal vanity, would they constitute 'reparations'? And do I even owe reparations?

"And finally—I am in love, passionately so. My love is my life! If, without disclosing my reasons, I should propose marriage to a young woman who is accustomed to luxury, to elegance, to a life rich in enjoyment of the arts, a girl who loves listening idly to Rossini's music from a box at the Bouffons opera house—well, if I propose that she should deprive herself of one hundred fifty thousand francs for the sake of some doddering old folks or some hypothetical invalids, she'll laugh and turn her back on me, or her companion will tell her I'm a cruel prankster. If in an ecstasy of love I should urge the delights of a modest existence in a little house on the banks of the Loire, if I ask her to sacrifice her Parisian life in the name of our love, first of all that would be a virtuous lie, and second I might have a sorry experience and lose the heart of a girl who loves dancing, is mad about fine clothes, and for the time being is mad about me. She'll be carried off by some slim dandy of an officer with a pretty curled mustache who plays the piano, makes much of Lord Byron, and cuts a fine figure on horseback. What to do? Messieurs, I beg you—tell me!"

The upright fellow, the Puritan gentleman who looked like Jeanie Deans's father in the Waverley novel, whom I had briefly mentioned before and who till now had said not a word, shrugged his shoulders and said, "Idiot! Why on earth did you ever ask him if he came from Beauvais!"

Paris, May 1831
Translated by Linda Asher

SARRASINE

To Monsieur Charles de Bernard du Grail

I WAS LOST in one of those deep meditations that can overtake anyone, even the most frivolous man, in the midst of uproarious revelries. Midnight had just sounded from the clock of the Élysée-Bourbon. Sitting in the recess of a window, concealed behind the undulating drape of a moiré curtain, I had full leisure to contemplate the garden of the house where I was a guest for the evening. Unevenly daubed with snow, the trees stood out dimly against the gray of an overcast sky, brightened only a little by moonlight. In that unearthly ambiance they looked vaguely like specters half wrapped in their shrouds, a monumental image of the famed dance of the dead. And then, turning in the other direction, I could admire the dance of the living!—a splendid salon, its walls ornamented with silver and gold, candles aglow in the gleaming chandeliers. There swarmed, darted, and fluttered the most beautiful women of Paris, sumptuous, resplendent, ablaze with diamonds! Flowers on their heads, at their bosoms, in their hair, strewn over their gowns, in garlands at their feet. It was all delicate shivers of delight, the lace, silk, and taffeta shimmering about their elegant flanks with every step. Here and there flashed an overheated glance, eclipsing the glint of the diamonds, further arousing already overwrought hearts. There were tilts of the head full of meaning for lovers, and demeanors discouraging for husbands. The gamblers' cries with each unexpected play of the cards, the clinking of the gold, all this mingled with the music, the hum of the conversation, and to complete the rapture of that crowd, drunk on all the enchantments this world has to offer, wafting perfumes and an atmosphere of euphoria excited the imagination to a fever pitch. Thus, to my right, the somber, silent image of death; to my left, the mannered bacchanalia of life; here a cold, drear, mourning-draped nature; there a jubilant humankind. For my part, at the junction of these two so disparate scenes, which, a thousand times re-created in all manner of forms, make of Paris the world's most amusing city and its most philosophical, mine was a motley half-festive, half-morbid mood. My left foot kept time with the music; the other might have been in a coffin, for my leg was chilled by one of those drafts that freeze half your body while the other half feels the damp warmth of the salons, not an uncommon happenstance at the ball.

"I don't believe Monsieur de Lanty has owned this house long?"

"He has. It was ten years ago that he bought it from Marshal de Carigliano."

"Ah!"

"These people must have an enormous fortune?"

"Most assuredly."

"What a party! There's a kind of shamelessness to its opulence."

"Do you suppose they're as rich as Monsieur de Nucingen or Monsieur de Gondreville?"

"But don't you know?"

Looking more closely, I recognized the speakers as members of that curious race that, in Paris, occupies itself exclusively with questions of "Why?", with "How?" "Where does he come from?" "Who are they?" "What might be the matter?" "What did she do?" They lowered their voices and wandered off in search of an isolated divan on which to continue their conversation more comfortably. Never had a more fruitful mine been opened for excavators of mysteries. No one knew in what land the Lanty family originated, nor what trade, what swindle, what piracy or inheritance had brought them a fortune estimated at several million. Everyone in the family spoke Italian, French, Spanish, English, and German with a flawlessness that suggested a long sojourn among those varied peoples. Were they Gypsies? Were they grifters?

"Suppose they were the devil incarnate," said several young politicians. "They throw a wonderful party."

"What does it matter to me if the Comte de Lanty pillaged some Casbah? I'd gladly marry his daughter!" cried a guest with a philosophical streak.

And indeed, who would not have married Marianina, a girl of sixteen, her beauty a living image of the Oriental poets' most fabulous dreams? Like the sultan's daughter in the tale of *The Magic Lamp*, she should have gone about veiled. Her singing put to shame the incomplete talents of any Madame Malibran, Madame Sontag, or Madame Fodor, for in them one single dominant quality hindered the perfection of the whole, while Marianina combined and united in equal measure purity of tone, musical sensitivity, precision in meter and phrasing, soul and science, accuracy and emotion. This girl was the very model of the secret poetry that holds all the arts in one common bond, and which always flees those who strive after it. Sweet and modest, educated and witty, nothing could outshine Marianina, save perhaps her mother.

Have you ever come across one of those women whose dazzling beauty defies all the onslaughts of age, who at thirty-six seem more desirable than they must have been fifteen years earlier? Their faces bespeak the passion of their soul; they scintillate; each feature glows with intelligence, every pore is endowed with a particular radiance, especially by lamplight. Their seductive eyes attract, refuse, speak, or stay silent; their walk is innocently knowing; their voices exploit the melodious riches of sweetness and tenderness at their most enticing. Founded in experienced comparisons, their words of praise are a caress for the prickliest amour propre. One arch of their eyebrows, the faintest flick of an eye, a pursing of their lips, and a sort of terror assails all who depend on them for their life and their happiness. A girl inexperienced in love and easily swayed by fine words can always be seduced, but with such women as these, a man needs the discipline, like Monsieur de Jaucourt, not to cry out when an unknowing chambermaid breaks two of his fingers against the doorjamb as he hides in a closet. Is loving one of these redoubtable sirens not gambling with one's very life? And is that perhaps why we love them with such passion? The Comtesse de Lanty was just such a woman.

Filippo, Marianina's brother, inherited from the countess the same superhuman beauty as his sister. To say it all in a word, this young man was a living image of Antinous, if of slenderer build. But how becoming to youth are those slight and delicate proportions, when an olive tint, luxuriant eyebrows, and the fire in a velvet-soft eye promise a future of manly passions and gallant thoughts! If, in every young girl's heart, Filippo was lodged as an ideal, he was also lodged in the memory of every mother as the finest catch to be had in all of France.

The beauty, the fortune, the wit, the grace and intelligence of these two children came to them solely from their mother. The Comte de Lanty was short, ugly, and pockmarked, somber as a Spaniard, dull as a banker. On the other hand, he passed for a man of great shrewdness and acumen, perhaps because he rarely laughed and was forever citing the words of Metternich or Wellington.

This mysterious family possessed all the allure of a poem by Lord Byron, whose obscurities were translated differently by every denizen of the beau monde: a dark, sublime song, verse upon verse. Monsieur and Madame de Lanty's silence on their origins, on their past, on their links with the four corners of the world would not long have been a subject of surprise in Paris. There is perhaps no land where Vespasian's axiom is better understood. There, even stained with blood or filth, golden ecus betray nothing and mean everything. So long as high society can put a figure on your fortune, your class is that of the sums equivalent to yours, and no one asks to see your documents of title, for everyone knows how little they cost. In a city where social problems are resolved by algebraic equations, fortune hunters have every chance on their side. Were this family of Gypsy extraction, they were wealthy and glamorous enough that high society gladly allowed them their little mysteries. Unfortunately, however, the enigmatic history of the House of Lanty offered one subject of undying curiosity, something that would not have been out of place in a novel by Ann Radcliffe.

Observant and inquiring folk, those who insist on knowing in what shop you buy your candelabras or who ask you your rent when your apartment strikes them as fine, had noted the sporadic presence of a curious personage in the midst of the countess's parties, concerts, balls, and routs. This personage was a man. He first appeared on the occasion of a concert at the Lantys', drifting into the drawing room as if lured by Marianina's bewitching voice.

"I feel a chill all of a sudden," said one lady to another, standing not far from the doorway.

The stranger, then close beside her, went on his way.

"Isn't that odd! Now I'm hot," said the woman, once he was gone. "Call me mad if you like, but I can't help thinking that gentleman in black was the cause of it."

Soon the exaggeration native to high society spawned the birth and multiplication of the quaintest ideas, the strangest remarks, the most ridiculous tales concerning this enigmatic figure. Though not exactly a vampire, a ghoul, an artificial man, a sort of Faust or Robin Hood, he nonetheless, to hear those of a fantastical bent, had in him some part of all these anthropomorphic essences. Here and there one could find Germans who took these ingenious sallies of Parisian tittle-tattle for realities. The stranger was simply a little old man. Several of those young men accustomed to deciding the future of Europe each morning with a few well-turned sentences sought to see in that creature some nefarious criminal, some possessor of untold fortunes. Novelists recounted the old man's life and told you in truly picturesque detail of the atrocities he'd committed in the service of the Prince of Mysore. Bankers, a more down-to-earth folk, invented their own specious story. "Bah," they said, pityingly shrugging their broad shoulders, "that little old man is a Genoese head!"

"Monsieur, if the question is not indiscreet, would you be so kind as to explain what you mean by Genoese head?"

"Monsieur, it is a man on whose life hangs an enormous sum of money; no doubt the income of this family depends on that old man's good health."

I recall hearing a mesmerist at Madame d'Espard's, who on the most dubious historical evidence proved that the old man was none other than the great Balsamo, alias Cagliostro, preserved under glass. According to this latter-day alchemist, the Sicilian adventurer had eluded death and whiled away his days making gold for his grandchildren. The bailiff of Ferrette, for his part, claimed to have recognized that singular personage as the Count de Saint-Germain. Spoken in fanciful tones, with the jeering air that is the mark of our modern society without beliefs, these absurdities kept alive a whole host of vague suspicions concerning the House of Lanty. And by the curious workings of circumstance, that family lent credence to these conjectures through their rather mysterious behavior with the old man, whose existence they shielded, in a sense, from all inquiry.

He had only to cross the threshold of the rooms he was meant to occupy chez Lanty to set off a tremendous to-do among the family. One might have thought it an event of great moment. Only Filippo, Marianina, Madame de Lanty, and an aged servant had the privilege of helping the stranger to walk, to stand up, to sit down. They watched over his slightest gesture. He seemed some magical creature, on whom everyone's happiness, life, or fortune depended. Was it fear or affection? Try as they might, the society crowd could find no key to that conundrum. Concealed for months at a time in the depths of an unknown sanctuary, this household spirit emerged all at once, as if furtively, unbidden, and appeared in the drawing room like those fairies of days gone by, descending from their flying dragons to disrupt the grand occasions to which they had not been invited. Only the most practiced observer could then discern the anxiety of the houses' masters, singularly adept as they were at concealing their sentiments. Now and again, however, even as she danced a quadrille, the artless Marianina cast a panicked glance toward the old man she was charged with watching over amid the mingling crowds. Or else Filippo hastily slipped through the throng to his side, where he stayed, tender and attentive, as if that strange creature might be broken by any contact with men, by even the slightest puff of breath. The countess tried to come near, never signaling her intention to join him; then, adopting a manner and an expression no less servile than affectionate, no less submissive than tyrannical, she spoke two or three words to which the old man nearly always deferred, and he disappeared, led—or, more precisely, tugged along—by her hand. If Madame de Lanty was not nearby, the count would employ a thousand stratagems to approach him, but he seemed to have difficulty making himself heard by the old man and treated him like a spoiled child whose mother indulges his whims or fears his mutiny. Foolishly, certain indiscreet souls ventured to question Comte de Lanty, but that cold, reserved man never seemed to understand the meddlers' inquiries. And so, after many attempts, rendered vain by the entire family's vigilant reticence, the quest to discover the secret they guarded so closely was abandoned. The well-bred spies, the gossipmongers, the politicians all threw up their hands and troubled themselves with that mystery no more.

But at the time of these events those glittering salons may still have held a handful of philosophers who, taking an ice or a sorbet, or setting their empty punch glass on a sideboard, quietly remarked to each other, "I wouldn't be at all surprised to learn that these people are felons. That old man, always hidden away, appearing only at equinoxes or solstices, seems to me the very image of a murderer..."

"Or a swindler..."

"It's much the same thing. Sometimes it's far worse to kill a man's fortune than to kill the man himself."

"Monsieur, I placed a bet of twenty louis, I have forty coming to me."

"But, monsieur, there are only thirty left on the table."

"Very uneven crowd in this place. You daren't gamble here."

"It's true. Say, soon six months since we last saw the Spirit. Do you believe it's a living being?"

"Heh heh, at the very most..."

These last words were spoken in my vicinity by strangers who wandered off just as I was summing up my reflections in one final thought, black mingled with white, life with death. No less than my eyes, my fevered imagination contemplated by turns the party, its splendor now at a peak, and the dark tableau of the gardens. I know not how long I meditated on those two sides of the human coin; in any case, I was abruptly awoken by a young woman's stifled laughter. The image that then offered itself to my gaze left me dumbstruck. By an extraordinary caprice of nature, the semi-funereal fantasy that was twisting and turning in my mind had suddenly broken free: It was standing before me, personified, alive, burst like Minerva from Jupiter's brow, full-grown and strong, it was at once one hundred years old and twenty-two, it was living and dead. Escaped from his room like a madman from his cell, the old man must have discreetly taken cover behind a row of guests raptly listening as Marianina sang the last notes of the cavatina from *Tancredi*. He might almost have appeared from below the floor, hoisted by some theatrical mechanism. Motionless and somber, he stood for a moment watching the festivities, whose murmur had no doubt faintly reached his ears. He stared all around him, almost like a sleepwalker, his attention so fixed on the scene that he stood in the heart of the crowd without seeing the crowd. He had materialized unannounced beside one of Paris's most breathtaking creatures, an elegant young dancer, a woman of delicate physique, with one of those faces as fresh as a child's, white and pink, and so slight, so transparent, that a man's gaze might almost run straight through it, as the rays of the sun penetrate a pristine pane of glass. There they stood before me, the two of them, together, united, so close each to the other that the stranger brushed against both her gauzy dress and her garlands of flowers, both her slightly crimped hair and her loose, floating sash.

I had brought this young woman to Madame de Lanty's ball. As this was her first visit to that house, I forgave her her stifled laugh, but I silenced her with a curt and imperious sign, ordering her to show some respect for her neighbor. She sat down nearby me. The old man would not be parted from that delectable creature, to whom he had capriciously attached himself with the mute, seemingly gratuitous obstinacy to which the aged are prone, in which they are very like children. He was forced to pull up a folding chair to sit near the young lady. He moved with the mechanical awkwardness of a paralytic, sluggish and tentative. He sat down slowly, cautiously, mumbling a few unintelligible words. His broken voice was like the sound of a stone falling into a well. The young lady gave my hand a powerful squeeze, as if she were standing terrified atop a high precipice, and she shivered when the old man noted her stare and turned toward her two eyes without warmth, two murky eyes comparable only to dulled nacre.

"I'm afraid," she murmured into my ear.

"No need to whisper," I answered. "He's very hard of hearing."

"You know him, then?"

"Yes."

With this she found the courage to make a brief study of that creature with no name in our human tongues, form without substance, being without life, or life without will. She had fallen under the spell of the tremulous curiosity that compels women to seek out dangerous sensations, to gaze on chained tigers, to peer at boas, protected by only the most tinglingly tenuous barrier. The old man was stooped like a day laborer, but it was nonetheless plain that he had once been of average height. His excessive thinness and delicate limbs proved that his build had always been slight. His black silk breeches fluttered around his fleshless thighs, draping like a slack sail. An anatomist would immediately have recognized the symptoms of a dreadful consumption on seeing the withered legs that supported that strange body. They looked in every way like two crossed bones on a gravestone. An overpowering horror at the fate that awaits us all gripped the heart on discovering the ravages decrepitude had wrought on that fragile machine. The stranger wore a white waistcoat, embroidered in gold, as was once the fashion, and his linens were dazzlingly white. A rather dingy jabot of English lace, whose opulence a queen would have envied, made yellow ruffles on his breast, but on him that lace was more rag than ornament. At the center of the jabot, a diamond of incalculable price blazed like the sun. That outmoded flourish, that flagrant, tasteless treasure set off the bizarre creature's face all the more. The frame harmonized with the portrait. His dark face was angular and rutted every which way. His chin was hollow; his temples were hollow; his eyes were deep-set in yellowed orbits. His jawbones, sharply defined by an emaciation beyond words, created cavities in the middle of each cheek. Unevenly illuminated, these depressions produced curious patterns of shadow and light that stripped his countenance of its last sameness with the human face. On top of all this, the passing years had so strongly glued that face's fine yellow skin to its bones that it was covered by a multitude of wrinkles, some circular, like the ripples of water disturbed by a child's pebble, some in the form of an asterisk, like a crack in a window, but all of them as deep and dense as the pages of a closed book. There are aged men who bring us face-to-face with more hideous portraits, but above all else, it was his glistening rouge and white powder that made the specter before us seem an artificial creation. Under the lamplight, the eyebrows of his mask had a sheen that revealed a careful application of paint. Happily for the eye, saddened at the sight of such ruination, his cadaverous skull was concealed beneath a blond wig whose countless curls bore witness to an exceptional vanity. Indeed, the feminine coquetry of this phantasmagorical creature was rather overtly declared by the gold hoops that hung from his ears, by the rings whose fine stones gleamed on his ossified fingers, and by a watch chain that glimmered like the gems of a necklace on a woman's throat. Finally, the blue-tinged lips of this sort of Japanese idol were fixed in an unwavering smile, an implacable, mocking smile not unlike a skull's. Silent, still as a statue, he exuded the musky odor of old gowns exhumed from a duchess's wardrobe by her heirs in the course of an inventory. If he turned his eyes toward the assembled guests, the movement of those lifeless orbs seemed the work of some hidden artifice, and when those eyes fell still, he who examined them soon doubted they had ever moved. To see, beside these human ruins, a young woman whose neck, arms, and throat were naked and white; whose rounded forms, blooming with beauty, whose hair, lush and vital above an alabaster forehead, inspired love; whose eyes did not receive the light but disseminated it; who was silken and fresh; whose airy curls and perfumed breath seemed too heavy, too hard, too powerful for that shadow, for that man of dust—ah! it truly was life and death, my thought incarnate, an imaginary arabesque, a chimera, half hideous but divinely feminine about the bust.

"And yet there is no lack of such marriages in society," I said to myself.

"He smells of the graveyard," cried the young woman in horror, nestling against me as if seeking assurance of my protection, her violent tremors conveying the depth of her fear. "He's horrible! I can't stay here a moment longer. If I look at him again, I'll be sure death itself has come for me. But is he alive?"

She laid one hand on the phenomenon, with that special boldness women derive from the vehemence of their desires; but all at once a cold sweat broke from her pores, for the moment she touched the old man, she heard a rattling cry. That grating voice, if voice it was, had escaped from an almost perfectly dry gullet. This croak was quickly followed by a small childlike cough, violent and distinctive in its sound. Hearing that cough, Marianina, Filippo, and Madame de Lanty turned to look at us with furious eyes. The young woman would gladly have been at the bottom of the Seine. She seized my arm and pulled me away toward a boudoir. Men and women alike, everyone stepped aside to make way for us. At the far end of the reception rooms, we entered a small semicircular chamber. My companion dropped onto a divan, quivering with terror, unsure where she was.

"Madame, you are mad," I told her.

"But," she replied, after a moment of silence that I spent admiring her, "is it my fault? Why does Madame de Lanty let ghosts wander at liberty in her home?"

"Come now," I said, "you're behaving like those other fools. You take a little old man for a specter."

"Be quiet," she shot back, with that scornful, imperious air women so expertly adopt when they want to be right. "What a wonderful boudoir!" she cried, looking around her. "Blue satin looks so lovely on a wall. How fresh it is! Ah, what a fine painting!" she added, standing up and approaching a magnificently framed canvas.

We stood for a moment lost in contemplation of that marvel, the work of some supernatural paintbrush, it seemed, depicting Adonis reclining on the skin of a lion. Softened by an alabaster shade, the ceiling lamp lit the canvas with a gentle glow that brought out all its beauty.

"Can such a perfect creature exist?" she asked me, once she had studied the exquisite grace of his body, his pose, his coloring, his hair—in short, everything—with a sweetly approving smile.

"He's too beautiful for a man," she added, subjecting him to the same minute scrutiny she would have given a female rival.

Oh, how deeply did I then feel the very pangs of jealousy that a poet had fruitlessly struggled to make me believe in—a jealousy of engravings, of paintings, of statues, of that exaggerated human beauty an artist creates, obeying a doctrine that demands that all things be idealized!

"It's a portrait," I told her, "from the talented hand of Joseph-Marie Vien. But that great painter never saw the original, and your admiration will perhaps be less fervid when you learn that the model for this nude was a statue of a woman."

"But who is it?"

I hesitated.

"I want to know," she added, sharply.

"I believe," I told her, "that this Adonis represents a . . . a . . . a relative of Madame de Lanty."

To my chagrin, I saw her utterly rapt in her admiration of that figure. She sat down in silence. I took my place beside her and clasped her hand, and she never so much as noticed! Forgotten for a portrait! Just then the silence was broken by the delicate sound of a rustling gown and a woman's footfalls. Young Marianina came in, her innocent expression enhancing her radiant beauty even more than her natural elegance or the freshness of her gown and makeup. She walked slowly, one arm encircling, with maternal attentiveness and filial solicitude, that specter in human garb who had driven us from the music room, leading him, watching him with a sort of apprehension as he slowly set down his unsteady feet, one after the other. At last they made their laborious way to a door concealed in the wall. Marianina knocked gently. Immediately, as if by magic, a tall wiry man, a sort of household spirit, appeared in the doorway. Before entrusting the old man to this mysterious guardian, the child respectfully kissed that walking corpse, and in her chaste caress was a hint of that winsome flirtatiousness whose secret is known to only a few privileged women.

"*Addio, addio!*" she said, with the prettiest inflections of her young voice.

She even added an admirably skillful melisma to the last syllable, but quietly and as if seeking to portray the effusions of her heart by a poetic expression. The old man stood on the threshold of that secret room, suddenly struck by some memory. In the deep silence that enveloped us, we could hear a heavy sigh escaping his breast; he pulled off the finest of the rings burdening his skeletal fingers and placed it in Marianina's bosom. The girl broke into a laugh, took out the ring, slipped it over a gloved finger, and tripped off toward the salon, where the first measures of a contra dance were playing. She caught sight of us.

"Ah! You were here!" she said, blushing.

She stared at us inquiringly, then ran off to her partner with all the lighthearted exuberance of her age.

"What does this mean?" my young friend asked me. "Is he her husband? I must be dreaming. Where am I?"

"You!" I answered. "You, madame, who are so full of feeling, you who, so perfectly understanding the most rarefied emotions, can cultivate the most fragile sentiments in a man's heart without depleting it, without breaking it on the first day, you who take pity on all heartache, you who combine the wit of a Parisienne with a passionate soul worthy of Italy or Spain—"

She could hear the vexed sarcasm underlying my words; seeming to pay it no mind, she interrupted me: "Oh! You're remaking me to suit your own tastes. A strange sort of tyranny that is! You want me to be something other than *me*."

"Oh! I want nothing," I cried, crushed by her stern manner. "Is it at least true that you like hearing tales of the lively passions aroused in our hearts by the ravishing women of the south?"

"It is. What of it?"

"Well, in that case I shall come to you tomorrow night around nine o'clock, and I will lay bare this entire mystery."

"No," she answered defiantly, "I want to know now."

"You haven't yet given me the right to obey you when you say 'I want.'"

"At this moment," she answered, heartbreakingly adorable, "I am burning to know that secret. Tomorrow, I might not even listen to you . . ."

She smiled, and we parted; she still as proud, as formidable, and I every bit as ridiculous as ever. She had the audacity to waltz with a young aide-de-camp, leaving me by turns furious, sulking, admiring, affectionate, jealous.

"Until tomorrow," she told me toward two in the morning, as she was leaving the ball.

"I won't go," I thought. "I'll have no more to do with you. You are more capricious, perhaps a thousand times more wayward than . . . than my imagination."

The next evening we were sitting before a lively fire in an elegant little salon, she on a love seat, I on some cushions, almost at her feet, looking up into her eyes. The street outside was silent. The lamp cast a gentle glow. It was one of those evenings that enrapture the soul, one of those moments one never forgets, one of those hours full of tranquillity and desire, whose charm will later be looked back on with enduring wistfulness, even once all our wishes have been granted. Who can erase the radiant mark left by the first stirrings of love?

"Go on, then," she said, "I'm listening."

"But I don't dare begin. Parts of this tale are treacherous for the narrator. If I grow too enthusiastic, you will silence me."

"Speak."

"I obey…

"Ernest-Jean Sarrasine was the only son of a prosecutor of the Franche-Comté," I began, after a pause. "His father had more or less honestly amassed an annual revenue of six to eight thousand pounds, a professional's income which in those days and in the provinces passed for a colossal sum. Having only one child, the good lawyer Sarrasine spared no expense for his education, hoping to make of him a magistrate and to live long enough to see the grandson of Matthieu Sarrasine, a simple laborer of Saint-Dié, sit on a lily-emblazoned bench and sleep through the sessions for the greater glory of the parliament. But heaven did not have that joy in store for the prosecutor. Entrusted at an early age to the Jesuits, young Sarrasine proved a most turbulent pupil. He had the typical childhood of a man of great talent. He studied only what he wished, he was often rebellious, and sometimes he spent hours lost in meandering meditations, now contemplating his schoolmates as they played, now picturing Homer's heroes in his mind's eye. When he did happen to join in their frolics, he displayed a fearsome intensity. His scuffles with classmates rarely ended without bloodshed. If he was the weaker combatant, he bit. By turns active and passive, now unable to keep up with the lessons, now far beyond them, his unconventional nature earned him the fear of his masters and schoolmates alike. Rather than acquire the elements of the Greek language, he drew portraits of the father parsing some passage from Thucydides; he sketched the mathematics teacher, the prefect, the valets, the proctor, and covered the walls with aimless drawings. Rather than exalt the Lord, he amused himself during services by carving figures into the back of a bench; or, if he had succeeded in stealing a piece of wood, he sculpted some female saint. If he had no wood, stone, or pencils, he modeled his fancies in bread. Whether copying the figures in the paintings that adorned the choir or simply improvising, he always left some hastily done study on his seat, whose licentious character drove the younger priests to despair—and, claimed the gossips, brought a smile to the lips of the elderly Jesuits. At last, if we are to believe the school's chronicles, he was expelled for having sculpted a figure of Christ from a thick log as he waited his turn in the confessional one Good Friday. The impiety that graced this statue was too enormous for the artist to go unpunished. And to make matters worse, he'd had the audacity to place that distinctly irreverent figure on top of the tabernacle!

Seeking refuge from the threat of paternal malediction, Sarrasine came to Paris. His powerful will was of the sort that admit to no obstacle, and so, heeding the dictates of his genius, he entered the studio of Edmé Bouchardon. He worked all day long and in the evening went to beg for his subsistence. Astounded at the young artist's progress and intelligence, Bouchardon soon realized the depth of his student's poverty; he offered his aid, took a liking to him, and treated him like his own child. Then, when Sarrasine's genius was revealed by one of those works in which the mature talent to come battles the excesses of youth, the kindly Bouchardon tried to restore him to the good graces of the prosecutor, whose fatherly wrath subsided before the authority of the great sculptor. All of Besançon congratulated itself on having brought a future great man into the world. In his flattered vanity's first rush of joy, the parsimonious lawyer offered his son the wherewithal to cut a respectable figure in society. For some time the long, laborious studies that sculpture demands tamed Sarrasine's impetuous nature and restless mind. Foreseeing the violence with which the passions would surely rage in that youthful soul, perhaps as furiously unbridled as Michelangelo's, Bouchardon smothered his ardency under continual labors. He succeeded in maintaining Sarrasine's fervor within acceptable limits, now forbidding him to work, now proposing distractions when he saw him obsessed by some project, now assigning him arduous tasks just when he was about to give himself over to dissipation. But kindliness was always the most powerful weapon for subduing that passionate soul, and it was only by arousing his gratitude with paternal affections that the master acquired a real hold over his pupil. At the age of twenty-two, Sarrasine was wrenched away from Bouchardon's salutary influence on his mores and habits. He paid the price of his genius by winning the sculpture prize funded by the Marquis de Marigny, Madame de Pompadour's brother, that great benefactor of the arts. Diderot hailed Bouchardon's student's sculpture as a masterpiece. It was with profound sorrow that the sculptor to the king watched the departure for Italy of a young man whose profound ignorance of the ways of this world he had so scrupulously protected. For six years Sarrasine had shared Bouchardon's table. No less obsessed with his art than Canova would later prove, he rose at dawn, made for the studio, and stayed there late into the night, living only with his muse. If he went to the Comédie-Française, it was only at his master's insistence. Profoundly ill at ease at Madame Geoffrin's, and in all the social circles into which Bouchardon sought to introduce him, he preferred to spend his time alone and forwent all the pleasures of that licentious age. He had no mistress other than Sculpture, apart from Clotilde, one of the Opéra's brightest stars—and even that affair would be a short-lived one. Sarrasine was rather homely, always badly dressed, and so untamed in his nature, so immoderate in his ways that the celebrated nymph, fearing some catastrophe, soon returned the sculptor to the arms of the Arts. Sophie Arnould made some sort of quip on the subject, expressing, I believe, her surprise that her friend had ever stood a chance against statues.

Sarrasine left for Italy in 1758. As he traveled, his imagination was fired by the deep golden light, by the magnificent monuments scattered all through that fatherland of the arts. The statues, the frescoes, the paintings, everything filled him with wonder, and stirred by competitive zeal, he arrived in Rome burning to inscribe his name between those of Michelangelo and Monsieur Bouchardon. Thus, in the beginning, he divided his time between the studio and the study of the works of art so abundant in Rome.

He spent two full weeks in the ecstatic state that the queen of ruins inspires in all youthful imaginations, and then one evening he happened onto the Teatro Argentina, before which a great crowd had gathered. Asking the cause, he was answered by two names: 'Zambinella! Jommelli!' He entered and found a seat in the parterre, pressed in between two remarkably fat *abati* but close to the stage and with a rather fine view. The curtain went up. This was his first encounter with that music whose praises he had heard so eloquently sung by Monsieur Jean-Jacques Rousseau one evening at the Baron d'Holbach's. The young sculptor's senses were lubricated, so to speak, by Jommelli's sublime harmonies. The languorous manner-isms of those perfectly interwoven Italian voices plunged him into a rapturous ecstasy. He sat silent, motionless, oblivious even to the compression exerted by the two priests. His soul flooded into his ears and eyes. His every pore seemed to be listening. All at once a roar of applause, loud enough to bring down the whole edifice, hailed the entrance of the prima donna. She coyly advanced to the lip of the stage and greeted the public with infinite grace. The light-ing, the enthusiasm of a vast crowd, the illusion of the stage, the be-witchments of her costume (for the fashion of those times was singularly enticing): all this conspired to her advantage. Sarrasine cried out in pleasure. There before his marveling eyes stood that ideal beauty whose perfections he had thus far sought out only in bits and pieces, looking to one model, often ignoble, for the curve of an impeccable leg; to another for the contours of the breast; to this one for her white shoulders; finally taking the neck of a young girl, and the hands of this woman, and the gleaming knees of that child; never encountering, beneath the cold skies of Paris, the sumptuous, fluid creations of ancient Greece. In La Zambinella he found—united, delicate, and perfectly alive—all the exquisite proportions for which he so yearned, all the perfections of a femininity of which a sculptor is at once the sternest and the most passionate critic. Her mouth was expressive, her eyes amorous, her skin brilliant white. And to this, which would surely have delighted a painter, add all the wonders of those Venuses so revered by the Greeks and re-created by their chisels. The artist never tired of admiring the inimitable grace with which her arms were joined to her torso, the haunting curve of her neck, the harmonious lines of her eyebrows, her nose, then the perfect oval of her face, the purity of its youthful forms, and the ef-fect of the lush, curving lashes that fringed her long and voluptuous eyelids. She was more than a woman, she was a masterpiece! In that undreamt-of creation there was love to delight any man and beauty to earn the raves of any critic. Sarrasine's eyes devoured this work of Pygmalion, descended from her pedestal for him alone. When La Zambinella sang, a tumult filled his soul. The artist felt a sudden chill, then a rush of heat scintillating in his most intimate depths, in what we call the heart, for want of a more precise word! He did not applaud, he said nothing, he felt a wave of madness, a sort of frenzy that stirs us only at the age when desire has something terrible and infernal about it. Sarrasine wanted to leap onto the stage and take her in his arms. His physical strength—multiplied a hundredfold by a desperation that cannot be explained, since these phenomena were taking place in a sphere inaccessible to human scrutiny—was struggling, with painful violence, against its constraints. To see him, one would have thought him a cold and dull-witted man. Fame, learning, future, existence, laurels, everything came crashing down. 'Earn her love or die': such was the ultimatum that Sarrasine addressed to himself. Utterly intoxicated, he no longer saw the theater, nor the spectators, nor the actors; he heard no music. More than that, all distance between himself and La Zambinella was abolished; he possessed her; glued to her person, his eyes took her over. By the grace of an almost diabolical potency, he could feel the breath conveying her voice, smell the powder that scented her hair, see every contour of that face, count the blue veins that tinged her satin skin. Finally, that agile voice, so fresh, so clear, supple as a thread to which every slight puff of breath gives a new form, curling it, extending it, looping it, that voice so deeply shook his soul that more than one involuntary cry burst from his breast, born of convulsive delectations too rarely supplied by human passions. Soon he had no choice but to flee the theater, his trembling legs almost refusing to carry him. He was drained, weak as a timid and anxious man who has given himself over to some towering fit of rage. So great had been his pleasure—or, perhaps, so terrible his torment—that his life had poured out of him like water from an overturned vase. He felt an emptiness inside him, an annihilation very like the listlessness of a convalescent after some serious illness. Invaded by an inexplicable sadness, he sat down on the steps of a church. His back pressed to a column, he fell into a meditation as tangled as a dream. Passion had left him utterly undone.

He returned home and threw himself into one of those paroxysms of activity that reveal the presence of a new order in our existence. Rapt in that first surge of love, as much pleasure as pain, he tried to quell his impatience and agitation by drawing La Zambinella from memory. It was a sort of material meditation. On one sheet La Zambinella appeared in that seemingly cold, placid pose so beloved of Raphael, of Giorgione, of all the great painters. On another, she held her head delicately turned to one side, as if listening to herself as she finished a trill. Sarrasine sketched his mistress in every possible attitude: He depicted her unveiled, sitting, standing, lying, both chaste and amorous, his pencil's frenzied fantasies materializing all the impulsive ideas that vie for our imagination's attention when we think intensely of a mistress. But his untamable thoughts did not stop at drawing. He saw La Zambinella, he talked to her, he entreated her, he ran through a thousand years of life and happiness with her, placing her in every situation imaginable, trying on, so to speak, a shared future. The next day he sent a footman to rent a private box beside the stage for the remainder of the season. Then, like every young man with a powerful soul, he inflated in his mind the difficulties of his undertaking, and as a prelude to better things, he offered his passion the opportunity to gaze on his mistress without hindrance. This golden age of love, in which we delight in our own emotion and are made happy almost by ourselves, was not to last long for Sarrasine. Nevertheless, events overtook him when he was still under the spell of that budding hallucination, as innocent as it is sensual. Over some eight days, he lived an entire life. In the morning he kneaded the clay from which he would fashion a superb likeness of La Zambinella, despite all the veils, skirts, corsets, and knotted ribbons that distanced her from him. In the evening, settling early into his box, alone, outstretched on a sofa, he invented for himself, like a Turk in the embrace of opium, a happiness as rich and unsparing as he wished. First he gradually inured himself to the overpowering emotions inspired by his mistress's singing; then he trained his eyes to look on her, and soon found himself able to contemplate her with no fear of the muted explosion of fury that had shaken him that first evening. His passion grew more profound as it grew more pacific. On top of all this, the unsociable sculptor guarded his solitude—peopled with imaginings, decorated with the caprices of desire, full of happiness—against any intrusion by his comrades. So powerful was his love, and so naïve, that he fell prey to all the youthful uncertainties that besiege us in our first amorous experience. Realizing that he would soon have to take action, bestir himself, learn where La Zambinella lived, determine if she had a mother, an uncle, a guardian, a family—musing, in short, on the measures required to see her, to speak with her—he felt his heart swelling so powerfully at such ambitious ideas that he postponed these considerations until the next day, happy in his physical torment no less than in his mental delight."

"But," said Madame de Rochefide, interrupting me, "I have yet to see any sign of Marianina or her little old man."

"You've seen nothing but him," I cried, cross as any author whose startling twist has been spoiled. "For several days," I went on after a pause, "Sarrasine so faithfully appeared in his box, and gazed so lovingly at La Zambinella, that his passion for her voice would have been the talk of all Paris had this adventure happened there; but in Italy, madame, at the theater, everyone attends for his own sake, with his own passions, with a heartfelt interest that precludes operaglass espionage. Nevertheless, the sculptor's frenzy would not long escape the other singers' notice. One evening, the Frenchman saw them laughing at him in the wings. Who knows where that might have led, had La Zambinella not then made her entrance. She cast Sarrasine one of those eloquent glances that often say more than women wish. That look was nothing short of a revelation. Sarrasine was loved! 'If this is some mere passing fancy,' he thought, already accusing his mistress of exaggerated ardor, 'she has no idea of the tyranny she is about to fall prey to. I hope to see that fancy last as long as I live.' At that moment, the artist was wrested from his reverie by three light raps outside his box. He opened the door. An old woman entered, with a mysterious air. 'Young man,' she said, 'if you wish to find joy, then take care, wrap yourself in a cape, pull a large hat down low over your eyes, and come to Via del Corso, in front of the Hotel di Spagna, at around ten o'clock this evening.' 'I'll be there,' he answered, dropping two louis into the duenna's wrinkled hand. He slipped out of his box after nodding to La Zambinella, who timidly lowered her sensuous eyelids like a woman happy to have made herself understood at long last. He ran home to rifle his wardrobe and dressing table for all the charms they could offer him. As he was leaving the theater, a stranger had held him back by one arm. 'Take care, Frenchman,' he murmured into Sarrasine's ear. 'This is a matter of life and death. Cardinal Cicognara is her protector, and he's not a man for half measures.' Had a demon opened the gaping abyss of hell between Sarrasine and La Zambinella, he would at that moment have crossed it with one single stride. Like the horses of the immortals depicted by Homer, the sculptor's love had taken a mighty leap, flying over vast expanses in a second. 'If Death itself were awaiting me outside the house, I'd go all the faster,' he answered. '*Poverino!*' cried the stranger, vanishing. For one in love, are words of warning not merely a fresh offering of pleasure? Never had Sarrasine's footman seen his master tend so fastidiously to his appearance. His best sword (a gift from Bouchardon), the cravat given him by Clotilde, his sequined morning coat, his silver satin vest, his gold snuffbox, his precious watches—everything was pulled from his coffers, and he adorned himself like a girl about to parade past her first lover. At the appointed hour, drunk with love and boiling over with impatience, Sarrasine ran to the meeting place named by the old woman, his nose buried in a cloak. The duenna was waiting. 'You took your sweet time!' she said. 'Come.' She hurried the Frenchman through several small streets, then stopped before a rather opulent palace. She knocked. The door opened. She led Sarrasine through a labyrinth of stairways, corridors, salons lit only by the tenuous glow of the moon, and soon arrived at a door with bright lights and a joyous clamor of voices streaming through the cracks. On a word from the old woman, Sarrasine was admitted into these mysterious digs, dazzled to find himself in a salon as brilliantly lit as it was sumptuously furnished, amid which stood a nicely laid table, laden with august bottles, with merry decanters, their red-tinged facets gleaming. He recognized the singers from the theater, interspersed with a number of charming women, all of them ready to begin an artists' orgy that lacked only him. Sarrasine fought back a surge of disappointment and put on a festive face. He was hoping for a dimly lit boudoir, his mistress close by a coal fire, a jealous rival two steps away, love and death, confidences exchanged in low tones, heart to heart, perilous kisses, faces so close that La Zambinella's hair would caress his brow, burdened with desire and burning with joy. 'Long live folly!' he cried. '*Signori e belle donne*, you will allow me to take my vengeance later; for the moment, let me simply express my gratitude for the welcome you offer a poor sculptor.' Once he had received the affectionate compliments of most of those present, whom he knew by sight, he tried to approach the bergère in which La Zambinella nonchalantly lolled. Oh, how his heart beat on spying a delicate foot, shod with those mules that, may I say, madame, once gave women's feet a form so enticing and voluptuous that I don't see how men could resist it. The clinging white stockings with green clocks, the short skirts, the pointed, high-heeled mules of the reign of Louis XV might well have played some small part in the moral undoing of Europe and the clergy."

"Just a small part?" said the marquise. "Have you read nothing?"

"La Zambinella," I resumed, smiling, "had boldly crossed her legs, and as she bantered she swayed the topmost one this way and that, a duchess's pose, ideally suited to her airy, provocatively languid sort of beauty. She had changed out of her costume and wore a bodice that girdled a slender waist, the effect heightened by panniers and a satin dress embroidered with blue flowers. Its treasures teasingly concealed beneath a lace drape, her breast was purest white. Coiffed rather like Madame du Barry, her face, although enveloped in a large bonnet, seemed only the more charming, and her powder suited her perfectly. To see her this way was to adore her. She smiled graciously at the sculptor. Deeply unhappy that his first words to her must have witnesses, Sarrasine sat down politely beside her and engaged her in a conversation on music, extolling her prodigious talent; but his voice was shaking with love, fear, and hope. 'What are you afraid of?' asked Vitagliani, the most celebrated singer in the troupe. 'Fear not, you've no rivals here.' The tenor smiled in silence. That smile repeated itself on the lips of all the guests, whose attention had a hidden slyness that a lover was not likely to notice. This public airing of his love was like a dagger plunged into Sarrasine's heart. Although endowed with a certain force of character, and although no circumstance could ever alter his feelings, it might not yet have occurred to him that Zambinella was almost a courtesan, and that he could not have both the pure raptures that make a young girl's love so delicious and the fiery transports that a woman of the theater requires in payment for her passion's delights. He reflected, and resigned himself. Supper was served. Sarrasine and La Zambinella sat down side by side, without ceremony. In the first half of the feast, the artists observed some restraint, and the sculptor was able to chat with the soprano. He found in her wit and finesse, but she was surprisingly ignorant, as well as fragile and superstitious. Her intellect was as slight as her physique. When Vitagliani uncorked the first bottle of champagne, Sarrasine read in his neighbor's eyes a distinct fright at the little explosion of escaping gases. The love-struck sculptor interpreted that involuntary feminine flinch as a sign of excessive sensitivity. The Frenchman was charmed by this weakness. How protective is a man in love! 'My strength will be yours, like a shield!' Is that sentence not written deep beneath every amorous declaration? Too overcome with passion to whisper sweet trifles into her perfect ear, Sarrasine was, like all lovers, by turns earnest, merry, and meditative. Although seeming to listen to the other guests, he heard not a word that they spoke, so engrossed was he in the pleasure of sitting beside her, of brushing her hand with his, of serving her. He was lost in a secret joy.

Notwithstanding the eloquence of several shared glances, he was bewildered by La Zambinella's reserve. To be sure, it was she who first pressed her foot against his, teasing him with all the wiles of a besotted, uninhibited woman, but on hearing Sarrasine utter a quip that revealed the excessive impetuosity of his nature, she suddenly draped herself in a girlish modesty. Before long their supper gave way to unbridled revelry; inspired by the Peralta and Pedro Ximenez, the tablemates broke into song. Delightful duos ensued, Calabrian airs, Spanish seguidillas, Neapolitan canzonettas. There was intoxication in every eye, in the music, in their hearts and their voices. The room was suffused with an enchanting exuberance, a convivial abandon, an Italian good humor unimaginable to those who know only the soirees of Paris, the routs of London, or the clubs of Vienna. Japes and words of love flew back and forth like bullets in battle, through the laughter, the impieties, the invocations addressed to the Holy Virgin or *al Bambino*. One guest lay down on a sofa and slept. A young girl listened to a declaration of love, unaware that she was pouring sherry onto the tablecloth. Amid this chaos, La Zambinella sat mute, as if gripped by apprehension. She refused to drink, ate perhaps a little too much, but a healthy appetite can be an adorable thing in a woman. Admiring his mistress's demureness, Sarrasine began to think seriously of the future. 'No doubt she wants to be married,' he told himself. And then he reveled with all his heart in the joys of that marriage. His entire lifetime did not seem enough to exhaust the wellspring of happiness he found deep in his soul. His neighbor Vitagliani refilled his glass so many times that, toward three in the morning, though not thoroughly drunk, Sarrasine found his ardor getting the better of him. In a moment of intense desire, he swept the woman away from the others and into a sort of adjoining boudoir, toward whose door he had cast more than one longing glance. She was armed with a dagger. 'If you come one step closer,' she said, 'I will have no choice but to sink this blade into your heart. Don't you see, you would soon despise me. I have come to respect your character too highly to simply abandon myself to you. I don't want to fall from the grace of the sentiments you are so good as to feel for me.' 'Ah! Ah,' said Sarrasine, 'arousing a passion is no way to extinguish it. Are you then already so corrupted that, though an old woman in your heart, you behave like a young courtesan, stoking the emotions that bring her business?' 'But today is Friday,' she answered, quivering at the Frenchman's insistence. Sarrasine, who was not a churchgoer, let out a laugh. Leaping like a young roebuck, La Zambinella bounded into the other room, where the party was still raging. When Sarrasine burst in after her, he was greeted by an infernal laugh. He saw La Zambinella unconscious on a sofa. She was pale, as if utterly drained by the extraordinary effort she had just expended. Although Sarrasine knew little Italian, he heard his mistress whispering to Vitagliani, 'But he'll kill me!' This strange scene left the sculptor mortified. His reason came flooding back. At first he simply stood motionless; then, finding his tongue, he sat down beside her to pledge his respect. He summoned the strength to cast off his desire, even as he spoke to her in the most exalted of discourses, and to convey his love, he pressed into service all the treasures of eloquence, that worker of wonders, that obliging spokesman whom women so rarely refuse to believe.

Soon the revelers were surprised by the first gleams of morning; with this, one of the women suggested an outing to Frascati. The idea of a day at Villa Ludovisi was hailed with spirited hurrahs. Vitagliani went off to hire carriages. Sarrasine had the pleasure of driving La Zambinella in a phaeton. Once out of Rome, the revelers' gaiety, subdued for a moment by their battle with sleep, abruptly returned. They all seemed entirely at ease in this curious existence, these unending pleasures, this artistic vivacity that made of life a perpetual party, in which laughter was never troubled by serious thoughts. Only the sculptor's companion seemed defeated by exhaustion. 'Are you ill?' Sarrasine asked her. 'Would you rather go home?' 'I haven't the strength to withstand all these excesses,' she answered. 'I need to be treated with special care, but with you beside me, I feel so happy, so fine! If not for you, I would never have stayed at that supper; a night without sleep robs me of all my freshness.' 'How delicate you are!' Sarrasine replied, staring at the charming creature's delightful little features. 'Orgies do harm to my voice.' 'Now that we're alone,' cried the artist, 'and you need no longer fear the vehemence of my passion, tell me you love me.' 'Why?' she answered. 'What purpose would that serve? You thought me pretty. But you are French, and your feelings will pass. Oh! You would never love me as I want to be loved.' 'And how is that?' 'Not for the sake of vulgar passion but purely. I abhor men perhaps even more than I loathe women. My only refuge is friendship. The world is empty for me. I am a cursed creature, condemned to understand felicity, to feel it, to desire it, and yet, like so many others, to see it flee me at every turn. Please, signore, in times to come, remember: I never deceived you. I forbid you to love me. I can be a devoted friend, for I admire your force and your character. I need a brother, a protector. Be all that for me, but nothing more.' 'Not love you!' cried Sarrasine. 'But, dear angel, you are my life, my joy!' 'One word from me and you would push me away in horror.' 'Coquette! Nothing can frighten me. Tell me you will rob me of my future, tell me I'll be dead in two months, tell me one single kiss will mean my damnation.' And with this he kissed her, La Zambinella struggling to extract herself from his fervent embrace. 'Tell me you're a demon, tell me I must sign away my fortune, my name, my renown! Would you have me not be a sculptor? You need only speak the word.' 'And if I was not a woman?' La Zambinella asked timidly, in a sweet, crystalline voice. 'A fine joke that is!' cried Sarrasine. 'Do you truly believe you can fool the eye of an artist? Have I not spent ten days devouring, studying, wondering at your perfections? Only a woman can have that rounded, yielding arm, those elegant curves. Ah! You're fishing for compliments!' She smiled sadly. 'Cursed beauty!' she murmured, raising her eyes to the heavens. There was in her gaze a despair so profound and so poignant that a shudder ran through Sarrasine. 'Oh, French signore,' she said, 'forget forever a moment of folly. I have only the highest regard for you, but do not ask me for love; that emotion has been forever snuffed out in my heart. I have no heart!" she cried, weeping. 'The stage where you first saw me, the applause, the music, the great fame to which I have been condemned, that is my life, I have no other. A few hours from now you will not look on me with the same eyes; the woman you love will be dead.' The sculptor made no reply. A mute fury had overtaken him, constricting his heart. He could only stare at this extraordinary woman, his eyes afire. That fragile voice, La Zambinella's attitude, her manners, her gestures so full of sadness, melancholy, and despair, all this reawoke the urgent passion in his soul. Every word was a goad. They had now arrived in Frascati. Clasping his mistress to help her alight, he found her trembling from head to toe. 'What's the matter?' he cried as she paled. 'It would kill me if you were suffering any pain that I might have caused, however innocently.' 'A serpent!' she said, pointing at a garter snake gliding by, alongside a ditch. 'I'm terrified of those hateful beasts.' Sarrasine crushed the snake's head with one stamp of his foot. 'Where can you possibly find the courage?' asked La Zambinella, contemplating the dead reptile with visible horror. 'Well now,' said the artist with a smile, 'dare you still claim you are not a woman?' They rejoined their companions and strolled through the woods of Villa Ludovisi, which then figured among the properties of Cardinal Cicognara. The day went by too fast for the smitten sculptor, but it was filled with a host of incidents that revealed all the vanity, all the frailty, all the preciousness of that feeble, languorous soul. She was in every way a woman, with her sudden frights, her unreasoning caprices, her instinctive emotions, her abrupt bursts of daring, her bravado, the delicious refinement of her sentiments. At one moment, as the merry little band of singers ventured out into the countryside, they caught sight of a distant knot of men, heavily armed and disreputably dressed. On the word 'Those men are brigands,' they turned hurriedly back toward the shelter of the grounds of the cardinal's villa. In that tense moment, Sarrasine noted La Zambinella's extreme pallor and realized that she lacked the strength to walk any farther; he took her in his arms and carried her for some time at a run. Nearing a neighboring vineyard, he set his mistress down. 'Explain to me,' he said to her, 'how this extraordinary frailty, which in any other woman would be tiresome and repellent, any sign of which would almost suffice to extinguish my love, why in you it so charms and delights me?' He paused, then went on: 'Oh! How I love you! Your weakness, your terror, your pettiness, they all add some mysterious sort of grace to your soul. I think I would despise a strong woman, a Sappho, courageous, full of passion and energy. O fragile, gentle creature! How could you be otherwise? That angelic voice, that tender voice would have been the very height of incongruity had it come from any body but yours.' 'I can give you no hope,' she answered. 'Stop this talk, lest you be mocked. I cannot forbid you to enter the theater, but if you love me, or if you are wise, you will come there no more. Listen to me, monsieur,' she said, gravely. 'Oh! Be silent,' the infatuated artist answered. 'Obstacles only fan the flames of love in my heart.' La Zambinella stood in a pose as exquisite and modest as ever, but she said nothing, as if some awful thought had shown her a terrible imminent sorrow.

When it came time to return to Rome, she climbed into a four-seat berline, cruelly ordering the sculptor to take the phaeton back alone. Along the way, Sarrasine resolved to abduct La Zambinella. He spent the entire day making plans, each more convoluted than the last. At nightfall, just as he was going out to inquire into the address of his mistress's palace, he found a comrade of his on the doorstep. 'My dear friend,' said the visitor, 'I am requested by our ambassador to invite you to his home this evening. He's planned a magnificent concert, and when I tell you that Zambinella will be there—' 'Zambinella!' cried Sarrasine, ecstatic to hear the name spoken. 'I'm mad about her!' 'As are we all,' his friend replied. 'But if you truly are my friends, you, Vien, Lautherbourg, and Allegrain, you will lend me your aid for a small undertaking after the party,' answered Sarrasine. 'There's no cardinal to be killed, I hope, no—' 'Nothing of the sort,' said Sarrasine, 'I ask of you nothing honest folk could not do.' Soon the sculptor had in hand all he required for the success of his scheme. He was among the last guests to arrive at the ambassador's, but he came in a traveling coach drawn by vigorous horses and driven by one of the ablest and most serviceable *vetturini* in Rome. A great crowd crammed the ambassador's palace; only with difficulty did the sculptor, a stranger to all present, fight his way into the salon where Zambinella was singing. 'I suppose it's for the sake of the cardinals, bishops, and abbots in attendance,' asked Sarrasine, 'that she is dressed as a man, that she has a snood behind her head, crimped hair, and a sword at her side?' 'She? What she is that?' replied the old lord to whom Sarrasine was speaking. 'La Zambinella.' 'La Zambinella?' the Roman prince snorted. 'Are you joking? Where do you come from? Has any woman ever set foot on the stages of Rome? And do you not know what sort of creatures play women's roles in the Papal States? It is I, monsieur, who gave Zambinella his voice. I paid that rogue's every expense, down to his singing master. And do you know, the ingrate never so much as set foot in my house again! And to think: If he makes a fortune, he will owe it entirely to me.' Prince Chigi might well have gone on talking for some time; Sarrasine had stopped listening. An awful truth had pierced deep into his soul. He was speechless with shock. He stood still, eyes glued to that false soprano. His fiery gaze exerted a sort of magnetic influence on Zambinella, for after a moment the musico whirled around to face Sarrasine, and suddenly his celestial voice cracked. He trembled! An involuntary murmur rose from the crowd, which he had up to then held as if bound to his lips. His discomposure complete, he broke off his song and sat down. Glimpsing from the corner of his eye the direction of his protégé's gaze, Cardinal Cicognara turned toward the Frenchman; he bent to one of his ecclesiastical aides-de-camp, as if to ask the sculptor's name. On obtaining the desired answer, he looked the artist over and whispered some order to an abbot, who hurried off at once. In the meantime, Zambinella recovered his poise and began anew the air that he had so capriciously interrupted, but he performed it badly, and despite all the crowd's urgings refused to sing another note. This was his first display of the unpredictable willfulness for which he would later become famous, as famous as for his talent and vast fortune, which he is said to owe no less to his voice than to his great beauty. 'She's a woman,' said Sarrasine, thinking himself alone. 'There's some secret intrigue behind all this. Cardinal Cicognara is deceiving the pope and the entire city of Rome along with him!'

The sculptor dashed out of the salon, gathered his friends, and led them to a dark, secret spot in the palace's courtyard. Seeing that Sarrasine was gone, Zambinella seemed to recover some semblance of tranquillity. Toward midnight, after wandering for some time through the salons, in the manner of a man looking for an enemy, the musico left the party. On the palace's threshold, he was deftly seized by a group of men, who gagged him with a handkerchief and bundled him into Sarrasine's hired carriage. Zambinella huddled in one corner, too terrified to move. Before him he saw the terrible face of the artist, as silent as the dead. The trip was a short one. Abducted by Sarrasine, Zambinella soon found himself in a dim, barren studio. The singer sat numbly on a chair, not daring to glance at the nearby statue of a woman on which he saw his own features. He did not speak a word, but his teeth chattered. He was paralyzed with fear. Sarrasine paced back and forth in deep agitation. Suddenly he stopped before Zambinella. 'Tell me the truth,' he asked, in a choked, quiet voice. 'Are you a woman? Cardinal Cicognara...' Zambinella fell to his knees, his only answer a bowed head. 'Ah! You are a woman,' cried the artist, beside himself, 'for surely even a...' He left his sentence unfinished. 'No,' he resumed, 'he would never be so base.' 'Ah! Do not kill me,' cried Zambinella, dissolving into tears. 'It was only to please my friends that I deceived you. They wanted some fun.' 'Fun!' the sculptor answered, in an infernally caustic voice. 'Fun, fun! You dared to toy with the passion of a man, you of all people?' 'Take pity on me,' Zambinella answered. 'I should put an end to your life here and now!' cried Sarrasine, furiously drawing his sword. 'But,' he went on with cold disdain, 'were I to plunge this blade into the very depths of your soul, would I find any sentiment to snuff out, any vengeance to satisfy? You are nothing. Man or woman, I would kill you! But...' Sarrasine made a gesture of disgust that forced him to turn his head, and his eye landed on the statue. 'And all this is an illusion!' he cried. Then, turning back to Zambinella, 'For me, a woman's heart was a refuge, a home. Do you have sisters who resemble you? No. Well then, die! But no, you shall live. By allowing you your life, am I not consigning you to something still worse than death? I care nothing for my blood nor my life, only my future and my fortunes in love. Your frail hand has sent my happiness crashing to earth. What hopes might I strip you of, for all those you have blighted? You have lowered me to your level. *Loving* and *being loved* are henceforth words without meaning for me, as they are for you. From this moment on, the sight of a real woman will always fill me with thoughts of this imaginary woman.' He gestured despairingly toward the statue. 'In my memory there will ever be a celestial harpy who will sink her claws into my every manly emotion, and who will stamp all other women with the mark of imperfection. Monster! You who can bring no new life into being, you have emptied my world of women forever.' Sarrasine sat down before the distraught singer. Two large tears welled up in his dry eyes, rolled down his virile cheeks, and fell to the ground, two tears of rage, two bitter, stinging tears. 'No more love! I am dead to all pleasure, to all human sentiment!' He snatched up a hammer and hurled it at the statue with such excessive force that he missed his mark. Thinking he had destroyed that monument to his folly, he picked up his sword and raised it high, making ready to dispatch the singer. Zambinella cried out sharply. At that moment three men entered, and all at once the sculptor fell to the ground, pierced by the blades of three stilettos. 'On behalf of Cardinal Cicognara,' said one of the intruders. 'This is a blessing worthy of a Christian,' the Frenchman answered in his final breath. These somber emissaries told Zambinella of the anxieties that had assailed his protector, who was waiting at the door in a closed carriage, ready to take him away the moment he was freed."

"But," said Madame de Rochefide to me, "what has this to do with the little old man we saw at the Lantys'?"

"Madame, Cardinal Cicognara took possession of the statue of Zambinella and had it sculpted in marble. Today it can be seen in the Albani Museum. It was there that, in 1791, the Lanty family discovered it and commissioned a copy from Vien. The portrait that showed you Zambinella at twenty, a moment after you'd seen him at one hundred, later served as a model for Girodet's *Endymion*, whose essence you recognized in that Adonis."

"But this Zambinella? Who is she? Or he?"

"Why, madame, Marianina's great-uncle. Perhaps now you can

imagine Madame de Lanty's interest in concealing the source of a fortune that comes from—"

"Enough!" she interrupted, with a commanding gesture.

We sat for a moment in deepest silence.

"Well?" I asked.

"Ah!" she cried, standing and pacing restlessly through the room. She came and looked at me, then said in a choked voice, "You have put me off life and passion for a long time to come. The monster aside, do not all human sentiments end just that way, in crushing disappointment? As mothers, our children destroy us by their wickedness or their distance. As wives, we are betrayed. As lovers, we are cast aside and forgotten. And friendship! Does it even exist? I would devote my life to God tomorrow, did I not have the gift of standing like an inaccessible rock amid all the tempests of life. If the Christian's future is only one more illusion, at least it goes on unshattered until we are dead. Leave me now."

"Ah!" I said. "You know how to punish a man."

"Am I wrong?"

"Yes," I answered, with a sort of courage. "As a conclusion to this story, fairly well known in Italy, I can offer you a consoling idea of the progress that contemporary civilization has achieved. They no longer make those wretched creatures there."

"Paris," she said, "is a very hospitable land; here all are welcome, fortunes draped in shame no less than fortunes bathed in blood. Crime and infamy have free rein and meet with nothing but sympathy; virtue alone finds no altar. Yes, only in heaven do pure souls have a place of their own! I say it with pride: No one will ever know me!"

And the marquise sat lost in thought.

Paris, November 1830
Translated by Jordan Stump

A PASSION IN THE DESERT

"THAT PERFORMANCE was terrifying!" she cried out as she left Monsieur Martin's menagerie.

She was there to contemplate the dashing performer *working* with his hyena, as the advertising poster put it.

"How did he manage," she went on, "to tame his animals to the point where he is so certain of their affection that—"

"That accomplishment, which seems so strange to you," I interrupted her, "is in fact something very natural."

"Oh!" she cried, allowing an incredulous smile to play over her lips.

"So you think that animals have no passions?" I asked her. "Here's proof that we can give them all the vices belonging to our stage of civilization."

She looked at me in astonishment.

"But," I continued, "seeing Monsieur Martin for the first time, I confess that, like you, I could not contain my surprise. At that time I found myself seated next to an old veteran with a missing right leg. He struck me as an impressive figure. He had one of those intrepid heads marked by war and inscribed by Napoleonic battles. That old soldier had an aura of frankness and cheer about him that always makes me favorably disposed. No doubt he was one of those unflappable troopers who laugh at a comrade's final rictus, cheerfully strip or enshroud him, command cannonballs to be fired with dispatch, deliberate swiftly, and deal with the devil without a qualm. After paying close attention to the menagerie's owner as he was leaving the loge, my companion pursed his lips in a gesture of mocking disdain, with the sort of pout that allows superior men to single out the gullible. And when I exclaimed at Monsieur Martin's courage, he smiled and said to me with a knowing look, shaking his head: 'Same old story.'

"'Same old story? What do you mean?' I asked him. 'I would be much obliged if you would explain this mystery to me.'

"After spending several moments exchanging introductions, we went to dine at the first restaurant we came across. Over dessert, a bottle of champagne coaxed this curious old soldier to refresh his memories in all their clarity. He told me his tale and I saw that he was right to cry out, 'Same old story!'"

As I was seeing my companion home, she begged and pleaded with me until I agreed to write up the soldier's confidences for her. The following day she received this episode from a saga that could be entitled "The French in Egypt."

During the expedition undertaken in Upper Egypt by General Desaix, a soldier from Provence fell into the hands of the Maghrebis and was taken by those Arabs into the desert situated beyond the cataracts of the Nile. In order to put sufficient distance between themselves and the French army and so ensure their peace of mind, the Maghrebis undertook a forced march, stopping only at night. They made camp around a water source hidden by palm trees where they had buried provisions some time before. Having no idea that their prisoner might take it into his head to flee, they were content to bind his hands, and all went to sleep after eating a few dates and feeding their horses. When the bold man from Provence saw his enemies incapable of keeping watch over him, he used his teeth to steal a scimitar, then, employing his knees to steady the blade, he cut the cords that bound his hands and freed himself. He instantly grabbed a rifle and a dagger, provisions of dried dates, a small sack of barley, some powder and bullets, strapped on a scimitar, hopped on a horse, and headed quickly in the direction he thought the French army must have taken. Impatient to join his bivouac, he rode his already tired mount so hard that the poor animal expired, its flanks torn to shreds, leaving the Frenchman in the middle of the desert.

After walking for some time in the sand with all the courage of an escaped convict, the soldier was forced to stop at nightfall. Despite the beauty of the sky during the Oriental night, he hadn't the strength to continue on his way. Fortunately, he was able to climb a promontory crowned by several palm trees, whose long visible fronds had awakened the sweetest hopes in his heart. His fatigue was so great that he stretched out on a piece of granite whimsically shaped like a camp bed and slept without a thought to defend himself. He had made the sacrifice of his life. His last thought was even a regret. He repented having left the Maghrebis, whose nomadic life was beginning to please him, now that he was far from them and quite helpless.

He woke with the sun, whose pitiless rays were falling directly on the granite and generating an unbearable heat. Now, our man from Provence had had the poor judgment to place himself on the other side from the shade projected by the verdant and majestic tops of the palm trees... He looked at those solitary trees and shivered! They reminded him of the elegant capitals, crowned with the long leaves, that distinguish the Saracen columns of the Arles cathedral. But after counting the palms, he cast his glance around him and felt the most terrifying despair sink deep into his soul. He saw a limitless ocean. The blackened sand of the desert extended unbroken in every direction, and it glittered like a steel blade struck by harsh light. He did not know whether this was a sea of ice or of lakes smooth as a mirror. Borne on waves, a mist of fire whirled above this moving earth. The sky was an Oriental burst of desolate purity, for it left nothing to the imagination. Sky and earth were on fire. The silence was frightening in its savage and terrible majesty. The immensity of the infinite pressed on the soul from all sides: not a cloud in the sky, not a breath of air, no undulation in the depths of the sand that shifted in small, skittering waves on the surface. Finally, the horizon ended like a sea in good weather, at a line of light as slender as the edge of a sword. The man from Provence squeezed the trunk of one of the palm trees as if it were the body of a friend; then, in the shelter of the straight, spindly shade that the tree inscribed on the granite, he wept, sitting and resting there, deeply sad as he contemplated the implacable scene that lay before him. He cried out to test his solitude. His voice, lost in the crevices of the heights, projected a thin sound into the distance that found no echo; the echo was in his heart: He was twenty-two years old, he loaded his rifle.

"There'll always be time enough!" he said to himself, laying the weapon of his liberation on the ground.

Looking in turn at the black and the blue spaces around him, the soldier dreamed of France. He caught the delightful scent of Parisian rivulets, he remembered the cities he had passed through, the faces of his comrades, and the most trivial circumstances of his life. And his southern imagination soon conjured the stones of his dear Provence in the play of heat that undulated above the extended sheet of the desert. Fearing all the dangers of this cruel mirage, he went down the other side of the hill he had climbed the day before. He felt great joy in discovering a kind of grotto naturally carved into the gigantic crags of granite that formed the base of this small peak. The remains of a mat told him that this refuge had already been inhabited. Then, several feet farther on, he saw palm trees laden with dates. The instinct that attaches us to life awoke in his heart. He hoped to live long enough for the passage of some Maghrebis, or perhaps indeed he would soon hear the noise of cannon; for just now Bonaparte was marching through Egypt.

Revived by this thought, the Frenchman whacked down several clusters of ripe dates whose weight seemed to bend the date palm's branches, and as he sampled this unanticipated manna he was certain that the grotto's inhabitant had cultivated the palm trees. The delicious, cool flesh of the date provided clear evidence of his predecessor's labors. The man from Provence shifted unthinkingly from dark despair to an almost mad joy. He climbed back up to the top of the hill and busied himself for the rest of the day cutting down one of the infertile palm trees that had provided him with a roof the previous night. A vague memory made him think of the animals of the desert, and foreseeing that they might come to drink at the watering hole lost in the sands that appeared at the base of the rocky outcropping, he resolved to guard against their visits by putting a barrier at the door of his hermitage. Despite his enthusiasm, despite the strength he drew from his fear of being devoured as he slept, he found it impossible to cut the palm tree into several pieces in the course of the day, but he succeeded in felling it.

When toward evening this king of the desert finally fell, the noise of its collapse echoed in the distance, like a groan uttered by the solitude. The soldier shivered as if he had heard some voice announcing disaster. But like an heir who does not grieve for long at a parent's death, he stripped the fine tree of the long, broad green leaves that define its poetic decoration and used them to repair the mat on which he would sleep. Worn out by the heat and his labors, he slept under the red walls of his damp grotto.

In the middle of the night his sleep was disturbed by an extraordinary noise. He sat up, and in the deep silence he recognized the sound of something breathing with a savage energy that could not belong to a human creature. A deep fear made even greater by the darkness, by the silence, and by the fancies of his sudden awakening chilled his heart. He barely even felt his scalp crawl when his dilated pupils glimpsed in the darkness two faint yellow beams. At first he attributed these lights to some reflection of his own eyes, but soon the vivid brightness of the night helped him by degrees to distinguish objects within the grotto, and he perceived an enormous animal lying two steps away from him. Was it a lion, a tiger, or a crocodile? The man from Provence did not have enough education to know in what subspecies to place his enemy, but his fright was all the more violent since his ignorance caused him to assume all these disasters at once. He endured the cruel torture of hearing, of grasping the irregularities of this breathing without losing any of its nuances, and without daring to make the slightest movement. An odor as strong as a fox's breath but more penetrating, more serious, we might say, filled the grotto, and when the man from Provence had taken it in with his nose, his terror was at its height, but he could no longer doubt the existence of the terrifying companion whose royal lair served as his bivouac.

Soon the rays of the moon sailing toward the horizon lit up the den and the subtly gleaming skin of a spotted panther. This royal Egyptian beast was sleeping rolled over like a large dog, peaceful possessor of a sumptuous nook at the door of a grand house. Its eyes opened for a moment, then closed again. It had its face turned toward the Frenchman. A thousand jumbled thoughts passed through the soul of the panther's prisoner. At first he wanted to kill it with a rifle shot, but he saw that there was not enough space between them to aim properly—the barrel would have extended beyond the animal. And what if he were to wake it up? This hypothesis stopped him in his tracks. Listening to the beating of his heart in the silence, he cursed the pounding pulsations of his blood, dreading to disturb the sleep that allowed him to find a solution to his advantage. He put his hand twice on his scimitar, planning to cut off his enemy's head, but the difficulty of cutting through such a tough hide forced him to give up his bold project. "Fail to kill it? Surely that would be a death sentence," he thought. He preferred the odds of combat and resolved to wait for daylight. And daylight was not long in coming. The Frenchman then was able to examine the panther; its muzzle was tinged with blood. "She's had a good meal!" he thought, without worrying whether the feast had been one of human flesh. "She won't be hungry when she wakes up."

It was a female. The fur of the white belly and thighs glimmered. Several little velvety spots formed pretty bracelets around the paws. The muscular tail was also white but tipped with black rings. The upper part of the coat, yellow as matte gold but very smooth and soft, bore those characteristic spots shaped like roses that distinguished panthers from other kinds of *Felis*. This calm and formidable hostess purred in a pose as graceful as that of a cat reclining on the cushion of an ottoman. Her bloody paws, twitching and well armed, lay beneath her head, whose sparse, straight whiskers protruded like silver wires. If she had been in a cage, the man from Provence would surely have admired the grace of this beast and the vigorous contrasts of strong colors that gave her simarre an imperial splendor, but just now he felt his viewing disturbed by its ominous aspect.

The panther's presence, even asleep, made him experience the effect produced by the hypnotic eyes of a snake on, they say, a nightingale. The soldier's courage failed for a moment before this danger, although he would surely have been exalted facing cannon spewing a hail of shot. However, an intrepid thought blossomed in his soul and halted at its source the cold sweat running down his forehead. Acting like men whom misfortune has pushed to the end of their rope, challenging death to do its worst, he saw a tragedy in this adventure without being conscious of it, and resolved to play his role with honor, even to the final scene.

"The day before yesterday, perhaps the Arabs would have killed me," he said to himself. Considering himself a dead man already, he bravely waited with restless curiosity for his enemy to awake. When the sun appeared, the panther silently opened her eyes; then she violently extended her paws, as if to loosen them up and dissipate any cramps. At last she yawned, displaying the fearsome array of her teeth and her grooved tongue, as hard as a grater. "She's like a little mistress!" thought the Frenchman, seeing her rolling around and making the gentlest, most flirtatious movements. She licked the blood that stained her paws, wiped her muzzle, and scratched her head with repeated gestures full of delicacy. "Good! Make your toilette," the Frenchman thought to himself, recovering his cheer by summoning courage. "We'll wish each other good morning." And he grabbed the short dagger he had taken from the Maghrebis.

Just then the panther turned her head toward the Frenchman and stared at him without moving. The rigidity of those metallic eyes and their unbearable clarity made the man from Provence shiver, especially when the beast walked toward him. But he gazed at her caressingly and steadily, as if attempting to exert his own animal magnetism, and let her come near him; then, with a movement as gentle, as amorous as if he had wanted to caress the prettiest woman, he passed his hand over her entire body, from head to tail, using his nails to scratch the flexible vertebrae that ran the length of the panther's yellow back. The beast voluptuously raised her tail, her eyes softened, and when the Frenchman completed this self-interested petting for the third time, she made one of those purring noises by which our cats express their pleasure. But this murmur came from a gullet so powerful and so deep that it sounded in the grotto like the last drones of a church organ. The man from Provence, understanding the importance of his caresses, redoubled his efforts to stun and stupefy this imperious courtesan. When he felt certain of extinguishing his capricious companion's ferocity, remembering that her hunger had been so fortunately satisfied the evening before, he rose to leave the grotto. The panther let him go, but when he had climbed the hill, she leaped with the lightness of monkeys jumping from branch to branch and came to rub herself against the soldier's legs, curving her back like a cat. Then, looking at her guest with an eye whose brightness had become less rigid, she uttered a wild call, which naturalists compare to the noise of a saw.

"How demanding she is!" cried the Frenchman, smiling. He tried to play with her ears, caress her belly, and scratch her head hard with his nails. And seeing his success, he tickled her skull with the point of his dagger, looking for the moment to kill her. But the hardness of the bones made him tremble at the possibility of failure.

The sultana of the desert noted with approval her slave's talents by raising her head, stretching out her neck, marking her intoxication by her repose. The Frenchman suddenly thought that in order to kill this savage princess in one blow, he would have to stab her in the throat, and he raised his blade just as the panther, no doubt sated with this play, lay down graciously at his feet, giving him looks now and then which, despite an inborn rigidity, displayed something like benevolence. The poor man from Provence ate his dates, leaning against one of the palm trees, but he glanced inquiringly at the surrounding desert in every direction, searching for liberators, and at his terrifying mate, keeping an eye on her uncertain clemency. The panther looked at the place where the date pits were falling every time he threw one of them, and then her eyes expressed a skeptic's suspicion. She examined the Frenchman with a calculating caution that concluded in his favor, for when he had finished his meager meal she licked the soles of his shoes, and with her rough, strong tongue miraculously cleaned the encrusted dust from their creases.

"But when she gets hungry?" thought the Provençal soldier. Although this idea caused him a shiver of fear, he began out of curiosity to measure the proportions of the panther, certainly one of the most beautiful examples of the species, for she was three feet high and four feet long, not counting her tail. This powerful weapon, thick around as a gourd, was nearly three feet long. Her head, as large as the head of a lioness, was distinguished by a rare expression of refinement; a tiger's cold cruelty was dominant, of course, but there was also a vague resemblance to the facial features of a cunning woman. Just now the face of this solitary queen revealed something like Nero's drunken gaiety: She had quenched her thirst for blood and wanted to play. The soldier tried to come and go, and the panther let him move freely, content to follow him with her eyes, less like a faithful dog than like a large angora cat made restless by everything, even her master's movements. When he returned, he noticed the remains of his horse next to the fountain, where the panther had dragged the cadaver. Around two-thirds of it had been devoured. This spectacle reassured the Frenchman. It was easy to explain the panther's absence and the respect she had shown him while he slept.

This first happiness emboldened him to attempt the future: He conceived the mad hope of getting on well with the panther all that day, engaging every means to win her over and ingratiate himself. He came near her once more and had the inexpressible happiness of seeing her wave her tail with a subtle movement. So he sat near her without fear and they began to play together. He took her paws, her muzzle, he twisted her ears, rolled her onto her back, and scratched her warm, silky flanks hard. She participated willingly, and when the soldier tried to smooth the fur of her paws, she carefully retracted her claws, curved like steel blades. The Frenchman, who kept one hand on his dagger, was still of a mind to plunge it into the overly trusting belly of the panther, but he was afraid of being instantly strangled in her last wild convulsion. And besides, his heart filled with a kind of remorse that begged him to respect a harmless creature. He felt he had found a friend in this boundless desert. Unbidden thoughts came to him of his first mistress, whom he had called ironically by the nickname "Mignonne" because she was so violently jealous that as long as their passion lasted, he was afraid of the knife with which she used to threaten him. This memory of his youth prompted him to try and impose the name on the young pantheress, whose agility, grace, and softness he now admired less fearfully.

Toward the end of the day, he had become used to his perilous situation, and he almost enjoyed its anguish. His companion had become used to looking at him when he called in a falsetto voice: "Mignonne." By sunset, Mignonne uttered a deep and melancholy cry several times.

"She is well brought up!" thought the cheerful soldier. "She is saying her prayers!" But this unspoken pleasantry came to him only when he had noticed his companion's peaceful attitude. "Go on, my little blonde, I will let you go to bed first," he said to her, counting heavily on escaping by foot as quickly as possible while she slept and finding another shelter for the night. The soldier waited impatiently for the moment of his getaway, and when it came, he walked vigorously in the direction of the Nile, but scarcely had he gone a quarter of a league in the sands than he heard the panther leaping behind him, periodically uttering a harsh cry, still more terrifying than the heavy sound of her leaps.

"Come now!" he said to himself. "She's taken a shine to me... Perhaps this young panther never met anyone before, it is flattering to have won her first love!" At this moment the Frenchmen fell into one of those quicksand traps travelers so dread and from which it is impossible to extricate yourself. Feeling caught, he let out a cry of alarm, and the panther grabbed him by the collar with her teeth. And jumping powerfully backward, she pulled him from the abyss, as if by magic. "Ah, Mignonne," cried the soldier, caressing her enthusiastically. "We're bound to each other now in life and death. But no practical jokes, all right?" And he retraced his steps.

From then on the desert seemed populated. It held one being to whom the Frenchman could talk and whose ferocity was softened for him, although he could not grasp the reason for this unbelievable friendship. However powerful the soldier's desire to remain standing and on the alert, he slept. Upon waking, he could not see Mignonne; he climbed the hill, and in the distance he glimpsed her moving by leaps and bounds according to the habit of those animals for whom running is out of the question because of the extreme flexibility of their spinal column. Mignonne arrived with her chops bloodied and received the necessary caresses from her companion, testifying by several deep purrs how happy she was with him. Her eyes turned with even more sweetness than the evening before on the man from Provence, who spoke to her as to a domestic animal.

"Ah, ah, mademoiselle, such a respectable girl you are, aren't you? Do you see that? We love to be cuddled. Aren't you ashamed? Perhaps you've eaten some Maghrebi? Well, well! They're animals like you! But at least don't go deceiving a Frenchman ... or I will not love you anymore!"

She played the way a young dog plays with his master, rolling, sparring, patting each other by turns, and sometimes she aroused the soldier by putting her paw on him with a solicitous gesture.

Several days passed this way. Her company allowed the man from Provence to admire the sublime beauties of the desert. From the moment he found there alternating hours of fear and tranquillity, provisions, and a creature who occupied his thoughts, his soul was buffeted by contrasts ... It was a life full of opposites. Solitude revealed all its secrets to him, wrapped him in its charms. In the sunrise and sunset he discovered unfamiliar dramas. A shiver went down his spine when he heard the soft whistling of a bird's wings above his head—a rare passing creature—and saw the clouds merge together, multihued, ever-changing travelers! During the night he studied the effects of the moon on the oceans of sands where the simoon produced waves, undulations, and rapid changes. He lived the Orient's day, he admired its marvelous pomp, and often, after enjoying the terrifying spectacle of a hurricane on that plain where the rising sands produced dry, red mists, fatal clouds, he saw the night come on with delight, followed by the life-giving coolness of the stars. He listened to the imaginary music of the spheres.

Then solitude taught him to savor the treasure of daydreams. He spent whole hours remembering trivia, comparing his past life to his life in the present. Finally, he was fascinated by his panther, for he had a need for love. Whether his will, powerfully projected, had modified his companion's character, or she found abundant nourishment thanks to the combat unleashed in these deserts, she respected the life of the Frenchman, who no longer mistrusted her, seeing her so well tamed. He spent the greater part of his time sleeping, but he was forced to keep watch, like a spider in the middle of his web, so as not to miss the moment of his deliverance if someone should pass in the sphere bounded by the horizon. He had sacrificed his shirt to make a flag, hung on the top of a palm tree stripped of its foliage. Instructed by necessity, he knew how to find the means of keeping it flying by holding it out with sticks, for the wind might not have moved it at the very moment when the anticipated traveler would be looking in the desert.

It was during the long hours when hope abandoned him that he amused himself with the panther. He had come to know the different inflections of her voice, the expression in her eyes, had studied the caprices of all the spots that moderated the gold of her robe. Mignonne no longer growled even when he took her by the tuft at the end of her formidable tail in order to count the graceful decoration of black and white rings that shone in the sun like precious stones. He took pleasure in contemplating the supple, delicate lines of her contours, the whiteness of her belly, the grace of her head. But it was especially when she frisked about that he took such pleasure in watching her, and the agility, the youth of her movements always surprised him. He admired her suppleness when she began to leap, crawl, glide, burrow, cling, roll over, flatten herself, dash forward in every direction. She was lightning fast in passion, a block of granite slipping forward, and she froze at the word "Mignonne."

One day under a fiery sun, a huge bird was gliding in the sky. The man from Provence left his panther to examine this new guest, but after a moment's pause, the sultana let out a low growl. "God help me, I think she is jealous," he cried to himself, seeing her eyes harden. "Virginie's soul must surely have passed into this body!"

The eagle disappeared in the sky while the soldier admired the panther's crouching haunches. There was such grace and youth in her shape! She was as pretty as a woman. The blond fur of her coat was matched by the delicate tint of matte white tones that colored her thighs. The profuse light from the sun made that vivid gold and those brown spots shine with ineffable allure. The man from Provence and the panther looked at each other with an intelligent understanding, the coquette trembled when she felt her friend's nails scratch her skull, her eyes shone like two beams, then she closed them firmly.

"She has a soul," he said, studying the calmness of this queen of the sands, gold and white like them, like them solitary and burning…

"Ah well," my companion said to me, "I have read your plea in favor of animals. But how did it end between two beings so well suited to understand each other?"

"Ah, that's it…They ended the way all grand passions end, through a misunderstanding! One or the other believes he has been betrayed, pride prevents understanding, stubbornness prompts a falling out."

"And sometimes in the most exquisite moments," she said. "One look, one exclamation is enough. Now will you finish this story?"

"It's terribly difficult, but you understand what the old fellow had already confided in me when, finishing his bottle of champagne, he cried: 'I don't know how I'd hurt her, but she turned on me as if enraged, and with her sharp teeth she bit me in the thigh, weakly no doubt. As for me, believing that she wanted to devour me, I plunged my dagger into her throat. She rolled over letting out a cry that froze my heart, I saw her struggling while looking at me without anger. I would have given anything in the world, even the Legion of Honor that I didn't yet have, to bring her back to life. It was as if I'd murdered a real person. And the soldiers who had seen my flag and who ran to my rescue, found me in tears . . . Well, monsieur,' he continued after a moment of silence, 'since then I've gone to war in Germany, Spain, Russia, and France. I've faithfully dragged my carcass all over and I've seen nothing equal to the desert . . . ah, how beautiful it is!'

"'What do you feel there?' I asked him.

"'Oh, it can't be put into words, young man. Besides, I don't always regret my stand of palm trees and my panther . . . it's only when I feel sad. In the desert, you see, there is everything and there is nothing.'

"'Still, can you explain it to me?'

"'Well,' he went on, letting a gesture of impatience escape him, 'it is God without men.'"

Paris, 1832
Translated by Carol Cosman

ADIEU

To Prince Frédéric Schwarzenberg

"COME along now, deputy, representative of the people and the Centrist Party, forward! We'll have to do better than this if we want to sit down to dinner along with the others. Lift your feet! Jump, marquis! There, that's the stuff. You leap those ruts like a veritable stag!"

These words were spoken by a hunter sitting lazily at the edge of the forest of L'Isle-Adam, savoring the last puffs of a Havana cigar as he awaited his companion, who must have lost his bearings in the dense woods a good while before. Four panting dogs waited beside the speaker, their eyes trained, like his, on the gentleman thus addressed. In order to fully grasp the sting of these regular harangues, we must understand that the other hunter was a short, corpulent man, whose prominent belly betokened a girth of truly ministerial dimensions. It was thus with some difficulty that he trudged through the furrows of a vast, newly harvested field, his progress greatly hampered by the stubble; to compound his miseries, the solar rays obliquely striking his face bathed it in a copious flow of sweat. Preoccupied by the urgent imperative of keeping upright, he bent now forward, now back, imitating the jolts and shudders of a carriage on a particularly rough road. It was one of those September days whose blazing, equatorial heat brings the grapes of the vineyards to full ripeness. A coming storm could be sensed in the air. Although several wide bands of azure still separated the enormous dark clouds on the horizon, pale golden billows could be seen advancing at an ominous speed, drawing a light curtain of gray underneath them, west to east. Only in the upper reaches did the wind exert its force; below, the atmospheric pressure held the earth's vapors confined in the lowlands. Deprived of air by the ranks of tall trees that surrounded it, the little valley that the hunter was now crossing was as hot as a furnace. Burning and silent, the forest seemed thirsty. The birds and insects did not make a sound; the treetops scarcely swayed. Those who harbor some memory of the summer of 1819 will thus surely sympathize with the poor ministerial deputy as he toiled to join his mocking companion, who was studying the position of the sun as he smoked and had gauged the time at somewhere near five in the evening.

"Where the devil are we?" asked the fat hunter, wiping his forehead and leaning on a tree in the field, almost face-to-face with his companion, for the moment not feeling up to the challenge of jumping the broad trench that separated them.

"You're asking me?" laughed the other, now lying stretched out in the tall yellow grasses that crowned the embankment. He tossed his cigar stub into the ditch, crying, "By Saint Hubert, I swear, I will never again venture into parts unknown with a magistrate, not even one such as you, my dear d'Albon, my old school friend!"

"But Philippe, have you forgotten how to read French? Perhaps you left your mind back in Siberia," the fat man retorted, casting a comically pained glance at a signpost some hundred paces away.

"Message received!" answered Philippe, who picked up his rifle, leapt to his feet, and bounded into the field toward the signpost. "This way, d'Albon, this way! About-face, left," he shouted to his companion, pointing toward a broad, paved lane. "Baillet–L'Isle-Adam road," he read. "Which means that the Cassan road must be this way, since it surely turns off from the L'Isle-Adam road."

"Just so, *mon colonel*," said Monsieur d'Albon, giving up fanning himself with his cap and placing it on his head.

"Onward, then, my honorable councillor," answered Colonel Philippe, whistling to the dogs, which already seemed to obey him more eagerly than they did their owner, the magistrate. "I do hope you realize, monsieur le marquis," he said tauntingly, "we still have more than two leagues to cover! That village off there must be Baillet."

"Good God!" cried the Marquis d'Albon. "Go on to Cassan if you like, but you'll go alone. I'd sooner wait here, storm or no storm. You can send a horse out to me from the château. See here, Sucy, that was a cruel trick you played on me. We were supposed to be going out for a nice little hunt, sticking close by Cassan, rooting about on grounds I know well. But no! No such pleasure for us! Instead you've had me sprinting like a greyhound since four in the morning, with only a couple of cups of milk for breakfast! Oh, should you ever have a case to bring up before the court, I'll make quite sure you lose, even if you're in the right a hundred times over!"

Dejected, he sat down on one of the milestones at the foot of the signpost, took off his rifle, his empty game bag, and let out a long sigh.

"Oh France! Behold thy deputies!" hooted Colonel de Sucy. "My poor d'Albon, if like me you'd spent six years in the remotest depths of Siberia..."

He left his sentence there and raised his eyes heavenward, as if his sorrows were a secret known only to God and himself.

"Come now! Walk!" he added. "If you go on sitting there, you're done for."

"What do you expect, Philippe? It's such an old habit for a judge! Word of honor, I can't manage another step! If at least I'd killed a hare!"

The two hunters' appearance presented a rather remarkable contrast. Aged forty-two years, the good deputy could easily have passed for thirty; the soldier, aged thirty, seemed at least forty. Both wore the red rosette of the Officer of the Legion of Honor. The locks of hair peeking out from beneath the colonel's cap were a mingling of black and white, like the wing of a magpie; fine blond curls graced the magistrate's temples. The one was tall, slender, taut, and the wrinkles of his pale face betrayed great passions or terrible woes; jovial as an Epicurean, the other's countenance radiated robust good health. Both were deeply tanned by the sun, and the stains on their long leather gaiters attested to every ditch, every marsh they had traversed.

"Come along now," cried Monsieur de Sucy. "Onward! One short hour's walk and we'll be in Cassan, with a fine dinner before us."

"I'll wager you've never been in love," answered the councillor, his tone humorously plaintive. "You're as pitiless as Article 304 of the Penal Code!"

With this, Philippe de Sucy gave a violent start; his broad forehead furrowed, and his face turned as dark as the sky. Although the memory of some unspeakable anguish contorted his features, he did not shed a tear. Like all men of great strength, he was able to still his emotions, to choke them back into the depths of his heart; perhaps, like many of pure character, he found it somehow indecent to reveal a grief whose depth was beyond human expression, and which might well be mocked by those who cannot be bothered to understand it. Monsieur d'Albon was graced with the kind of sensitive soul that divines others' sorrows and feels intensely all the upset a slip of the tongue can unwittingly cause. He did not trouble his friend's silence but stood up, his weariness forgotten, and followed him wordlessly, pained to have touched a wound that must not yet have healed.

"One day, my friend," said Philippe, clasping his hand and thanking him for his mute remorse with a heartrending gaze, "one day I shall tell you my story. Today, I couldn't possibly."

They walked on in silence. Once the colonel's desolation seemed to subside, the councillor rediscovered his own fatigue. With the instinct—or rather the longing—of a desperate man, his gaze probed the depths of the forest; he questioned the treetops, interrogated the broad avenues, in hopes of discovering some sort of dwelling where he might seek hospitality. Arriving at an intersection, he thought he spotted a wisp of smoke rising through the trees. He stopped, looked more closely, and made out several dark green boughs of pine amid a dense, tangled thicket.

"A house! A house!" he cried, joyous as the sailor who shouts out "Land ho!"

And in a burst of alacrity he dashed through a dense thicket, while the colonel followed mechanically after, lost in a deep reverie.

"Better an omelet here, and some plain homemade bread, and a crude chair, than all the divans and truffles and Bordeaux in Cassan."

These words were a cry of delight, wrested from the councillor by the sight of a wall in the distance, off-white amid the brown of the forest's gnarled trunks.

"Ah! Ah! Why it looks like some ancient priory!" the Marquis d'Albon cried out again on encountering a venerable iron fence, through which, in the midst of a large private park, he saw a building of monastic design. "Oh, those clever monks! Those scoundrels knew just where to build!"

This second outburst expressed the magistrate's astonishment at the poetic hermitage he now found before him. The house sat halfway up a slope, on the backside of the mount at whose summit stands the village of Nerville. Forming a vast circle around the residence, the lofty, aged oaks of the forest created an atmosphere of deepest seclusion. The main building, once home to the monks, faced south. The park might have covered some forty arpents. The house adjoined a green meadow, prettily crisscrossed by several limpid streams and dotted with ponds, whose pleasing arrangement betrayed no trace of artifice. Green trees stood here and there, their forms graceful, their foliage varied. Cunningly contrived grottos, vast terraces with crumbling staircases and rusting handrails, everything colluded to make this wild Thebaid a place like no other, an elegant union of artistry's creations and nature's most picturesque effects. Human passions seemed bound to find peace beneath those tall trees, which defended that retreat against the clamors of the world, just as they tempered the sun's withering heat.

"What a shambles!" said Monsieur d'Albon to himself, admiring the somber cast these ruins gave their surroundings, which seemed to have been visited with some sort of malediction. It had the air of a cursed place, abandoned by men. Everywhere ivy had splayed out its tortuous tendons and rich green mantles. Brown, greenish, yellow, or red mosses daubed the trees, benches, roofs, and stones with their romantic tints. The worm-eaten window frames had been scoured by rain and rutted by age; the balconies were broken, the terraces dilapidated. Some of the shutters were held by one single hinge. The ill-fitting doors seemed no obstacle for an intruder. Burdened by glistening clumps of mistletoe, the branches of the neglected fruit trees stretched into the distance, offering no harvest. Tall grasses grew in the walkways. These signs of decay produced a deeply poetic effect and inspired meditative thoughts in the onlooker's soul. A poet would have lingered there, lost in prolonged melancholy, musing on that disorder so rich in harmonies, that destruction in no way devoid of grace. Just then, several shafts of sunlight burst through the crevasses in the clouds, illuminating this half-wild scene with streaks of a thousand varied colors. The brown roof tiles glinted, the moss shone, fantastic shadows played over the fields, beneath the trees; the dulled colors awoke, arresting contrasts contended, the green boughs stood out darkly in the light. Suddenly the sun dimmed again. The landscape, which seemed to have spoken, now fell silent and once more turned somber, or rather muted, like the most muted hue of an autumn dusk.

"It's Sleeping Beauty's castle," the councillor whispered, now seeing this house only through a proprietor's eyes. "Who on earth might this place belong to? Only a fool would choose not to live in such a fine spot."

All at once a woman shot from beneath a walnut tree to the right of the iron fence and raced silently past the councillor's eyes, fleet as the shadow of a cloud. This apparition left him speechless with surprise.

"Why, d'Albon, what's the matter?" the colonel asked.

"I'm rubbing my eyes to see if I'm sleeping or awake," the magistrate answered, pressing close to the fence, hoping for another glimpse of the wraith.

"She must be under that fig tree," he said, pointing to the branches overhanging the wall, to the left of the fence.

"'She'? Who?"

"How should I know?" Monsieur d'Albon shot back. "A very

strange woman just appeared right here before me," he said softly. "She seemed to belong more to the shadows than the world of the living. She was so slight, so wispy, so vaporous—she must be transparent. Her face was white as milk. Her hair, her eyes, her clothing, all black. She looked at me as she passed by, and I'm not a fearful man by nature, but that cold, still gaze of hers froze the very blood in my veins."

"Was she pretty?" asked Philippe.

"I don't know. Her eyes were all I could see of her face."

"The devil take our dinner in Cassan," cried the colonel, "let's stay right here. I've a childish urge to take a closer look at this curious property. Do you see those red-painted window frames, those red lines on the moldings of the shutters and doors? Does this not seem the house of the devil? Perhaps he inherited it from the monks. Come, after the black-and-white woman! Forward!" cried Philippe with forced gaiety.

Just then the two hunters heard a cry, rather like the shriek of a mouse caught in a trap. They stood still and listened. The leaves of a few overgrown bushes rustled in the silence, like the hiss of a rushing wave, but although they strained to detect some further sound, the earth remained silent, guarding the secret of the stranger's footsteps, assuming that she had indeed walked on her way.

"Now that's very odd," cried Philippe, following the walls that surrounded the park.

Soon the two friends arrived at a forest path that led to the village of Chauvry. Following it toward the Paris road, they arrived at a large gate and beheld the mysterious dwelling's main façade. On this side, the disarray was complete. Huge cracks wandered over the walls of the house, whose three sections were built at right angles. The damaged roofs, the fallen tiles and slate shingles heaped on the ground, everything suggested utter neglect. A few pieces of fruit had dropped from the trees and lay rotting on the ground, uncollected. A cow grazed on the lawn, trampling the flower beds, while a goat plucked the shoots and green fruits from a grapevine.

"Here all is harmony, and disorder itself is in a sense ordered," said the colonel, pulling the chain of a bell, but the bell had no clapper.

The hunters heard only the oddly piercing squeak of a rusted spring. Decrepit though it was, the little door in the wall beside the gate resisted all their efforts to open it.

"Oh! Oh! This is all becoming very strange," the colonel said to his companion.

"If I weren't a judge," answered Monsieur d'Albon, "I'd say that woman in black was a witch."

He had just spoken these words when the cow ambled to the gate and raised its warm muzzle, as if eager to look upon human beings. Suddenly a woman, if such could be called the indefinable creature that had risen to its feet from beneath a clump of bushes, gave a tug on the cow's rope. This woman wore a red handkerchief on her head; from beneath it strayed locks of blond hair that looked rather like the tow on a distaff. She wore no fichu over her breast. Several inches too short, a black-and-gray striped skirt of coarse wool left her legs exposed. She might almost have belonged to one of the redskin tribes celebrated by Cooper, for her bare legs, neck, and arms seemed to have been painted the color of brick. No spark of intelligence animated her flat face. Her bluish eyes held neither expression nor warmth. A few sparse white hairs served as her eyebrows. Between her twisted lips several teeth could be seen, crooked and irregular, but white as a dog's.

"Ho there! Woman!" cried Monsieur de Sucy.

She drifted toward the gate, staring simplemindedly at the two hunters, having forced a shy smile upon catching sight of them.

"Where are we? What is this house? Whose is it? Who are you? Are you from this place?"

These questions, and a host of others put to her in quick succession, met only with guttural growls, more animal than human.

"She's deaf and dumb, can't you see?" said the magistrate.

"*Bons-Hommes!*" cried the peasant girl.

"Oh! She's right. This might well be the old Bons-Hommes monastery," said Monsieur d'Albon.

The questions resumed. But the peasant girl blushed like a backward child, played with her wooden shoe, twisted the cow's rope (the animal had gone back to grazing), stared at the two hunters, inspected every element of their dress; she yelped, she growled, she clucked, but she did not speak.

"What's your name?" said Philippe, staring into her eyes as if to place her under his power.

"Geneviève," she answered, with a mindless laugh.

"So far the cow is the most intelligent creature we've met," said the magistrate. "I'll fire my rifle—no doubt that will bring someone."

But the colonel brusquely stayed d'Albon's hand as he reached for his weapon. Pointing into the distance, he showed his friend that woman in black who had so piqued their curiosity. She was meandering along a garden path, as if lost in deep meditation, giving the two friends a moment to study her more closely. She was dressed in a threadbare gown of black satin. Her long hair fell in curls over her forehead, about her shoulders, past her waist, taking the place of a shawl. No doubt long used to this dishevelment, she rarely troubled to shake the hair from her temples, but when she did, she tossed her head so sharply that no second attempt was required to whisk that thick veil away from her forehead or eyes. Like an animal's, her movements showed remarkable physical confidence, so quick and precise as to seem almost miraculous for a woman. The two hunters looked on astonished as she leapt onto the branch of an apple tree and perched there, light as any bird. She plucked a few fruits, ate them, then dropped to the ground with that fluid ease we find so wondrous in squirrels. Her limbs had an elasticity that spared her every move even the appearance of discomfort or effort. She played on the grass, rolled head over heels like a child, then suddenly threw out her feet and hands and lay on the lawn, as languorous, graceful, and uninhibited as a young cat asleep in the sun. Hearing a distant rumble of thunder, she quickly rolled over and rose onto all fours, with the prodigious agility of a dog hearing a stranger's approach. Owing to this unusual position, her black hair suddenly fell into two wide swaths that hung swinging from either side of her head, granting the two spectators of that singular scene a vision of shoulders so white that the skin glowed like daisies of the meadow, and a neck whose perfection hinted at a body of a most exquisite form.

She let out a grating cry and rose to her feet. So nimbly, so smoothly did each movement follow upon the last that she seemed less a human creature than one of those daughters of the sky celebrated in the poems of Ossian. She strolled toward a pool of water, delicately shook one leg to throw off her shoe, and dipped in her alabaster white foot with visible delight, no doubt marveling at the gemlike undulations it made. Then she knelt at the edge of the basin and, like a child, played at immersing her long tresses and then briskly raised her head to watch the water drip off, drop by drop, like strings of pearls shot through by the sun.

"That woman is mad," cried the councillor.

Geneviève gave a loud, throaty shout, evidently addressed to the madwoman, who sat bolt upright, pushing the hair back from her cheeks. With this, the colonel and d'Albon caught a clear glimpse of her features; spotting the two friends, she bounded to the fence, agile and swift as a doe.

"Adieu!" she said, in a voice both sweet and harmonious, but that melody, so eagerly awaited by the hunters, seemed to contain no trace of sentiment and no trace of thought.

Monsieur d'Albon gazed admiringly on her long lashes, her thick black eyebrows, her glowing white skin unmarred by any tinge of red. A few delicate blue veins alone contrasted with her paleness. When the councillor turned toward his friend to voice his astonishment at the sight of this singular woman, he found him lying flat on the grass, as if lifeless. Monsieur d'Albon fired his rifle in the air to call for aid, shouting *"Help! Help!"* as he tried desperately to rouse the colonel. At the sound of the gunshot, the woman suddenly ran off fast as an arrow, shrieking in fright like a wounded animal and racing in circles over the meadow, giving every sign of profound terror. Hearing a calèche rattling down the L'Isle-Adam road, Monsieur d'Albon waved his handkerchief to beseech the sightseers' assistance. The calèche turned immediately toward Bons-Hommes, and within it Monsieur d'Albon spied the faces of Monsieur and Madame de Grandville, his neighbors. They hurried out of the carriage and offered it to the magistrate. By chance, Madame de Grandville had with her a bottle of smelling salts, which was administered to Monsieur de Sucy. The moment he opened his eyes, the colonel looked toward the meadow, where the strange woman was endlessly running and shouting, and he let out a cry both indistinct and eloquent in its expression of horror, then he closed his eyes once again, gesturing to his friend as if begging to be hurried away from this sight. Monsieur and Madame de Grandville urged the councillor to take their calèche, obligingly offering to continue their excursion on foot.

"Who is this woman?" asked the magistrate, pointing at the stranger.

"She's thought to come from Moulins," answered Monsieur de Grandville. "She calls herself the Comtesse de Vandières. Word has it she's mad, but as she's been here only two months, I cannot vouch for the truth of those rumors."

Thanking Monsieur and Madame de Grandville, d'Albon started off for Cassan.

"It's her," cried Philippe, recovering his senses.

"Who?" asked d'Albon.

"Stéphanie. Ah! Dead and living, living and mad! I thought it would be the end of me."

Understanding all the gravity of the crisis afflicting his friend, the prudent magistrate questioned him no further and took pains not to upset him. He was anxious to arrive at the château, for the change he could see in Colonel Philippe made him fear that the countess might have contaminated him with her terrible illness. On reaching avenue de L'Isle-Adam, d'Albon sent the footman ahead to summon the village doctor; thus, when the colonel was laid in his bed, the surgeon was already at his side.

"Had the colonel's stomach not been nearly empty," he said, "he would surely have died. It was his depletion that saved him."

Once he had dictated the immediate measures to be taken, the doctor left to prepare a sedative potion. The next morning Monsieur de Sucy's condition had improved, but the doctor insisted on watching over him personally.

"I will admit, monsieur le marquis," said the doctor to Monsieur d'Albon, "my first fear was a brain lesion. Monsieur de Sucy has had a terrible shock, and he is a man of strong passions, but with him it's the first blow that decides everything. Tomorrow he may well be out of danger."

The doctor was not mistaken, and the next day he permitted the magistrate to see his friend.

"My dear d'Albon," said Philippe, pressing his hand, "I want a favor from you! Hurry straight to Bons-Hommes, find out all you can about that woman, and then come back quick as you can! I'll be counting the minutes."

Monsieur d'Albon leapt onto a horse and galloped to the former abbey. As he drew near, he saw a tall, thin man standing before the fence, a man of amenable mien, who answered in the affirmative when the magistrate asked if this ruined house was his home. Monsieur d'Albon revealed the motive of his visit.

"Was it you, then, monsieur," cried the stranger, "who fired that cursed shot? You very nearly killed my poor patient."

"See here, monsieur, I fired in the air."

"You would have done less harm to the countess if you'd hit her."

"In that case we're even, for the sight of your countess nearly killed my friend, Monsieur de Sucy."

"Would that be the Baron Philippe de Sucy?" cried the doctor, joining his hands. "Was he in Russia, at the crossing of the Berezina?"

"That's right," d'Albon answered. "He was captured by the Cossacks and taken to Siberia. He returned to us some eleven months ago."

"Come in, monsieur," said the stranger, showing the magistrate into a salon on the ground floor of his house. Some destructive force had been at work in this room, but in a capricious and unpredictable manner. Precious porcelain vases sat in pieces beside a clock whose glass dome remained intact. The silk curtains over the windows were torn, the double muslin drapes untouched.

"You see here," he said to Monsieur d'Albon as they entered, "the ravages wrought by the charming creature to whom I have devoted my existence. She is my niece; despite the impotence of my art, I hope one day to restore her to reason by means of a method that, alas, only the rich can afford."

Then, rambling like all those who live solitary lives, preyed on by an irremediable sorrow, he recounted the following adventure, whose relation has here been adapted and stripped of the many digressions interjected by the narrator and the councillor.

———

When, toward nine in the evening, he withdrew from the heights of Studyanka, which he had defended all through that day of November 28, 1812, Marshal Victor left behind some thousand men whose charge was to protect one of the two surviving bridges over the Berezina as long as humanly possible. This rear guard had fought valiantly to save a vast crowd of stragglers, who, numb with cold, had gathered around the retreating army's abandoned equipment and refused to go on. In the end, the heroism of those devoted troops would prove useless. By a stroke of misfortune, the soldiers who poured onto the banks of the Berezina found a massive array of coaches, caissons, and materiel left behind by the army as it crossed the river on November 27 and 28. Inheritors of riches beyond their wildest dreams, wits dulled by the cold, these wretches settled into the unoccupied campsites, broke up the equipment to build huts, made fire with whatever was at hand, butchered the horses for food, stripped the carriages of their felt or canvas for blankets, and slept; slept, rather than pressing on, rather than tranquilly crossing the Berezina under cover of darkness—that same Berezina that an unimaginable twist of fate had already rendered so deadly for the armed forces of France. These pitiable soldiers' apathy can only be understood by those who remember traversing those vast deserts of snow, with no other drink than snow, no other bed than snow, no other prospect than a horizon of snow, no other food than snow, except for a few frozen beets, a few handfuls of flour, perhaps a bit of horsemeat. Dying of hunger, of thirst, of sleeplessness and exhaustion, the wretches had happened onto a riverbank where they found wood, fires, food, countless abandoned vehicles, campsites, in short an entire improvised city. The village of Studyanka had been wholly dismantled, divided, transported from the heights down to the plain. However *dolente* and perilous that city, its miseries and dangers could not have seemed more welcoming to people who saw before them only the fearsome wastelands of Russia. In short, it was an enormous sanctuary, in existence for not yet twenty hours. Whether by weariness of life or delight in an unhoped-for comfort, that mass of men was impermeable to any thought other than rest. To be sure, the artillery of the Russians' left flank fired relentlessly on that horde, which appeared as a massive blot in the snow, here black, there aglow with flames, but to the numbed multitudes those implacable cannonballs seemed only one more inconvenience to be borne. It was like a thunderstorm whose bolts inspired only derision, for wherever they fell their victims would already be ailing or dying, if not already dead. At every moment, fresh packs of stragglers appeared. These walking corpses scattered at once, staggering from bonfire to bonfire, begging for a place to rest; then, having generally been turned away, they joined up again to obtain by brute force the hospitality they'd been refused a moment before. Deaf to the voices of a small number of officers who predicted that the coming day would be their last, they exhausted their courage and energy—the very courage and energy they would need to cross over the river—in the fabrication of a shelter for the night, in the confection of an often deadly meal. The death that awaited them no longer seemed so terrible a horror; at least it would allow them an hour of sleep. The word *horror* they reserved for their hunger, for their thirst, for the cold. When there was no more wood to be found, no more fire, nor canvas, nor shelter, fierce clashes erupted between the empty-handed newcomers and those so wealthy as to enjoy some manner of hearth.

The weakest perished. At length the moment came when a group of men fleeing the Russians found nothing but snow for their campsite, and there they lay down, never to rise again. Gradually this mass of half-annihilated beings grew so dense, so deaf, and so dulled—or perhaps so happy—that Marshal Victor, Duke de Bellune, he who had so heroically defended them in battle against Wittgenstein's twenty thousand Russian troops, had no choice but to force his way through that human forest in order to cross the Berezina with the five thousand warriors he was bringing to the emperor. Rather than make way, the dejected masses allowed themselves to be crushed, and they died in silence, smiling at their extinguished fires, never thinking of France.

Not until ten o'clock in the evening did the Duke de Bellune find himself on the opposite bank. Before starting over the bridges and on toward Zembin, he had entrusted the fate of the rear guard of Studyanka to Éblé, that savior of all those who survived the calamities of the Berezina. Toward midnight, the great general, with a particularly courageous officer at his side, left the little riverside hut that served as his shelter and contemplated the spectacle of the enormous encampment that covered every inch of ground from the Berezina to the Borisov–Studyanka road. The Russians' cannon had ceased their roar; on that expanse of snow, countless scattered fires, paling and seeming to cast no light, illuminated faces with nothing human about them. Some thirty thousand wretches from all the varied nations whose forces Napoleon had thrown at Russia were gathered on the riverbank, at great risk to their lives, brutishly unconcerned for their fate.

"So many to be saved," said the general to the officer. "Tomorrow morning the Russians will be the masters of Studyanka. We've no choice but to set fire to the bridge as soon as we catch sight of them. And so, my friend, summon your courage! Find your way up to the heights, and tell General Fournier he has no time to lose: He must vacate his position at once, drive through these crowds, and cross the bridge. Once he's set off, follow close behind him. Find a few able men to assist you and set fire to the campsites, the equipment, the caissons, the coaches, everything! No pity! Herd all these men onto the bridge! Leave everything with two legs no choice but to take shelter on the opposite bank. Fire is now our only hope. Oh, if Berthier had allowed me to destroy that damned gear, this river would have swallowed up no one but my poor *pontoniers*, those fifty heroes who saved the army and who will be forgotten by all!"

The general put his hand to his brow and stood silent. He sensed that Poland would be his grave, and that no voice would ever be raised in support of those glorious men who willingly leapt into the waters—the waters of the Berezina!—to sink trestles for the bridges. Today only one of their number is still living, or more precisely languishing, in a provincial village, unknown! The aide-de-camp set off. That devoted officer had scarcely taken a hundred paces toward Studyanka when General Éblé roused a few of his ailing pontoniers and started off on his mission of mercy, setting fire to the campsites around the bridge, forcing the crowd of sleeping soldiers to rise and cross the Berezina. In the meantime, after considerable struggles, the young aide-de-camp had arrived at the one wooden house still standing in Studyanka.

"Is this hut so full, then, comrade?" he said to a man standing outside.

"You're a hard man if you can get in here," the officer answered, never turning around, still hacking at the house's wooden wall with his sword.

"Is that you, Philippe?" said the aide-de-camp, recognizing a comrade by the sound of his voice.

"Yes. Ah! It's you, my friend," answered Monsieur de Sucy, looking at the aide-de-camp, only twenty-three years old, like himself. "I thought surely you'd be across that accursed river by now. Have you come to bring us cakes and jam for our dessert? I can promise you a warm welcome," he added, pulling away a strip of bark and giving it to his horse, by way of fodder.

"I'm looking for your commander. On behalf of General Éblé, I must tell him to make for Zembin fast as he can! You have just enough time to plow your way through that crowd of living corpses. And then I'm to set them on fire, so they'll get up and walk."

"You're almost making me warm! I'm sweating already. Listen, I have two friends I must save. Ah, without those two dormice, my friend, I'd be a dead man at this moment! It's for their sake that I'm looking after my horse rather than eating it. For pity's sake, do you have a crust of bread? It's been thirty hours since I last had something in my belly, and I've fought like a madman to keep up what little warmth and courage I have left."

"Poor Philippe! I have nothing, nothing. But is your general here?"

"Don't try to get in! This barn's for our wounded. Go a little farther uphill. On your right, you'll come upon a sort of pigsty, that's where you'll find the general. Adieu, my good fellow. If we ever again dance *la trénis* on a Paris floor…"

There was no way to finish this sentence: The wind was blowing so viciously that the aide-de-camp had to walk in order not to freeze, and Major Philippe's lips were too cold for words. Soon silence reigned, broken only by groans from the house and the muffled sound of Monsieur de Sucy's starving, enraged horse, chewing the frozen bark of the trees from which the house was built. The major resheathed his cutlass, briskly took up the reins of the precious animal whose life he had managed to safeguard, and despite its resistance tugged it away from the wretched food it was downing so desperately.

"Off we go, Bichette! Off we go. Only you can save Stéphanie now, my beauty. Come on! We'll rest later—or more likely die."

Wrapped in a pelisse to which he owed his continued existence and hardiness, Philippe set off at a run, stomping the packed snow to warm his feet. After no more than a hundred paces the major caught sight of a well-fed fire at the spot where, that morning, he'd left his coach in the care of an old trooper. A dreadful foreboding flooded over him. Like all those driven by an overpowering emotion amid this debacle, he found within himself the strength to rescue his friends, a strength he would never have had to save himself. Soon he was within a few paces of a sheltered hollow, well protected from the cannonballs, where he had left a young woman, his childhood companion and his most precious belonging!

A few paces from the carriage, some thirty stragglers huddled around an enormous blaze, diligently stoking it with planks, boxes from the caissons, carriage wheels, and side panels. No doubt these soldiers were the latest newcomers to the crowd that filled the broad plain from Studyanka to the fateful river with a sort of sea of heads, fires, and huts, a living ocean stirred by vague currents, from which rose a vague hum, sometimes punctuated by fearsome shouts. Possessed by hunger and despair, the wretches had likely ransacked his carriage. The aged general and young woman they'd found inside, sleeping on bundles of baggage, wrapped in overcoats and pelisses, now sat slumped by the fire. One door of the carriage was broken. On hearing the horse and the major approaching, the mob let out a shout, a cry of rage inspired by hunger.

"A horse! A horse!"

Their many voices were one.

"Get away! Look out!" cried two or three soldiers, training their weapons on the horse.

Philippe leapt down and stood before his mare, saying, "Brigands! I'll toss you into that fire of yours, every last man of you. There are dead horses up the hill! Go and get them."

"Oh, the officer's quite a clown, isn't he!" a giant of a grenadier shouted back. "One . . . two . . . will you get out of the way? No? Very well, suit yourself."

A woman's cry rang out over the gunshot. Happily, Philippe was not hit, but Bichette sank to the ground, locked in a frantic struggle with death; three men rushed forward and finished her off with their bayonets.

"Cannibals! Let me at least take the blanket and my pistols," said Philippe, dismayed.

"You can have the pistols all right," answered the grenadier. "As for the blanket, this soldier's had nothing in his gut for two days, and he's standing here shivering in his miserable rags. He's our general..."

Philippe made no reply as he gazed on a man in worn shoes and a pair of trousers with holes in ten places, a forlorn, rime-crusted forage cap on his head. He quickly took up his pistols. Five men dragged the mare nearer the fire and set about cutting it up, deft as any Paris butcher's boy. With miraculous speed, the pieces of meat were removed and dropped onto the embers. The major went to join the woman who had shrieked in despair on recognizing him. He found her sitting dully on a carriage cushion, warming herself; she stared at him in silence, never smiling. Not far away, Philippe spied the soldier he'd ordered to guard the carriage; the poor man was wounded. Outnumbered, he had yielded to the stragglers assailing him, but like a dog that has defended his master's dinner to the end, he'd taken his share of the spoils and fashioned himself a sort of shawl from a white sheet. At the moment he was busy turning over a piece of the mare, and on his face the major saw unmingled joy at the feast to come. The Count de Vandières, whose mind had three days before slipped into a sort of second infancy, sat on a cushion near his wife and stared at the flames, their warmth beginning to dispel his torpor. Philippe's arrival, the danger he'd faced, all this had left no impression on him, no more than the altercation that preceded the pillaging of the carriage. Sucy clasped the young countess's hand, as if to convey his affection and his sorrow at seeing her reduced to these depths of misery, but he said nothing as he sat down on a nearby snow mound, now melting and trickling, and surrendered to the pleasure of warmth, forgetting all peril, forgetting everything. In spite of himself, an expression of almost mindless joy fell over his face, and he waited eagerly for his allotted strip of horsemeat to be done roasting. The aroma of that charred flesh inflamed his hunger, and his hunger silenced his heart, his courage, and his love. Without anger, he contemplated the fruits of his carriage's despoliation. The men around the bonfire had shared among them the blankets, cushions, pelisses, gowns, everything that belonged to the count, the countess, and the major. Philippe turned around to see if there was anything more to be found in the chest. By the light of the flames, he saw the gold, diamonds, and silverware strewn on the ground, of interest to no one. To a man, every living soul that chance had brought to this fireside sat enveloped in an appalling silence, doing only what he thought necessary for his own well-being. There was something grotesque about such destitution. Haggard with cold, every face was caked with a layer of mud, rutted from eye to jaw by falling tears, making the thickness of that mask plain to see. The soldiers were disfigured further by long matted beards. Some of the men were wrapped in women's shawls; others wore horses' shabracks, soiled blankets, rags dusted with melting hoarfrost; some had one foot in a boot and the other in a shoe—in short, there was no one whose garb did not exhibit some quaint peculiarity. Amid these many causes for amusement, they remained serious and somber. The silence was troubled only by the crackling of the wood, the hiss of the flames, the distant murmur of the camp, and the saber blows inflicted on Bichette by the hungriest of the men in their eagerness to remove the choicest morsels. The weariest slept, and if one happened to roll into the fire, no one bothered to pull him to safety. If he wasn't dead, reasoned these inflexible logicians, a good burn would surely spur him to find a more suitable spot. If the wretch awoke in the fire and died, no one pitied him. A few of the soldiers looked at each other, each as if justifying his own unconcern by the other's indifference. Twice the young countess witnessed this sight and said nothing. Finally the pieces of meat on the embers were cooked, and everyone sated his own hunger, with the ravenousness that we find repellent in animals.

"Thirty infantrymen on one horse! There's a first time for everything!" cried the grenadier who had shot the mare.

Such was the one quip that expressed the native wit of the French.

Soon most of these pitiful soldiers bundled themselves up in whatever they were wearing, lay down on planks or anything else that might shield them from the snow, and slept, caring little for tomorrow. Once the major was warm and his hunger appeased, his eyelids grew heavy with an invincible need for rest. He gazed at the young woman all through the ensuing brief contest with slumber. She slept with her face turned to the fire, showing her closed eyes and a part of her forehead; she was wrapped in a lined pelisse and a thick dragoon's greatcoat, her head on a bloodstained pillow; an astrakhan hat, secured by a handkerchief knotted under her chin, protected her face from the cold so far as it could; she'd tucked her feet beneath the coat. Curled on the ground as she was, she truly looked like nothing at all. Was she the last of the camp followers? Was she that magnificent woman, a lover's pride and joy, the queen of the Parisian balls? Alas! Not even the eye of her most devoted friend could find any lingering trace of femininity in that pile of drapes and rags. Love had succumbed to the cold, in the heart of a woman. Through the thick veils that the most irresistible of all sleeps was pulling over the major's eyes, he saw the husband and wife only as two shapeless spots. The flames of the bonfire, those prostrate human figures, that terrible cold raging three steps away from a tenuous warmth, everything was a dream. An unwelcome thought intruded into Philippe's tormented mind. "If I sleep we'll all die; I don't want to sleep," he told himself. He was sleeping. An hour later he was awakened by a terrible clamor and an explosion. The thought of his duty and of his lover's danger fell leadenly on his heart once again. He let out a shout, like a lion's roar. He and his adjutant were the only ones up. Before them they saw a sea of flame raging through a horde of men in the shadow of the night, devouring the campsites and huts; they heard shrieks of despair, howls; they spied thousands of defeated bodies and furious faces. At the heart of that hell, between two ranks of corpses, a column of soldiers was forcing its way toward the bridge.

"That's the rear guard retreating," cried the major. "Now there's no hope."

"I've spared your carriage, Philippe," said a friendly voice.

Turning around, Sucy recognized the young aide-de-camp by the light of the fire.

"Ah! It's no good," answered the major. "They've eaten my horse. And in any case, how am I supposed to get that addle-headed general and his wife up and walking?"

"Pick up a burning brand, Philippe, and threaten them!"

"Threaten the countess!"

"Adieu!" cried the aide-de-camp. "I only just have the time to cross that cursed river, and I must! I have a mother back in France! What a night! These wretches would rather stay here in the snow; most of them would sooner burn than stand up. It's four in the morning, Philippe! In two hours, the Russians will be stirring. I promise you, you'll see the Berezina clogged with corpses once again. Philippe, think of yourself! You have no horse, and you can't carry the countess. There's no other way, can't you see? Come with me!" he said, taking him by the arm.

"But my friend, the thought of abandoning Stéphanie!"

The major clasped the countess in his arms and pulled her to her feet, shaking her with a desperate violence to force her awake; she looked at him with a fixed, deadened stare.

"We must walk, Stéphanie, or we'll die here."

The countess's only response was to try to drop back to the ground and return to her slumbers. The aide-de-camp snatched up a burning brand and waved it in Stéphanie's face.

"We'll save her in spite of herself!" cried Philippe, picking up the countess and placing her in the coach.

He came back and beseeched his friend's aid. The two of them lifted the old general, unsure if he was dead or alive, and set him down beside his wife. One by one, the major approached all those asleep on the ground and rolled them over with his foot, relieving them of what they had pillaged; he piled the clothes atop the two spouses and threw a few roasted strips of his mare into a corner of the carriage.

"What are you planning to do?" asked the aide-de-camp.

"Pull them," said the major.

"You're mad!"

"I am indeed!" cried Philippe, crossing his arms over his chest.

All at once a desperate idea seemed to come to him.

"Here, you," he said, grasping his adjutant's good arm, "I'm leaving her in your care for an hour! Mark this well: You must die before you allow anyone to come near this carriage."

The major picked up the countess's diamonds with one hand; with the other he drew his saber and began to rain furious blows down on the sleepers who looked to him most intrepid. He succeeded in waking the gigantic grenadier and two other men of indeterminate rank.

"We're done for," he told them.

"I'm aware of that," answered the grenadier. "All the same to me."

"Well then, since we're dead either way, is it not better to give up one's life for a beautiful woman and just possibly see France again?"

"I'd rather sleep," said one man, curling up in the snow. "And if you trouble me again, Major, you'll find my saber in your gut!"

"What's the plan, officer?" the grenadier asked. "This man is drunk! He's a Parisian—likes his comforts, you know!"

"Brave grenadier, this is yours," cried the major, showing him a diamond necklace, "if you will follow me and be prepared to fight like a madman. The Russians are ten minutes away on foot; they have horses; we're going to make for their forward battery and help ourselves to a couple."

"But what about the sentinels, Major?"

"One of us three—" he began, then broke off and looked at the aide-de-camp. "You're coming, Hippolyte, aren't you?"

Hippolyte nodded.

"One of us," the major went on, "will deal with the sentinel. But for all we know those damned Russians are sleeping too."

"Ho, Major, you've got grit! But you'll take me along in your berline?" said the grenadier.

"Yes, if you don't meet your maker up there. Should by any chance I perish, Hippolyte and you, grenadier, promise you'll give your all to keep the countess safe."

"Agreed!" cried the grenadier.

They started toward the Russian lines, toward the batteries that had so relentlessly pummeled the hopeless, supine masses on the riverbank. A few moments later, the galloping hooves of two horses resounded over the snow, and the reawakened battery fired several volleys that passed over the sleepers' heads; the horses' steps rang out as furiously as blacksmiths pounding iron. The devoted aide-de-camp had not survived. The sturdy grenadier was safe and sound. Philippe had taken a bayonet in one shoulder while defending his friend; nevertheless, he clutched the horse's mane, and his legs squeezed the animal like a powerful vise.

"God be praised!" cried the major, finding his carriage just where he'd left it, and his adjutant standing tranquilly beside it.

"If you're a just man, officer, you'll see to it I get the Cross of Honor. We did some nice work up there, didn't we? Showed them a thing or two!"

"We haven't done anything yet! Let's hitch up the horses. Take these ropes."

"It's not enough."

"Well then, grenadier, give that crowd of layabouts a good going-over, and help yourself to their shawls, their linens—"

"Say, this joker's dead!" cried the grenadier, divesting the first one he came to. "Well, what do you know, they're all dead!"

"All of them?"

"Every one! Looks like that horsemeat didn't agree with them—that or the generous helping of snow on the side!"

These words sent a shiver through Philippe. The cold was twice as bitter as before.

"God! To think of losing a woman I've saved twenty times over..." The major shook the countess by her shoulders, crying, "Stéphanie! Stéphanie!"

The young woman opened her eyes.

"Madame! We're saved."

"Saved," she repeated, falling back.

They hitched up the horses as best they could. Holding his saber in his good hand and the reins in the other, his pistols at his sides, the major climbed onto the first horse, the grenadier onto the second. His feet frozen stiff, the old adjutant had been heaved cross-wise into the carriage atop the general and the countess. Spurred on by the saber, the horses hurtled forward, speeding the carriage down onto the plain, where difficulties without number awaited the major. Soon there was no way to go on without crushing the men, women, even children asleep on the ground. The grenadier did what he could to rouse them, but they stubbornly refused to move. Monsieur de Sucy searched in vain for the path that the rear guard had cleared: It had vanished like a ship's wake on the water. They advanced at a crawl, continually halted by soldiers threatening to kill the horses.

"Do you want to get through?" asked the grenadier.

"If it costs me every drop of blood in my body, if it costs me the whole world," answered the major.

"Then forward! You can't make an omelet without breaking eggs!"

And the grenadier of the guard spurred the horses over the slumbering bodies, bloodied the wheels, toppled the huts, left two furrows of corpses in that field of heads. Let it nonetheless be said that he never failed to cry out, in a thundering voice, "Out of the way, you moldering bastards!"

"These poor people!" cried the major.

"Bah! It's this or the cold, this or the cannon!" said the grenadier, urging the horses ever on, pricking them with the point of his saber.

A calamity that should have befallen them long before, which they had thus far been spared only by miraculous good fortune, now put a sudden halt to their progress. The carriage tipped over.

"I had an idea this would happen!" cried the imperturbable grenadier. "Oh! Oh! Our friend is dead."

"Poor Laurent," said the major.

"Laurent! From the Fifth Cavalry?"

"Yes."

"He's my cousin. Ah well! Not much fun in this life at the moment. I don't imagine he'll miss it."

Only after an interminable, irreparable delay was the carriage righted and the horses untangled. Awakened and wrenched from her torpor by the violent jolt, the young countess had thrown off her wraps and stood up.

"Philippe, where are we?" she whispered, looking around her.

"Five hundred paces from the bridge. We're heading over the Berezina. And then, once we reach the other side, Stéphanie, I'll torment you no longer, I'll let you sleep, we'll be safe, we can go on untroubled to Vilnius. May God grant that you never know the price paid for your life!"

"You're wounded!"

"It's nothing."

The hour of the catastrophe had sounded. Daybreak was announced by the Russians' guns. Masters of Studyanka, they unleashed a withering fire over the plain; in the first light of morning, the major spied their columns advancing, positioning themselves on the heights. A cry of alarm erupted from the multitudes; a moment later they'd all leapt to their feet. Instinctively sensing their peril, they hurtled toward the bridge like a mighty wave. The Russians poured down from the heights, fast as a brush fire. Men, women, children, horses, everything bolted onto the bridge. Happily, the major and the countess were still at some distance from the riverbank. General Éblé had just set fire to the trestles on the opposite side. The cries of warning addressed to those now packed onto that life raft fell on deaf ears; no one would turn back. Not only did the bridge give way under their weight; in their frantic race toward the murderous riverbank, a great mass of humanity poured into the Berezina like an avalanche. No shriek could be heard, only a dull sound like a stone falling into water, and a moment later, the river was clotted with corpses. So fierce was the backlash created by those retreating onto the plain in hopes of escaping that death, and so violent their collision with those still advancing, that many were asphyxiated on the spot. The Count and Countess de Vandières owed their life to the carriage. After trampling and breaking so many dying bodies, the horses were soon crushed to death in their turn, overrun by the human cyclone sweeping over the bank. The major and the grenadier survived purely by main force. They killed so as not to be killed. This hurricane of human faces, this surge of bodies animated by one single movement left the bank of the Berezina deserted for a few moments. The herd had poured back onto the plain. If some threw themselves into the river from the bank, it was less in hopes of reaching the other side, which for them meant France, than simply of fleeing the Siberian wastelands. For a few particularly audacious souls, desperation became a guardian angel. An officer reached the other bank by leaping from one lump of ice to the next; a soldier crawled miraculously over floating corpses. In the end, the vast crowd realized that the Russians would not kill twenty thousand unarmed men, numb with cold, their senses dulled, who made no attempt to defend themselves, and with a horrible resignation settled down to await their fate. The major, the grenadier, the old general, and his wife were thus left alone, just steps away from what had once been a bridge. These four stood silent and dry-eyed amid a field of dead bodies, in the company of a few able soldiers, a few officers whose fighting spirit had been revived by the circumstances, numbering perhaps fifty. Two hundred paces away, the major descried what was left of the carriage bridge, swallowed by the river two days before.

"We'll build a raft!" he cried.

No sooner had those words been spoken than everyone sped off as one toward the ruined bridge. A mob set about gathering iron clamps, hunting for pieces of wood, for ropes, for everything required to construct a raft. Under the major's command, some twenty armed soldiers and officers stood guard, protecting the workers against any attack the crowd might launch on realizing their intentions. An imprisoned man's yearning for freedom can sometimes energize him and inspire him to miraculous feats, but that is as nothing next to the need compelling these pitiable Frenchmen to act.

"The Russians! The Russians are on their way!" the guards warned the workers.

And the wood creaked and groaned, the vessel grew wider, higher, deeper. Generals, soldiers, colonels, everyone helped to transport wheels, iron bars, ropes, and planks, bowing under their weight:

It was a living image of the building of Noah's ark. Beside her husband, the young countess gazed on this spectacle, regretting her inability to take part in the labors; nevertheless, she helped to tie knots to strengthen the rigging. Finally the raft was finished. Forty men heaved it into the water, a dozen soldiers holding the ropes that moored it to the bank. Seeing their craft afloat on the Berezina, the builders immediately leapt aboard, a loathsome spirit of self-interest animating them all. The major had foreseen that the first surge would be violent, and so clasped Stéphanie and the general by the hand to hold them back, but a shiver ran through him when he saw the vessel packed from one end to the other, the passengers pressed together like spectators on the parterre of a theater.

"Savages!" he cried. "It was I who gave you the idea of building a raft; I saved your lives, and you refuse to leave room for me."

A muddled tumult of voices was the only response. By means of long poles braced against the riverbank, a group of men on the raft were preparing to cast off with one mighty thrust, hoping to propel it straight toward the other bank, cutting through the corpses and floating ice.

"By thunder! I'll toss you overboard right enough, if you don't make way for the major and his two friends," cried the grenadier, raising his saber to halt the launch, and—braving awful bellows of fury—forcing those on board to further close ranks.

"I'm going to fall! I'm falling!" came the cries of his companions. "Push off! Forward!"

The major looked dry-eyed at his mistress, who gazed toward the heavens in sublime resignation.

"Better to die with you!" she said.

There was something comical in the situation of the raft's passengers. Rage though they might, none dared disobey the grenadier, for they pressed together so tightly that to jostle one would be to topple them all. Faced with this threat, a captain resolved to be rid of the troublesome soldier. Sensing the officer's hostile intentions, the grenadier seized him and flung him into the water, saying, "Ah! Ah, ducky, so you want a drink? Be my guest! Room for two more!" he cried. "Come along, Major, toss that little woman this way and get yourself over here! Leave the dotard where he is, he'll be dead by tomorrow."

"Hurry!" roared a voice composed of a hundred voices.

"Come along now, Major! These people are getting itchy, and I don't believe you can blame them."

The Comte de Vandières threw off his coverings and stood on the bank, displaying his general's uniform.

"We must save the count," said Philippe.

Stéphanie squeezed her lover's hand, threw herself on his neck, and embraced him with a fearsome intensity.

"Adieu!" she said.

They had understood each other perfectly. The Comte de Vandières found the strength and presence of mind to leap onto the craft. Stéphanie followed, after casting Philippe one last glance.

"Major, would you like my place?" shouted the grenadier. "Life's nothing to me. I've neither wife nor child nor mother."

"I'm leaving these two in your care," cried the major, pointing toward the count and his wife.

"Don't you worry, I'll look after them like my own flesh and blood."

Philippe stood still, watching. The raft was propelled toward the opposite bank with such force that when it touched ground a mighty shudder ran through it from one end to the other. The count tumbled into the river; as he fell, a sheet of ice sheared off his head and launched it far into the distance, like a cannonball.

"What did I tell you, Major?" cried the grenadier.

"Adieu!" cried a woman.

Philippe de Sucy fell to his knees, frozen with horror, defeated by the cold, by regret, by exhaustion.

"My poor niece's mind was destroyed," added the doctor after a moment of silence. "Ah! monsieur," he went on, clasping d'Albon's hand, "how cruel life has been to that fragile woman, so young and so delicate! Separated by an appalling misfortune from the grenadier, a man by the name of Fleuriot, for two years she had no choice but to follow after the army, a plaything for a bunch of ruffians. As I understand it, she had no shoes to wear, only the most meager dress, went for months with no one caring for her or feeding her; now sheltered in a charity house, now chased away like an animal. God alone knows what miseries that poor woman nevertheless survived. She was locked up with the mad folk in a small German town, and meanwhile her family, thinking her dead, was dividing her legacy. In 1816 Grenadier Fleuriot recognized her in a Strasbourg inn, not long after she'd escaped from her prison. The local peasants told him the countess had been living in the forest for an entire month, that they'd tracked her like an animal, hoping to capture her, but in vain. I was then staying a few leagues from Strasbourg. Hearing tell of a wild girl, I was curious to discover the truth of these ridiculous tales. What a shock when I found the countess before me! Fleuriot told me all he knew of that terrible story. I brought the poor man back to the Auvergne with my niece, and there I had the misfortune of losing him. He had a kind of power over Madame de Vandières. He alone could persuade her to dress. Only rarely, in the beginning, did she utter that word *Adieu!*, which constitutes the whole of her language. Fleuriot did all he could to reawaken her mind, but he failed, and succeeded only in making her speak that sad word a little more often. The grenadier had a gift for distracting her, for occupying her with play, and through him, I hoped, but . . ."

For a moment Stéphanie's uncle sat silent.

"Here," he resumed, "she found another creature, whose company seems to suit her: An idiot peasant girl, who, ugly and backward as she is, was once in love with a mason. This mason wanted to marry her, for she owns a bit of land. For a year, poor Geneviève was the happiest woman there had ever been on the face of this earth. She looked after herself, and on Sundays went off to dance with Dallot; she knew love; there was a place in her heart and her mind for emotion. But Dallot had second thoughts. He found a girl still possessed of her wits, and of more land than Geneviève, and so he left her. The poor thing lost what little intelligence love had inspired in her, and now she can only herd cows or gather hay. She and my niece are, in a sense, bound together by the invisible chain of their shared fate and by the sentiment that was the cause of their madness. Come and see for yourself," said Stéphanie's uncle, leading the Marquis d'Albon to the window.

And the magistrate did indeed see the pretty countess sitting on the ground between Geneviève's legs. Armed with a huge tortoise-shell comb, the peasant girl was devoting all her attention to untangling Stéphanie's long black hair. The countess sat patiently, now and then letting out a stifled cry whose tone betrayed a purely instinctual pleasure. Monsieur d'Albon shivered as he contemplated the countess's unguarded pose, her animal carelessness, the signs of an utter absence of soul.

"Philippe! Philippe!" he cried. "Yesterday's sorrows are as nothing. Is there no hope, then?"

The old doctor looked heavenward.

"Adieu, monsieur," said Monsieur d'Albon, pressing the old man's hand. "My friend is waiting. You shall meet him soon."

"So it truly is her," cried Sucy after the Marquis d'Albon had spoken a few words. "Ah, I still had my doubts!" he added, tears falling from his dark eyes, usually so severe.

"It is indeed the Countess de Vandières," rejoined the magistrate.

The colonel leapt out of bed and threw on some clothes.

"Now hold on, Philippe!" said the magistrate, aghast. "Are you out of your mind?"

"But I'm not ill anymore," the colonel answered, plainly. "This news has vanquished all my miseries. What ailment could possibly hope to compete with thoughts of Stéphanie? I'm off to Bons-Hommes, I'll see her, I'll talk to her, I'll cure her! She's a free woman. And joy will be ours, or there is no such thing as Providence. Do you really believe that poor woman can hear my voice and not recover her reason?"

"She's already seen you and not recognized you," the magistrate gently replied, noting his friend's overly high hopes and eager to sow a few salutary doubts.

The colonel winced slightly on hearing those words, but soon his smile returned, and he brushed them aside with a quick wave. No one dared stand in his way. A few hours later he had settled into the former priory with the doctor and the Comtesse de Vandières.

"Where is she?" he cried as he entered.

"Shh!" answered Stéphanie's uncle. "She's asleep. Look, here she is."

Philippe saw the poor madwoman huddled on a bench in the sun. Her head was shaded from the heat by a forest of unkempt hair draped over her face; her arms hung elegantly groundward; her body had a doe's delicate grace; her feet were effortlessly tucked beneath her; her breast rose at regular intervals; her skin displayed that porcelain whiteness for which we admire the limpid faces of children. Motionless beside her, Geneviève held a small branch that Stéphanie must have snapped from the very top of a poplar, and she gently waved it over her dozing friend to chase off the flies and cool the air. The peasant girl looked at Monsieur Fanjat and the colonel; then, like an animal recognizing its master, she slowly turned back to the countess and went on watching over her, never showing the slightest sign of surprise or intelligence. It was a stifling hot day. The stone bench seemed to sparkle, and from the meadow rose those mischievous vapors that flutter and shimmer like gold dust over grass, but Geneviève seemed oblivious to the consuming heat. The colonel violently clasped the doctor's hands. Tears rolled down the soldier's virile cheeks and fell into the grass at Stéphanie's feet.

"Monsieur," said the uncle, "for two years my heart has broken every day. Soon you will be exactly like me. You may not weep, but you will feel your grief all the same."

"You've looked after her," said the colonel, equal parts gratitude and jealousy in his eyes.

These two men understood each other. Again clasping hands, they stood motionless, contemplating the wonderful tranquillity that sleep had draped over the charming creature before them. Now and then Stéphanie sighed, and that sigh, which had every appearance of sensibility, left the poor colonel trembling with joy.

"Alas," Monsieur Fanjat said gently, "do not be fooled, monsieur. You see her now as full of reason as she will ever be."

Those who have spent hours looking on in delight as a loved one lies slumbering, someone whose eyes will smile at them on awakening, must surely understand the sweet, terrible emotion that now gripped the colonel. Here that sleep was an illusion; her awakening would be a death, and the most horrible of all deaths. Suddenly a young goat came bounding to the bench and sniffed at Stéphanie. Roused by the sound, she lightly rose to her feet, inspiring no alarm in the impulsive animal, but on spotting Philippe she fled to the cover of an elderberry hedge, her four-legged companion at her heels; then she threw out the small birdlike cry that the colonel had heard near the fence when the countess first appeared to d'Albon. Finally she climbed into a laburnum tree, perched among its green boughs, and peered at the "stranger" as intently as the forest's most curious nightingale.

"Adieu, adieu, adieu!" she said, her tone unmarked by any trace of intelligence.

It was the indifference of a bird whistling its song.

"She doesn't know me!" cried the colonel, despairing. "Stéphanie! It's Philippe, your Philippe, Philippe."

And the poor soldier strode toward the tree. When he was three paces away, the countess shot him a glance as if to challenge him, though with a sort of fright in her eyes; then, in one leap, she fled from the laburnum to a locust tree, and from there to a Norway spruce, where she swung from branch to branch with an incredible agility.

"Don't chase after her," Monsieur Fanjat told the colonel. "You would create an aversion that may well become insurmountable. I'll help you to make yourself known to her and to tame her. Come to this bench. Pay the poor creature no mind, and you'll soon find her creeping your way, ever so slowly, to examine you."

"For her of all people not to recognize me, to flee me!" the colonel repeated, sitting down with his back against a tree whose boughs shaded a rustic bench, and he bowed his head over his breast. The doctor said nothing. Soon the countess nimbly climbed down from her spruce tree, flitting this way and that like a will-o'-the-wisp, sometimes swaying with the undulations of the wind-tossed boughs. On each branch she paused to peer at the stranger, but at last, seeing him so still, she dropped onto the grass, stood, and slowly stole toward him through the meadow. She stopped at a tree some ten feet from the bench, and Monsieur Fanjat quietly said to the colonel, "Carefully reach into my right-hand pocket and take out a few lumps of sugar. Show them to her, and she'll come to you. For you, I will gladly forgo the pleasure of giving her these sweets myself. She loves sugar with a passion; you'll soon have her approaching you and recognizing you without the slightest hesitation."

"When she was a woman," Philippe answered sadly, "she had no taste for sweets."

The colonel clasped the lump of sugar between his right thumb and index finger and proffered it to Stéphanie, who once again let out her savage cry, bounding eagerly toward Philippe, then stopped, thwarted by the instinctive fear he aroused in her. Again and again, she looked at the sugar and then looked away, like those poor dogs whose masters forbid them to touch a morsel of food until, after a drawn-out recitation, the last letter of the alphabet has been spoken. Finally animal passion triumphed over fear; Stéphanie leapt toward Philippe, timidly put out her brown hand to seize her quarry, touched her lover's fingers, clutched the sugar, and vanished into a thicket. This devastating spectacle left the colonel deeply forlorn. He dissolved into tears and fled into the drawing room.

"Is love then less courageous than friendship?" Monsieur Fanjat asked him. "Monsieur le baron, I have hope. My poor niece's condition was once far more dire than this."

"Is such a thing possible?" Philippe cried.

"She went about naked."

The colonel made a gesture of horror and paled; thinking he glimpsed certain disturbing symptoms in that pallor, the doctor came and took his pulse, and found him in the grips of a violent fever. At his unyielding insistence, the colonel was put to bed, while the doctor prepared a mild dose of opium to ensure him a restful sleep.

Some eight days went by, the Baron de Sucy continually tortured by fits of mortal anguish; soon his eyes had no tears left to shed. So often shattered, his soul could not inure itself to the spectacle of the countess's madness, but he made his peace, so to speak, with this cruel state of affairs and found moments of relief in his sorrow. His heroism knew no bounds. He found the courage to tame Stéphanie with offers of sweetmeats; he devoted so much thought to this ritual, he so skillfully calibrated each modest new step toward the conquest of his mistress's instinct—the last lingering shred of her intelligence—that she was soon more at home here than ever before. Every morning, on rising, the colonel hurried down to the garden, and if, after a long search for the countess, he could not guess in what tree she was gently swaying, or in what corner she had nestled to play with a bird, or on what roof she was perched, he had only to whistle the well-known air "Partant pour la Syrie," to which the memory of an episode from their love affair was attached. Immediately Stéphanie came running, light as a fawn. She had grown used to the sight of the colonel, and he no longer frightened her; soon she took to sitting on his knees, encircling him with her lithe, slender arm. In this position, so dear to lovers, Philippe slowly offered the greedy countess a few sweets. Sometimes, when she had eaten them all, she searched through his pockets, her gestures as mechanically purposeful as a monkey's. Once she was satisfied that there was nothing more to be had, she looked at Philippe with an empty gaze, devoid of thought or recognition, and began to play with him; she tried to take off his boots to see his foot, she ripped his gloves, donned his hat; but she passively allowed him to run his hands through her hair, let him take her in his arms, and received ardent kisses without pleasure. When his tears flowed, she stared at him in silence; the whistling of "Partant pour la Syrie" she understood perfectly, but he could not make her speak her own name: *Stéphanie*. In all these heartbreaking endeavors, Philippe was buoyed by a hope that never deserted him. If, on a beautiful fall morning, he saw the countess peacefully sitting on a bench beneath a yellowing poplar, the pitiable lover lay down at her feet and gazed into her eyes as long as she would allow it, hoping to spy in them some new glimmer of lucidity; sometimes he fell prey to illusion and believed he had glimpsed a vibrancy in their hard, immobile gleam, a softening, a liveliness, and he cried out: "Stéphanie! Stéphanie! You can hear me, you can see me!" But she listened to the sound of that voice as she would to a noise, to the wind rustling the leaves, to the lowing of the cow on whose back she liked to clamber; and the colonel wrung his hands in despair, a despair whose sting never waned. His sorrow only grew with the passage of time and these pointless, repeated attempts. One evening, beneath a tranquil sky, in the silence and calm of that bucolic haven, the doctor glanced at the couple and saw the baron loading a pistol. The old physician understood that Philippe had given up hope; instantly the blood drained from his face, leaving him light-headed and weak, and if he succeeded in overcoming that impairment it was because he preferred his niece mad and living to dead. He came running.

"What are you doing?" he said.

"This one is for me," the colonel answered, pointing to the loaded pistol beside him on the bench. "And this one for her," he concluded, stuffing the wadding into the barrel of the weapon in his hand.

The countess was stretched out on the ground, playing with the bullets.

"Then you don't know," the doctor calmly replied, hiding his horror, "that last night while she was sleeping I heard her say 'Philippe!'"

"She spoke my name!" cried the baron, dropping his pistol. Stéphanie snatched it up at once, but he wrenched it from her hands, picked up the weapon from the bench, and ran off.

"Poor dear child!" the doctor cried, relieved at the success of his fabrication. He pressed the madwoman to his bosom and went on: "He would have killed you, the selfish brute! Because he is suffering, he wants to see you dead. He doesn't know how to love you for yourself, my child! But we forgive him, don't we? He's irrational. And you? You're only mad. No, God alone may call you to His side. We think you unhappy because you no longer join in our sorrows, fools that we are! But," he said, pulling her onto his knees, "you're happy, nothing upsets you; you live life like a bird, like a deer."

She pounced on a young blackbird that was hopping nearby on the ground, clasped it in her hands with a little cry of pleasure, smothered it, gazed at its dead body, and left it at the foot of a tree without another thought.

At first light the next day, the colonel came down to the garden, searching for Stéphanie, believing in happiness; failing to find her, he whistled. When his mistress appeared, he took her by the arm, and walking together for the first time, they made for a bower of yellowing trees, their leaves falling in the light breeze of morning. The colonel sat down, and Stéphanie settled unprompted onto his knees. Philippe was trembling with delight.

"My love," he said to her, fervently kissing the countess's hands, "I am Philippe."

She looked at him curiously.

"Come," he added, pressing her to him. "Do you feel my heart beating? All this time, it has beaten only for you. I still love you. Philippe isn't dead, he's right here, beneath you. You are my Stéphanie, and I am your Philippe."

"Adieu," she said, "adieu."

The colonel quivered, for he believed he could see his joy spreading to his mistress. His heartfelt cry, born of a surge of hope, that last desperate bid of an undying love, a delirious passion, was reawakening his lover's reason.

"Ah! Stéphanie, we will be happy."

She let out a shriek of pleasure, and her eyes revealed a faint flicker of awareness.

"She recognizes me! Stéphanie!"

The colonel felt his heart swell, his eyes grow moist. But just then he saw that the countess was showing him a piece of sugar she'd discovered in his pocket as he spoke. He had taken for human thought what was only the faint glimmer of reason that a monkey's cunning implies. Philippe fainted. Monsieur Fanjat found the countess sitting on the colonel's still body. She was chewing her sugar, voicing her delight with coos that any visitor would have admired if, when she still had her reason, she had merrily attempted to imitate her parakeet or her cat.

"Ah! My friend," cried Philippe, recovering his senses, "I die every day, every moment! I'm too much in love with her! If in her madness she retained some small trace of her womanhood, I could bear it. But to see her still a savage, devoid even of modesty, to see her—"

"You were hoping for madness as we see it at the opera," the doctor said sharply. "Is your loving devotion subject to preconditions, then? What, monsieur! For you I have forgone the sad pleasure of feeding my niece, to you I have left the joy of playing with her, I have kept for myself only the most burdensome tasks. I watch over her while you sleep, I . . . Come, monsieur, abandon your hopes for her. Leave this sad hermitage. I have learned to live with that dear little creature; I understand her madness, I foresee her every move, I share her secrets. One day you shall thank me."

The colonel left Bons-Hommes, to return only once. The doctor was distraught to have inflicted such grief on his guest, whom he was coming to love no less than his niece. If only one of the two lovers was to be pitied, it was surely Philippe: Was he not bearing the burden of a horrific sorrow all alone? The doctor made inquiries and learned that the poor colonel had retired to a property he owned close by Saint-Germain. Placing his faith in a dream, the baron had conceived a plan to restore the countess's reason. Unbeknownst to the doctor, he spent the rest of the fall making ready for that ambitious undertaking. A small river flowed through his grounds; in the winter it flooded a broad marsh that bore some resemblance to the wetlands of the Berezina's right bank. The nearby hilltop village of

Satout completed the backdrop for that grim decor, like Studyanka looming over the floodplain. The colonel assembled a crew of workers to dig a canal that would stand in for the insatiable river where France's greatest treasures, Napoleon and his army, were lost. Relying on his memories, Philippe created a copy of the riverbank where General Éblé had constructed his bridges. He sank trestles, then burned them in such a way as to evoke the blackened, ravaged beams that told the stragglers the road to France was now closed to them forever. The colonel brought in a load of debris, similar to the fragments with which his companions in sorrow had built their raft. To complete the illusion on which he had founded his last hope, he lay waste to his gardens. He ordered enough tattered uniforms and costumes to clothe several hundred peasants. He erected huts, campsites, batteries, then incinerated them. In short, he omitted nothing that might re-create that most horrible of all scenes, and he succeeded admirably. In the first days of December, when the snow had covered the ground in a thick mantle of white, he recognized the Berezina. Several of his comrades-in-arms, too, instantly recognized the scene of their past miseries, so chillingly lifelike was this counterfeit Russia. Monsieur de Sucy would not speak a word of this tragic re-creation, which was much discussed in certain Parisian circles at the time and diagnosed as a symptom of eccentricity.

One day in early January 1820, the colonel climbed into a carriage not unlike the one that had conveyed Monsieur and Madame de Vandières from Moscow to Studyanka, and set off for the forest of L'Isle-Adam. It was drawn by horses matching those he'd risked his life to snatch from the ranks of the Russians. He wore the filthy, incongruous clothing, the arms, the headgear that were his on November 29, 1812. He had gone as far as to grow out his beard and hair, and to avoid washing his face, so that this horrible likeness might be complete.

"I understand what you're thinking," cried Monsieur Fanjat, as the colonel climbed out of the carriage. "Don't let her see you, if you want your plan to succeed. This evening I'll give my niece a small dose of opium. While she sleeps, we'll dress her just as she was in Studyanka, and we'll place her in the carriage. I'll follow you in a berline."

At two in the morning, the young countess was carried to the vehicle, laid on cushions, and wrapped in a rough blanket. Several peasants stood by to provide light for this curious abduction. Suddenly a sharp cry pierced the night's silence. Philippe and the doctor turned to see Geneviève emerging half naked from the ground-floor room where she slept.

"Adieu, adieu, it's all over, adieu," she cried, weeping bitter tears.

"Why Geneviève, what is it?" said Monsieur Fanjat.

Geneviève shook her head despairingly, raised her arms to the heavens, gazed at the carriage, let out a long moan, displayed a profound terror, and silently withdrew to her room.

"This bodes well," cheered the colonel. "The girl is sorry to be losing her friend. Perhaps she can *see* that Stéphanie will recover her reason."

"May God grant it," said Monsieur Fanjat, who seemed deeply affected by this incident.

In his studies of madness, he had more than once read of cases of prophecy and second sight among the mentally afflicted, a phenomenon that may also, travelers tell, be found among the savage tribes.

Just as the colonel had planned it, Stéphanie was sent on her way across the simulated Berezina floodplain toward nine in the morning and was awakened by the detonation of a small mortar shell some hundred paces from her carriage. This was a signal. A thousand peasants burst into a terrible roar, like the desperate howl that erupted, to the Russians' terror, when through their own fault twenty thousand stragglers saw themselves bound over to death or slavery. Hearing that cannon and that clamor, the countess leapt from the carriage, raced crazed with panic through the snow, caught sight of the burned camps, the fateful raft being launched into the icy Berezina. Major Philippe was there, swinging his saber to hold back the crowd. Madame de Vandières let out a scream that chilled every soul and ran straight to the colonel, whose heart was hammering in his chest. Lost in thought, she looked vaguely around her at this strange tableau. For a moment, brief as a flash of lightning, her eyes took on the clarity without intelligence that we admire in a bird's shining eye; then she passed her hand over her forehead, staring intently before her as if in deep meditation, contemplating this living memory, this past life here translated before her. Suddenly she turned her head toward Philippe, and *she saw him*. Dread silence had fallen over the crowd. The colonel breathed heavily, not daring to speak; the doctor was weeping. A hint of color appeared on Stéphanie's beautiful face, then, from one tint to the next, she finally regained the radiance of a girl glowing with freshness and youth. Soon her face was colored a fine crimson. Animated by an ardent intelligence, life and happiness spread over her like a burgeoning fire, one flame touching off the next. A convulsive tremor ran from her feet to her heart. And then these varied phenomena, having instantaneously burst into life, were joined in a sort of common bond when a celestial ray, a living flame, lit Stéphanie's eyes. She was living, she was thinking! She shivered, perhaps in terror! God himself unbound that dead tongue a second time, and once more poured his fire into that extinguished soul. Her will came flooding back in an electric torrent, energizing that body from which it had so long been absent.

"Stéphanie!" cried the colonel.

"Oh! It's Philippe," said the poor countess.

She fell into the colonel's trembling arms, and the crowd looked on awestruck as the two lovers embraced. Stéphanie melted into tears. But all at once her tears went dry; she stiffened, as if struck by lightning, and said, weakly, "Adieu, Philippe. I love you. Adieu!"

"Oh! She's dead," cried the colonel, loosening his grasp.

The old doctor caught his niece's lifeless body, embraced her as a young man might have done, carried her some distance away, and sat down with her on a pile of wood. He looked at the countess, laying a weak, convulsively trembling hand on her heart. It beat no longer.

"It's true, then," he said staring now at the unmoving colonel, now at Stéphanie's face, over which death was spreading its resplendent beauty, its fleeting glow, the promise, perhaps, of a glorious future. "Yes, she is dead."

"Ah! That smile," cried Philippe, "just look at that smile! Can it be?"

"She's already gone cold," answered Monsieur Fanjat.

Monsieur de Sucy strode a few steps away, freeing himself from that terrible sight, but he stopped to whistle the tune that the madwoman knew so well. Not seeing his mistress come running, he staggered off like a drunken man, still whistling, but never once turning back.

In society, General Philippe de Sucy passed for a most amiable man, and above all a very merry one. Not a few days ago, a lady complimented him on his good humor and irrepressible temperament.

"Ah! Madame," he answered, "I pay for my pleasantries very dearly, in the evening, when I find myself alone."

"Are you ever alone?"

"No," he answered with a smile.

Had some shrewd observer of human nature seen the Comte de Sucy's expression at that moment, he might well have shivered.

"Why do you not marry?" continued the lady, who had several daughters at boarding school. "You're rich, you have a title, a noble ancestry of long date; you have talent, a fine future ahead of you, everything smiles on you."

"Yes," he answered, "but there is one smile that's killing me."

The next day the lady was shocked to learn that Monsieur de Sucy had blown out his brains in the night. This extraordinary event was widely and diversely discussed in society; everyone sought to uncover the cause. Depending on the tastes of the inquirer it was gambling, or love, or ambition, or secret dishonors that explained this catastrophe, the last scene of a drama begun in 1812. Two men alone, a magistrate and an elderly doctor, knew that the Comte de

Sucy was one of those strong men to whom God has granted the sad power to emerge each day triumphant from a horrible battle with a secret monster. Let God take His mighty hand from them, if only for a moment, and they succumb.

Paris, March 1830
Translated by Jordan Stump

Z. MARCAS

*To Monseigneur le Comte Guillaume de Wurtemberg, in token of
the author's respectful gratitude*

I NEVER saw anyone, even among the remarkable men of our time, whose appearance was more striking than this man's; studying his physiognomy inspired, first, a sense of melancholy and, ultimately, a nearly painful sensation. There was a kind of harmony between the person and the name. That "Z." preceding "Marcas," which always appeared on letters addressed to him and which he never failed to include in his own signature, that last letter of the alphabet brought to mind some sense of fatality.

MARCAS! Say it over to yourself, that two-syllable name: Don't you hear some sinister meaning to it? Don't you feel as if the man who bears it must be destined for martyrdom? However strange and wild, still the name does have the right to go down to posterity: It is properly constructed, it is easy to pronounce, it has that brevity desirable in famous names.

Is it not as gentle as it is bizarre? Also, doesn't it seem unfinished? Far be it from me to declare that names have no influence on destiny. Between the facts of a life and a man's name there are mysteries and inexplicable concordances, or visible discordances, that are surprising; often distant but consequential correlations come to light. Our globe is full, everything is possible. We may yet some day turn again to the occult sciences.

Don't you see some thwarted stride in the shape of that "Z"?

Doesn't it look like the arbitrary, whimsical zigzag of a tormented life? What wind could have blown onto this letter that occurs in scarcely fifty words in whatever languages even use it? Marcas's first name was Zéphirin. Saint Zéphirin is widely worshiped in Brittany. Marcas was Breton.

Look again at the name: Z. Marcas! The man's whole life is evident in the weird assemblage of those seven letters. Seven! The most significant of the Kabbalah numbers. The man died at thirty-five, thus his life counted seven lustrums. Marcas! Doesn't it evoke the idea of something precious shattering in a fall, with or without a sound?

I was finishing my law degree in 1836, in Paris. At the time I lived on rue Corneille, in a building occupied entirely by students, one of those buildings where the stairwell twists upward at the rear, lighted first from the street, then through grilled transoms, and farther up by a skylight. There were forty rooms, furnished the way students' rooms are furnished. What more would a young man need in a room: a bed, a few chairs, a chest of drawers, a mirror, and a table. As soon as the sky turns blue, the student opens the window. But in that street there was no pretty neighbor to flirt with. Across the way, the Odéon Théâtre, long closed, blocked the view with its blackened walls, its small gallery windows, its vast slate roof. I wasn't rich enough to have a good room; I couldn't even afford a room to myself. Juste and I shared one with two beds on the top floor.

On our side of the stairwell, there was only our room and another small one occupied by Z. Marcas, our neighbor. Juste and I lived for about six months utterly unaware of his presence. An elderly woman who ran the house had in fact told us the small room was occupied, but she added that we would not be disturbed in the slightest, the tenant was extraordinarily quiet. In fact, for six months we never saw our neighbor and we heard not a sound from the room despite the flimsiness of the wall between us—one of those partitions built of slats and plaster so common in Paris buildings.

Our room, seven feet high, was lined in cheap blue wallpaper scattered with flowers. The painted floor had never known the polishers' brushes. Thin mats lay alongside the beds. The chimney pipe stopped short above the roof and gave off so much smoke that we had to attach an extension to it, at our own expense. Our beds were painted wooden cots like the ones in boarding schools. On the mantelpiece stood only two copper candlesticks with or without candles in them, our two pipes, a little tobacco in a packet or loose, as well as some small heaps of cigar ash dropped there by visitors or ourselves. A couple of calico curtains slid along rods at the window, on either side of which hung the small cherrywood bookshelves familiar to anyone who ever strolled the Latin Quarter and on which we stacked the few books needed for our courses. The ink was always solid in the inkwell, like lava caked in the crater of a volcano. These days, can't any inkwell become a Vesuvius? Our distorted pens we used for cleaning our pipestems. Contrary to the laws of credit, paper was even scarcer in our place than coin.

How could young folk be expected to stay at home in furnished rooms like that? So students would often study in the cafés, in the theater, along the walks in the Luxembourg Gardens, in girlfriends' quarters—anywhere, even at the law school—rather than in their rooms, which were awful for studying but charming for chatting and smoking. Spread a cloth on the table, lay out a last-minute dinner sent in from the best cookhouse in the neighborhood, four settings and two girls, catch the scene in a lithograph, and even a prig couldn't help but smile at it.

All we thought about was having a good time. The reason for our dissolute behavior was the very grave nature of the current political situation: Juste and I could see no place for us in the professions our parents insisted we should pursue. For every vacant post there are a hundred lawyers, a hundred doctors. Hordes of applicants block those two pathways, which are supposed to be the route to success but are more like two great arenas where men kill one another, not with knives or guns but with intrigue and slander and by horrendous toil, intellectual combat as murderous as the battles in Italy were for France's Republican troops. Today, when everything is intellectual competition, a man must be capable of sitting in his chair at a desk for forty-eight hours straight just as a general had to sit for two days in his saddle on horseback.

The crush of candidates has forced the medical field to divide into categories: the doctor who writes, the doctor who teaches, the political doctor, and the militant doctor—four different ways of being a doctor, four sectors already full to bursting. As for the fifth sector—the one involving doctors who peddle remedies—there is competition there, too, carried on by rivals posting squalid advertisements onto walls throughout Paris.

And in every courtroom there are nearly as many lawyers as there are cases. The lawyer has been thrown back onto journalism, politics, literature. And the state, under siege for the lowliest posts in the justice system, has taken to requiring applicants to have independent means. The pear-shaped skull of some rich grocer's son wins out over the square head of a talented but penniless youngster. Doing his utmost, deploying all his energy, a young man setting out from zero can wind up after ten years somewhere below where he started. Today, talent needs the kind of luck that favors the incompetent; in fact, if a skilled man rejects the vile arrangements that bring success to rampant mediocrity, he will never get on at all.

While we understood our times perfectly well, we also understood ourselves, and we preferred a thinking man's idleness to aimless agitation, loafing and pleasure to useless labors that would have taxed our enthusiasm and worn the edge off our intelligence. We analyzed the social situation while we laughed, smoked, and strolled around. But our thinking, our long discussions were no less wise, no less profound for going about them this way.

Even though we were fully aware of the abject state to which the young generation was condemned, we were still astonished at the government's brutal indifference toward anything to do with intellect, or thought, or poetry. What looks we exchanged, Juste and I, as we read the newspapers and watched the political goings-on, scanned the debates in the chambers, discussed the behavior of a court whose willful ignorance was matched only by the courtiers' servility, the mediocre quality of the men who formed a hedge around the newly restored throne—all of them without wit or vision, without achievement or learning, without influence or nobility. What a compliment to the old court of Charles X is this one, if it can even be called a court! What hatred for the nation, handing citizenship to vulgar talentless foreigners who go on to be enthroned in the Chamber of Peers! What a miscarriage of justice! What an insult to our own distinguished youth, to the ambitions sprung from our own soil! We watched all these developments like theater, and we groaned over them without taking a position for ourselves.

Juste, whom no one came to seek out and who would never seek out anyone himself, was, at twenty-five, a profound political thinker, a man with an extraordinary capacity to grasp obscure connections between present events and events yet to come. He told me in 1831 what was going to occur, and those things actually did come to pass: assassinations, conspiracies, the dominance of the Jews, France's constraints on any real movement, the shortage of good minds in the upper echelons, and the abundance of talented men in the lower ranks, where the noblest hearts are smothered beneath cigar ash.

What was to become of him? His family wanted him to be a doctor. But wouldn't that mean spending twenty years to establish a practice? You know what did become of him? No? Well, he *is* a doctor, but he has left France—he is in the East. At this very moment, he may be fainting with exhaustion in a desert, he may be dying beneath the pummeling of a barbarian horde, or he may be the prime minister to some Hindu prince.

My own vocation is action. Finishing school at twenty, I could join the army only as a common soldier, and unenthusiastic at the dreary prospect of a lawyer's life, I set about acquiring a seaman's skills. I shall do as Juste did: I mean to quit France, where in order to make any place at all for oneself requires expending the time and energy needed for the very loftiest activities. Do as I do, my friends: I'm off to where a man makes his own destiny as he pleases.

These grand resolutions were coolly decided in that little room in the house on the rue Corneille, as we went along, stopping in at the

Musard dance hall, flirting with the street girls, leading a wild, seemingly careless life. Our resolutions, our ponderings floated formless for a long while. Our neighbor Marcas was a kind of guide who led us to the edge of the precipice or the torrent and made us understand it, who showed us what our future would be if we let ourselves fall over. He put us on guard against making compromises with poverty in the name of hope, accepting a precarious position to fight from, succumbing to the wiles of Paris, that great courtesan who will take you up and drop you, who smiles on you and then just as lightly turns away, who wears down the firmest purpose with specious delays, and where Bad Luck is sustained by Chance.

Our first encounter with Marcas was rather dazzling. Coming in separately before dinner after a day at the schools, we always went up to our room and waited there for one another, to discuss any change in our evening plans. One day, at four o'clock, Juste saw Marcas on the stairs; I had passed him in the street. It was November by now, and Marcas had no cloak; he wore thick-soled shoes, heavy felt trousers, and a blue frock coat buttoned up to the chin, with a stiff collar that lent an even more military look to his torso given his black neckerchief. There is nothing unusual about such an outfit, but it did suit the style of the man and his face. My first impression at the sight of him wasn't surprise or amazement, or sorrow, or interest, or pity, but a curiosity that combined traces of all those responses. He moved slowly, with a gait that suggested a deep melancholy, head crooked forward but not lowered like a man who feels himself to be guilty. His head, large and strong, seemed to contain the resources required for a highly ambitious man and looked heavy with thought, bent beneath the weight of some mental grief, but his expression showed no sign of any remorse. As for his face, a single word would describe it, according to a folk tradition that says every human face resembles some animal: Marcas's was the lion. His hair looked like a mane, his nose was short, flattened, broad, and cleft at the tip like a lion's. A strong groove divided his forehead into two prominent lobes; his furry cheekbones looked the sharper for the thinness of the flesh below; his huge mouth and hollow jaws—all were marked by a bold pattern of creases brought out by a complexion full of yellowish tones. This almost fearsome visage seemed brightened by two lights—eyes that were black but infinitely kind, calm, profound, full of thought. If I may express it so, those eyes were humiliated. Marcas was afraid to look at people—less for his own sake than for those on whom he might level his compelling gaze: He possessed a certain power, and he was reluctant to wield it; he wanted to spare passersby, so he feared to be noticed. This was not modesty but resignation, and not the Christian resignation that involves charity but the resignation advised by reason that sees our talents going useless, the impossibility of entering and living within the setting where we ought to be. At moments that gaze could shoot lightning. From that mouth one expected a thunderous voice; it was much like the mouth of Mirabeau.

"I just saw an extraordinary man in the street," I told Juste as I came in.

"That must be our neighbor," he answered, and described exactly the figure I had passed. "A man who lives like a wood louse must look that way."

"Such humility, and such dignity!"

"The one is the effect of the other."

"So many hopes dashed, so many plans thwarted!"

"Seven leagues' worth of ruins! Obelisks and palaces and towers: the ruins of Palmyra in the desert." Juste laughed.

So we named our neighbor "the Ruins of Palmyra." On our way out to dine in the gloomy restaurant on rue de la Harpe where we had meal tickets, we asked about the man in number 37, and thus we learned the wondrous name "Z. Marcas." Like the children we were, we took to repeating it a hundred times in a hundred different ways, clownish and melancholic, that name whose sound lent itself so neatly to our game. Sometimes Juste would hiss the "Z" like a rising rocket, make a brilliant flash of the next syllable, then enact its fall to earth in the brief, blunt thud of the ending.

"Ah...well, where and how does he make a living?" we wondered. From that question to the playful espionage born of curiosity, it took us only a moment to start our project. Instead of wandering the streets that night, we returned to the house, each with a book in hand, and sat down to read and listen. In the absolute silence of our garret we heard the soft, regular sound of the breathing of a man asleep.

"He's sleeping," I said, as the first to make it out.

"At seven o'clock!" Doctor replied. I called Juste "Doctor"; he called me "Attorney General."

"A person has got to be pretty unhappy to sleep as much as our neighbor does," I said, as I climbed onto the dresser holding an enormous knife with a corkscrew in its handle. At the top of the partition I bored a round hole the size of a five-sou coin. It hadn't occurred to me that there would be no light at the far side; I put my eye to the hole and all I saw was darkness. At one in the morning, having finished our books and starting to undress, we heard sounds from our neighbor's room: He rose from his bed, struck a match, and lit his candle. I climbed back onto the dresser and spied Marcas seated at his table copying out what looked like legal documents. His room was half the size of ours; the bed stood in a recess beside the door, for the hallway ended at his threshold and its width added to his space. But apparently the land beneath the building was irregular, for that wall met the mansard ceiling at a slant. He had no fireplace, just a small white porcelain stove trimmed in green, with its pipe leading out onto the roof. The window in the slanted wall was hung with worn red curtains. An armchair, a table, and a flimsy nightstand made up the furnishings. His linens hung in a cupboard. The wallpaper was stained. Probably no one but a housemaid had ever lived there until Marcas arrived.

"What did you see?" Doctor asked as I jumped down.

"Look for yourself," I replied.

The following morning, at nine o'clock, Marcas was still in bed, asleep. He had breakfasted on a cervelat sausage—on a plate, among some bread crumbs, lay the remains of that mainstay we knew so well. He woke only at about eleven and sat down again to the copying he had begun during the night, which lay open on the table. Downstairs, we asked the price for that room and we were told it cost fifteen francs a month.

In a few days we knew all about Z. Marcas's way of life. He drew up documents, probably at so much per page, for a transcription service with offices in the courtyard of the Sainte-Chapelle. He worked through half the night; after sleeping six to ten hours he would return to his table and go on copying until three in the afternoon, then leave to deliver his copies before dinner. He would eat on rue Michel-le-Comte at Mizerai's for about nine sous, then go home to sleep until six o'clock. We reckoned that Marcas said no more than fifteen sentences in the course of a month; he spoke to no one, and he said not a word to himself there in his horrid little garret.

"Really, the Ruins of Palmyra are terribly silent!" exclaimed Juste.

That silence, in a man whose appearance was so impressive, seemed deeply significant to us. Sometimes, running across him, we would exchange very interested looks, but they were never followed by any overture. Gradually the man became the object of our private admiration, though we could not explain it to ourselves. Was it his plain, private habits? The monastic routine? The hermit-like frugality? The idiot toil that left the mind free to be neutral or active, and which suggested expectation of some happy event or some exceptional attitude toward life?

We spent a good while exploring the Ruins of Palmyra, and then forgot about him; we were so young. And then carnival arrived! The Parisian carnival that will overtake the old Venice carnival and in a few years draw the whole of Europe to Paris, that is if certain wretched police commissioners do not oppose it. Gambling ought to be tolerated during carnival, but the stupid moralists who had it outlawed are narrow-minded bean counters who will only bring back the necessary evil when it is clear that France regularly leaves millions on German gaming tables.

The merry carnival reduced us to awful poverty, along with all the other students. We stripped ourselves of our luxury possessions, having already sold our extra suits, our extra boots, our extra waistcoats, whatever we had two of except our friends. We ate bread and sausages, we walked carefully to spare our shoes, we settled down to work. We owed two months' rent and expected at any moment to be presented with a bill listing sixty or eighty charges amounting to forty or fifty francs. We quit our noisy passage through the tiled foyer at the bottom of the stairs; rather, we often crossed it in silence with a single leap from the last step right into the street. The day our pipe tobacco ran out, we realized that for the past several days we had been eating our bread without any kind of butter. The grief was enormous.

"No more tobacco!" said Doctor.

"No more overcoat!" said Attorney General.

"Ah, you rascals! Dressing up like the Coachman of Longjumeau! You thought you'd live like dockworkers, snack in the morning and lunch at Very's, maybe even at the Rocher de Cancale! Well, it's back to dry crusts, gentlemen! You'd best" (here I broadened my voice) "go sleep under your beds, you're not worthy to sleep on top of them—"

"Yes, but Attorney General! No more tobacco!" Juste cried.

"It's time to write to our aunts, our mothers, our sisters that we're out of linens, that working in Paris could wear out even iron-mail underclothes. And we'll solve an interesting chemistry problem: turning linens into silver."

"We've still got to live till they reply."

"Well, I'll see about engineering a loan from friends who haven't run through their capital yet."

"What can you get?"

"Maybe ten francs!" I boasted.

Marcas had heard the whole conversation: It was noontime. He knocked on our door and said, "Gentlemen, here is some tobacco. You can pay me back later."

We stood dumbstruck—not at the offer, which we accepted, but at the richness, the depth, the fullness of that voice; it could only be compared to the low string on Paganini's violin. Marcas vanished without waiting for our thanks. We looked at each other, Juste and I, in utter silence. To be rescued by someone obviously poorer than ourselves! Juste sat down to write to all his familial sources, and I went off to negotiate the loan.

I collected twenty francs from a hometown friend. In those hard but rollicking days gambling still went on, and mining its veins, tough as any mineral lode in Brazil, young people could risk a little and just possibly dig out a few chunks of gold. My countryman had some Turkish tobacco that a sailor had brought back from Constantinople, and he gave me the amount we had received from Z. Marcas. I sailed the rich cargo back to port, and we went in triumph to repay his black *caporal* with a voluptuous blond hank of Turkish tobacco.

"You didn't want to owe me anything," he said. "But you give me gold for copper. You're children . . . good children . . ."

Those three sentences, each spoken at a different pitch, bore different tonalities. The words were nothing, but the tone—oh! The tone turned us into decade-old friends in a moment.

Marcas had covered over his worksheets when he heard us approach, and we understood that it would be indiscreet to mention his livelihood; we were ashamed then to have spied on him. His closet stood open, revealing just two shirts, a white cravat, and a razor. The straight razor made me shudder. A mirror worth perhaps a few francs hung by the window. The man's simple, spare gestures had a kind of primitive nobility. We looked at each other, Doctor and I, as if to determine what to say. Seeing me caught short, Juste asked jokingly, "Are you involved in literature, sir?"

"Certainly not!" Marcas answered. "I wouldn't be this wealthy."

"I thought," I said, "that these days poetry was the only thing that could consign a man to a room as bad as ours."

My sally made Marcas smile, and that smile warmed his yellow face. "Ambition is no less demanding for people who do not succeed," he said. "So, you boys starting out in life: Stick to the beaten paths! Don't aim high—it will be the end of you!"

"You advise us to stay just what we are?" Doctor smiled.

The banter of youth has such contagious, childlike charm that Juste's teasing line made Marcas smile again.

"What experiences could have given you such a dreadful philosophy?" I asked him.

"Once again I forgot that chance is the result of an elaborate equation, and we cannot know all of its roots. When we start at zero on our way to one, the odds are incalculable. For ambitious people, Paris is one immense roulette wheel, and every young man believes he's got the winning strategy."

He offered us the tobacco I had brought him by way of inviting us to smoke with him. Doctor went to fetch our pipes; Marcas filled his own and then, carrying it, he came to sit at our place; in his room he had only a desk chair and his armchair. Nimble as a squirrel, Juste slipped downstairs and reappeared with a boy carrying three bottles of Bordeaux, a slice of Brie, and some bread.

"Well," I said to myself, "that's fifteen francs right there!" And indeed, Juste gravely laid a hundred sous in change on the mantelpiece.

There are immeasurable differences between social man and the man who lives as close as possible to nature. Once he was captured, Toussaint Louverture died without uttering another word. Napoleon, on his rock, babbled like a magpie; he kept trying to explain himself. Z. Marcas committed the same error, but for our sake alone. Silence and all its majesty are found only in the savage. There is no criminal who, given the chance to drop his secrets into the bloody basket along with his head, doesn't instead feel the purely social need to tell them to somebody. No, I'm wrong: We have seen one of those Iroquois from the Faubourg Saint-Marceau raise Parisian character to the level of the savage's: A man—a Republican, a conspirator, a Frenchman, an old man—outdid everything we knew of an African's resolve, and anything Fenimore Cooper ascribed to the redskins in the way of calm disdain in the midst of defeat. Morey, that Cuauhtémoc of the Montagne Sainte-Geneviève, maintained a posture unseen in the annals of European justice.

This is what Marcas told us that morning, interlacing his tale with tartines smeared with cheese and moistened by wine. All the tobacco disappeared. Occasionally carriages crossing place de l'Odéon and buses trundling around it would send up their dim rumble to us, as if to attest that Paris was still there.

His family was from Vitré; his father and mother lived on fifteen hundred francs a year. Marcas was educated tuition-free in a seminary, then refused to become a priest: He felt inside himself the flame of a huge ambition, and he came on foot to Paris at the age of twenty with two hundred francs in his pocket. He read law, working the while at an attorney's office where he rose to chief clerk. He took his doctorate in law; he knew the old and the new codes; he could more than match the most illustrious barristers. He knew *The Law of Nations* and was familiar with all the European treaties and international customs. He had studied men and events in five capital cities: London, Berlin, Vienna, Petersburg, and Constantinople. No one knew legislative precedent better than he; for five years he had reported on the chambers for a daily newspaper. He could improvise; he spoke admirably and at length in that deep, rich voice that had struck us to the soul. Telling the story of his life, he showed himself a great orator, concise and grave, with a penetrating eloquence. He had Berryer's qualities of warmth, his impulses to appeal to the masses; he had Monsieur Thiers's finesse and skill, but he would have rambled less, been less awkward in his closings. He expected to move rapidly into power without becoming tangled in doctrines, which may initially be necessary for a man of the opposition but which can burden a statesman later on.

Marcas had learned everything a true statesman must know, so he was astonished when he witnessed the profound ignorance of those already established in public service. For him such a vocation meant study, but nature had also been generous, granting him much that cannot be acquired by study alone: a lively grasp, insight, self-discipline, a supple mind, swift judgment, decisiveness, and—the special genius of such figures—fertile resourcefulness.

When he felt adequately prepared, Marcas returned to France but to a country wracked by internal divisions born of the triumph of the Orléans branch over the elder Bourbon branch. Clearly the political battleground is different. Civil war in France cannot last for long now, and it will not be waged in the provinces; from now on struggle will be brief, fought right at the seat of government, and it will end the intellectual struggle that superior minds fought in the past. This state of affairs will persist as long as France has this singular political system, which is unlike that of any other country; there is no more equivalence between the English government and ours than there is between the two nation's physical terrains.

So Marcas's place was in the political press. As a poor man, and thus unable to stand for election, he would have to give prompt evidence of his abilities. He decided on the most costly sacrifice a superior man can make: to work under some rich, ambitious deputy. Like a new Bonaparte, he sought his Barras; like Colbert, he hoped to find a Mazarin. He rendered enormous service and rendered it promptly; he made no display of it, he never boasted, he never complained of ingratitude; he rendered service in the hope that his deputy would make it possible for Marcas to be elected deputy himself. All Marcas wanted was a loan to buy a house in Paris, to meet the requirements of the election law. All Richard III wanted was a horse.

Within three years, Marcas built his man into one of the country's fifty would-be power centers: the racquets which a couple of shrewd players wield to bat cabinet posts back and forth, the way a puppeteer knocks Punch and the Constable about in his little theater stall, always with profit in mind. This man only existed through Marcas's skill, but he was intelligent enough to appreciate his aide's value, to know that once Marcas came to the fore he would remain there as an indispensable figure, whereas he himself would be relegated to the antipodes of the Luxembourg Palace. He therefore set impossible obstacles in Marcas's path to advancement and masked his strategy with protestations of heartfelt devotion. Like all small men, he was expert at dissembling; then he moved ahead in the ingratitude game: He had to kill Marcas so as not to be killed by him. These two men, seemingly so close, hated each other once the one had tricked the other.

The politician was named to a ministry; Marcas stayed behind with the opposition forces to keep them from attacking his man—and he even managed, by an ingenious maneuver, to win him their praise. To avoid rewarding his lieutenant, the new minister claimed that obviously he could not, suddenly and without some subtle preparations, appoint a man so strongly identified with the opposition. Marcas had counted on the appointment to enable him to marry and to qualify to stand for election. He was thirty-two years old, and he foresaw that the chamber would soon dissolve. Finding the minister acting in such flagrant bad faith, he overthrew him, or at least contributed importantly to his fall, and dragged him through the mire.

Any fallen minister seeking to return to power must arrange to look formidable; this man, drunk on royal flattery, had believed his position would last a long while. Now, however, he acknowledged his wrongdoing and did a small financial favor for Marcas, who had gone into debt during their quarrel: He underwrote the journal Marcas worked on and had him appointed editor in chief. Thus Marcas was indirectly subsidized as well, and although he despised the man, he agreed to an apparent alliance with him. Without yet revealing all the many aspects of his excellence, Marcas advanced farther than he had the first time around while using only half his skills. The new government lasted a mere hundred and eighty days before it was swallowed up. But Marcas had been working closely with a few deputies, manipulated them like pastry dough, and left them all with a lofty idea of his talents. His puppet-chief was again named to a ministry, and the newspaper became a ministerial organ.

The man then merged the paper with another, solely in order to do away with Marcas, who in the merger was forced to give over to a rich, insolent rival with a well-known name and one foot already in the stirrup. Marcas fell back into the direst poverty; his patron/protégé was fully aware of the abyss into which he had thrown his aide. Where could he go? The governmental journals, quietly warned off, would have nothing to do with him. The opposition papers were unwilling to take him on. Marcas could join neither the Republicans nor the Legitimists, two parties whose victory would mean the upending of the current situation.

"Ambitious men love current events," he told us with a smile.

He managed a living by writing an occasional article on business; he worked at one of the encyclopedias produced out of speculation rather than learning. Finally someone started a paper that was destined only to publish for two years but which sought out Marcas as editor. He renewed his acquaintance with his minister's enemies; he joined the faction that sought to bring down the government; and once his own pickax set to work, the administration was overthrown.

When we met, it was already six months since Marcas's paper had gone under; he had not found another position anywhere. He was reputed to be a dangerous man; the calumny gnawed at him that he had just killed off an enormous financial and industrial operation with a few articles and a pamphlet. He was called the mouthpiece of a banker who was said to have paid him extremely well and from whom he could supposedly expect some favors in return for his dedication. Disgusted with men and politics, wearied by a five-year struggle, Marcas—viewed rather as a mercenary soldier than as a great captain, broken by the need to make a living which kept him from making other headway, despairing over the influence of money on thought, gripped by severe poverty—withdrew into his garret, earning thirty sous a day as the absolute lowest sum required for his needs. Meditation stretched a kind of wilderness around him. Now he had to read the papers to keep current with events; Pozzo di Borgo had lived in that condition for a period. Marcas was probably plotting some serious attack, learning to cover his tracks and punishing himself for his mistakes by living in Pythagorean silence; he didn't tell us the reasons for his behavior.

It is impossible to describe the scenes of high comedy that lay beneath this algebraic account of his life: the futile rituals offered at the feet of elusive Fortune, the long chases through the Parisian underbrush, the endless errands of a panting petitioner, the efforts spent wooing idiots, the elaborate projects that finally miscarried because of some foolish woman, the meetings with shopkeepers who expected their investments to bring them not only sizable interest but a box at the theater and a peerage besides, the hopes that rose to a crest then crashed onto a rocky reef, miracles worked to bring together opposing interests in projects that functioned well for a week and then fell apart, the vexation time and again of seeing a fool decorated with the Legion of Honor (a fellow as ignorant as an errand boy preferred over a man of talent), and then what Marcas called the stratagems of stupidity: You hit on a prospect, he seems convinced, he nods, it is all coming together, and then the next morning the rubber wad that was momentarily molded into a useful shape has regained its old form overnight—it's even become inflated and the whole business must begin over again. You keep reworking it until you recognize that what you are dealing with is not a man but some gummy mass that dries out in the sun. These thousand setbacks, this huge waste of human energy poured onto barren terrain, underscores the difficulty of doing good, the incredible ease of doing ill: two major games played, twice won and twice lost; the hatred of a statesman, a blockhead with a face painted on it, and a wig, but a figure people believed in—all those large and small things had not undone Marcas but only temporarily knocked him down. On days when money came in, his hands never held on to it; he afforded himself the heavenly pleasure of sending it all on to his family—to his sisters, his brothers, his old father. He himself, like the fallen Napoleon, needed only thirty sous a day to live, and any energetic fellow can make thirty sous a day in Paris.

When Marcas had finished recounting the story of his life, interspersed with reflections, maxims, and observations that bespoke a great politician, a few more queries and discussions among us on the direction of matters in France and Europe sufficed to persuade us that Marcas was indeed a true statesman—for the quality of a man can be promptly and readily measured when he consents to step onto the terrain of problems: Certain shibboleths can reveal a superior person, and we belonged to the tribe of modern Levites without yet dwelling in the temple. As I have said, our frivolous life was a cover for plans that Juste, for his part, has already carried out; mine will soon come to pass.

After our exchange, we all three left the house, and despite the cold we went to walk a little before dinner in the Luxembourg Gardens. Our discussion, still somber, touched on the painful points of the political situation. Each of us had his own view, observation, statement, jest, or maxim. The talk wasn't only of life at the colossal scale laid out before us by Marcas, the veteran of political battle, nor was it the horrible monologue of the shipwrecked navigator cast up in the garret atop the Hotel Corneille; rather, it was a conversation in which two thoughtful young men, having come to a judgment on their times, were exploring their own futures under the guidance of an accomplished man.

"Why," Juste asked him, "did you not bide your time and follow the example of the only man to emerge since the July Revolution, by always just keeping his head above water?"

"Haven't I said that we never know all the roots of chance? Carrel was in exactly the same position as the orator you mean: Carrel the morose young man, that bitter character, carried a whole government in his head; the one you are talking about had just one idea—to climb onto the rump of every event as it came along. Of the two, Carrel was the better man. Well, the one became a government minister, and Carrel remained a journalist; that incomplete but shrewd fellow, the minister, is still alive, but Carrel is dead. I would point out that that fellow has spent fifteen years making his way, and he has still only partly made it; he could get caught anytime and ground up between two carts on the high road. He has no home; he hasn't a palace, a stronghold of royal favor, like Metternich, nor like Villèle the sheltering roof of a reliable majority. I don't believe the present situation will still exist in ten years. So supposing such a sorry good fortune, I am too late; in order not to be swept aside in the upheaval I foresee, I would have to be already established in a high position."

"What upheaval?" Juste asked.

"August 1830," Marcas answered in solemn tones, stretching a hand toward Paris. "August—the child born of Youth, who tied up the sheaves of grain, and of Intellect, who had cultivated the harvest—August 1830 failed to provide for youth and intellect. Youth is going to explode like the boiler of a steam engine. Youth has no outlet in France; it is gathering an avalanche of unrecognized abilities, of legitimate and unsatisfied ambitions; the young are rarely marrying, families don't know what to do with their children. What shock will come and shake loose these masses I do not know, but they will surge forward into the current situation and overturn it. There are laws of flux that reign in the sequence of generations, which the Roman Empire failed to recognize when the barbarians arrived. Today's barbarians are intelligent minds. Pressure is rising among us now, slowly, quietly. The government is behaving criminally: It doesn't recognize youth and intelligence, the two powers to whom it owes everything; it has let its hands be bound by the absurdities of the contract; it is setting up to be a victim. Louis XIV, Napoleon, England were and are all hungry for intelligent young people; in France, the young are imprisoned by the new legalities, by the noxious requirements of the election rules, by the wrong thinking of the ministerial constitution. Look at the roster of the elective chamber: You will not find a single deputy under thirty. Richelieu's young people or Mazarin's, the young of Turenne and Colbert, of Pitt and Saint-Just, of Napoleon and Prince Metternich—none of their youthful constituents would have a seat here. Burke, Sheridan, Fox would not be elected. Even if the age of political majority were set at twenty-one, and if the eligibility requirements were cleared of every sort of limiting condition, the regional departments still would only elect these present deputies, people with no political talent whatsoever, who cannot speak without slaughtering grammar, and among whom, over these ten years, scarcely a single statesman has emerged. We can generally make out the forces tending toward some disaster, but we cannot foresee the disaster itself. Right now we are driving our whole younger generation to turn republican because they believe the republic will bring their emancipation! They remember that the representatives of the people were young, and the young generals! This government's foolishness is matched only by its avarice."

That day went on echoing in our lives; Marcas confirmed us in our determination to leave France, where talented young people bursting with energy are being crushed beneath the weight of mediocre climbers, envious and insatiable.

We dined together on rue de la Harpe. From that night on we gave him our most respectful affection, and he gave us practical training in the sphere of ideas. The man knew everything; he had thought deeply about everything. He scanned the political globe, seeking the places where opportunities were the most plentiful and the most favorable for the success of our plans. He set out lines of study for us, and he urged us to move quickly, explaining the importance of timing, arguing that a massive exodus would soon begin, that its effect would be to strip France of its best energy, its young talent; that these necessarily nimble minds would choose the best destinations and that it was crucial to get there first. From then on, we would often work late by lamplight. Our generous teacher wrote us memoranda—two for Juste and three for me—marvelous instructions, full of the sort of information that only experience can yield, with guidelines that only genius can lay out. In those pages, perfumed with tobacco, jammed with writing in an almost hieroglyphic cacography, there were pointers toward fortune and uncanny predictions regarding various developments in America and Asia that have since, even before Juste and I could leave, come true.

Marcas, like us in fact, had reached utter destitution; he earned his daily living, but he had neither linen, nor coats, nor shoes. He didn't pretend to be a better person than he was; he had dreamed of luxury along with his dream of power. He didn't view his present self as the true Marcas; he left its current shape to the whim of daily life. He lived on the breath of his ambition, dreamed of revenge, and reproached himself for harboring so hollow an attitude. The true statesman ought above all to be indifferent to vulgar passions; like the scholar, he should care only for matters within his expertise. Through those days of poverty Marcas seemed to us a great, even an awesome man: There was something terrifying in his gaze, which looked onto a world past the one that strikes the eyes of ordinary men. He was the focus of our constant study and amazement, for youth feels an urgent need to admire (who among us has not experienced this?);

the young are eager to attach to something and naturally lean toward offering themselves to the service of figures they think superior, just as they dedicate themselves to great causes. We were particularly bemused by his indifference to sentimental matters: Women had never disturbed his life. Whenever we mentioned the subject, that eternal topic of conversation among Frenchmen, he would only say, "Dresses cost too much!" He saw the look Juste and I exchanged, and he went on: "Yes, they cost far too much. The woman you buy—and that's the least expensive sort—takes a great deal of money; the woman who gives herself free takes all our time! A woman snuffs out all activity, all ambition. Napoleon reduced woman to what she ought to be; on that point he was great. He did not fall into ruinous fantasies like Louis XIV and Louis XV; still, he had his secret lovers."

We discovered that like Pitt, who took England to wife, Marcas carried France in his heart; he worshipped her, never had a thought that was not for his country. He was gnawed by rage at holding in his very hands the remedy for the ailment whose tenacity so saddened him and at his incapacity to apply it, but worse was his rage at France's status as lower than Russia and England. France in third place! The cry recurred constantly in his conversation. The country's intestinal upset had moved into his own gut! He called the chamber's quarrels with the court cheap belowstairs squabbling revealed by so many shifts, such constant agitation, that damaged the nation's well-being.

"They give us peace by selling off the future," he said.

One evening, Juste and I were busy in our room, plunged in deep silence. Marcas was at work on his copying. He had refused our help with the task despite our strongest urgings; we had offered to take turns copying in his stead, so that he would have only a third of the dreary labor to do himself; he grew angry, and we stopped insisting. We heard the sound of expensive boots in our corridor and looked up at each other. The newcomer knocked at Marcas's door, which was always left on the latch. We heard our great man say "Come in!" and then "You—here, monsieur?"

"Yes, it is I," replied the former minister, Emperor Diocletian to the unknown martyr.

The two men talked for a while in low tones. Our neighbor's voice emerged only rarely, as occurs in a meeting where the interested party begins by setting out his purpose, but suddenly Marcas burst forth at some proposal we had not caught.

"You would laugh at me if I took you seriously!" he cried. "The Jesuits are over, but Jesuitism is eternal! There's no good faith in your Machiavellianism or in your generosity. You know how to count, but no one can count on you. Your royal court is made up of owls afraid of the light, old men who are either terrified of the young or pay them no attention. And the government does the same as the court. You've searched out the leftovers of the Empire, just as the Restoration court recruited Louis XIV's old Voltigeur troops! So far, people have taken your cowardly, timid evasions for smart maneuvering, but the dangers will come, and the young generation will rise up as they did in 1790. Our youth did some fine things back then. Now you keep changing ministers like a sick man changing positions in bed. These fidgetings show the decrepitude of your government. Your system of political evasions will be turned against you because the country will tire of all this equivocation. The nation won't tell you outright that it's tired of it; an invalid never knows exactly *how* he's dying—the *why* is for the historian to say—but die you surely will, for failing to ask the youth of France for their strength and vigor, their dedication and ardor; for scorning capable people, for not picking them out, with love, from this beautiful generation; for always, in every sphere, choosing mediocrity. You come to ask my support, but you are a part of that decrepit mob made hideous by their self-interest, the crowd that trembles, that cringes, that wants to reduce France to a mean thing because you yourselves are mean things. My strong nature, my ideas would be like poison to you. You've tricked me twice, twice I've brought you down, and you know it. For us to join forces a third time, it would have to be very serious. I would kill myself if I allowed you to dupe me again, for I would lose faith in my own person: Not you but I would be to blame."

Then we heard humble appeals, hot pleadings to not deprive the nation of its finest talent. There was talk of "patriotism"; Marcas uttered some sardonic grunts of "Hmpf hmpf!" he mocked his would-be employer. The politician grew more explicit: He acknowledged the superiority of his former counselor and swore to see to it that Marcas would stay on in the administration and become a deputy. Then he offered him a position of real eminence, saying that he, the minister, would take a subordinate role to Marcas, that he could only be the lieutenant to such a figure. He was expected to join the new cabinet, he said, and did not want to return to power unless Marcas held a post that was worthy of him; he had mentioned that condition to the others, and Marcas was understood to be indispensable.

Marcas refused.

The minister said, "I've never before been in a position to keep my commitments; here is a chance to be faithful to my promises, and you reject it."

Marcas did not reply. The fine boots rang in the corridor again, moving toward the stairwell.

"Marcas! Marcas!" the two of us shouted, rushing into his room. "Why refuse? The man meant what he said. His conditions were honorable. And besides, you'd be working with the other ministers!"

In the blink of an eye we listed a hundred reasons why Marcas should agree: The future minister's tone was honest; without seeing him, we were sure he was not lying.

"I have no clothes," Marcas said.

"We'll take care of that," Juste said, looking over at me.

Marcas was brave enough to trust us; a light flared in his eyes. He ran a hand through his hair, baring his forehead in one of those gestures that reveal a belief in good fortune, and when he had, so to speak, unveiled his face, we saw a man who was utterly unknown to us: Marcas sublime, Marcas in power, the mind in its element, the bird released into the air, the fish returned to the water, the horse galloping across the steppe. It was transitory: The forehead darkened again, and he had a kind of vision of his destiny. Halting Doubt followed close upon the heels of White-Winged Hope. We left him.

"Well," I said to Doctor, "we promised, but how will we manage it?"

"We'll think overnight," Juste replied, "and in the morning we'll see what ideas we've had."

The next morning we took a walk in the Luxembourg Gardens. We reviewed the events of the night before, both of us surprised at Marcas's feeble capacity for confronting life's smaller difficulties—he who was cowed by nothing when it came to solving the most complex problems of theoretical or practical politics. But these great natures are all susceptible to tripping over a grain of sand, to fumbling the most promising projects for lack of a thousand francs. It is the story of Napoleon who for lack of boots did not go off to the Indies.

"What have you come up with?" asked Juste.

"Well, I have a way to get a full outfit on credit."

"Where?"

"At Humann's."

"How is that?"

"Humann, my good fellow, never goes to his clients, the clients come to him, so he doesn't know whether I am rich; all he knows is that I dress well and carry off the suit he makes for me. I'll tell him that I've just been handed an uncle from the provinces whose indifference in matters of dress is a huge problem for me in the fine houses where I hope to marry, and that he wouldn't be Humann if he sent his bill before three months."

Doctor found this an excellent idea for a vaudeville act but a deplorable one for real life, and he doubted it could succeed. But I swear to you, Humann did dress Marcas and, artist that he is, managed to dress him as a political figure should be dressed.

Juste gave Marcas two hundred francs, the earnings off two watches bought on credit and immediately handed over to the pawnshop. Myself, I said nothing about the six shirts and all the necessary linen that cost me only the pleasure of asking for them from the forelady of a lingerie shop with whom I had spent some time during carnival. Marcas accepted it all with no more thanks than was appropriate. He did inquire how we had come by all this treasure, and we made him laugh for the last time. We gazed upon our Marcas the way shipowners who have exhausted their every last credit and all their resources to fit out a vessel must look on as it hoists sail.

Here Charles fell silent; he seemed pained by his memories.

"Well?" we all cried. "What happened?"

"I'll tell you in a few words, as this is a story, not a novel. We saw nothing of Marcas for some time. That government lasted three months; it fell after the parliamentary session. Marcas came back to us penniless, exhausted from work. He had plumbed the crater of power; he climbed out of it with the beginnings of brain fever. The illness progressed fast; we nursed him. Juste brought in the chief physician from the hospital where he had started as intern. I was living alone in our room and was a very attentive caretaker, but the care and the science—it was all futile. In that month of January 1838, Marcas himself felt that he had only a few days to live. The minister whose soul he had been for six months never came to see him, didn't even send for news. Marcas made clear his deep contempt for the administration; he seemed to doubt the very future of France and this doubt had made him ill. He thought he saw treason at the heart of the government—not a palpable, actionable betrayal by particular acts but a betrayal produced by a whole system, by the subjection of the national interests to selfish ends. His belief in the abasement of the country was so strong that his illness worsened daily from it.

"I was witness to proposals made him by a leader of the opposition group he had been fighting. His hatred for the men he had tried to serve was so violent that he would have consented joyfully to join the coalition taking shape among these ambitious men who harbored at least one idea: the idea of shaking off the yoke of the court.

But Marcas answered the negotiator with the phrase of the Hôtel de Ville: 'It is too late!'

"Marcas did not leave enough to provide for his burial. Juste and I went to great pains to spare him the shame of the pauper's cart, and the two of us alone followed behind the hearse bearing Z. Marcas's coffin, which was thrown into the common grave at the Montparnasse cemetery."

We looked at one another sadly as we listened to this story, the last one Charles Rabourdin told us, the day before he boarded a brig at Le Havre for the Malay Islands—for we all knew more than one Marcas, more than one victim of a political dedication that is rewarded by betrayal or oblivion.

Les Jardies, 1840
Translated by Linda Asher

GOBSECK

To Monsieur le Baron Barchou de Penhoen,

*Of all us students at Vendôme, you and I are, I believe, the
only ones who have met anew in the course of literary careers,
we who were already exploring philosophy at the age when we
ought to have been exploring the* De viris! *This is the story I was
writing at the time of our recent encounter and when you were
engaged in your fine works on German philosophy. Thus we have
neither of us missed our vocation. I hope you will experience as
much pleasure from seeing your name inscribed here as I had in
writing it.*

AT ONE o'clock of a night in the winter of 1829–1830, two guests
who were not family members still lingered in the drawing room of
the Vicomtesse de Grandlieu. One, a handsome young man, left the
house upon hearing the clock toll the hour. While his carriage clattered out of the courtyard and the viscountess saw only her brother
and a family friend finishing their game of piquet, she approached
her daughter, who stood by the mantelpiece pretending to study a
lampshade as she listened to the departing carriage in a way that justified her mother's fears.

"Camille, if you go on behaving as you did this evening with the
young Comte de Restaud, you will compel me to end his visits here.
Listen, my child: If you trust in my love for you, do let me guide you
in life. At seventeen a person is not equipped to assess the future, nor
the past, nor certain social considerations. I would offer this one remark: Monsieur de Restaud has a mother who would eat through

millions of francs, a woman who comes of modest stock, a Mademoiselle Goriot. She caused all sorts of talk in times past, and she behaved
so very badly toward her father that she certainly does not deserve to
have such a good son. The young count adores her and stands by her
with a degree of filial care that is highly praiseworthy, and he is extremely good to his brother and sister as well. But however admirable his own conduct," the viscountess continued, with a worldly-wise
look, "so long as his mother is alive, any family would shudder to
entrust young Restaud with a daughter's future and fortune."

"I've overheard a few words that make me eager to intervene between you and Mademoiselle de Grandlieu," the family friend called
from across the room. He turned back to his opponent: "I've won
this game, count. I'm abandoning you to run to your niece's aid."

"That is what they mean by 'having a lawyer's ears,'" said Madame de Grandlieu. "My dear Derville, how could you have heard
what I was saying so quietly?"

"I could tell from your expression," Derville answered, moving to
an easy chair by the fire.

The uncle settled in beside his niece, and Madame de Grandlieu
took a seat on a hearth stool between her daughter and Derville.

"It is time, madame la vicomtesse, to tell you a story that should
change your views on Comte Ernest de Restaud's prospects."

"A story!" cried Camille. "Do tell us, please, sir!"

Derville sent Madame de Grandlieu a glance that said the tale
was intended for her. By reason of her fortune and the venerable an-
tiquity of her name, the viscountess was one of the most prominent
ladies in the Faubourg Saint-Germain. And if it seems unlikely that
a Paris attorney could address her with such familiarity and behave
so freely in her house, the phenomenon is easily explained.

Madame de Grandlieu had returned to France in 1815 with the
Restoration of the royal family. She took up residence in Paris, living
initially on only the pension that Louis XVIII granted her from
the civil list funds, an intolerable situation. The Hôtel de Grandlieu
had been confiscated and sold by the Republic; the young Derville
had occasion to discover some technical flaws in the sale and claimed

that the house must be returned to Madame de Grandlieu. On a contingency basis, he brought suit to that effect and prevailed. Encouraged by that success, he wrangled well enough with some hospice or other and brought about the restitution of her family's timberlands. He went on to recover Grandlieu shares in the Orléans Canal Company, as well as some sizable buildings that the emperor had awarded to some other public institutions. Thus reestablished by the young lawyer's skills, Madame de Grandlieu's estate was already yielding an income of some sixty thousand francs a year when the new indemnification law restored further enormous sums to her. A man of great probity, informed and modest, and good company besides, the young attorney became a family friend.

Although his work for Madame de Grandlieu earned him the esteem, and the business, of the finest houses in the Faubourg Saint-Germain, he did not exploit his reputation as an ambitious man would have done. He resisted the viscountess's urging to sell his law practice and enter the magistrature, a career in which her patronage would have helped him to quick advancement. Except for spending an occasional evening at the Grandlieu house, he went out into society only to keep up relations with clients. It was good luck that his talents had been brought to light through his dedication to Madame de Grandlieu, for otherwise he might have risked his practice dying off; Derville did not have the soul of an attorney. Lately, since Comte Ernest de Restaud had begun attending the Grandlieu salon and Derville noticed Camille's interest in the young man, the attorney had become as assiduous a visitor to madame's house as any dandy from the Chaussée d'Antin newly admitted into the Faubourg's social circles. A few days before this evening, sitting by Camille at a ball, he had nodded toward the count and said, "A pity that lad hasn't got a few millions, isn't it?"

"Is it a pity? I don't think so," the girl had replied. "Monsieur de Restaud is very talented, he is knowledgeable, and the minister he works for thinks highly of him. I have no doubt he will become a very notable person. 'That lad' will have all the fortune he likes, the day he has power."

"Yes, but suppose he were already rich now?"

"If he were rich," Camille said, flushing, "then every girl in the room would be competing for him." She nodded toward the quadrille dancers.

"And then," said the attorney, "Mademoiselle de Grandlieu would no longer be the only one he'd look to. Is that why you're coloring? You do rather like him, don't you? Come, say it."

Camille rose abruptly.

"She loves him," Derville thought.

From that day on, Camille had been especially attentive to the lawyer, now that she understood that he approved of her inclination for the young Ernest de Restaud. Till then, though she was quite aware of her family's debt to Derville, she had displayed more respect than real friendship for him, more courtesy than warmth; her manner, and her tone of voice, had always kept him on notice of the social distance between them. Gratitude is a debt that the next generation is not always happy to count among the family obligations.

"This situation," Derville told Madame de Grandlieu after a moment, "calls to mind the only romantic story in my life. You're already laughing," he said, "at hearing a lawyer claim to have had a romance in his past. But like everyone else, I was once twenty-five, and by that age I had already seen some curious things. I must start by telling you about a person whom you could never have known: This man was a usurer . . ."

———

Can you possibly picture that pallid, wan face, one to which I wish the Academy would allow me to apply the term "lunar"—it was like a vermeil piece with the gilt worn off. His hair lay flat to his head, scrupulously combed down and ashen gray. His face was as impassive as Talleyrand's, the features immobile as a bronze casting. His small eyes were as yellow as a ferret's and almost lashless, and they seemed to cringe at the light, but the visor of an old cap shielded them from it. His pointed nose tapered to a narrow tip that made you think of a gimlet, and his lips were thin, like the lips of the alchemists and the wizened old men in paintings by Rembrandt or Metzu. The man spoke low, his tone was soft, and he never became agitated. His age was a question: It was impossible to say whether he was old before his time or had managed his youth so economically as to make it last forever.

In his room, everything was clean and threadbare, from the green baize on his desk to the bedcover. It was like the chilly sanctum of those old maids who spend their days rubbing down their furniture. In winter he kept the embers in his hearth smoldering beneath layers of ash and never let them flame up. His every act, from the hour he woke to his evening fit of coughing, was regular as a pendulum. He was a kind of automaton, rewound each night by sleep. If you touch a woodlouse as it crosses a sheet of paper, it will stop short and play dead; in the same way, this man would stop speaking in mid-sentence while a carriage passed in the street, so as not to strain his voice. Like Fontenelle, he was sparing with his vital energies and concentrated all his human feeling on the self. Thus his life flowed as quietly as the sand in an hourglass. Occasionally his victims would raise a ruckus and carry on; then there would come a great silence, as in a kitchen when a duck has its throat slit. Toward evening this banknote man would turn into an ordinary human, and his metals metamorphosed into a human heart. If he was pleased with his day, he would rub his hands together and the crevassed folds of his face would let off a smoke of gaiety—there is no other way to describe the silent play of those muscles, an effect akin to Leatherstocking's hollow laughter. In even his fiercest transports of pleasure, though, his conversation was still monosyllabic and his face remained empty of expression.

This was the neighbor whom chance provided me in the house where I lodged on rue des Grès when I was still just an assistant clerk and finishing my third year at the law faculty. The house has no courtyard, and it is damp and gloomy. The building is divided into a series of cell-like rooms of equal size; their only light comes from the street-front windows, and their only exit is onto a single long corridor lit by dim transoms. The claustral arrangement indicates that the building was once part of a convent. In the melancholy air of the place, a well-born lad's high spirits would die away before he even entered my neighbor's door; the man's house and the man resembled each other, you might say, like an oyster and its rock.

I was the only person he had anything to do with, socially speaking; he would come to ask me for a light or to borrow a book or a newspaper, and on the occasional evening he would allow me into his cell where we would chat when he was in a good mood. These marks of trust were the fruit of four years of proximity and of my orderly way of life; through lack of money, my life was much like his own. Did he have relatives or friends? Was he rich or poor? No one could have answered such questions. I never saw money in his room. His funds must have been stored in the vaults of the Bank of France. He would collect on his bills himself, running about Paris on legs as bony as a stag's. In fact he was a martyr to his own cautious ways: One day, he chanced to be carrying some money, and a gold double Napoleon coin somehow fell out of his pouch. A tenant climbing the stairs behind him picked it up and handed it to him. "That's not mine!" he exclaimed, looking startled, as if to say, "Gold? mine? Would I be living like this if I were rich?"

Mornings, he made his own coffee on a tin brazier that stood always in the dark corner of his grate. He had his dinner sent in from a cookshop. Our elderly porteress came upstairs daily to tidy the room.

Well, by an odd chance, the sort of detail Sterne would call predestination, this man's name was Gobseck. When in later days I handled his legal business, I learned that at the time we met he was about seventy-six years old. He was born in 1740, on the outskirts of Antwerp, of a Jewish mother and a Dutch father, and was named Jean-Esther van Gobseck. You remember back when all of Paris was obsessed with the murder of a woman called La Belle Hollandaise? When I happened to mention the crime to my neighbor, he told me, showing neither the slightest interest nor the least surprise, "That was my great-niece." Those words were all that could be drawn from him on the death of his only near kin, his sister's granddaughter. I learned from the court records that La Belle Hollandaise was indeed named Sara van Gobseck. When I asked him once by what curious circumstance his niece bore his own last name, he smiled and replied, "The women in our family have never married." The odd fellow had never cared to see a single person of the four generations of women among his relatives. He wanted nothing to do with any heirs and could not conceive that his riches should ever belong to anyone but himself, even after his death.

His mother had sent him off at the age of ten as a cabin boy to the Dutch East Indies, and he had knocked about there for twenty years. Thus the creases in his sallow brow harbored secrets of dreadful events, sudden terrors, unexpected turns, romantic escapades, sublime joys: hunger was borne, love trampled underfoot, a fortune threatened, lost, and regained; life a thousand times in peril, and saved perhaps by quick decisions whose urgency justified their ruthlessness.

He had known Monsieur de Lally and Monsieur de Kergarouet, Monsieur d'Estaing, the bailiff Suffren, Monsieur de Portenduère, Lord Cornwallis, Lord Hastings, Tippu Sahib's father, and Tippu Sahib himself. The Savoyard who served Mahadaji Sindhia, the King of Delhi, and did so much to establish the power of the Marathas—Gobseck had done business with him, as well as with Victor Hugues and a number of famous pirates, having spent a long time in St. Thomas. So determined was he to try every path to fortune that he had gone hunting for the treasure of that tribe of savages so famous around Buenos Aires. He was familiar with all the events of the American War of Independence. But when he spoke of the Indies or the Americas, which he never did with anyone else and rarely did with me, he seemed to feel he'd committed an indiscretion and appeared to regret it. If humanity, if sociability were a religion, he could be considered an atheist. I had hoped to plumb his character, but I confess to my shame that it remained quite opaque to me. I sometimes even wondered which sex he belonged to; if all usurers are like him, I believe they are neuter in gender. Had he kept to his mother's religion, and did he consider Christians his prey? Had he turned Catholic, Muslim, Brahmin, or Lutheran? I never learned a thing about his religious views. He seemed indifferent rather than a nonbeliever.

One evening I entered the room of this man who had turned himself into gold, the man whom his victims—his clients, as he said—called "Papa" Gobseck, either as a euphemism or perhaps with sarcasm. I found him in his armchair, motionless as a statue, his eyes fixed on the mantelpiece as if he were reviewing his account statements there. A smoky lamp on a once-green base cast a glow that, far from throwing color on his face instead brought out its pallor. He looked at me in silence and pointed to my waiting chair. "What could this creature be thinking?" I said to myself. "Does he even know if a God exists, or an emotion, or women, or happiness?" I pitied him as I would a sick creature. But I understood, too, that in addition to his millions in the bank, he could also lay mental claim to the whole earth, which he had roamed, mined, weighed up, evaluated, and developed.

"Hello, Papa Gobseck," I said. He turned his head toward me, his thick black eyebrows pulled together slightly; that characteristic expression from him was the equivalent of the merriest smile from a southerner. "You're looking as gloomy as the day you heard about the bankruptcy of that bookseller you admired for his cleverness, despite being a victim of it."

"I, a victim?" he said, surprised.

"To get him to settle, didn't you let him pay you in discounted notes, and then when he was back in business he redeemed them for full value rather than at the discount?"

"He was sharp, yes," Gobseck replied, "but I got even later."

"What is it then, some overdue bills to protest? Today is the thirtieth, I think."

It was the first time I had ever spoken to him of money. He looked up teasingly, and then, in his soft voice with tones like those produced by a flute student with a poor embouchure, he said, "I'm playing."

"So, you do sometimes play?"

"Do you think the only poets in the world are the people who publish verses?" he asked, shrugging and throwing me a pitying look.

"Poetry... in that head?" I said to myself, for at the time I knew nothing about his life.

"What finer existence can there possibly be than mine?" he went on, and his eyes glowed. "You're young, you think with your blood, you look at your glowing embers and see women's faces, whereas I see only cinders in mine. You believe in everything; I believe in nothing. Hold on to your illusions, if you can. I'll show you life as it is, minus the discount. Whether you travel the world or stay close to hearth and wife, there always comes a certain age when life is simply a habit carried out in some chosen setting. From then on happiness consists in applying our faculties to a given reality. Apart from these precepts, everything else is false. My own principles have always shifted to match those of the men I live among—I have had to adjust them according to latitude: what Europe admires, Asia punishes; what's a vice in Paris is a requirement once you sail past the Azores. Nothing on this earth is absolute; everything is only convention that changes with the local climate. For anyone who's had to leap into a multitude of social molds, convictions and moral rules become empty words. What stays in us is the one true feeling nature put there: the instinct for self-preservation. In your European societies, it's called self-interest. If you'd lived as long as I have, you would know that there is only one material thing whose value is reliable enough to be worth caring about: That thing is GOLD. Gold represents every sort of human power. I have traveled, I have seen that everywhere there are plains or mountains—plains are tiresome and mountains are tiring, so place makes no difference. As to behaviors, man is everywhere the same: Everywhere the struggle between the poor and the rich is a given; everywhere it is inevitable, so much the better to be exploiter than exploited; everywhere you find sinewy men who labor and indolent men who torment themselves; pleasures are the same everywhere; everywhere the senses grow jaded and only one sentiment endures: vanity! Vanity is always about the self.

Vanity is only satisfied with floods of gold. Our fantasies take time, or physical means, or care in order to be realized. Well, gold contains every potential and provides every reality. Only madmen and invalids are happy to shuffle cards every night to see if they'll win a few sous in the end. Only fools will spend their time wondering about what goes on around them, whether Madame So-and-so slept alone or with a companion, whether she has more blood than lymph, more temperament than virtue. Only idiots believe they serve their fellow man by working out political principles to foretell events that will always be unpredictable. Only simpletons like to chatter about theater folk and quote their sayings; or like an animal in its cage, pace daily the same trail if a little broader; dressing for other people, eating for other people, boasting about a horse or a carriage that the next fellow cannot acquire for another three days. Isn't that in a nutshell the life you Parisians lead? Let's look at existence from a higher vantage point. Happiness lies either in strong emotions that wear out life or in routine activities that give existence the relentless rhythm of an English-style machine. At a higher level than such gratifications is the curiosity—considered noble—to plumb nature's secrets or to achieve a kind of imitation of her effects. Is this not—in two words—art or science, passion or calm? Well, I tell you, every human passion, writ larger by the play of social interests, they all come and parade before me in my life of calm. Furthermore, that scientific curiosity of yours, a kind of struggle with man always getting the worst of it—I replace it with insight into the springs that set mankind moving. In a word, I possess the world with no effort at all, and the world has no grip on me.

"Listen," he went on, "an account of my morning's adventures will give you an idea of my pleasures."

He rose, bolted the door, pulled shut an old tapestry curtain whose rings creaked along the rod, and returned to his seat.

"This morning," he said, "I had only two bills to collect, the others I had passed on to clients as loans yesterday evening. That already puts me ahead, because I always charge in advance for the cost of collection—forty sous to hire a good carriage, for instance. Wouldn't it be a fine thing if a client had me running all over Paris for a six-franc fee, when I answer to no one, and when I pay only seven francs in taxes!

"So then, the first bill, for a thousand francs, came to me from a handsome young dandy in a beaded waistcoat who wore a monocle, drove a tilbury carriage pulled by an English horse, and so on. It was endorsed by one of the finest women in Paris, the wife of a rich landowner, a count. Why had the countess underwritten a bill of exchange, which is worth nothing legally but worth a great deal in practice? These unfortunate women are terrified of the scandal a publicly protested bill could set off in their household and would give their very selves as payment rather than default. I wanted to find out the secret value of that bill of exchange: Was it stupidity, imprudence, love, or charity?

"The second bill, for the same amount, was signed 'Fanny Malvaut'—it had been given to me by a cloth merchant on the verge of collapse. No one who has any credit at the bank comes to my office, where the first step from the door to my desk declares a hopeless situation: an imminent bankruptcy and above all the refusal of credit by every banker in town. So all I ever see are stags at bay, hounded by packs of creditors.

"The countess lived on rue du Helder and my Fanny on rue Montmartre. What a mass of conjectures I mulled as I left my house this morning! If these two women were not able to pay, they would receive me with greater respect than if I were their own father. How many contortions and wiles would the countess muster for the sake of a thousand francs? She would take on an affectionate manner, use that cajoling tone peculiar to an endorser of notes, murmur endearments, plead, even beg. And I"—here the old man turned his pale gaze on me—"I am unshakable!" He continued, "I am the Avenger, I am the embodiment of Remorse!

"Well, enough imaginings. I arrive at the house ..."

"Madame la comtesse is still asleep," a chambermaid tells me.

"When will she be available?"

"At noon."

"Is madame unwell?"

"No, monsieur, but she returned from a ball at three in the morning."

"My name is Gobseck. Tell her I called and that I shall return at twelve o'clock."

And I leave, marking my visit on the carpet lining the stone staircase. I like to soil the carpets of the rich, not out of spite but to make them feel the claw of necessity.

On rue Montmartre, arriving at a shabby building, I push open a crooked carriage gate and enter one of those murky courtyards where the sun never shines. The porter's lodge is dark, the windowpane looks like the edge of a worn old robe—grimy, brown, cracked.

"Mademoiselle Fanny Malvaut?"

"She's gone out, but if you've come about a bill, the money is here for you."

"I'll come back," I said. Upon hearing that the porter had the money, I wanted to meet the young lady; I imagined she was pretty. I spent the morning looking through the prints on display along the boulevard; then as noon rang I crossed the parlor adjoining the countess's room.

"Madame has only just rung," the chambermaid tells me. "I don't believe she is ready for visitors yet."

"I will wait," I said, sitting down in an armchair.

In a moment the Persian blinds opened and the chambermaid returned to say, "Do come in, sir." From the sweetness of her tone, I understood that her mistress would not be paying me. But what a beautiful woman then appeared! She had hastily covered her naked shoulders with a cashmere shawl so closely wrapped that their nude form could be made out beneath. Her gown was trimmed with snowy ruffles that announced that some fine laundress earned a good two thousand francs a year there. Thick locks of the woman's black hair slipped free of a pretty plaid kerchief knotted carelessly around her head like a Creole woman. Her disordered bed was the picture of a sleepless night. A painter would have paid good money to spend a few moments observing the scene. Beneath a voluptuously slung canopy, a pillow tucked into a blue silk eiderdown, its lace edge in sharp relief against the azure quilt, bore the print of vague forms that stirred the imagination. At the feet of the lions carved into the mahogany bedposts lay a broad bearskin rug, upon which gleamed two white satin slippers flung down carelessly in exhaustion from the late ball. On a chair lay a rumpled gown, its sleeves touching the floor. Stockings that the faintest breeze might waft away twined around the leg of an armchair. White garters trailed along a chaise. An elegant fan, half spread, glowed on the mantelpiece. Drawers hung open; flowers, diamonds, gloves, a nosegay, a sash lay here and there. A light scent of perfume filled the air. All was luxury and disorder, beauty and disharmony; for her or for her worshipper, trouble crouching below was already lifting its head, grazing them with its sharp teeth.

The countess's drawn face resembled that bedroom strewn with the remains of a festive night. I felt pity for the scattered baubles that only the night before, arrayed together, had roused excitement and envy. These vestiges of a love corroded by remorse, this picture of a life of dissipation, of luxury and riot, evoked a Tantalus-like effort to clutch at fleeting delights as they slip out of reach ... Red marks on the young woman's face showed the delicacy of her skin, but her features seemed somehow coarsened and the brown rings beneath her eyes looked unusually dark. Still, nature flowed so powerfully in her that these signs of excess did not lessen her beauty. Her eyes sparkled. Like some Herodias from Leonardo's brush (I used to deal in paintings), she was magnificent with life and vigor; there was nothing mean about her contours or features; she inspired love, and I sensed she must be even stronger than love. She was entrancing. It is a long while since my heart had beat so hard. So I was already repaid enough! I would readily give a thousand francs for a sensation that so recalled the days of my youth.

"Sir," she said, offering me a chair, "would you be kind enough to wait?"

"Until noon tomorrow, madame," I replied, as I refolded the paper I had presented her. "I cannot legally protest the note before then."

At the same time, I was thinking, "Pay up for your luxury, pay for your name, pay for your ease, pay for the monopoly you live by! To keep their holdings safe, the rich invented courtrooms and judges, and the guillotine—a candle that draws the ignorant fluttering up to be burnt. But for you who sleep upon silk and beneath silk, what waits is remorse, grinding teeth hidden behind a smile, and those fantastical lion jaws biting at your heart."

"Protest the note! Do you actually intend to do that?" she exclaimed, staring at me. "You have so little consideration for me!"

"Madame, if the king himself owed me a debt and failed to pay, I would file a complaint against him, and even quicker than against any other debtor."

At that moment we heard a discreet knock at the door.

"I am not in!" the young woman declared imperiously.

"But Anastasie, I wish to see you!"

"Not just now, my dear," she replied, her tone slightly less harsh, but still far from gentle.

"Nonsense, you are talking to someone now," the voice retorted, and a man entered who could be none other than the count. The countess looked at me, and I understood instantly: She had become my slave.

"Young man, there was a time when I might have been foolish enough not to protest an unpaid bill. In 1763 in Pondicherry, I let a woman off and she took me for a fine ride. I deserved it—why had I ever trusted her?"

"What is your business here, sir?" the count asked me. I saw the woman trembling from head to foot; the sleek white skin of her neck turned rough with what people call "gooseflesh." And I—I was laughing without twitching a muscle.

"Monsieur is a merchant I have dealings with," she said. The count turned his back to me; I drew the note partway out of my pocket again. Seeing this inexorable gesture, the young woman crossed the room and handed me a diamond. "Take this," she said, "and go."

We exchanged the two assets, and with a bow I left the room. The diamond was easily worth twelve hundred francs to me. Outside in the courtyard I came across a crowd of lackeys brushing their uniforms, waxing their boots, scrubbing sumptuous carriages. I said to myself, "This is what brings these people to my office. This is what impels them to legally steal millions and betray their country. The great lord, or his would-be imitator, will plunge his whole self into the mud to keep a spot of it from hitting his boots if he were to go about on foot." Just then the main gate opened to make way for the tilbury carriage of the young man who had given me the co-signed bill of exchange.

"Monsieur," I said when he had climbed down, "please return this two hundred francs to the countess and tell her that for the next week I will hold available the security she left with me this morning."

He took the two hundred francs and allowed himself a sardonic smile, as if to say, "Ha! She did pay it...Well, so much the better!"

I could read the countess's future on that face. This cold, handsome, blond gentleman, this soulless gambler, will ruin himself, ruin her, her husband, and their children, he will devour their fortunes and wreak more havoc in the Paris drawing rooms than a regiment's worth of mortar shells.

I went back to rue Montmartre to see Miss Fanny. I climbed a very steep staircase to the fifth floor and entered a two-room apartment where all was as neat as a new coin. I saw not a trace of dust on the furnishings of the first room, where I was received by Miss Fanny. She was a Parisian girl, simply dressed, her face fine and fresh, her gaze forthright. Her chestnut hair, smoothly coiffed, was looped into two curves at her temples, and set off the elegance of blue eyes as clear as crystal. Daylight filtered through small curtains at the casements and cast a soft gleam on her modest face. Around her, several pieces of cut fabric revealed her customary occupation: She worked as a seamstress. She seemed the very spirit of solitude. I presented her the signed bill of exchange, remarking that I had failed to find her in earlier that morning.

"But I had left the money with the porter," she said.

I pretended not to hear her. "Mademoiselle goes out very early, it seems?"

"I do not leave this room often, but when a person works all night, it is sometimes necessary to visit the baths."

I looked at her. With a single glance I understood everything about her life: This was a girl consigned by misfortune to a life of labor, her family most likely farmers, for she had some of those freckles common to country folk. Her features gave off a sense of goodness. I felt I had entered an atmosphere of sincerity, of candor, and my lungs seemed refreshed. The poor innocent was a believer: Above her plain-painted wood bed hung a crucifix with two sprigs of bay leaf. I was rather touched; I even felt inclined to charge her only twelve percent on her bill and thus help her to set up in some suitable little business. But then I thought, "Oh, but she might have a little cousin who would use her signature to raise money and live off the poor girl," and I left, stifling my generous impulse, for I have often observed that while a charitable act may do no harm to the benefactor, it is death to the one who receives it.

"Tonight, when you came into my room, I was musing that Fanny Malvaut would make a good little wife; I was comparing her pure, solitary life to the countess's: That woman has already sunk to bills of exchange, and she will go tumbling on down to the depths of vice!

"Well now," Gobseck continued after a deep silence, during which I watched him with some curiosity, "do you think it's nothing, this power to see into the most secret recesses of the human heart, to engage another person's life, to see it all stripped naked? It is always drama, always different: hideous wounds, deathly sorrows, love scenes, griefs likely to end beneath the waters of the Seine, a young man's pleasures that lead to the scaffold, despairing laughter, and sumptuous celebrations. Yesterday a tragedy: A good-hearted father hangs himself because he can no longer feed his children. Tomorrow a comedy: A young fellow will try an updated version of the *Monsieur Dimanche* scene on me. People rave about the eloquence of the latest preachers; I have wasted a little time listening to them, and they might persuade me to change my opinions but, as someone once said, never my actions. Well, I tell you: Those fine preachers, and your Mirabeaus and Vergniauds and such—they are all just stammering amateurs compared to the orators who come in and perform for me.

"It may be a girl in love, or an old shopkeeper sliding toward collapse, a mother desperate to cover up her son's misdeeds, a starving artist, or some prominent figure who's slipping in favor and for lack of money may lose the fruit of his work—they've all made me shudder with the power of their words. These sublime actors perform for me alone, and they cannot manage to deceive me. My gaze is like God's: I can see into their hearts. Nothing is hidden from me. No one refuses the man who ties and unties the purse strings. I am rich enough to buy the consciences of those who rule over the actions of ministers, from their office boys to their mistresses: Is that not power? I can have the loveliest women and their sweetest caresses: Is that not pleasure? Power and pleasure—do these two words together not sum up your whole social order?

"There are a dozen of us here in Paris, all silent unknown kings, the arbiters of your destinies. Life is a machine fueled by money, is it not? The truth is this: Means are always tangled up with ends; you can never separate the soul from the senses, spirit from matter. Gold is the spiritual ground of your contemporary societies. Our bunch are bound together by similar interests; we meet on certain days of the week at Café Thémis, by the Pont Neuf. There we uncover the mysteries of finance. There is no fortune that can keep the truth from us; we know every family's secrets. We keep a kind of black book where we track the most important bills issued and redeemed, drafts on the public credit system, on the bank, in trade. We are casuists of the stock exchange; we sit as a Vatican council judging and analyzing the slightest activities of everyone with any level of wealth —and our assessments are always right. One of us watches the judicial sector, another the financial sector; one the administrative world, another the commercial world. Myself, I follow eldest sons, the artists, fashionable society, the gamblers—the liveliest segment of Paris life. Everyone tells us his neighbor's secrets; betrayed love and ruffled vanity are great gossips; vice and disappointment and vengeance are the sharpest detectives. Like myself, my colleagues have all enjoyed everything, had our fill of everything, and we've reached the point of enjoying power and money for the simple sake of power and money. Right here in this place," he said, waving a hand about his bare cold room, "the fiercest lover, a man who anywhere else explodes at a word and draws his sword at a remark—here he will stand and implore me with his hands clasped! Here the most arrogant merchant, the vainest beauty, the most formidable general—all of them come here to plead, they beg and beseech, their eyes wet with rage or sorrow. Here in this room they kneel and pray—the most renowned artist or writer, people whose names will pass down to posterity. And in *here*," he added, touching a hand to his brow, "inside here is a set of pitiless scales that weigh the wealth, the estates, the interests of all Paris.

"So now: Do you still think there are no ecstasies beneath this blank mask whose impassive stillness has so often puzzled you?" he inquired, offering me his colorless face with its smell of money.

I returned to my room in a daze. This dry little old fellow had grown vast. Before my eyes he had become a phantasm, the very power of gold made flesh. Life, mankind, filled me with horror. "Is it true, then, that everything must come down to money?" I wondered. That night, I remember, it was very late before I slept. I saw mounds of gold all around me. The lovely countess filled my mind; to my shame, I confess that she completely eclipsed the image of the simple chaste creature absorbed in a life of labor and obscurity. But the next morning, through the mists of waking, gentle Fanny appeared to me in all her beauty; I thought of nothing else but her.

"Would you like a glass of sugar water?" the viscountess broke in on Derville.

"Very much," he replied.

"But I see nothing in your story that could concern us," said Madame de Grandlieu as she rang for the drink.

"Sardanapalus!" Derville cried, his customary exclamation. "Surely Mademoiselle Camille will be interested to hear that her happiness used to depend entirely on this Papa Gobseck, but that with the old man's death just now, at eighty-nine, Monsieur de Restaud will soon come into a nice fortune. This will require some explanation. And as to Fanny Malvaut—you know her: She is my wife!"

"The poor boy," said the viscountess. "He'd proclaim it in front of twenty people, with his usual openness."

"I would shout it out to the whole universe," said the attorney.

"Drink up, my poor Derville. You will never be anything but the happiest and best of men."

The old uncle raised his dozing head. "I left you at rue du Helder, in some countess's house," he said. "What have you done with her?"

Derville resumed his tale.

———

A few days after my conversation with the old Dutchman, I presented my thesis, won my law license, and soon became an attorney. The old miser's confidence in me increased enormously. He took to consulting me—without pay—about various thorny projects he was undertaking, investments founded on solid investigation but which other counselors would have considered unwise. This man, whom no one had ever influenced in the slightest, listened to my advice with a kind of respect. And in truth he always did quite well with it.

Time passed, and I was named head clerk of the firm where I had been working for three years; I left my lodgings at rue des Grès and moved into my employer's house; I would have room, board, and a salary of one hundred fifty francs a month. A wonderful day! When I went to say farewell to my neighbor the usurer, he gave no sign of either friendship or regret, he did not ask me to come see him, he merely gave me one of those looks that, from him, somehow implied the gift of second sight. A week later, though, I did receive a visit from the old man; he brought me a rather difficult case, an expropriation; and he continued to make use of my free consultations as readily as if he were paying for them.

After two years in my new situation, through 1818 and 1819, my employer, a man who lived extravagantly and spent freely, found himself in serious difficulties and was forced to sell his practice. Although at that time a professional office didn't yet command the exorbitant prices of today, my employer was still practically giving his away, asking only one hundred fifty thousand francs. I thought that an energetic man, skilled and intelligent, could manage to live respectably, meet the interest payments on such a sum, and pay off the principal in ten years, if he inspired trust. But as the seventh son of a small tradesman from Noyon, I didn't have a sou to my name, and the only capitalist I knew in the world was Papa Gobseck. An ambitious idea, and some inexplicable glimmer of hope, gave me the courage to go see him, and so one evening I slowly made my way to rue des Grès. My heart pounded in my chest as I knocked at the door to the gloomy house. I recalled everything the old miser used to tell me, back when I never imagined what violent anxieties stormed on this threshold. I was now about to beg and entreat like so many others . . .

"Well, no!" I told myself. "An honest man should maintain his dignity in every circumstance. Not even a fortune is worth groveling for. I'll look just as confident as he is."

Since I'd left the place, Papa Gobseck had taken over my room to avoid having a new neighbor; he had set a small grilled window into the door, which he didn't open until after he looked through the grille and saw my face.

"Well, now!" he said in his thin fluting voice. "So your employer is selling his practice?"

"How do you know that? He has told no one but me!"

The old man's lips stretched into a crease at the corners, exactly like curtains, and the silent smile was accompanied by a cold gaze.

"It took such an event to bring you here," he added dryly after a pause, during which I stood confused.

"Listen to me, Monsieur Gobseck," I began again, with what calm I could muster, standing before this old man who stared at me with impassive eyes, their clear fire making me uneasy.

He gestured as if to say "Go on."

"I know you're not easily moved, so I will not waste any eloquence trying to describe the situation of a penniless clerk whose only hope lies in you, and who knows no heart in the world but yours that could understand his prospects. But we can leave heart aside: Business is business, nothing mawkish like a novel. So here are the facts: In my employer's hands, the practice brings in some twenty thousand francs annually, but I believe that in mine it could be doubled. He wants to sell it for one hundred fifty thousand francs. I feel, right in here," I said, tapping my forehead, "that if you were to lend me the funds to buy it, I could repay you within ten years."

"Now that's proper talk," Papa Gobseck replied, offering his hand and shaking mine. "Never before in my business," he continued, "has anyone laid out more clearly the purpose of his visit."

He looked me over from head to foot. "Any guarantees?" he asked. "None, I can see," he concluded after a pause. "How old are you?"

"Twenty-five, in ten days," I replied. "Otherwise, I could not qualify to—"

"Correct!"

"So then—"

"Possibly."

"Good Lord, I'll have to move fast or other buyers will bid the price up!"

"Bring me your birth certificate tomorrow morning, and we will discuss your plan. I'll think it over."

The next morning at eight, I was at the old man's door. He took the document in his hands, put on his spectacles, coughed, spat, wrapped himself in his black greatcoat, and read through the whole sheet from the local registry. Then he flipped it over, flipped it back again, looked up at me, coughed again, twisted about on his seat, and said, "We will try to arrange the matter."

I jumped.

"I take fifty percent interest on my money," he said, "sometimes one hundred, two hundred, five hundred percent."

I paled at his words.

"But given our acquaintance, I will take twelve and a half per year..." He hesitated. "Well... for you I'll settle for thirteen percent annually. Will that suit you?"

"Yes," I replied.

"But if that's too much," he parried, "stand up for yourself, Grotius!" He often addressed me as the great Dutch jurist to tease. "When I ask thirteen percent, I am doing my job. It's your job to decide whether you can pay it. I don't like a man who agrees with everything. Is it too much?"

"No," I said, "I'll just expect to work a little harder."

"Well, in any case," he teased, with a sly sidelong glance, "your clients will pay for it."

"No, absolutely not!" I exclaimed. "I will be the one paying. I would rather cut off my hand than take advantage of my clients."

"Then good evening to you," said Papa Gobseck.

"But fees are set by the state," I said.

"Not for time spent on mediation, or clients coming to terms under your guidance, or negotiated agreements—for such things you can bill a thousand francs, even six thousand, depending on the amounts involved—and then for consultations, outside conferences, expenses, memoranda and drafts, professional terminology. You must learn to seek out these aspects of business. I will recommend you as a very learned and able attorney. I'll send you so much work that your colleagues will die of jealousy. Werbrust, Palma, Gigonnet—my friends will all give you their expropriation cases, and Lord knows they have plenty of those! So you'll have two practices: the one you're buying and the one I'll set up for you. You should almost pay me fifteen percent on my hundred and fifty thousand."

"All right, but no more," I said with the firm tone of a man who means to grant nothing further. Papa Gobseck softened; he seemed pleased with me.

"I will pay your employer myself, to establish a solid primary-debtor position on the purchase and the surety bond."

"Fine, whatever guarantees you like."

"And you'll write me bills of exchange for the amount yourself: fifteen notes for ten thousand francs each, made out to an unnamed third party."

"Yes, with a note in writing that this is a duplicate copy, not a different purchase—"

"Oh, no," Gobseck broke in. "Why should I trust you more any than you trust me?"

I kept silent.

"And," he continued in a comradely tone, "you'll handle my business affairs without a fee for as long as I live, yes?"

"All right, so long as there is no outlay on my part."

"Correct!" he said. "Now then," continued the old man, whose face showed the strain of adopting that companionable manner, "you'll allow me to come to your office?"

"With pleasure."

"Yes, but mornings will be very difficult. You'll have business to attend to and so will I."

"Then come in the evening."

"Ah, no," he replied emphatically. "You must go out socially, to see your clients. And I have my friends to see, in my café."

"His friends!" I thought to myself. "Well, then—why not come at dinnertime?"

"Fine," said Gobseck, "at five, then, after the stock exchange closes. So, very good: You will see me Wednesdays and Saturdays. We'll chat about business as a couple of friends. Ah . . . you know, I'm a jolly fellow at times. Just give me a partridge wing and a glass of champagne, and we'll talk. I know a lot of things that can be revealed now, and that will teach you to know men—and especially women."

"Done, for a partridge and a glass of champagne."

"Do nothing foolish, or you'll lose my trust. Don't go in for some grand style at home: Hire yourself an elderly housemaid, just one. I will come around to see how you're getting on. I have an investment riding on you, after all, heh heh heh . . . I must keep abreast of your activities. That's all, then, come back this evening with your employer."

As we reached the door, I said to the old fellow, "Could you tell me, if it is not indiscreet to ask, what was the significance of my birth certificate in all of this?"

Jean-Esther van Gobseck hunched his shoulders, smiled wickedly, and replied, "Young people are thick. Learn this, then, Monsieur Lawyer—something you ought to know, to keep from being taken in: Under the age of thirty, honesty and talent are still qualities solid enough to lay money on; past that age, a man is no longer a sure thing." And he closed his door.

———

"Three months later I became an attorney, and soon after that, madame, I had the good fortune to see to the restitution of your properties. Winning those cases brought me some recognition. Despite the enormous interest I had to pay to Gobseck, in less than five years I was free of debt. I married Fanny Malvaut, whom I love deeply. Similarities in our two lives, in our work, and in our progress constantly strengthen our feelings for each other. An uncle of hers, a farmer who'd got rich, died and left her seventy thousand francs, which helped me to pay off the loan. From that day on, my life has been nothing but happiness and prosperity.

"But that's enough about me; nothing is so tedious as a happy man. To return to our characters: A year after I bought my practice, I was drawn, almost despite myself, into a gentlemen's luncheon. The occasion was the paying off of a bet that a friend of mine had lost to a young man then much in vogue in fashionable social circles. Monsieur de Trailles, the flower of dandyism at that moment, enjoyed a tremendous reputation—"

"But he still does," the count broke in, interrupting the attorney. "There's nobody who carries off an outfit with more dash or drives a tandem better than he. Maxime has the talent of gambling, eating, and drinking with more elegance than anyone in the world. He knows horses, hats, paintings. The women all go mad for him. He spends a good hundred thousand francs a year and yet no one can say if he has a single hectare of land or one investment to his name. The very model of a knight-errant of our salons, boudoirs, and boulevards, an amphibian breed as much woman as man, Comte Maxime de Trailles is a remarkable figure—good at everything and good for nothing, both feared and mocked, knowing everything and nothing, as likely to commit a good deed as an offense, one minute base and noble the next, more likely smeared with mud than stained with blood, quicker to apprehensions than remorse, more interested in good digestion than good thinking, feigning passion and feeling nothing. A brilliant link between the criminal and high society, Maxime de Trailles is a man of that eminently intelligent class that occasionally spins out a Mirabeau, a Pitt, a Richelieu, but more often gives us the Comtes de Horn, the Fouquier-Tinvilles, the Coignards."

"Well," Derville said after listening to the old statesman, "I had heard a good deal about this person from poor old Goriot, a client of mine, and I had managed on several occasions to avoid the dangerous honor of his acquaintance when we crossed paths in society. However, my friend was so insistent that I should come to his luncheon that I couldn't refuse without looking like a prude. Madame, you would be hard-pressed to imagine a gentlemen's luncheon. It is a business of rare magnificence and affectation, the splurge of a miser driven by vanity to one great day of display..."

When you first arrive, you are astonished at the beauty and order laid out before you, a table dazzling with silver, crystal, damask linens. Life is in full flower there: The young men are graceful, smiling, their voices are low, they behave like new brides, everything around them fresh and virginal. Two hours later, you'd think it was a battle-field after the battle: broken glass everywhere, napkins rumpled and ripped; revolting dregs of half-eaten food; a head-shattering uproar, with smart toasts; an onslaught of salty epigrams and bad jokes; flushed faces and swollen eyes that can no longer express a thing; and blurted confidences that say everything. There's an infernal racket, fellows smash bottles, roar out songs, someone shouts a challenge, someone else hangs tenderly on a neck or starts a fight, the room gives off a hideous stench of a hundred odors and a hubbub of a hundred voices; nobody knows any longer what he's eating, or drinking, or saying; some are morose and others babble; this one is a monomaniac who keeps repeating the same word like a bell tolling, that one tries to get a hand on the tumult; the soberest fellow in the room proposes an orgy. If some levelheaded passerby should step into the room he'd think he had fallen into a bacchanal.

In all this confusion, Monsieur de Trailles was busy wheedling his way into my good graces. I had more or less held on to my own sanity; I was on guard. For his part, though he pretended to be decently drunk, he was in full control and keeping a firm eye on business. In fact, I don't know how this happened, but by the time we left the Grignon rooms at nine that night, he had me utterly bewitched, and I had promised to take him the next day to see our Papa Gobseck. What with his golden tongue, the words "honor," "virtue," "countess," "honest woman," "bad luck" were magically scattered through his talk. Waking up the next morning and trying to recall what I had done the night before, I had great difficulty collecting my thoughts. In the end, the story seemed to be that the daughter of one of my clients was in danger of losing her reputation, as well as the respect and love of her husband, unless she could get hold of fifty thousand francs in the course of the morning. Something about gambling debts, bills from the coach maker, money lost to something or other... My distinguished companion had assured me that the woman was rich and it would require only a few years of careful spending to repair the damage to her fortune. Only then did I start to see the reason for the fellow's urgency. I confess, to my shame, that I never suspected that it was important for Papa Gobseck to make up with this dandy.

As I was dressing, Monsieur de Trailles arrived. "Monsieur le comte," I said formally, "I don't see why you should need me to introduce you to Monsieur van Gobseck. He's the most courteous, the mildest of any of the capitalists. He will give you money if he has it—that is, if you provide him adequate security."

"Monsieur," he replied, "it would never enter my mind to force you to do me a service, even though you did promise."

"Sardanapalus!" I said to myself. "Am I going to let this fellow think I am not a man of my word?"

He went on: "I had the honor of telling you yesterday that I had, most inconveniently, quarreled with Papa Gobseck. Now, because there is hardly another lender in Paris who could spit out a hundred thousand francs on a moment's notice, especially on the first day of the month, I asked you to make my peace with him. But we'll just leave it at that." Monsieur de Trailles gazed at me in a politely insulting manner and prepared to leave my room.

"Wait ... I am ready to take you there," I conceded.

When we reached rue des Grès, the dandy looked up and down the street with an unease that surprised me. His face turned pale, then flushed a dark, sickly yellow; a few drops of sweat appeared on his brow as we neared Gobseck's house. As we stepped down from his gig, a hired cab turned into rue des Grès. My hawkeyed companion made out a woman sitting deep inside the carriage. An expression of nearly savage joy livened his face; he called to a small boy walking by and gave him his horse to hold. We climbed the stairs to the old bill-discounter's rooms.

"Monsieur Gobseck," I said, "I bring you one of my most intimate friends," and murmured into his ear, "whom I trust like the devil." I went on aloud: "I would be obliged if you would offer him your kind services (at your usual rates) to help him out of a difficulty (if it suits you)."

Monsieur de Trailles bowed before the usurer, sat down, and prepared to listen, assuming a courtier's posture of obsequious modesty that would have charmed you, but my Gobseck sat unmoved and impassive in his chair at the chimney corner. He looked like the statue of Voltaire we see at night beneath the peristyle of the Théâtre-Français; as if in greeting, he slightly lifted the worn cap covering his head, and the patch of yellow skull he disclosed completed the resemblance to a marble figure.

"I only have money for my own clients," he said.

"So then, you're irritated that I already looked elsewhere to ruin myself?" The count laughed.

"Ruin yourself!" Gobseck retorted, with irony.

"Are you going to say that it's impossible to ruin a man who has nothing? But I defy you to find a better investment prospect than this in the whole of Paris," exclaimed the stylish fellow, standing up and pivoting on his heels. That half-serious buffoonery left Gobseck utterly unaffected. "Am I not an intimate friend of the Ronquerolles, the Marsays, the Franceschinis, the two Vandenesses, the Ajuda-Pintos—that is, of all the most sought-after young men in Paris? I play cards with a prince and an ambassador, whom you know. I draw my income from London, Carlsbad, Baden-Baden, Bath. Surely that is the most brilliant industry of all?"

"True."

"You make me into a sponge, for God's sake, you encourage me to swell up and out into the world, and then at a crucial moment you squeeze me dry. But you are all sponges yourselves, and death will come and squeeze you too!"

"Possibly."

"Without us spendthrifts, where would you be? We two are one, we're body and soul together."

"Correct."

"Well then, how about a nice handclasp, my good Papa Gobseck, and a little magnanimity from you—if all I've said is true, correct, and possible?"

"You come to me," replied the usurer coldly, "because Girard, Palma, Werbrust, and Gigonnet are fed up with your bills of exchange, which they are offering everywhere at a fifty percent loss.

Now, since they probably gave you only half the face value in the first place, the notes are not worth twenty-five percent. Your servant, sir! Can I," Gobseck went on, "decently lend a single franc to a man who owes thirty thousand and hasn't got a sou? You lost ten thousand francs the day before yesterday at Baron de Nucingen's party."

"Monsieur," replied the count with startling impudence, staring down the old man, "my affairs are no concern of yours. A man with a due date ahead is not a man in debt."

"True!"

"My bills will be paid when they are due."

"Possibly!"

"And right now, the question between us is simply whether I can present you with sufficient security for the sum I have come to borrow."

"Exactly."

The clatter of a cab filled the room as it stopped at the doorstep.

"I will show you something that may satisfy you," cried the young count, and he went out.

"Oh, my boy!" exclaimed Gobseck, standing and opening his arms to me when the borrower had vanished. "If he has some worthwhile collateral, you've saved my life! This would have been the death of me. Werbrust and Gigonnet thought they were putting one over on me. Thanks to you, I'll have a good laugh tonight at their expense!"

There was something frightening about the old man's exhilaration. It was the only time I ever saw him expansive. His ecstasy lasted a brief moment, but in my memory it will live forever.

"Please do me the favor of staying here a little," he said. "I'm armed, and I'm a sure shot, as a man must be who has hunted tigers and held his own on deck when it was conquer or die, but I don't trust that elegant rascal." He returned to the chair at his desk. His face was again colorless and calm.

"Ah!" he said, turning to me. "I believe you are about to see the beautiful creature I once told you about; I hear an aristocrat's step in the hallway."

And indeed, the young man returned escorting a woman I recognized as the countess whose noontime rising Gobseck had described to me, one of old Goriot's daughters. The countess didn't see me right away; I was standing in the window recess, my face to the glass. Stepping into the moneylender's damp, dim room, she cast a mistrustful glance at Maxime. She was so lovely that, despite her faults, I felt pity for her. An awful anguish was riling her heart; her noble, proud features were contorted in an expression of pain that was barely disguised. The young man had become an evil genie in her eyes. I admired Gobseck for foreseeing the future of these two beings from that one bill four years earlier. I thought, "This angel-faced monster probably rules over her with every possible mechanism: vanity, jealousy, erotic pleasure, the ways of her world."

———

"But," here the Vicomtesse de Grandlieu broke in on Derville, "the woman's very virtues were weapons in his hands—he brought her to tears of devotion, he roused the generosity that comes so naturally to our sex, and then he took advantage of her feelings to charge her a very high price for sinful pleasures!"

"I must admit," said Derville, oblivious to the signals of the viscountess, "I hardly mourn the fate of that unlucky woman, so splendid to the world's eyes and so repugnant to anyone who could read her heart. I did shudder, though, at the sight of her assassin, this young fellow with his brow so untroubled, his mouth so fresh, his smile so winning, his teeth so white—the look of an angel. At that moment the two of them stood before their judge, who was scrutinizing them the way an old sixteenth-century Dominican monk must have watched a couple of Moors being tortured, down in the dungeons of the Inquisition."

———

"Monsieur," the countess asked Gobseck, "is there a way to obtain the price of these diamonds but keep the right to buy them back?" Her voice trembled as she held out a jewel box to him.

"Yes, madame, there is," I interjected, stepping forward and revealing myself. She glanced over, recognized me, shuddered, and threw me that look which in every land means "Not a word!"

I went on: "There is a procedure we call a 'sale with right of redemption,' which consists in ceding and transferring a property, real or personal, for a fixed period of time, at the expiration of which one may retrieve the object in question against payment of a prearranged sum."

She breathed more easily. Count Maxime frowned; he suspected quite rightly that the usurer would now offer a smaller amount for the diamonds, since their value would fluctuate. Gobseck, still seated unmoving at his desk, had fitted a loupe against his eye and was silently looking through the jewel case. If I live a hundred years, I will never forget the sight of his face: His pale cheeks colored; his eyes, which seemed to collect the stones' sparkle, shone with a supernatural blaze. He rose, moved to the window, and held the diamonds close to his toothless mouth as if he would devour them. He mumbled vague words, lifting bracelets, brooches, pendants, necklaces, tiaras one by one, holding them to the light to judge their clarity, their whiteness, their cut; he pulled them out of the jewel box and put them back, picked them up again, jostled them to bring out their every glint, more a child than an old man, or rather child and old man both at once.

"Beautiful diamonds! These would have brought three hundred thousand francs before the Revolution. What brilliance! They're true Asia diamonds, from Golconda or Visapur! Do you know what these are worth? No, no, Gobseck is the only person in Paris who can appreciate them. Under the Empire it would have cost more than two hundred thousand to put together such a set." He shook his head in disgust and added, "But diamonds are dropping in value every day now. Brazil has been pouring them out since the end of the war, the market is glutted with stones that aren't so white as the ones from India. And nowadays women are wearing them everywhere, not only at court. Does madame go to court?" Muttering these awful remarks he went on examining the stones, one after the other, with unspeakable pleasure. "Not a flaw!" he exclaimed. "There's one here ... Here's something, a streak ... Fine diamond, this one."

His colorless face was so brilliantly illuminated by the blazing jewels that I thought of those murky old mirrors you see in country inns, which absorb the surrounding light and send nothing back, so that a traveler who looks for his image in the glass sees a fellow in an apoplectic spasm.

"Well now!" said the young count, slapping Gobseck on the shoulder. The aged child gave a start. He let go the trinkets, set them on his desk, sat down, and became the moneylender once again—hard, cold, polished as a marble column.

"How much do you need?"

"One hundred thousand francs, for three years," said the count.

"Possible!" said Gobseck, and from a mahogany box—his own sort of jewel case!—he drew scales of irreproachable accuracy. He weighed the stones and—heaven knows how—his practiced eye calculated the weight of the settings as well. Throughout the operation the old miser's face struggled between excitement and sternness. The countess was sunk in a stupor; watching her, I felt she was looking at the depths of the chasm she was falling into. There was still some remorse in the woman's soul; perhaps it would take only a small effort, a charitable hand offered, to save her. I decided to try.

"Do these diamonds belong to you personally, madame?" I asked in a clear voice.

"Yes, monsieur," she replied, with a haughty look.

"Draw up the purchase and redemption contract, chatterbox!" Gobseck snarled, standing and pointing me to his seat at the desk.

"Madame is probably a married woman?" I asked her further.

She nodded curtly.

"I will not draw up the contract," I declared.

"And why not?" asked Gobseck.

"Why not?" I said, drawing the old man into the window niche to speak privately. "This woman is under her husband's authority; the contract would be null and void; you couldn't claim ignorance of a fact that is stated in the document itself. You would be required to produce the diamonds deposited with you, whose weight, value, and cut would be described right there."

Gobseck interrupted me with a nod and turned to the two culprits. "He is right," he said. "This is a different situation entirely. Eighty thousand francs cash, and you leave the diamonds with me!" he added in a hollow, fluting voice. "In matters of personal property, possession equals title."

"But—" objected the young man.

"Take it or leave it," Gobseck said, handing the jewel case back to the countess. "There are too many risks in it for me."

"You would do best to throw yourself on your husband's mercy," I murmured into her ear, leaning toward her. The usurer doubtless understood my words from the movement of my lips, and he threw me a cold look. The young man's face turned livid. The countess's hesitation was palpable. The young count went to her, and though he spoke very low, I heard: "Farewell, dear Anastasie, I wish you happiness! As for me, tomorrow my cares will be over."

"Monsieur," cried the countess, "I accept your offer."

"Well now," replied the old man, "you are very difficult to bring around, my lovely lady."

He wrote a check for fifty thousand francs drawn on the Bank of France and handed it to the countess. "Now," he said with a smile that rather resembled Voltaire's, "the balance of thirty thousand francs I will give you in my own bills of exchange . . . and no one would ever contest their validity. They are as good as gold bullion. Monsieur de Trailles said earlier, 'My bills will be paid when they are due.'" Gobseck brought out a bundle of notes signed by the young count, all of them contested the day before at the request of a fellow lender who had probably then sold them cheap to Gobseck. The young man gave a roar that contained the phrase "Old scoundrel!"

Papa Gobseck didn't turn a hair; from a box he lifted out a pair of pistols and said coldly, "As the insulted party, I shall fire first."

"Maxime, you owe the gentleman an apology," the trembling countess exclaimed softly.

"I had no intention of offending you," the young man stammered.

"I am sure of that," Gobseck replied tranquilly. "Your only intention was to not pay your bills of exchange."

The countess rose, bowed, and left in what must have been a state of deep dread.

Monsieur de Trailles was obliged to follow her, but before going out he turned to us. "If the slightest indiscretion should escape your lips, gentlemen," he said, "I will have your blood or you will have mine."

"Amen," Gobseck exclaimed, as he put away his pistols. "But to gamble his blood, a man must have some in his veins, little one, and you have nothing but muck in yours."

When the door had closed and the two carriages were gone, Gobseck rose and began to dance about, chanting, "I've got the diamonds! I've got the diamonds! The beautiful diamonds, such diamonds! And cheap! Ah, ah, Werbrust and Gigonnet! You thought you could trick old Papa Gobseck! *Ego sum papa!* I am the master of you all! Fully paid for, the interest too! Won't they feel like fools tonight when I tell them this story, between a couple of games of dominoes!"

That dark exuberance, that ferocity of a savage, over the possession of a few shiny pebbles made me shudder. I was silent, stunned.

"Ah, you're still here, my boy!" he said. "Let's go eat together, we'll have a good time at your place—I don't keep house here, and all those restaurant folk, with their purées and their sauces and their wines, they'd poison the devil himself!"

The look on my face abruptly returned him to his cold impassivity. "You don't understand all this," he said, taking his seat again by the fire and setting a tin saucepan of milk on the grate. "Would you like to have breakfast with me?" he went on. "There may be enough here for two."

"Thank you," I replied, "I don't breakfast until noon."

Just then rapid footsteps sounded in the corridor. The unknown arrival stopped at Gobseck's door and rapped several times in what seemed a fury. The moneylender went to look through the grille, then opened the door to a man of about thirty-five who must have looked harmless to him, despite the man's anger. The newcomer was dressed simply; he resembled the late Duc de Richelieu. It was the count (whom you have probably met, madame? If you'll permit the liberty—he had the aristocratic look of the statesmen from your neighborhood).

"Monsieur," the man said to Gobseck, who had resumed his calm stolid demeanor again, "my wife just left here?"

"Possibly."

"What, monsieur—do you not understand me?"

"I have not had the honor of meeting madame, your wife," replied the usurer. "I've received a good many visitors this morning: women, men, young ladies who looked like young men and young men who looked like young ladies. It would be rather difficult for me to—"

"Enough foolishness, sir! I am talking about the woman who left your office a moment ago."

"How should I know whether she is your wife?" asked the usurer. "I have never had occasion to see you before."

"You are mistaken, Monsieur Gobseck," said the count with heavy irony. "We met in my wife's room, one morning. You came to collect a note she had underwritten, a note she did not owe."

"It was not my business to discover how she came to underwrite the note," replied Gobseck, shooting a mischievous look at the count. "I had taken it over from a colleague. And by the way, monsieur," said the moneyman, his voice neither agitated nor hurried as he added coffee to his mug of milk, "allow me to remark that it is not clear by what right you come and lecture me here in my office: I have been an adult since the sixty-first year of the past century."

"Monsieur, you have just bought for a pittance family diamonds that did not belong to my wife."

"Without feeling any obligation to discuss my business with you, count, I will say that if madame took your diamonds, you should have circulated a notice warning jewelers not to buy them. She might have sold them separately."

"Monsieur!" cried the count. "You knew my wife."

"True."

"She is under her husband's authority."

"Possibly."

"She had no right to dispose of those diamonds."

"Correct."

"Well then, monsieur?"

"Well then, monsieur: I do know your wife; she is under her husband's authority, fine (she seems to be under the authority of several people). But I...do...not...know...your diamonds. If madame the countess can sign bills of exchange, then presumably she can carry on business herself, can buy diamonds, can acquire them to sell—that is clear!"

"Good day, sir!" cried the count, white with fury. "There are courts of law."

"Correct."

"This gentleman," the count added, pointing to me, "was witness to the sale."

"Possibly."

The count turned to leave. Suddenly, feeling the situation was grave, I intervened between the two belligerent parties.

"Count," I said, "you are right, and Monsieur Gobseck is not at all in the wrong. You could not sue the purchaser without implicating your wife, and the ugly aspects of the affair would not fall upon her alone. I am an attorney, yet I owe it to my own self, still more than to my professional position, to declare that the diamonds you speak of were bought by Monsieur Gobseck in my presence. But I believe that you would be wrong to contest the legality of the sale of items that are, besides, not easily identified. In equity, you would win; in law, you would lose. Monsieur Gobseck is too honest a man to deny that the sale was profitable to him, especially since both my conscience and my duty would require me to say it was. But were you to bring suit, count, the outcome would be uncertain. So I would advise you to come to terms with Monsieur Gobseck, who can claim he acted in good faith, but to whom you would in any case still have to return the purchase money. Agree to a redeemable sale, for a period of seven or eight months, or even a year—time enough to allow you to repay the sum madame borrowed—unless you prefer to buy the jewels back today, providing security for the payment."

The moneylender sat dipping his bread into his coffee bowl and chewing it with what seemed utter indifference, but at my phrase "come to terms" he looked over at me as if to say, "Smart fellow—he's learned a thing or two from my lessons!"

I retorted with a hard look that he understood perfectly: The whole business was deeply dubious, ignoble; it was becoming urgent to negotiate a way out. Gobseck couldn't have recourse to denials; I would have told the truth. The count thanked me with a gracious smile. After a discussion in which Gobseck displayed enough skill and avidity to stymie the diplomatic cunning of a whole parliament, I prepared a document by which the count acknowledged receiving from the usurer a sum of eighty-five thousand francs, interest included, and Gobseck pledged to return the diamonds to him upon the repayment of the full amount.

"Such waste," exclaimed the husband as he signed. "What could possibly bridge such a chasm?"

"Sir," Gobseck asked gravely, "have you any children?"

The question made the count flinch, as if an expert physician had suddenly put a finger on the very center of a pain. The husband didn't reply.

"Well," continued Gobseck, understanding the man's sorrowful silence, "I know your story by heart. This woman is a demon whom you may still love; I can certainly believe it, I was very much taken with her myself. But you may want to salvage your wealth, keep it for one or two of your children. Well, then, do this: Throw yourself into the social whirl, gamble away your wealth, and come around often to see Gobseck the moneylender. People will call me a Jew, an Arab, a usurer, a pirate, saying that I ruined you—I don't care! If someone insults me, I lay him low! No one handles a pistol or a sword as well as yours truly here, and people know it! Then find a friend with whom you can arrange a counterfeit sale of all your holdings." He turned to me and asked, "Isn't that what they call a *fideicommissum* —a trust?"

The count seemed entirely absorbed in his thoughts. He said, "You will have your money tomorrow, sir—have the diamonds ready for me," and he left.

"That fellow seems as stupid as an honest man," said Gobseck coldly, when the count had gone.

"Say, rather, as stupid as a man of passion."

"The count owes you a fee for drawing up the document," Gobseck cried, seeing me leave.

A few days after that episode, which initiated me into the dreadful mysteries of the life of a woman of fashion, the count stepped into my law office.

"Monsieur," he said, "I have come to consult you on some very serious matters; I have the utmost confidence in you, and I hope to give you proof of that. Your conduct with Madame de Grandlieu is beyond all praise."

———

"So you see, madame," Derville turned from his story now to the Vicomtesse de Grandlieu, "that you have paid me a thousand times over for what was a very simple service." He then resumed . . .

———

I bowed respectfully to the count and replied that I had only done the duty of a decent man.

"Well, monsieur," the count said, "I have gathered a good deal of information on the remarkable person to whom you owe your situation. From what I know of him, I recognize Gobseck as a philosopher of the Cynic school. Would you consider him an honest man?"

"Count," I replied, "Gobseck is my benefactor—at fifteen percent," I laughed, "but his avarice doesn't authorize me to paint his portrait for a stranger's sake."

"Do speak, monsieur! Your candor cannot harm either Gobseck or yourself. I don't expect to find an angel in a moneylender."

"Papa Gobseck," I began, "is deeply convinced of one governing principle: He believes money is a commodity that a person may in good conscience sell high or low, according to the situation. In his eyes, by charging a high rate for the use of his money, a capitalist becomes a kind of advance partner in a profit-making business or venture. Apart from his financial principles and his philosophical notions on human nature, which allow him to act as an apparent usurer, I am convinced that outside his business activities he is the most scrupulous, most upright person in Paris. Two different men exist at once in him: He is a miser and a philosopher, petty and great. If I were to die leaving children behind, I would name him their guardian. This is my sense of Gobseck from my experience with him. About his past life I know nothing. He may have been a pirate, he may have circled the world trafficking in diamonds or men, in women or state secrets, but I swear no human soul has been through more nor been more thoroughly tested. The day I brought him the money to pay off my debt, I asked him, speaking carefully, what had brought him to charge me such enormous interest, why—since he did want to do me a favor as a friend—he had not allowed himself to do a complete one. His answer: 'Son, I spared you a sense of obligation, by giving you the right to feel you owed me nothing, and so we came out the best of friends.' That reply, count, will give you a better picture of the man than any possible words could."

"I have made up my mind, irrevocably," said the count. "Prepare the necessary documents to transfer ownership of my estate to Gobseck. I will trust you alone, monsieur, to devise the counter deed, in which Gobseck will declare that this is a simulated sale, and that he pledges to return my fortune, which is to be administered by him as he does so well, to my eldest son when the boy comes of age.

"Now, Monsieur Derville," he continued, "I must tell you this as well: I am afraid to keep this crucial document in my house. My son's attachment to his mother makes me uneasy about entrusting him with it. Dare I ask you to hold it for me? In case of death, Gobseck would make you the legatee to the property he holds for me. This should take care of all contingencies."

The count fell silent for a moment; he seemed very agitated. "I beg your pardon, monsieur," he said after a pause. "I am in great physical pain, and I am seriously concerned for my health. Recent troubles have disturbed my life in very cruel ways and have forced me to take this important measure."

"Monsieur," I told him, "first, let me thank you for your trust in me. But I must justify it by pointing out that by these measures you are completely disinheriting your... other children. They do bear your name. If only because they are the children of a woman you once loved, even if less so now, they have the right to a certain quality of life. I will not accept the task by which you hope to honor me unless their future is assured."

These words caused a violent reaction from the count. Tears filled his eyes, and he gripped my hand, saying, "I did not yet know you well enough. You have just caused me both joy and pain. We will provide for those children by stipulations in the counter deed."

I saw him out of my office, and it seemed to me his features shone with a sense of satisfaction from that act of justice.

"So you see, Camille," Derville turned to the girl, "how easily young women enter the abyss. It can take as little as a quadrille, a song at the piano, a ride in the countryside, to trigger some dreadful mistake. A person might succumb to the appealing voice of vanity or pride, to faith in a smile, or just to folly or thoughtlessness! Then shame, remorse, destitution—those are three Furies into whose hands women inevitably fall when they cross the boundaries."

"My poor Camille is longing to fall asleep," the viscountess interrupted the attorney. "Go, darling, go to bed. Your heart has no need for such terrors to keep pure and virtuous."

Camille de Grandlieu understood her mother and left the room.

"You went a bit too far there, dear Monsieur Derville," said the viscountess. "Attorneys are not mothers or preachers."

"But the newspapers are a thousand times more—"

"Poor Derville!" the viscountess interrupted him. "I swear, I hardly recognize you! Do you actually think that my daughter reads the newspapers? . . . Go ahead now," she said after a pause.

"Three months after the count's sale to Gobseck was officially registered—"

"You can call him the Comte de Restaud, now that my daughter has left the room," said the viscountess.

"So I shall!" the attorney continued.

———

Some time went by after my encounter with Comte de Restaud, and I had still not received the counter deed that I was to hold safe for him. In Paris, an attorney gets swept up in a current that distracts him from paying as much attention to his clients' affairs as the clients themselves do, apart from some few exceptions. One day, though, the moneylender was dining with me, and as we rose from the table I asked if he knew why I had heard nothing more from the Comte de Restaud.

"There are excellent reasons for that," he replied. "The gentleman is close to dying. He is one of those good souls who don't know how to kill their pain and are always getting killed by it. Living is a job, a task a person has to take the trouble to learn how to do. When a man has known life, has gone through its troubles, his fiber becomes stronger, and it takes on a flexibility that gives him mastery over his feelings; it turns his nerves into steel springs that can bend without breaking. If his stomach can take it, a man with that kind of preparation should live as long as the cedars of Lebanon, those famous trees."

"The count is really dying?" I said.

"Possibly," said Gobseck. "You'll have a juicy piece of business settling the estate."

I looked at the man and, to probe him a little, said, "Explain to me, please, why we, the count and I, are the only people you take any interest in?"

"Because you are the only ones who trusted me without quibbling," he answered.

Although his response did allow me to believe that Gobseck would not misuse his position if the counter deed should be lost, still I resolved to go and see the count. I pled some pressing errand, and we parted. I hurried directly to rue du Helder and was shown into a sitting room where the countess was playing with her children. Hearing me announced, she rose brusquely and came to meet me, and without a word she sat down and motioned me to an empty chair by the fire. Her face assumed that impenetrable mask beneath which society women so skillfully hide their strongest feelings. Troubles had already withered that face; all that remained to indicate its former grace was the marvelous structure that had made it so remarkable.

"It is essential, madame, that I speak with the count—"

"If you did, you would be more privileged than I," she replied, interrupting me. "Monsieur de Restaud will see no one. He barely allows his doctor in, and he refuses any care, even from me. Sick people have such strange fantasies! They are like children, they don't know what they want."

"Perhaps, like children, they know very well what they want."

The countess flushed. I almost repented my Gobseck-like retort. "But," I went on, to change the tone, "it can't be, madame, that Monsieur de Restaud is constantly alone."

"He has his eldest son with him," she said.

However intently I stared at the countess, she did not redden again, and I sensed she was even more firmly determined not to let me into her secrets.

"You should understand, madame, that my visit is not frivolous; some important interests of his—" I bit my lip, feeling that I had made a bad start. And the countess instantly took advantage of my clumsiness.

"My interests are not at all separate from my husband's, monsieur," she said. "There is no reason not to speak to me directly."

"The business that brings me here concerns only the count," I replied firmly.

"I will see that he is told of your visit."

Her polite tone and manner did not fool me; I understood that she would never allow me to approach her husband. I chatted for another moment about unimportant matters, thinking to observe her further, but like every woman with a plan in mind, she dissembled with that rare perfection which, in persons of your sex, madame, constitute the highest degree of perfidy. Dare I say it—I feared she might go to any lengths, even commit a crime. My apprehension arose from seeing—in her gestures, her glances, her manner, and even the intonations of her voice—that her sights were firmly set on the future. I left her.

Now I will tell you the rest of the story, including some elements that emerged over the course of time, and details I later grasped through Gobseck's insight, or my own.

When Comte de Restaud appeared to plunge into a whirl of dissipation and to squander his fortune, something occurred between the two spouses whose nature will never be known, but which caused the count to judge his wife still more unfavorably than before. Once he fell ill and was forced to take to his bed, he made clear his aversion to the countess and to her two younger children: He forbade them to enter his bedroom, and when they tried to evade the rule, their disobedience brought on crises so dangerous for his condition that the doctor urged the countess not to infringe on her husband's orders.

Madame de Restaud had watched the family's land and properties, even the mansion where she lived, pass successively into Gobseck's hands—Gobseck who, in regard to their fortune, embodied the fantastical figure of an ogre—and she surely grasped her husband's intentions. Monsieur de Trailles, being rather too vigorously pursued by his creditors, had gone off traveling in England. He alone might have explained to the countess what secret precautions against her Gobseck had suggested her husband take. It is said she long resisted giving her signature as the law requires for any sale of family holdings, but her husband did finally obtain it. The countess believed he was liquidating all his property, and that whatever small amount of money was so far realized probably lay in a safe somewhere in a notary's office or perhaps in the Bank of France. But she figured that the count must have kept with him some document that would eventually allow the eldest son to recover any estate the count still owned. She therefore established a strict surveillance zone around her husband's room. She reigned as a despot in the house, which was subjected to her feminine espionage. She spent the entire day in the parlor adjoining his bedroom, where she could hear his faintest words and slightest movements. At night, she had a bed laid for her in the parlor, and she barely slept. The doctor was in full accord with her concerns: Her devotion seemed admirable. With a cunning natural to a schemer she managed to disguise her husband's revulsion for her and was so persuasive in feigning sorrow over it that she won a kind of fame. Some prudes even conceded that she was redeeming her sins. But constantly before her eyes loomed a vision of the poverty that lay in store for her upon the count's death if her presence of mind should flag for a moment. And so this woman, driven from the sickbed where her husband lay groaning, drew a magic circle around it. Distant from him and near to him, in disgrace and all-powerful, the apparently devoted wife lay in wait for death and fortune, like that insect that carves a spiral pit in soft earth and waits at the bottom for its doomed prey, listening for any falling grain of sand. Even the harshest critic couldn't refuse to acknowledge that the countess carried motherly concern to an extreme. People said her own father's death had been a lesson to her. She adored her children; she had kept the spectacle of her misdeeds hidden from them, and their young age allowed her to achieve her goal—to have them love her. She had given them the finest, the most brilliant education. I confess that I couldn't help but feel admiration and pity for this woman, and Gobseck still teases me about it. By then, the countess had come to acknowledge Maxime's low character, and with tears of blood she was repenting the sins of her past life. I do believe that. However odious the steps she took to regain her husband's wealth, were they not dictated by maternal love and by the desire to repair the wrongs she had done her children? Then, too, like many women who have suffered the storms of a passion, she may have felt the need to return to a virtuous life. Perhaps she only learned the price of that virtue when she came to gather the bitter harvest sown by her errors.

Each time young Ernest stepped out of his father's room, the countess put him through an inquisitorial interrogation about everything the count had said and done. The boy lent himself willingly to his mother's questions, which he attributed to loving concern, and he would reply with more than she even asked.

My visit was a sudden revelation for the countess; she saw me as the agent of the count's vengeful actions, and she determined I should not come near the dying man. Impelled by some dark foreboding, I was very anxious to talk with Monsieur de Restaud, for I was uneasy about the fate of the counter deed. If it fell into the countess's hands she could turn it to her own uses, and that would lead to endless lawsuits between her and Gobseck. I knew the moneylender well enough to be certain that he would never return the properties to the countess, and there were many complicated elements in the structure of these title transfers that only I could navigate. In hopes of heading off a horde of troubles, I went to see the countess a second time.

I have noticed, madame (Derville said to the viscountess as if confiding a secret), certain behaviors to which we pay too little attention in society. By nature I am an observer, and as I handle certain business matters where human passions come very sharply into play, I automatically bring an analytic eye to bear. Now, I often see, always with fresh surprise, that two adversaries more often than not sense one another's hidden motives and ideas. Between enemies, you sometimes find a similar lucidity of mind, the same sort of intellectual insight, as between lovers reading each other's soul.

So when the countess and I met this time, I suddenly understood the reason for her antipathy toward me, however well she concealed her feelings beneath her graceful civility and consideration: I had been forced on her as a confidant; I knew her secret, and it is impossible for a woman not to hate a man in whose presence she blushes. From her standpoint, she guessed that while I was the person in whom her husband had put his trust, he had not yet handed me his fortune. Our conversation, which I will spare you, I will always remember as one of the most dangerous struggles I have ever known. The countess, whom nature endowed with the qualities required for irresistible seduction, was in turn supple and proud, cajoling and confident; she even went so far as to try to pique my interest, to waken love in my heart, so as to dominate me. She failed. When I bade her good night I caught a look of hatred and fury that made me shudder. We parted enemies. She would have liked to annihilate me, and I . . . I felt pity for her, and to certain personalities that response is the cruelest insult. The same feelings colored my parting remarks. I believe I left her with a deep dread in her soul when I told her that however she went about matters, she was bound to lose everything.

"If I could meet with the count," I told her, "at least your children's well-being would—"

"I would be at your mercy," she cut in with revulsion.

Now that the issues were so frankly set out between us, I resolved to save that family from the destitution that lay ahead of them. I was determined even to commit legal improprieties if need be to accomplish my goal, and this is how I prepared for it: I brought suit against the Count de Restaud for moneys he supposedly owed to Gobseck, and I won a judgment. The countess naturally kept the outcome quiet, but I now had acquired the right to seal the premises immediately upon the count's death. I then bribed one of the house staff, who promised to come fetch me when his master was about to expire, even in the middle of the night, so that I could step in immediately, frighten the countess by threatening to seal her house, and thus salvage the counter deed. I later learned that the woman had been studying the civil code as she sat listening to the moans of her dying husband. What frightful images would be produced by the souls of people hovering around deathbeds, if only we could paint thoughts! And money is always the impelling motive for schemes being conceived, plans taking shape, plots being woven! But we can leave aside some of these details, which are fairly tedious in themselves, though they would offer some sense of the woman's miseries, and her husband's too, as well as a glimpse into the secrets of similar households.

For two months Count de Restaud, resigned to his fate, lay in bed, alone in his room. A fatal illness slowly enfeebled his body and spirit. In the grip of an invalid's bizarre imaginings, he refused to let his room be tidied and rejected any sort of care, even bed-making. This extreme apathy was imprinted on everything around him: The furniture in the room stood in disarray, dust and spiderwebs covered the most delicate objects. This previously elegant man, so fastidious in his refined tastes, was content now to fester in the sorry spectacle of that room where the mantelpiece, the desk, the chairs were piled with a jumble of sickroom objects: pillboxes empty or full, smeared flasks, scattered undergarments, cracked plates, an open warming pan on the hearth, a bathtub full of old mineral water. The sense of destruction spoke in every detail of this repellent chaos. Death had become apparent in objects before it invaded the person. The count could not bear daylight, so the window blinds were pulled shut and the darkness added still more to the gloom of the sad place. The invalid had grown very thin. His eyes still shone; life seemed to have taken its last refuge there. The livid whiteness of his face was horrible, and was made starker yet by the great length of his hair—he would not let it be cut and it hung in long flat hanks along his cheeks. He looked like a crazed desert hermit. Bitter sorrow had killed off all the natural human impulses in this man, barely fifty years old, a man the whole city had known as so brilliant, so blessed.

Early one morning in December 1824, he looked up at his son Ernest who was sitting at the foot of his bed gazing at him in sorrow. "Are you in pain, Father?" the young viscount asked.

"No!" the man replied with a frightening smile. "It is all here, and here around my heart!" He pointed to his head, then pressed his fleshless fingers to his bony chest, in a gesture that sent Ernest into tears.

"Maurice, why hasn't Monsieur Derville come to see me?" the count suddenly demanded of his manservant, who he believed was deeply attached to him but who was instead thoroughly caught up in the countess's interests. "What is this, Maurice!" cried the dying man. Abruptly he sat up in bed and seemed to have recovered all his presence of mind. "I've sent you to fetch my lawyer seven or eight times these past two weeks, and he's still not come. Do you think you can play games with me? Go find him right now, this minute, and bring him back. If you don't carry out my orders I will get up and go myself!"

"Madame," the servant said as he left the bedchamber, "you heard the count. What should I do?"

"Pretend to go to the attorney's office, then come back and tell monsieur that his counsel has gone forty leagues away on an important case. You can add that he is expected back at the end of the week."

To herself she thought, "Sick people are often deluded about their condition; he'll wait for the fellow to return." The doctor had declared the night before that the count was unlikely to live another day.

When the houseman returned two hours later and told his master the heartbreaking news, the dying man grew agitated. "Ah, my Lord! My Lord!" he kept repeating. "I trust in You alone!"

He gazed at his son for a long while, and finally, his voice grown still weaker, he said, "Ernest, my child, you are very young, but you have a good heart. I'm sure you understand that a promise to a dying man, to a father, is a sacred thing. Do you feel you could keep a secret, could bury it so deep inside yourself that even your mother would never suspect you are hiding something? My son, you are now the only one in this house who I can rely on. You won't betray my secret?"

"No, Father!"

"Well then, Ernest, in a few moments I will give you a sealed packet that belongs to Monsieur Derville. You must keep it safe in a way that no one will know you even have it. Then later you must slip out of the house and put it into the little mailbox at the end of the street."

"Yes, Father."

"Come kiss me. You will be making my death less bitter, my darling boy. In six or seven years, you'll understand the importance of this secret, and you will be well rewarded for your skill and loyalty today. You'll know then how much I love you. Leave me now for a moment, and keep absolutely everyone—no matter who—from coming in here."

Ernest left the bedchamber and found his mother standing in the salon. "Ernest," she said to him, "come here." She sat down and, taking her son between her knees and pressing him hard to her heart, she kissed him. "Ernest, your father just told you something."

"Yes, Mama."

"What did he tell you?"

"I may not repeat it, Mama."

"Oh, my darling boy," cried the countess, kissing him again with enthusiasm, "what pleasure it gives me to see how discreet you can be! Never lie, and always keep your word: Those are two principles you must never forget."

"How beautiful you are, Mama! You've never lied, not you! I'm sure you never have."

"There have been times, dear Ernest, when I lied. Yes, I have sometimes broken my word, in circumstances where all the laws break down. Listen, my Ernest—you are old enough, sensible enough, to see how your father drives me away from him, refuses to let me care for him, and that is not natural, for you know how much I love him."

"Yes, Mama."

"My poor child," the countess said, weeping, "this terrible situation comes from lying insinuations. Wicked people have tried their best to separate me from your father, for their own greed. They want to do us out of our money and take it for themselves. If your father were well, the discord between us would soon disappear, he would listen to me, and he is a good, loving man, so he would recognize his error. But his mind is disturbed, and his suspicions against me have hardened into a kind of madness—it stems from his sickness. His preference for you lately is another sign of his confusion: Before he fell ill you never felt that he loved Pauline and Georges any less than you. Everything is caprice with him now. This special attachment he feels for you could give him the idea of asking you to do special errands for him. If you don't want to ruin the family, my dear angel, if you don't want to see your mother begging for her bread one day like a pauper, you must tell her everything—"

"Ah, ah!" cried the count. He had flung open his door and now stood half naked on the sill, desiccated and fleshless as a skeleton. His strangled cry had a terrible effect on the countess; she sat frozen, as if struck dumb. Her husband was so fragile, so pale, that he seemed to emerge from the tomb.

"You have flooded my life with bitterness, and now you mean to trouble my death, twist my son's mind, make a vicious man of him!" he shouted hoarsely.

The countess ran and threw herself at the feet of this dying figure, who appeared even more ghastly from these final effusions of life, and she poured out a torrent of tears.

"Mercy! Have mercy!" she cried.

"Did you have mercy for me?" he asked. "I let you devour your own fortune, now you want to devour mine and leave my son with nothing!"

"Oh yes! Yes! Be pitiless toward me, be ruthless," she said, "but the children! Sentence your widow to a convent—I will obey, I will do anything you command me, to expiate my sins against you—but let the children live content! Oh, the children! The children!"

"I have only one child," retorted the count, stretching his fleshless arm in despair toward Ernest.

"Oh, pity me! I repent, repent!" cried the countess, embracing her husband's feet, damp with her tears. Her sobs choked her speech; broken, incoherent words rose from her burning throat.

"After what you said to Ernest, you dare talk about repentance!" said the dying man, knocking his wife back with a thrust of his foot. "You turn me to ice," he added in a unfeeling tone that was horrifying. "You were a bad daughter, you have been a bad wife, you will be a bad mother."

The unhappy woman collapsed in a faint. The dying man returned to his bed, lay down, and in a few hours lost consciousness. The priests came to administer the sacraments. At midnight he died. The events of the morning had exhausted the remains of his vitality.

I arrived at midnight with Papa Gobseck. Amid all the commotion, we walked directly into the small sitting room outside the death chamber and found the three children in tears, along with two priests who were to spend the night by the body. Ernest ran over to me and said that his mother wished to be alone in the count's room. "Do not go in!" he said, his tone and expression touching. "She is praying in there!"

Gobseck began to laugh, that silent laughter that is peculiarly his. I was too moved by the emotion that lit Ernest's young face to share the miser's irony. When the boy saw us move toward the door, he ran and flattened himself against it, shouting, "Mama, there are two men in black here looking for you!"

Gobseck lifted the boy away as if he were a feather and opened the door. What a spectacle lay before us! A horrid chaos reigned in the room. Her hair tumbling loose from desperation, her eyes glittering, the countess stood speechless amid clothing and papers and rags strewn everywhere, a disorder appalling to see here in the presence of a dead man. Scarcely had her husband expired than the countess forced open all the drawers and the secretary; the carpet was covered in debris, overturned furniture, and boxes broken apart—everywhere were the signs of her violent hands. Her search might at first have been fruitless, but her expression and excitement now made clear to me that in the end she had indeed found the mysterious papers. I looked over at the bed, and with my instincts honed by professional experience, I could guess what had happened. The count's body lay in the groove between the bed and the wall, almost crosswise, nose twisted into the mattress, the corpse left there disdainfully like one of the paper envelopes on the floor now that he was nothing more than an envelope himself. His limbs, inflexible, gave him a grotesque, hideous look. The dying man must have hidden the counter deed beneath his pillow, as if to protect it from any other hands until death. The countess had guessed her husband's intent, which could also be seen in his final gesture, the clutch of his crooked fingers. The pillow had been flung off the bed and the countess's footprint was still visible on it. Before her on the floor I saw a packet stamped in several places with the count's coat of arms. I snatched it up and saw it was addressed to me. I stared at the countess with the shrewd severity of a judge questioning a suspect. Flames on the grate were devouring the contents of the packet. Hearing us approach, the countess had flung the papers into the fire. From her hasty glance at the first paragraphs, where I had set out provisions for her children, she must have thought she would be destroying a will that was to strip them of their fortune. A tortured conscience, along with the instinctive terror that a crime stirs in those who commit it, had undone her capacity to think. Caught in the act, now she could probably see the scaffold looming ahead, feel the law's branding iron. Gasping for breath, staring at us with haggard eyes, the woman waited to hear our first words.

"Ah, madame," I said, as I pulled from the grate a bit of paper that the fire had not fully consumed, "you have ruined your children! Those papers were their titles to your husband's property."

Her mouth contorted as if she might have a stroke.

"Hee hee!" cried Gobseck, and his exclamation struck us like a metal candlestick scraping across marble. After a pause, the old man addressed me, his voice calm: "So—you would have the countess believe that I am not the lawful owner of the properties the count sold me? As of a moment ago, this house belongs to me."

The blow of a truncheon on my head would have hurt and shocked me less. The countess could see the look of confusion I turned on the usurer.

"Monsieur . . . monsieur!" she said, unable to find other words.

"You are a trustee of this property, are you not?" I asked him.

"Possibly."

"And you mean to take advantage of madame's crime?"

"Exactly."

I quit the room, leaving the countess seated by her husband's bed weeping hot tears. Gobseck followed me out. When we reached the street, I turned away from him, but he came after me. He gave me one of those deep looks that pierce straight into a man's heart and said, in his fluting voice, now with an acrid edge to it, "Do you presume to judge me, boy?"

Since that night we have scarcely seen one another. Gobseck leased out the count's Paris mansion; he spends his summers on the Restaud country estates, living the life of a lord, constructing farm buildings, restoring mills and roads, planting woods. One day I met him on a path in the Tuileries. "The countess is leading a heroic life," I told him. "She's devoted herself entirely to bringing up her children, and she has raised them beautifully. The eldest boy is a fine fellow."

"Possibly."

"But," I went on, "shouldn't you give Ernest some help?"

"Help him!" cried Gobseck. "No, no. Hardship is our greatest teacher, hardship will teach him the value of money, of men and of women. Let him navigate the Paris seas. When he has become a good pilot, we will give him a ship."

I left him without trying to make out the meaning of his remarks.

Madame de Restaud passed on her repugnance for me to her son, and the young count would never engage me as his legal counsel. Still, a week ago I visited Gobseck to tell him of Ernest's love for Mademoiselle Camille, and to urge him to fulfill his obligations, now that the youth is coming of age.

The old moneylender had long become bedridden, suffering from the disease that would eventually carry him off. He said he would postpone his response until he could be up and attending to business properly. Of course he was not eager to hand anything over as long as he still had a breath in him; there could be no other reason for such a delaying tactic. Finding him much sicker than he believed he was, I stayed with him long enough to make out the progress of a passion that had aged into a kind of insanity.

Wanting no one else to live in the house he inhabited, he had made himself the principal tenant and left all the other rooms empty. Nothing had been changed in the one where he dwelled. The furnishings I knew so well from sixteen years back might have been preserved under glass, they were so completely unchanged. His loyal old porteress, married to a retired soldier who tended the office whenever she went upstairs to care for the master, was still his housekeeper, his right hand, his receptionist, and now she also functioned as his nurse. Despite his weak condition, Gobseck still received his clients and his revenues himself, and had so simplified his affairs that he could send the old soldier out on the occasional errand and manage the business from bed.

When France formally recognized the Republic of Haiti, Gobseck's familiarity with the old estates in Santo Domingo and his knowledge about the colonists and their successors got him named to the commission to liquidate property and distribute compensation from the new Haitian government. His canniness led him to create an agency for discounting the credits due to the colonists or their heirs. The business operated under the names of Werbrust and Gigonnet. Gobseck shared in the profits without putting in capital, for his expertise counted as his investment. The agency was like a distillery steaming off profits from the ignorant, the credulous, or claimants whose rights might be contested. As liquidator, Gobseck was able to negotiate with the large landowners who, looking to obtain higher evaluations or quicker settlements and payouts, would send him gifts in proportion to the size of their business. The presents constituted a kind of tax on funds he did not wholly control. Furthermore, for a low price his firm gave him accounts involving small or dubious claims, and those of people who preferred immediate payment, however minimal, to the uncertainties of disbursements from the new republic.

So Gobseck was the insatiable boa constrictor of this huge enterprise. Every morning he would receive his tributes and eye them like an Indian nabob deciding whether to sign a pardon. He would take all sorts of payment, from some poor devil's basket of fresh game to pounds of wax candles collected by a thrifty churchgoer, from a rich man's silver dinner service to a speculator's golden snuffbox. No one knew what became of all these gifts to the old usurer; everything went into his house and nothing came out. "On my faith as an honest woman," said the concierge, who was my old acquaintance too, "I think he swallows it all down but without ever getting any fatter, for he's as shriveled and thin as the bird in my cuckoo clock."

Then last Monday Gobseck sent for me by the old soldier, who arrived at my office and said, "Come quick, Monsieur Derville, the old man is about to turn in his last bills. He's gone yellow as a lemon, he's impatient to talk to you; death is moving in and his last hiccup is already rattling in his gullet."

When I stepped into the room of the dying man, I surprised him on his knees before the hearth; no fire was burning, but there was an enormous cold mound of ashes. Gobseck had dragged himself across the room from his bed, but he lacked the strength to get back to it and lie down, as well as any voice to complain.

"My old friend," I said to him, lifting him up and helping him back to his bed, "you're cold—why don't you make a fire?"

"I am not cold," he said firmly. "No fire! No fire! I'm going, boy, where to I don't know," he went on, flashing me a last blank, untender glance. "But I am leaving here! I have carphologia," he said, using the term to show that his mind was still clear and precise. "I thought I saw real gold piled around my room, and I left the bed to take an armful of it. Who will it all go to? I won't give it to the government! I made a will—find it, Grotius. La Belle Hollandaise had a daughter; I saw her one night on rue Vivienne. I think they call her 'The Torpedo,' she's as pretty as a picture—look for her, will you, Grotius? You're the executor of my will. Take whatever you want from here— Eat up! there are pots of foie gras, sacks of coffee, sugars, gold spoons. Give your wife the Odiot dinner service . . . But the diamonds, who gets them? Do you take snuff, boy? I've got all kinds of tobaccos, sell them at Hamburg, they go for half again higher there. Look, I have some of everything, and I have to leave everything! . . . Oh, come now, Papa Gobseck!" he said scolding himself. "Stop being so weak—get hold of yourself!"

He sat straight up in his bed; his face stood out sharp against the pillow like a bronze, he stretched a withered arm and bony hand forward along his coverlet and gripped it as if to hold himself upright, looked over at the hearth, as cold as his metallic gaze, and died, his mind fully intact. To us—the concierge, the old soldier, and me—he looked the image of those alert old Romans that Lethière painted standing behind the consuls in his *Brutus Condemning His Sons to Death*.

"The old rascal had real nerve," said the veteran in his soldier's style. I could still hear the dying man's insane enumeration of his riches, and my gaze, which had followed his earlier, went again to the mound of ashes. I was struck by its size. I took the fire tongs and plunged them into the mound. I hit a mass of gold and silver, doubtless made up of the payments brought in during his last illness, which his feeble state had kept him from hiding away, or perhaps his mistrust from sending to the bank.

"Run and fetch the justice of the peace," I told the old soldier. "The premises must be sealed instantly!"

Recalling Gobseck's last words, and what the old woman had told me earlier, I took the keys to the rooms on the first and second floors and went to have a look inside. In the first room lay the full meaning of the talk I had thought was his mad ranting: Here was a harvest of a greed that lives on unchecked until all that's left is the mindless instinct we often see among hoarders in the provinces. In the room next to the one where Gobseck had died were rotted pâtés and masses of food of all sorts, even shellfish, fishes sprouting mold—the mix of stenches nearly choked me. Worms and insects crawled everywhere. The bounty more recently arrived was tangled together with boxes of all shapes, cases of tea, bales of coffee. On the chimneypiece in a silver tureen were notices of shipments arrived to his name at Le Havre for cotton bales, vats of sugar, casks of rum, coffees, indigo dyes, tobaccos, a whole bazaar of products from the colonies! The room was piled high with furniture, silverware, lamps, and paintings and vases and books, rolled canvases without frames, and all sorts of curios. That enormous quantity of valuables may not have come entirely as gifts; they might have been deposited with Gobseck as collateral and never redeemed. I saw jewel boxes marked with coats of arms or monograms, fine linens and costly weapons, none with labels. Opening a book I had thought was simply lying out of place, I found thousand-franc notes in it. I swore to myself that I would inspect every last thing, tap the floorboards, the ceiling panels, the moldings, and the walls to locate all the gold he so passionately lived for, this Dutchman worthy of Rembrandt's brush. In all my career in the law never have I seen such a spectacle of greed and eccentricity.

Returning to his room, I found on his desk the cause of all the cumulative jumble and piles of treasure: Beneath a paperweight lay a pile of correspondence between Gobseck and the merchants to whom he must have regularly sold his bounty. Now, either because these men had already been victims of Gobseck's shrewd dealings or because Gobseck was asking too high a price for his foodstuffs or his artifacts, every one of the transactions had somehow been broken off. He had not sold his food items back to Chevet because Chevet would only take them at a thirty percent discount; Gobseck haggled over a few francs difference and meanwhile the products spoiled. For his silver serving pieces, he refused to pay delivery charges. For his coffees, he would not guarantee against short weights. Each transaction gave rise to disputes that suggested early symptoms of an infantile behavior, an incomprehensible stubbornness that comes to all old men in whom a powerful passion persists longer than a coherent mind. I said to myself, as he had said to himself, "Who will all these riches go to?"

"With a mind to the bizarre information he gave me about his only relative, his sole heiress, I feel bound now to rummage into all the houses of ill repute in Paris just so that I can drop an immense fortune onto some loose woman. But most important, madame, you should understand this: Comte Ernest de Restaud will soon with all the legal formalities come into a fortune that would permit him to marry Mademoiselle Camille, as well as provide comfortable incomes and dowries to his mother, the Countess de Restaud, and to his brother and sister."

"Well, dear Derville, we shall consider it," replied Madame de Grandlieu. "Monsieur Ernest will have to be very rich for his mother to be accepted into a noble family. It is true, though, that Camille could arrange never to see her mother-in-law."

"Madame de Beauséant did receive Madame de Restaud," said the old uncle.

"Well—at very large receptions," retorted the viscountess.

Paris, January 1830
Translated by Linda Asher

THE DUCHESSE DE LANGEAIS

To Franz Liszt

I. SISTER THERESA

IN A SPANISH town on an island in the Mediterranean, there is a convent of Barefoot Carmelites where the rule of the order instituted by Saint Teresa has been preserved with all the primitive rigor of the reformation undertaken by that illustrious woman. Extraordinary as this may seem, it is nonetheless the truth. While the religious houses on the peninsula and on the Continent were almost all destroyed or overturned by the outbreaks of the French Revolution and the Napoleonic Wars, this island was constantly protected by the English fleet, its wealthy convent and peaceable inhabitants sheltered from the general havoc and plunder. The storms of every kind that shook the first fifteen years of the nineteenth century were broken on this rock off the coast of Andalusia. If rumors of the emperor's name reached this shore, it is doubtful that the holy sisters kneeling in this cloister would have comprehended his fabulous trail of glory and the flamboyant grandeur of his meteoric life. In the Catholic world's memory, this convent's unchanged discipline made it a preeminent refuge. And the purity of its rule attracted from the farthest points of Europe sad women whose souls, unfettered by human ties, yearned for this long suicide accomplished in the bosom of God. Furthermore, no convent was so well suited to the complete detachment from things here below required by the religious life.

Yet on the Continent a great number of these houses are magnificently adapted to their surroundings. Some are shrouded in the depths of the most solitary valleys, others suspended above the steepest mountains or cast at the edge of precipices. Everywhere man has sought the poetry of the infinite, the solemn awe of silence; everywhere he has striven to draw closer to God, seeking Him on the peaks, in the depths of chasms, at the cliff's edge, and found Him everywhere. Yet nowhere but on this rock, half European and half African, could you find so many harmonies that all converged to lift the soul, to leaven the most sorrowful memories, to dull their sting, to put life's sufferings into a deep bed.

This monastery was built at the far edge of the island, at the highest point of the rock, which some great global upheaval broke cleanly off on the seaward side, where from every direction it offered the sharp crags of its heights eaten away to the high-water mark but no less unscalable. Any attempt to reach this rock is made impossible by the dangerous reefs that stretch out to sea, where the shining waves of the Mediterranean play over them. Only from the sea, then, can you grasp the four wings of the square building whose form, height, and openings have been scrupulously prescribed by monastic law. From the town side, the church entirely masks the solid construction of the cloister, whose roofs are covered with broad tiles that make it invulnerable to wind, storms, and the action of the sun. Thanks to the generosity of a Spanish family, the church crowns the town. The bold, elegant façade gives a fine, imposing face to this small seaside town. Surely we all have a vision of a terrestrial idyll of a town, whose huddled roofs, nearly all placed like an amphitheater around a pretty port, are surmounted by a magnificent Gothic three-sided porch, campaniles, small bell towers, and filigreed spires. Religion dominating life, putting men continually in mind of its End and the Way, is a very Spanish image! Now throw this image into the Mediterranean, under a burning sky; add some palms, several stunted but evergreen trees mingling their moving fronds with the sculpted foliage of the motionless architecture; see the fringes of foam whitening the reefs in vivid contrast to the sapphire blue of the sea; now turn and admire the galleries, the terraces built above each house where the inhabitants come to take the evening air among the flowers, between the treetops in their little gardens. Then, in the port, a few sails. Finally, in the serenity of early evening, listen to the music of the organs, the chant of prayers, and the admirable sounds of the bells ringing out to sea. Everywhere noise and calm, but more often calm presides.

Inside, the church is divided into three dark and mysterious naves. The fury of the winds doubtless prevented the architect from constructing those flying buttresses that ornament cathedrals almost everywhere and separate the chapels; as a result the walls that flanked the two smaller naves and sustained this vessel shed no light. On the outside, these strong walls presented the view of their gray mass leaning on huge piers placed at intervals. Inside, the great nave and its two small side galleries were lit entirely by the rose window suspended by a miracle of art above the entry, whose favorable exposure had allowed the luxury of stone lacework and other beauties particular to the style improperly called Gothic.

The larger part of these three naves was left to the townsfolk, who came to hear the Mass and prayers. The choir stood behind a grille and a heavily pleated brown curtain, slightly open in the middle so that nothing of the choir could be seen but the officiating priest at the altar. The grille itself was separated at equal intervals by pillars that supported an interior organ loft and the organ. And this construction with its carved wooden exterior was in harmony with the small columns of the galleries supported by the pillars of the great nave. If a curious person were bold enough to climb the narrow balustrade of these galleries to see into the choir, he would see nothing but the tall, octagonal stained-glass windows placed in equal panels around the high altar.

At the time of the French expedition to Spain to restore King Ferdinand VII once more to his throne, and after the taking of Cádiz, a French general came to this island to enforce recognition of the royal government. He prolonged his stay in order to see this convent and to find a way to gain entry to it. The enterprise was certainly a delicate one. But a man of passion, a man whose life had been, as it were, one long series of poems in action and who had always lived novels instead of writing them, a man of acts above all was sure to be tempted by something so seemingly impossible. To open the doors to a convent of women by legal means? The pope or the archbishop would scarcely have allowed it. As for trickery or force, an indiscretion would surely cost him his position, his entire military career, and his goal as well. The Duc d'Angoulême was still in Spain, and of all the faults committed with impunity by a man in the generalissimo's favor, this alone would have found him pitiless. Our general had solicited this mission in order to satisfy private motives of curiosity, although never had curiosity been more desperate. But this final attempt was a matter of conscience. The house of these Carmelites on the island was the only Spanish convent that had baffled his search. During the crossing, which took less than an hour, he felt hope rise in his soul. Then, although he had seen nothing of the convent but its walls, although he had not yet glimpsed the nuns' robes but only heard the chants of the liturgy, he encountered beneath these walls and in those chants slight clues that justified his slender hope. Indeed, however slight these presentiments so bizarrely awakened, never was a human passion more vehemently excited than the general's curiosity at that moment. But there are no minor events when it comes to the heart. It magnifies everything: It weighs the fall of a fourteen-year empire and the fall of a woman's glove on the same scale, and the glove nearly always weighs more than the empire. Now here are the facts in all their prosaic simplicity. After the facts, emotions will follow.

One hour after the general had landed on the island, royal authority was reestablished. A few Spanish republicans, who had taken refuge there by night after the fall of Cádiz, were allowed by the general to charter a vessel and sail to London. There was, then, neither resistance nor reaction. But this insular little restoration could not take place without a Mass, which the two divisions under the general's command were obliged to attend. Now the general had hoped that at this Mass he might to be able to obtain some information on the nuns sequestered in the convent, one of whom was perhaps dearer to him than life itself and more precious than honor. But he had no notion of the strictness of the order of Barefoot Carmelites.

His hopes were at first cruelly dashed. The Mass was, in truth, celebrated with great ceremony. In deference to the solemnity of the occasion, the curtains that usually hid the choir were open to display the riches, the valuable paintings and shrines ornamented with precious stones, whose brilliance eclipsed the numerous gold and silver ex-votos attached by the sailors of the port to the columns of the grand nave. The nuns had all taken refuge in the organ loft. However, in spite of this first failure, during the Mass of thanksgiving, the most secretly thrilling drama that ever battered a man's heart was played out before him.

The sister who was playing the organ stirred such intense enthusiasm that none of the soldiers regretted having come to the service. They even found pleasure in it, and all the officers were enraptured. As for the general, he appeared to remain calm and cold. The feelings stirred in him as the sister played various pieces of music are among a small number of things whose expression is not permitted to speech and renders it impotent, but which, like death, God, and eternity can be appreciated only in a slim point of contact with humanity. By singular chance, the organ music seemed to belong to the school of Rossini, the composer who brings the most human passion into musical art and whose works will one day inspire a Homeric respect. Among the scores penned by this genius, the nun seemed especially to have studied his *Moses*, no doubt because it embodies the highest expression of sacred music. Perhaps these two spirits— the great, gloriously European composer, the other an unknown nun—had met in the intuition of the same poetry. This was the opinion of two officers, true dilettantes, who must have regretted missing the Theater Favart in Spain.

At last, during the Te Deum, no one could fail to recognize a French soul in the music's sudden change of character. Joy in the triumph of the Most Christian King surely touched this nun's heart. She was certainly a Frenchwoman. Soon this patriotic feeling burst forth, pouring like shafts of light from a dialogue of organs as the sister introduced variations with all the delicacy of Parisian taste, vaguely mingled with allusions to our loveliest national airs. Spanish fingers would not have put such warmth into this gracious tribute to the victorious armies of France, revealing the musician's nationality.

"We find France everywhere, it seems," said a soldier.

The general had left during the Te Deum; it had been impossible for him to listen. The musician's playing revealed to him a woman loved to intoxication, who had so deeply buried herself in the heart of religion and so carefully hidden herself from the eyes of the world that until now she had escaped the stubborn, ingenious searches made by men armed with great power and superior intelligence. The suspicion roused in the general's heart became a virtual certainty with the vague reminder of a deliciously melancholy air, "Fleuve du Tage." The woman he loved had often played this prelude to a French ballad in her Parisian boudoir, and here in the convent church the nun had just used it to express an exile's regrets in the midst of triumphant joy. A dreadful sensation! To hope for the resurrection of a lost love, to find it still lost, to catch a mysterious glimpse of it after five years of pent-up passion, inflamed and increased with every vain attempt to satisfy it!

Who has not at least once in his life turned everything upside down, his papers, his house, impatiently rummaged in his memory seeking a precious object, and felt the ineffable pleasure of finding it after a day or two consumed in vain search—after hoping, despairing, after spending the most intense irritations of the soul for this important trifle that nearly became a passion? Well, extend this kind of rage over five years; put a woman, a heart, love in place of this trifle; transport this passion to the loftiest realms of feeling. Then imagine an ardent man, a man with a lion's heart and a leonine mane, one of those men who imposes himself and inspires terror and awe in those who think of him! Perhaps you will understand, then, the general's abrupt exit during the Te Deum, just as the prelude of a ballad he had once heard with delight in a gilt-paneled boudoir began to vibrate beneath the nave of this seaside church.

He walked down the steep street that led to the church and stopped only when the rumbling of the organ no longer reached his ears. Able to think only of his love, whose volcanic eruption was burning his heart, the French general only knew that the Te Deum was over when the Spanish congregation came pouring out of the church. Feeling that his conduct or his attitude might have seemed ridiculous, he went back to take his place at the head of the cortege, telling the alcalde and the governor of the town that a sudden indisposition had obliged him to take the air. Then, in order to prolong his stay on the island, he thought to exploit this pretext tossed off at first so carelessly, and pleading that his indisposition had grown worse, he declined to preside at the banquet offered by the island's authorities to the French officers. He took to his bed and sent a message to the major general that temporary illness forced him to leave the colonel in command of the troops. Such a commonplace but credible ruse freed him from all responsibilities during the time necessary to carry out his plans. As a man who was in essence Catholic and monarchist, the general informed himself of the schedule of services and affected the greatest attachment to religious practices, a piety that surprised no one in Spain.

The very next day, during his soldiers' departure, the general went to the convent to hear vespers. He found the church deserted by the inhabitants who, despite their piety, had gone to the port to see the troops set sail. The Frenchman, happy to find himself alone in the church, took care to let the echoing arches ring out with the clanking of his spurs. He walked there noisily, he coughed, he spoke out loud to himself to inform the nuns, and especially the musician, that if the French troops had departed, one Frenchman remained. Was this singular notice heard and understood? The general thought so. At the Magnificat, the organ seemed to answer him through its airborne vibrations. The soul of the nun flew toward him on the wings of music and was transported in the movement of its sounds. The music burst forth in all its power and filled the church with warmth. This song of joy, consecrated by the sublime liturgy of Latin Christianity expressing the exaltation of the soul in the presence of the living God, became the utterance of a heart nearly frightened by its happiness in the presence of a mortal love. This love still endured and had come to trouble her from beyond the tomb, where these women buried themselves in order to be reborn as brides of Christ.

The organ is surely the grandest, the most daring, the most magnificent of all the instruments created by human genius. It is a whole orchestra, and a skillful hand can play it to express everything. Is it not in some sense a pedestal on which the soul pauses before launching into space while in its flight attempting to trace a thousand pictures, to paint life, to traverse the infinite that separates heaven and earth? The more a poet listens to its vast harmonies, the more he realizes that only the hundred voices of this earthly choir can conquer the distances between men kneeling at prayer and the God hidden in the dazzling rays of the sanctuary. Only the organ is an intermediary strong enough to bear humanity's prayers to heaven in their omnipotent modes, in their diverse melancholy, with the shades of their meditative ecstasy, with the impetuous burst of their repentance and the thousand imaginings of every belief. Yes, beneath these long arches, the melodies imagined by the genius of the sacred find unexpected grandeurs, which they nurture and strengthen. In the dim light, the deep silence, the chanting that alternates with the thunder of the organ weaves a veil for God, and through it his luminous attributes shine forth.

This wealth of sacred things seemed to be tossed like a drop of incense upon the frail altar of love that sits opposite the eternal throne of a jealous and vengeful God. Indeed, the joy of the nun did not have the quality of grandeur and gravity that ought to harmonize with the solemnities of the Magnificat. She enriched it with graceful developments whose different rhythms spoke of a human gladness. In its brilliant trills a soprano might try to express her love, and her songs fluttered like a bird near its nest. Then at moments she leaped back into the past, now to frolic, now to weep. Her changing mode had something disordered about it, like the agitation of the happy woman at her lover's return. At last, after the shifting flights of delirium and the marvelous effects of this imagined recognition, the speaking soul turned back on itself. Shifting from a major to a minor key, the musician was able to inform her listener of her present lot. Now she told him of her long melancholy, her lingering moral malady. How each day she deadened the senses, each night erased some thought, gradually reducing her heart to ashes. After several soft undulations, her music shaded into a color of profound sadness, and soon the echoes of sorrow spilled forth in torrents. Then all at once the high notes rang out in a concert of angelic voices, as if to announce to the lost but not forgotten lover that the reunion of their two souls would take place only in heaven—a touching hope! Then the Amen. No more joy or tears in the melodies, no melancholy or regrets. The Amen was a return to God; this last chord was deep, terrifyingly solemn. The musician deployed all the nun's black flowing crepe, and after the final thundering of the bass pipes, which made the listeners tremble to the roots of their hair, she seemed to plunge back into the tomb from which she had momentarily risen. When the vibrations slowly died away, it seemed that the church, luminous until this moment, once again entered a profound darkness.

The general had been caught up and swiftly transported by the flight of this powerful spirit, following it into the regions it had just traveled. He fully understood the images unleashed by this burning symphony, and for him the chords flew far away. For him, as for the sister, this poem was the future, the present, and the past. Music—even theater music—for tender and poetic souls, for suffering and wounded hearts, is surely a text they may develop at the whim of memories. If a musician has the heart of a poet, certainly it takes poetry and love to hear and understand great musical works. Religion, love, and music are the threefold expression of a single fact, the need for expansion that stirs every noble soul. And these three poetries ascend to God, who untangles all earthly emotions. This holy human Trinity must be part of the infinite grandeurs of God, whom we can only imagine surrounded by the fires of love, the golden rays of music, light, and harmony. Is He not the beginning and the end of our works?

The Frenchman understood that in this desert, on this rock surrounded by the sea, the nun had seized upon music as an expression
of all the passion that still consumed her. Had she made her love an
homage to God or was it the triumph of love over God? Questions
difficult to answer. But surely the general could not doubt that in
this dead heart of the world he had found a passion still burning as
fiercely as his own. Vespers done, he returned to the alcalde, with
whom he was lodged. At first he was still prey to a thousand pleasures that a long-postponed satisfaction, painfully sought, lavished
on him, and he could see nothing beyond it. He was still loved. Solitude had increased the love in her heart, just as his love had grown
stronger as he breached the successive obstacles this woman had set
between them. This flowering of the soul reached its natural end.
Then came the desire to see this woman again, to contend with God
for her, to carry her away—a daring scheme that pleased this audacious man. After the meal, he went to bed to avoid questions, to be
alone, and to think clearly, and he lay plunged in the deepest meditations until daybreak. He rose only to go to Mass. He went to the
church and sat near the grille, his forehead touching the curtain,
and he would have torn it open, but he was not alone: His host had
accompanied him out of politeness, and the least imprudence might
compromise the future of his passion, spoiling all his hopes.

The organ was heard, but it was not played by the same musician.
For the general, it was all colorless and cold. Had his mistress been
devastated by the same emotions that had nearly felled a strong
man's heart? Had she so fully shared and understood a loyal and desired love that she now lay dying in her small cell? While a thousand
thoughts of this kind baffled the Frenchman's mind, the voice of the
woman he adored rang out nearby and he recognized its clear tim-
bre. This voice, slightly altered by a trembling that modest timidity
gave to young girls, cut through the chant like a prima donna's
through the harmony of a finale. It shone like gold or silver thread in
a dark frieze.

Surely it was she! Ever the Parisienne, she had not shed her coquetry when she left behind the adornments of the social world for

the headband and stiff muslin of the Carmelites. After signaling her love the evening before through praises addressed to the Lord, now she seemed to say to her lover: "Yes, it is me, I am here, I still love you, but I am sheltered from love. You will hear me, my soul will enfold you, and I will remain beneath the brown shroud of this choir, from which no one can tear me away. You will not see me again."

"It really is her!" said the general to himself, raising his head, for at first he had been leaning on his hands, unable to bear the crushing emotion that surged like a whirlwind in his heart when that familiar voice vibrated under the arches, accompanied by the murmur of the waves. The storm was outside and calm prevailed inside the sanctuary. Still, that rich voice continued to deploy all its tender ways: It fell like a balm on the lover's burning heart, it blossomed in the air, which a man would want to breathe more deeply, filled with the exaltations of a soul's love expressed in the words of the prayer. The alcalde came to join his guest and, finding him dissolved in tears at the elevation chanted by the nun, led him back to his house. Surprised to encounter such devotion in a French military man, the magistrate invited the confessor of the convent to dine and informed the general, who took the greatest pleasure in this news. During supper the confessor was the object of the Frenchman's attentions, and his not entirely disinterested respect confirmed the Spaniards in their high regard for his piety. He solemnly inquired about the number of nuns, asked for details on the convent's endowments and its treasures as if he wished to engage the good old priest on subjects that most concerned him. He informed himself on the way of life these holy women led. Were they allowed to go out of the convent or to be seen?

"Señor," said the venerable ecclesiastic, "the rule is strict. Women cannot enter a convent of the order of Saint Bruno without permission from Our Holy Father. The same strict rule is followed here. It is impossible for a man to enter a convent of Barefoot Carmelites unless he is a priest and attached by the archbishop to the service of the House. None of the sisters leaves the convent. However, the great saint Mother Teresa often left her cell. The visitor or the mother superior alone can allow a nun, with the authorization of the arch-bishop, to see outsiders, especially in the case of illness. Now, we are one of the principal houses of the order, and consequently we have a mother superior at the convent. Among other foreigners, we have a Frenchwoman, Sister Theresa, who directs the music in the chapel."

"Ah!" answered the general, feigning surprise. "She must have been pleased by the military triumph of the House of Bourbon."

"I told them the reason for the Mass—they are all a little curi-ous."

"But Sister Theresa may have interests in France, perhaps she would like to know something about it, to ask for news?"

"I do not think so; she would have sought me out for such knowl-edge."

"As a compatriot, I would be very curious to see her . . . if this were possible, if the mother superior would consent, if—"

"At the grille, and even in the presence of the reverend mother, an interview would be impossible for anyone whatsoever. But strict as the mother is, as a favor to a liberator of the Catholic throne and our holy religion, the rule might be relaxed," said the confessor, blink-ing. "I will speak to her."

"How old is Sister Theresa?" asked the lover, who dared not ques-tion the priest about the nun's beauty.

"She has no age," answered the good man, with a simplicity that made the general shiver.

The next day, before siesta, the confessor came to inform the Frenchman that Sister Theresa and the mother consented to receive him before vespers at the grille of the parlor. After siesta, which the general spent pacing back and forth along the harbor in the heat of midday, the priest returned to find him and led him into the con-vent by way of a gallery that bordered a cemetery. Several fountains, many green trees, and the rows of arches provided a coolness in har-mony with the silence of the place. At the end of this long gallery, the priest led his companion into a room divided into two parts by a grille covered with a brown curtain. In the more or less public half of the space, where the confessor left the general, a wooden bench ran along the wall and several chairs, also of wood, were set near the grille. The ceiling consisted of exposed beams made of live oak without any decoration. Daylight came through two windows situated in the nuns' portion of the room, although this weak light, poorly reflected by dark wood, scarcely lit the large black Christ, the portrait of Saint Teresa, and a painting of the Virgin that hung on the gray walls of the parlor. The general's feelings, in spite of their violence, took on a melancholy tinge. He grew calm in this domestic calm. Something of the grandeur of the tomb took possession of him beneath these cool boards. Wasn't this the eternal silence of the tomb, its deep peace, its sense of the infinite? In addition, the cloister's quiet and fixed thought, thought that slips into the air, into the dim light, into everything although it is written nowhere, looms still larger in the imagination. That great phrase "Peace in the Lord" enters here into the soul of the least religious as a living force.

The monk's life is scarcely conceivable; man in a monastery seems weak: He is born to act, to accomplish a life of work, which he renounces in his cell. But what virile vigor and touching weakness in a convent of women! A man can be pushed by a thousand feelings to bury himself in monastic life, he throws himself into it as he would jump off a cliff. But a woman comes here led only by one feeling: not to denature herself but to marry God. You may ask the monks: Why did you not struggle? But isn't a woman's withdrawal from the world always a sublime struggle? In short, the general found this mute visiting room and this convent lost in the sea full of himself. Love seldom reaches solemnity, yet surely love still faithful in the bosom of God was something solemn and something more than a man had the right to hope for in the nineteenth century, given the prevailing customs. The infinite grandeurs of this situation were able to act on the general's mind, and he was indeed beyond any thought of politics, honors, Spain, Parisian society, and was able to rise to the heights of this glorious conclusion. Besides, what could be more truly tragic? How much feeling united the two lovers in the middle of the sea on a granite ledge, yet they were separated by an idea, by an unbridgeable barrier! Observe the man say to himself, "Will I triumph over

God in her heart?" A slight rustling sound made him tremble, and the brown curtain was drawn back.

In the light he saw a woman standing there whose face was hidden by the length of pleated veil on her head. Following the rule of the order, she was clothed in a robe whose color has become proverbial. The general could not see the nun's naked feet, which would have borne witness to her alarming thinness; however, despite the numerous folds of the coarse robe so entirely covering her body, he could see that tears, prayer, passion, and her solitary life had already wasted her.

A woman's icy hand, no doubt the mother superior's, held back the curtain. The general examined the necessary witness to this interview, met the dark and penetrating look of an aged nun, almost a hundred years old. But hers was a clear, youthful look that belied the numerous wrinkles by which the pale face of this woman was furrowed.

"Madame la duchesse," he ventured, his voice full of emotion, to the nun who stood with bowed head. "Does your companion understand French?"

"There is no duchess here," answered the nun. "You are in the presence of Sister Theresa. The woman you call my companion is my mother in God, my superior here below."

These words—so humbly spoken by the voice that had once been in harmony with the luxury and elegance of her surroundings, the queen of fashionable Paris whose lips had once pronounced the language so lightly, so mockingly—struck the general like a bolt of lightning.

"My holy mother speaks only Latin and Spanish," she added.

"I know neither one. My dear Antoinette, make my apologies to her."

Hearing her name gently spoken by a man who had been so hard on her in the past, the nun felt a vivid inner emotion betrayed by the slight quivering of her veil, on which the daylight fell directly.

"My brother," she said, bringing her sleeve up under her veil, perhaps to wipe her eyes, "my name is Sister Theresa..." Then she turned toward the mother superior and spoke in Spanish words that the general perfectly understood, for he knew enough to understand and perhaps also to speak. "My dear mother, this gentleman presents his respects and begs you to excuse him if he cannot pay them himself, but he knows neither of the two languages you speak ..."

The old woman bowed her head slowly, an expression of angelic sweetness, enhanced by the consciousness of her power and dignity.

"Do you know this gentleman?" the mother asked her with a penetrating look.

"Yes, my mother."

"Go back to your cell, my daughter!" said the mother superior in an imperious tone.

The general slipped quickly behind the curtain to prevent the terrible emotions that shook him from showing on his face, and in the shadows, he thought he could still see the mother superior's piercing eyes. He was afraid of this woman, mistress of the fragile and fleeting happiness that had cost him such efforts, and he was trembling, this man whom a triple row of cannon had never frightened. The duchess was walking toward the door, but she turned back. "My mother," she said, in a stunningly calm tone of voice, "this Frenchman is one of my brothers."

"Stay then, my daughter!" said the old woman after a pause.

This admirable sophistry revealed such love and regret that a man less stalwart than the general might have felt faint at such keen pleasure in the midst of great peril—and for him this was something entirely new. How precious, then, were words, looks, and gestures when love must baffle the eyes of the lynx, the claws of the tiger! Sister Theresa came back.

"You see, my brother, what I have dared to do only to speak with you for a moment of your salvation, of the prayers my soul addresses each day to heaven on your behalf. I am committing a mortal sin. I have lied. How many days of penance it will take to expiate this lie! But I will suffer for you. You do not know, my brother, what happiness it is to love in heaven, to confess your feelings when religion has purified them, transported them into the highest spheres so that we are permitted to look only at the soul. If the doctrine and spirit of the saint to whom we owe this asylum had not borne me far above earthly anguish and set me, although far below the sphere where she dwells but surely above this world, I would not have seen you again. But I can see you and hear your voice and stay calm—"

"Ah, Antoinette," cried the general interrupting these words. "Let me see you. I love you now as passionately, as madly, as you wanted me to love you."

"Do not call me Antoinette, I beg you. Memories of the past hurt me. You must see here only Sister Theresa, a creature trusting in divine mercy…" And she added after a pause: "Control yourself, my brother. Our mother would separate us pitilessly if your face betrayed earthly passions or if you allowed tears to fall from your eyes."

The general bowed his head as if to gather himself. When he raised his eyes to the grille, he saw between two bars the emaciated, pale, but still ardent face of the nun. Her complexion, formerly blooming with all the enchantment of youth, in which the happy contrast of matte white played with the colors of a Bengal rose, had taken on the warm tone of an earthenware bowl lit by a weak light from within. The beautiful head of hair, once this woman's pride, had been shorn. A bandeau cinched her forehead and enveloped her face. The austerities of this life had left dark, bruised circles around her eyes, which at moments still sent out feverish rays, their usual calm merely a veil. In brief, all that remained of this woman was her soul.

"Ah! You shall leave this tomb, you have become my very life! You belong to me and were not free to give yourself, even to God. Did you not promise me to sacrifice everything at my slightest demand? Perhaps now you will find me worthy of this promise when you learn what I have done for you. I have sought you across the world. For five years, you have been in my thoughts every moment, my sole occupation. My friends, very powerful friends, as you know, have helped me with all their might to search through every convent in France, Italy, Spain, Sicily, and America. My love burned brighter with every vain search; I often made long journeys on a false hope; I have spent my life and the strongest throbbing of my heart beneath the dark walls of many cloisters. I am not speaking to you about unlimited fidelity—what is that? Nothing compared to the infinite longings of my love. If your remorse has been sincere, you must not hesitate to follow me today."

"You forget that I am not free."

"The duke is dead," he answered quickly.

Sister Theresa blushed.

"May heaven be open to him," she said with vivid feeling. "He was generous to me. But I was not speaking of such ties. One of my sins was wanting to break them all, without scruple, for you."

"You are speaking of your vows," cried the general, frowning. "I did not think that anything weighed in your heart but your love. Yet have no doubts, Antoinette, I will obtain a writ from the Holy Father to absolve your vows. I will go to Rome, certainly, to beg all the powers on earth. And if God could come down from heaven, I—"

"Do not commit blasphemy."

"Do not worry about God! Oh, I would love you even more if you would breach these walls for me, if this very evening you would hurl yourself into a boat below the rocks. We would go and be happy together, somewhere at the end of the world! And with me at your side, you would come back to life and health, under the wings of love."

"You must not talk like that," Sister Theresa went on. "You do not know what you have become for me. I love you much more than I ever did. I pray to God every day for you, and I no longer see you with the body's eyes. If you knew, Armand, the happiness of being able to surrender without shame to a pure friendship watched over by God! You do not know how happy I am to pray for heaven's blessings on you. I never pray for myself: God will treat me according to His will. But even at the cost of my eternal life I would like to be sure that you are happy in this world, and that you will be happy in the next for all the centuries to come. My eternal life is all that wretchedness has left me to offer you. Now I am aged by tears, I am neither young nor beautiful; besides, you would have contempt for a nun who became a wife, whom no feeling, not even maternal love, would absolve...What can you say to outweigh the innumerable reflections accumulated in my heart for five years, thoughts that have changed it, hollowed it, withered it? I should have made a less sorrowful gift to God!"

"What can I say, my dear Antoinette! I can say that I love you, that the affection, the love, a true love, the joy of living in a heart wholly ours, entirely ours, without reservation, is so rare a thing and so difficult that I doubted you, that I made you endure the harshest trials. But today I love you with all my soul's strength...If you follow me away from here, I will hear no voice but yours, I will see no other face—"

"Silence, Armand! You are cutting short the only moment we will be allowed in each other's presence here below."

"Antoinette, will you follow me?"

"But I am not leaving you. I live in your heart, not through an interest in worldly pleasures, vanity, selfish joy; I live here for you, pale and withered, in the bosom of God! If He is just, you will be happy—"

"All that is nothing but words! Pale and withered? And what if I want you and can be happy only by having you? Will you always know your duties, then, in your lover's presence? Does he not come first in your heart? Earlier you preferred society, yourself, who knows what else; now, it is God, it is my salvation. In Sister Theresa I can still see the duchess, ignorant of the pleasures of love and still insensitive under the guise of feeling. You do not love me, you have never loved—"

"Ah, my brother—"

"You do not want to leave this tomb, you love my soul, you say? Ah well, you will lose it forever, this soul, I shall kill myself—"

"My mother," cried Sister Theresa in Spanish, "I lied to you, this man is my lover!"

The curtain fell instantly. The general, stupefied, scarcely heard the interior doors slam shut.

"Ah! She still loves me!" he cried to himself, understanding the sublimity in the nun's cry. "She must be carried away from here..."

The general left the island, returned to headquarters, asked for leave—citing reasons of poor health—and returned promptly to France.

Here now is the adventure that lay behind the situation of the two persons in this scene.

2. LOVE IN A FASHIONABLE PARISH

What is called in France the Faubourg Saint-Germain is neither a quarter of Paris nor a sect nor an institution, nor anything that can be precisely defined. There are great houses in the Place Royale, the Faubourg Saint-Honoré, and the Chaussée d'Antin where people breathe the same air as in the Faubourg Saint-Germain. So the Faubourg is not entirely within the Faubourg. People born far from its influence can feel it and are attracted to this world, while certain others who are born there can be forever banished from it. For approximately forty years now, the manners, speech, in brief the tradition of the Faubourg Saint-Germain in Paris has played the role formerly taken by the court; the Hôtel Saint Paul did the same in the fourteenth century, the Louvre in the fifteenth, the Palace, the Hôtel Rambouillet, the Place Royale in the sixteenth, then Versailles in the seventeenth and the eighteenth centuries.

In every period of history, the Paris of the upper class and the nobility has had its center, just as the people's Paris always has its own. This periodic phenomenon offers ample reflection to those who would observe or depict the various social zones, and perhaps any inquiry into the causes of this centralization not only justifies the character of this episode but also serves serious interests, more pressing in the future than in the present, unless experience is as meaningless for the political parties as it is for the young.

In every era, the great lords, and rich people who will always ape the great lords, have kept their houses far from the more crowded parts of town. When the Duc d'Uzès, under the reign of Louis XIV, built his beautiful residence and put a fountain at the door on rue

Montmartre—an act of benevolence that made him, in addition to his virtues, the object of such popular veneration that the entire quarter followed his funeral cortege en masse—this corner of Paris was deserted. But as soon as the fortifications came down and the marshes beyond the boulevards were filled with houses, the d'Uzès family left this fine residence, which is occupied in our day by a banker. Then the nobility, out of their element in the midst of shops, abandoned the Place Royale and the center of Paris, and crossed the river in order to breathe at their ease in the Faubourg Saint-Germain, where palaces had already risen around the private residence built by Louis XIV for the Duc du Maine, this favorite among the bastards whom he legitimated. For people accustomed to the splendors of life, is there indeed anything more unseemly than the tumult, the mud, the shouting, the bad smells and narrow streets of the populous quarters? The habits of a trade or manufacturing district are completely at odds with the customs of the great. Commerce and Labor retire to bed just as the aristocracy is about to dine; the shopkeepers and artisans come noisily to life when the nobility and the wealthy have gone to sleep. Their calculations never coincide—the lower classes count their receipts, the nobility spare no expense. As a result, customs and manners are diametrically opposed.

No contempt is implied by this observation. An aristocracy is in a way the intellect of a society, just as the bourgeoisie and the proletariat are its organism and action. It follows that these forces are differently situated, and from their antagonism comes a seeming antipathy produced by the performance of different functions—all, however, for the common good. This social discord is so logically the outcome of every constitutional charter that any liberal inclined to complain about it as an attack against the sublime ideas under which ambitious members of the inferior classes conceal their designs, would find it highly ridiculous for Monsieur le Prince de Montmorency to live on rue Saint-Martin, at the corner of the street that bears his name, or for Monsieur le Duc de Fitz James, descendant of the royal Scots race, to have his private mansion on rue Marie Stuart, at the corner of rue Montorgueil. *Sint ut sunt, aut non sint*— "Let them be what they are, or let them not be"—these fine pontifical words can serve as a motto for the great of every country.

This social fact is obvious in every era and always accepted by the people; its reasons of state are self-evident: It is at once an effect and a cause, a principle and a law. The common sense of the masses never deserts them except when people of bad faith arouse them. This common sense rests on verities of a general order, as true in Moscow as in London, as true in Geneva as in Calcutta. Everywhere you find families of unequal fortune within a given space, you will see them form classes—patricians first, then the upper classes, and so on below them. Equality may be a *right*, but no power on earth is capable of converting it into a *fact*. It would enhance the happiness of France to popularize this thought. The benefits of political harmony are still obvious to the least intelligent masses. Harmony is the poetry of order. And order, reduced to its simplest expression, is the agreement of things: Unity, isn't that the simplest expression of order? Architecture, music, poetry, everything in France, more than in any other country, is based on this principle; it is inscribed on the foundation of its clear, pure language, and the native tongue will always be the most infallible index of a nation. You see its people, moreover, adopting the most poetic, modulated melodies; attracted to the simplest ideas; preferring supremely thoughtful, incisive motifs. France is the only country where some small phrase could bring about a great revolution. The masses have never rebelled except to bring men, things, and principles into harmony. No other nation has a better idea of the unity that should rule aristocratic life, perhaps because no other has better understood political necessity: History will never find her behindhand. France has often been mistaken, like a woman led astray by generous ideas, by a warmth of enthusiasm that may initially overtake calculation.

So to begin with, the most striking feature of the Faubourg Saint-Germain is the splendor of its mansions, its great gardens and their quiet, once upon a time in keeping with the princely fortunes drawn from its great estates. And this space between one class and the entire capital is but a material embodiment of the distances between ways of life that are bound to keep them apart. The head has its designated place in all creations. If by chance a nation allows its head to fall at its feet, sooner or later it is sure to discover that it has committed suicide. As nations do not want to die, they set to work at once to refashion a head. If they lack the strength for this, they perish, as did Rome, Venice, and so many others.

The distinction between the upper and lower circles of social activity introduced by their different ways of life necessarily implies that among the leading aristocracy, there is real capital value. In any state, under whatever form of government, when the patricians fail to maintain their complete superiority, they weaken and are soon overthrown by the people. The people always want to see money, power, and initiative in their leaders' hands, hearts, and heads: Their province is speech, intelligence, and glory. Without this triple power, all privilege collapses. Nations, like women, love force in those who rule them, and their love does not flourish without respect; they will not grant their obedience to someone who does not impose himself. An aristocracy fallen into contempt is like a lazy king or a husband in apron strings; it is a nullity on its way to nonexistence.

So the separation of the great, their separate way of life, in brief, the general customs of the patrician caste is at once a sign of real power and the reason for its death as soon as that power is lost. The Faubourg Saint-Germain let itself be laid low, temporarily, for refusing to recognize the obligations of its existence when it was still easy to perpetuate. It should have had the good faith to see in time, as the English aristocracy did, that the institutions have critical turning points—words no longer have the same meaning, ideas take on another guise, and the forms of political life are totally transformed without their foundations being deeply altered. These ideas demand further development, which forms an essential part of this story. They are given here as a definition of causes and an explanation of facts.

The grandeur of the aristocratic châteaus and palaces, the luxury of their details, the unstinting sumptuousness of the furnishings, the *atmosphere* in which the fortunate owner, born to riches, blithely and confidently moves; the habit of never stooping to calculate the trivial interests of daily existence, the leisure, the higher education required at an early age; in brief, the patrician traditions that give him social powers that his adversaries scarcely offset by their tenacious studies—these things should all lift the spirit of the man who possesses such privileges at an early age and stamp on his character that self-respect whose least consequence is a nobility of heart in harmony with the noble name he bears. This is true for some families. Here and there in the Faubourg Saint-Germain, you encounter persons of fine character, but they are clear exceptions to the rule of general egotism that has caused the ruin of this world apart. These privileges are the birthright of the French aristocracy, as they are of every patrician flowering formed on the surface of nations so long as their existence is based on the *estate*. The landed estate, like the financial estate, is the only solid foundation of an organized society. But the patricians hold these many advantages only to the extent that they maintain the conditions in which the people grant them. There is a kind of moral fiefdom whose *tenure* assumes service rendered to the sovereign, and here in France today the sovereign is surely the people. Times have changed, as have weapons. The knight banneret formerly wore a chain-mail tunic and a halberd, could skillfully handle a lance and show his pennant, and that was enough. Today he must prove his intelligence, and while in the old days, all he needed was a great heart, in our day he must have a good head as well. Skill, knowledge, and capital form the social triangle on which the escutcheon of power is inscribed, and it forms the basis of the modern aristocracy today.

A fine theory is as good as a great name. The Rothschilds, those modern Fuggers of the nineteenth century, are princes of deed. A great artist is really an oligarch; he represents an entire century and almost always becomes a law to others. Thus the art of the word, the high-pressure machinery of the writer, the genius of the poet, the merchant's constancy, the willpower of the statesman that concentrates a thousand dazzling qualities, the general's sword—the aristocratic class must have a monopoly today on these personal conquests made by a single man over a whole society in order to impose himself, as it formerly had a monopoly on material force. To remain at the head of a country, it must always be worthy of leading it, of being its mind and soul in order to direct its hands. How do you lead a people without having the powers to command? What would the marshal's baton be without the captain's innate power to wield it? The Faubourg Saint-Germain played with batons, believing that they were power itself. It reversed the terms of the proposition that called it into existence. Instead of throwing away the insignia that offended people and quietly retaining its power, it allowed the bourgeoisie to seize authority, clung fatally to its insignia, and constantly forgot the laws that its numerical weakness decreed. An aristocracy whose numbers scarcely constitute a small fraction of a society must today, as yesterday, multiply its means of action in order to counterbalance the weight of the popular masses in times of great crisis. In our days, those means of action must be real force and not historical memories.

The nobility in France, unfortunately still so inflated with its former vanished power, faced a kind of presumption against it, which made it difficult to defend itself. Perhaps this is a national defect. The Frenchman is less likely than other men to lower himself, moving only from the step where he finds himself to the next one up. He rarely laments the unhappiness of those over whom he has raised himself, but he always moans to see so much happiness above him. Though he may have a great heart, too often he prefers to listen to his mind. This national instinct pushes the French forward, this vanity wastes their fortunes and rules them as absolutely as the principle of thrift rules the Dutch. It has dominated the nobility for three centuries, which in this respect was preeminently French. The man of the Faubourg Saint-German, observing his material superiority, always concluded that he also possessed superior intellect. Everyone in France confirmed him in this belief, for ever since the establishment of the Faubourg Saint-Germain, the aristocratic revolution that began on the day when the monarchy left Versailles, the Faubourg Saint-Germain has always, with a few exceptions, depended on the power that in France must be based more or less in Faubourg Saint-Germain—hence its defeat in 1830.

In that period, it was like an army operating without a base. It had failed to take advantage of the peace to implant itself in the heart of the nation. It sinned through a lack of education and a total blindness to its larger interests. A certain future was sacrificed to a doubtful present. Perhaps this blunder in policy may be attributed to the following cause. The physical and moral distance that the nobility so keenly maintained between itself and the rest of the nation has had fatal results during the past forty years: sustaining personal feeling by killing caste patriotism. When the French nobility of former times was rich and powerful, gentlemen knew how to choose their leaders in moments of danger and to obey them. As their power waned, they grew undisciplined; and, as in the last days of the Roman Empire, every man wanted to be emperor. Regarding themselves as all equally weak, they believed they were all equally strong. Every family ruined by the Revolution, ruined by laws abolishing the right of primogeniture and forcing them to share their wealth equally among their offspring, thought only of itself instead of the larger family of the nobility. And it seemed to them that if each individual grew rich, the party would be strong. A mistake. Money, too, is merely an outward sign of power. All these families were made up of people who preserved the high traditions of refined manners, true elegance, fine language, noble restraint, and pride in harmony with the life they led; a life filled with petty occupations that become trivial when they are no longer merely accessories but become the center of life. There was a certain intrinsic merit in these families but this was strictly on the surface, leaving them merely a nominal value.

None of these families had the courage to ask themselves: Are we strong enough to wield power? They grabbed at power as the lawyers did in 1830. Instead of acting the protector, like a great man, the Faubourg Saint-Germain was as greedy as an upstart. When the most intelligent nation in the world understood that the restored nobility had organized power and the budget to its own profit, it fell mortally ill. The nobility wanted to be an aristocracy when it could only be an oligarchy, two very different systems, which anyone who is clever enough will understand by reading attentively the patronymics of the lords of the Upper House. Of course, the royal government had good intentions, but it constantly forgot that it owed everything to the people, even its happiness, and that France, that capricious woman, must be happy or beaten at whim. If there were more like the Duc de Laval, whose modesty made him worthy of his name, the throne of the elder branch would have been as secure as the House of Hanover today. In 1814, but especially in 1820, the French nobility had to rule over the most enlightened epoch, the most aristocratic bourgeoisie, and the most female country in the world. The Faubourg Saint-Germain could easily have led and amused a middle class in love with art and science and drunk with distinctions. But the petty leaders of this great intellectual era all hated art and science. They did not even know how to present religion in the poetic colors that would have endeared it to the people, although they needed its support. When Lamartine, Lamennais, Montalembert, and several other writers of talent were renewing or expanding religious ideas, gilding them with poetry, those men who were ruining the government made the bitterness of religion felt. Never was a nation more complacent, like an exhausted woman who becomes an easy one; never did power stumble more clumsily; France and woman prefer lapses from virtue.

If the nobility meant to establish a great oligarchical government, the Faubourg should have searched within its ranks for the coin of Napoleon, turned itself inside out to find a constitutional Richelieu. If this genius was not among its members, it should have sought him as far as the cold garret where he might lie dying, and it should have assimilated him, just as the English House of Lords constantly assimilates the chance aristocrat. Then they should have ordered this man to be ruthless, to chop off the dead wood, to prune the aristocratic tree. But in the first place, the great system of English Toryism was too large for small minds and to import it required too much time, for in France tardy success is no better than a fiasco. Besides, far from adopting a policy of redemption and seeking force where God has put it, these petty greats hated any capacity that did not issue from them; in brief, instead of being rejuvenated, the Faubourg Saint-Germain grew aged.

Etiquette, the other most crucial but secondary institution, might have been maintained if it had been kept for great occasions, but it became a daily battle, and instead of being a matter of art or ceremony, it became a marker of power. If from the outset the throne lacked a councillor equal to the circumstances, the aristocracy above all lacked the knowledge of its general interests, an instinct that might have made up for any deficiency. It balked at the marriage of Monsieur de Talleyrand, the only man who had one of those anvil minds in which new political systems are forged and nations gloriously revived. The Faubourg mocked ministers who were not gentlemen and did not provide gentlemen superior enough to be ministers. It could have rendered real service to the country by ennobling justices of the peace, by fertilizing the soil, by constructing roads and canals, by making itself an active territorial power, but it sold its lands to play the stock exchange. The Faubourg might have raided the bourgeoisie of its men of action and talent, whose ambition only undermined its authority, by opening its ranks to them. Instead, it preferred to fight them, unarmed, for tradition was all it had left of the reality it formerly possessed. To its misfortune, the nobility retained just enough of its former wealth to sustain its arrogance. Content with its memories, none of these families seriously thought to urge its older sons to take up arms, which the nineteenth century tossed so plentifully into the public square. The youth, excluded from political life, danced at Madame's while they should have been in Paris, working under the influence of young, conscientious talents, innocents of the Empire and the Republic, work that the head of each family should have begun in their administrative counties. There they might have won back the recognition of their titles by unremitting pleas in favor of local interests, by conforming to the spirit of the century, by reshaping the caste system to suit the taste of the times.

But gathered in its Faubourg Saint-Germain, where the spirit of ancient feudal conflicts and the former court lived on, the aristocracy was not at ease in the Tuileries and so was even easier to conquer in one place, in the Upper House, poorly organized as it was. Woven into the fabric of the countryside, it would have become indestructible; driven into its Faubourg, its back to the Château, or spread over the budget, one blow was enough to break the thread of its sputtering life, and the homely face of a small-time lawyer came forward to wield the ax. In spite of Monsieur Royer-Collard's admirable speeches, the hereditary peerage and its system fell under the lampoons of a man who boasted of having saved a few heads from the guillotine but who clumsily killed great institutions. Here we find examples and lessons for the future. If the French oligarchy hadn't had a future, it would be wretched cruelty to torture it after its demise; thoughts would turn only to its sarcophagus. Even though the surgeon's scalpel cuts deep, it sometimes gives the dying back their life. The Faubourg Saint-Germain could find that if it wants to have a leader and a system, it may be more powerful persecuted than it was triumphant.

Now it is easy to summarize this semipolitical aperçu. The nobility's lack of broader perspectives and its mass of small defects; everyone's blinkered desire to reestablish great wealth; a serious need for religion to sustain policy—all combined with a thirst for pleasure that tainted the religious spirit and spawned hypocrisy. The partial resistance of some loftier and clearer-thinking minds opposed the court rivalries, and the provincial nobility, often of a purer strain than the court nobility, was too often insulted and became disaffected: All of these causes merged to make the Faubourg Saint-Germain internally at odds. It was neither compact in its organization nor consequential in its acts, neither completely moral nor frankly dissolute, neither corrupt nor corrupting; it would neither wholly abandon its harmful practices nor adopt ideas that would have saved it. In short, however moronic a few persons might be, the party itself was nonetheless armed with all the great principles that constitute the life of nations. Then what did it take to make it lose its strength? It made difficulties in choosing those to be presented at court. The Faubourg had good taste, elegant disdain, but its fall was surely nothing very startling or chivalrous. The emigration of 1789 still exhibited some feeling; in 1830, the internal immigration exhibited nothing but interests. A few famous men of letters, a few oratorical triumphs at the speaker's platform, Monsieur de Talleyrand in the congress of Vienna, the conquest of Algeria, and several names that again became historic on the battlefields showed the French aristocracy the ways they could still participate in national life and once again win recognition of their titles, if it deigned to do so. The work of internal harmony prevails among living organisms. When a man is lazy, the laziness is revealed in everything he does. Similarly, the nature of a class of men is clearly written on its face, on the soul that animates the body.

Under the Restoration, the woman of the Faubourg Saint-Germain displayed neither the proud boldness of the former court ladies even in their lapses nor the modest grandeur of the belated virtues by which they expiated their sins and shed such brightness around them. There was nothing very frivolous or very serious about this woman. Her passions, with a few exceptions, were hypocritical; she compromised, as it were, with her pleasures. Several of these noble families led the bourgeois life of the Duchesse d'Orléans, whose marriage bed was so ridiculously displayed to visitors of the Palais Royal. At the most, two or three kept up the licentious customs of the Regency, inspiring a sort of disgust in cleverer women. This grand dame of the new school had no influence on the manners of the times, but she still could do much; as a last resort she could have offered the dignified spectacle of the women of the English aristocracy, but she foolishly hesitated among the old traditions, became necessarily devout, and concealed everything, even her finer qualities.

None of these Frenchwomen could create a salon in which society's leaders might take lessons in taste and elegance. Their voices, which formerly ruled in literature—that vivid expression of societies—now counted for nothing. When a literature has no general system, it fails to create a corpus and dies out with its century. When a people in any era is thus separately constituted in the midst of a nation, the historian almost always finds a central figure who embodies the virtues and vices of the group to which it belongs: for instance, Coligny among the Huguenots, Cardinal de Retz during the Fronde, Marshal de Richelieu under Louis XV, Danton during the Terror. This match between a man and his historical moment is in the nature of things. To lead a party in any era a man needs to be in agreement with its ideas, to shine in his time he must represent its ideas. The wise and prudent head of parties is always obliged to bow to the prejudices and follies of its following, and this is the cause of actions for which he later incurs the reproach of certain historians who sit removed from the terrible popular ferment, coldly judging the passions most crucial to the conduct of great secular struggles. And if this is true in the historical drama of the centuries, it is equally true in the more restricted sphere of disconnected scenes of the national drama called "The Manners of the Age."

At the beginning of the ephemeral life led by the Faubourg Saint-Germain during the Restoration, and to which, if there is any truth in the above reflections, it could give no stability, there was for a time a woman who was the most perfect type of her caste: at once strong and weak, great and petty. She was a woman artificially educated but in reality ignorant, full of lofty feelings but lacking any thought to coordinate them. She squandered the richest treasures of her soul in obedience to convention, ready to brave society but hesitant and in the end artificial in bowing to her scruples. She had more willfulness than character, was more impressionable than enthusiastic, with more head than heart, supremely woman, supremely coquette, and above all Parisian. This woman loved spectacle and celebration, was unreflective or reflective too late, of an imprudence verging on the poetic, ravishingly insolent but deeply humble. Like a very straight reed she had a certain strength, but like that reed she was ready to bend under a powerful hand. She spoke a great deal about religion but disliked it, and yet she was ready to accept it as a forgone conclusion. How can we explain such a complex creature, capable of heroism and forgetting to be heroic for the sake of back-biting; young and sweet-natured, not so much old at heart as aged by the maxims of those around her, schooled in their egotistical phi-losophy without any practice, with all the vices of a courtesan and all the nobility of an adolescent girl? She trusted nothing and no one, yet at times she allowed herself to believe in everything.

How could such a portrait of this woman be anything but incom-plete, a woman in whom the play of shifting hues clashed yet produced a poetic confusion, for there was in her a divine light, a radiance of youth that gave these muddled traits a kind of whole-ness. In her, grace served as unity. Nothing was feigned. Those pas-sions, that vague desire for greatness, the actual pettiness, the cool sentiments and warm impulses were natural and spontaneous, as much the result of her own situation as of the aristocracy to which she belonged. She knew she was all alone and set herself proudly above the social world, sheltered by her name. There was something like the egotism of Medea in her life, as in the life of the aristocracy that lay dying and refused to sit up or hold out its hand to any po-litical physician, to touch or to be touched. It felt so weak, conscious that it was already dust.

The Duchesse de Langeais, for that was her name, had been mar-ried for about four years when the Restoration was fully installed in 1816. By that time the uprising of the Hundred Days had enlight-ened Louis XVIII, who understood his situation and his century, in spite of his entourage. These courtiers nevertheless triumphed over this Louis XI lacking his battle-ax when he was felled by illness. The Duchesse de Langeais, a Navarreins by birth, came from a ducal family that from the time of Louis XIV had made it a principle never to abdicate its title through marriage. The daughters of this house were bound sooner or later to have, like their mother, a place at court. At the age of eighteen, Antoinette de Navarreins came out of the protected retreat where she had lived in order to marry the Duc de Langeais's elder son. The two families at this time were living far from the fashionable world, but the invasion of France allowed the Royalists to assume the return of the Bourbons as the sole conceivable conclusion possible to the miseries of the war. The Ducs de Navarreins and de Langeais, ever faithful to the exiled Bourbons, had nobly resisted all the temptations of imperial glory. And under the circumstances, they naturally followed the old family policy, and Mademoiselle Antoinette de Navarreins, beautiful and poor, was married to Monsieur le Marquis de Langeais only a few months before his father's death.

Upon the return of the Bourbons, the two families resumed their rank, their responsibilities, and their functions at court, and entered once again into the social whirl from which until then they had held themselves aloof. They became the most dazzling stars of this new political world. In that era of cowardice and sham conversions, the public consciousness was pleased to recognize in these two families their spotless fidelity, the consistency between private life and political character to which all parties reflexively render homage. But through a misfortune rather common in a time of transition, the most disinterested persons whose lofty views and wise principles would have gained France's confidence in the generosity of bold, new policies were turned away from affairs of state, and these fell into the hands of people interested in furthering extreme principles in order to give proof of their devotion. The Langeais and Navarreins families remained in the highest circle of the court, condemned to fulfill the obligations of etiquette amid the reproaches and mockeries of the Liberals. They were accused of gorging themselves on honors and wealth while their family estates grew no larger, and liberal allowances from the civil list were consumed as the expense of representation necessary to keep up every European monarchy, even a republican one.

In 1818, Monsieur le Duc de Langeais was in command of a military division, and the duchess, who was under the protection of a princess, had a place that authorized her, free of scandal, to remain in Paris far from her husband. The duke, in addition to his appointment, had a responsibility at court, where he came during leave, passing his command to an aide-de-camp. So the duke and the duchess lived entirely apart, in fact and in feeling, unbeknownst to the world. This marriage of convenience shared the usual fate of these family alliances. Two more antipathetic dispositions could not have been brought together; secretly they hurt each other's feelings, were secretly wounded, and went their separate ways. Each one then obeyed his nature, along with appearances. The Duc de Langeais, with a mind as methodical as the Chevalier de Folard himself, methodically surrendered to his tastes, to his pleasures, and left his wife free to follow hers, once he recognized in her an eminently proud spirit, a cold heart, a tendency to submit to the customs of the social world, a youthful loyalty that was bound to stay pure under the watchful eyes of great relatives, in the bright light of a prudish and bigoted court.

So the duke calmly played the grand seigneur of the previous century, abandoning to her own devices a twenty-two-year-old injured woman who had as part of her character one dreadful quality: She never forgave an injury when all her female vanities, her self-love, perhaps her virtues as well had been misunderstood and secretly wounded. When an outrage is public, a woman likes to forget it, she has opportunities to behave generously, she is womanly in her clemency. But women never pardon a secret offense because they despise secret cowardice, secret virtues, and secret loves.

Such was the position, unknown to society, in which Madame la Duchesse de Langeais found herself, without much reflecting on it, during the celebrations given on the occasion of the Duc de Berry's marriage. At this moment, the court and the Faubourg Saint-Germain roused themselves from their apathy and reserve. This was the true beginning of an unexpected splendor, which the government of the Restoration indulged to excess. At that time, the Duchesse de Langeais, whether out of calculation or vanity, never appeared in society without being surrounded or accompanied by three or four women equally distinguished by their name and fortune. As queen of fashion, the duchess had her ladies-in-waiting, who modeled their manners and wit on hers. She had chosen them cleverly from among several women who were as yet neither part of the court's inner circle nor at the heart of the Faubourg Saint-Germain, yet had the ambition to be so, simple angels of the second order who wished to rise within the neighborhood of the throne and mingle with the seraphic powers of the upper sphere known as *le petit château*. In this setting, the Duchesse de Langeais was stronger, more dominant and secure. Her ladies defended her against scandal and helped her to play the detestable part of the woman of fashion. She could toy with men and their passions, gather the praise that nourishes every feminine nature, and yet remain her own mistress.

In Paris among the loftiest company a woman is still a woman; she lives on incense, adulation, and honors. No genuine beauty, no admirable face is anything if it is not admired: Flattery and a lover are the proofs of her power. And what is power without recognition? Nothing. Imagine the prettiest woman alone in the corner of a salon—she would be sadness itself. When one of these creatures finds herself at the center of social glory, she wants to reign over all hearts, often because she cannot be the happy sovereign of one. That finery, that frippery, that style were all meant to please the poorest creatures you could meet, the mindless fops whose pretty face is their only merit, for whom all women would throw themselves away. These gilded wooden idols of the Restoration, with a few exceptions, had neither the antecedents of the petits-maîtres at the time of the Fronde nor the wit and manners of their grandfathers, yet they wished to be effortlessly something similar. They were brave, like all young Frenchmen, capable if they were put to the test, yet under the reign of worn-out old men they were kept on a leash. This was a cold, petty era, lacking all poetry. Perhaps it takes a long time for a restoration to become a monarchy.

For eighteen months, the Duchesse de Langeais had led this empty life, exclusively filled with balls, visits after the ball, objectless triumphs, ephemeral passions that are born and die in the course of an evening. When she entered a salon, all eyes turned toward her; she harvested flattering words and several passionate expressions, which she encouraged by gesture or glance but never allowed to go more than skin deep. Her tone, her manners, everything about her was authoritative. She lived in a sort of fever of vanity and perpetual enjoyment that deafened her. She was daring enough in conversation, she would listen to anything, depraved, as it were, to the surface of her heart. Yet upon returning home, she often blushed at what had made her laugh, at some scandalous story that supplied the details used to discuss theories of love she knew nothing about. Complaisant hypocrites commented to her on the subtle distinctions of modern passion—for women say everything among themselves, and more of them are ruined by each other than are corrupted by men. There was a moment, however, when the duchess understood that until a woman is loved, the world fails to recognize her beauty and wit. What did a husband prove? Simply that a young girl or a woman had a generous dowry or was well brought up, had a clever mother or satisfied the man's ambitions. But a lover constantly bears witness to her personal perfections. So Madame de Langeais learned while still young that a woman could be loved without being complicit, without proving it, giving pleasure only by the most meager displays of love. And there was more than one saintly hypocrite who showed her how to act out these dangerous dramas.

So the duchess had her court, and the number of those who adored her or courted her guaranteed her virtue. She was flirtatious, friendly, and charming until the end of the ball or the party, then the curtain dropped, and she found herself once again alone, cold, carefree, and ready to revive the following evening for more, equally superficial sensations. There were two or three utterly deceived young men who truly loved her and whom she mocked with perfect callousness. She said to herself, "I am loved, he loves me!" This certainty was enough. Like the miser satisfied to know that his whims might be granted, perhaps she did not go even as far as desire.

One evening she was at the home of one of her close friends, Madame la Vicomtesse de Fontaine, one of her humble rivals who cordially despised her and accompanied her everywhere. In such a barbed friendship, in which each one mistrusts the other and never disarms, confidences are cleverly discreet and not infrequently treacherous. After distributing small protective, fond, or disdainful greetings with the air natural to a woman who knew the worth of her smiles, her eyes fell on a man who was a total stranger but whose broad and serious aspect startled her. On seeing him, she felt something almost like dread.

"My dear," she said, turning to Madame de Maufrigneuse, "who is that newcomer?"

"A man you've heard of, no doubt: the Marquis de Montriveau."

"Ah! Is it he?"

She took her lorgnon and examined him quite impertinently, as she might have done a portrait meant to receive glances but not return them.

"Introduce me to him, then, he must be amusing."

"No one is more dull and serious, my dear, but he is all the fashion."

Monsieur Armand de Montriveau was at that moment the unwitting object of general curiosity and deserved it more than any of those fleeting idols Paris seems to need and adores for a few days in order to satisfy its periodic passion for infatuation and factitious enthusiasm. Armand de Montriveau was the only son of General Montriveau, one of those former aristocrats who served the Republic nobly and who perished at Joubert's side at Novi. The orphan had been placed under Bonaparte's orders at the school of Chalons, with several other sons of generals who died on the field of battle, under the protection of the French republic. Armand de Montriveau left this school without any sort of fortune, entered the artillery corps, and was still merely a major heading up a battalion at the time of the Fontainebleau disaster. In his branch of the service there was little opportunity for advancement. First of all, there are fewer officers than in other corps of the army; in the second place, the artillery was decidedly Liberal, not to say Republican, the emperor's fears inspired by a group of highly educated, thoughtful men, set against the military fortune of the majority among them. And contrary to usual practice, the officers who gained the status of generals were not always the most remarkable members of the army but rather mediocrities who inspired little fear. The artillery consisted of a separate unit within the army and belonged to Napoleon only on the fields of battle.

In addition to these general reasons, others inherent in Montriveau's person and his character might account for the slow progress of his career. Alone in the world, thrown from the age of twenty into this whirlwind of men that surrounded Napoleon, he had no interest outside himself and prepared to perish each day. Armand de Montriveau grew used to living only by his own moral compass and the consciousness that he had done his duty. Like all shy men, he was usually silent, but his shyness came by no means from a lack of courage; it was a kind of modesty that forbade any vain display. There was no arrogance in his intrepid conduct on the battlefield; he surveyed everything, could calmly give good advice to his comrades and lead them into a hail of bullets, crouching to avoid being hit. He was good, but his expression led one to imagine that he was haughty and severe. With a mathematical rigor in all things, he permitted no deviation from duty nor shirking the consequences of a deed. He never engaged in anything shameful and never asked anything for himself. In short, Armand de Montriveau was one of those great unknown men, philosophical enough to be skeptical of glory, living without much attachment to life because they have not found a way to develop the full extent of their strength or their feelings.

Montriveau was feared, admired, but hardly loved.

Men certainly allow you to rise above them, but they never forgive you for not descending to their level. Thus their feeling toward loftier natures is not unmixed with hatred and fear. Too much honor is, in their eyes, a tacit censure of themselves, something they forgive neither the living nor the dead.

After the farewells at Fontainebleau, Montriveau, however noble and titled, was put on half pay. His old-fashioned probity alarmed the War Ministry, where his attachment to vows made to the Imperial Eagle were well known. During the Hundred Days he was named colonel of the guard and left on the field of Waterloo. Retained in Belgium by his wounds, he was not part of the army of the

Loire, but the royal government would not recognize the promotions made during the Hundred Days, and Armand de Montriveau left France. Led by his enterprising spirit—that loftiness of thought previously satisfied by the hazards of war—and driven by his instinctive rectitude for projects of great utility, General Montriveau embarked on a plan to explore Upper Egypt and the unknown parts of Africa, especially the countries of central Africa, which excite so much interest among scholars today. His scientific expedition was long and unhappy. He had collected precious notes meant to resolve certain geographical or commercial problems so ardently sought in our times, and he had arrived, not without surmounting many obstacles, at the heart of Africa when treason delivered him into the hands of a savage tribe. He was stripped of everything, bound into slavery, and dragged for two years through the deserts, threatened with death at every turn and more mistreated than an animal at the whim of pitiless children. His physical strength and his mind's constancy allowed him to bear all the horrors of his captivity, but his miraculous escape nearly exhausted all his energy. He reached the French colony of Senegal half dead, in tatters, and with nothing but vague memories. The great sacrifices of his journey, the study of African dialects, his discoveries and observations were all lost. A single fact will reveal all his sufferings. During several days, the children of the sheik of the tribe that had enslaved him amused themselves by playing a game that consisted of throwing the small bones of a horse from as far as possible to hit his head and make them stay on it. Montriveau returned to Paris toward the middle of 1818, a ruined man, without protectors, indifferent to society. He would sooner have died twenty times over than ask for favors, even the recognition of his legitimate claims. Adversity and hardship had developed his energy even in small things, and the habit of preserving his self-respect in the face of that moral entity we call conscience led him to put a price on the most seemingly trivial acts. However, his merits and adventures became known through his acquaintance with the principal Parisian men of science and several informed military men. The details of his captivity and the incidents of his journey bore witness to such sangfroid, intelligence, and courage that he won without knowing it that transitory celebrity the salons of Paris lavish but for which artists who would perpetuate it must exert untold efforts. Around the end of this year, his position suddenly changed. From poor, he became rich, or at least he had all the external trappings of wealth. The royal government, seeking to attract men of merit to strengthen the army, at the time made several concessions to certain former officers whose known loyalty and character offered guarantees of fidelity. Monsieur de Montriveau was reinstated in the officer's corps, his rank of colonel restored; he received his back pay and was admitted into the Royal Guard. These favors, one after another, came to the Marquis de Montriveau though he had never made the slightest request. Friends had done for him what he would have refused to do for himself. Then, contrary to his habits, which were suddenly modified, he went out into society. There he was well received and met with testimonies of admiration on all sides. He seemed to have found some conclusion to his life, but with him everything happened within, there were no external signs. In society he was serious and composed, silent and cold. He had great social success precisely because he was such a contrast to the mass of conventional faces that furnished the salons of Paris, where he was, in effect, something quite new. His speech was concise, like the language of solitary people or savages. His shyness passed for arrogance and was highly pleasing. He was something strange and fine, and women were all the more taken with this original character since he escaped their clever flatteries, the circles they ran around the most powerful men, softening the most unbending spirits. Monsieur de Montriveau understood nothing of this petty Parisian monkey business, and his nature could answer only to the deep vibrations of fine feelings. He might have been promptly dropped without the poetry of his adventures and his life, without the admirers who sung his praises behind his back, without the triumph of self-regard that awaited any woman whom he courted.

The Duchesse de Langeais's curiosity about this man was as lively as it was natural. By chance, her interest in him had been piqued the evening before when she heard the story of one of Monsieur de Montriveau's travel adventures that made the most stirring impression on a woman's lively imagination. During an excursion to find the sources of the Nile, Monsieur de Montriveau had an argument with one of his guides that was surely the most extraordinary debate known in the annals of travel. He had to cross a desert and could go only on foot to the place he wanted to explore. One guide alone was capable of leading him there; no traveler before him had been able to penetrate this part of the country, where the intrepid officer hoped to find the solution to several scientific problems. In spite of his guide's warning and those of several old men of the region, he decided to undertake this terrible journey.

Gathering all his courage, already sharpened by the warning of ghastly difficulties ahead, he set out the next morning. After walking for an entire day on shifting ground that seemed to slip beneath him at every step, he experienced an unfamiliar fatigue and slept that evening on the sand. He knew that he would have to get up and on his way by dawn the following day, but his guide had promised him that toward midday they would reach their journey's end. This promise gave him courage and revived his strength, and in spite of his sufferings he continued on his way, cursing science under his breath. But he was ashamed to complain in front of his guide and kept his troubles to himself. After walking a third of the day, his strength failing and his feet bloodied by the march, he asked the guide if they would soon arrive. "In one hour," the guide told him. Armand found an hour's worth of strength in himself and continued on. The hour passed without his notice but the horizon remained the same, a horizon of sand as vast as the middle of the ocean, with no palm trees or mountains whose crests ought to have announced the end of his journey. He stopped, threatened the guide, and refused to go farther, reproaching the guide for murdering him, for tricking him; then tears of rage and fatigue rolled down his inflamed cheeks; he was bowed down by the recurrent pain of the march, and his throat felt parched by the desert thirst. The guide, standing quite still, listened to his complaints with an ironic expression while studying, with the seeming indifference of Orientals, the imperceptible random shifts of that almost blackish sand, like darkened gold. "I was mistaken," he remarked coldly. "It's been too long since I came this way. We are certainly on the right track but it will take another two hours." "This man is right," thought Monsieur de Montriveau.

So he continued on his way with some difficulty, following the pitiless African, as if he were bound by a thread to the guide, like a condemned man invisibly bound to his executioner. But two hours passed, the Frenchman spent his last drops of energy, and the horizon remained unsullied—he saw neither palm trees nor mountains. He could neither cry nor groan and simply lay down in the sand to die. But his look would have appalled the most intrepid man and seemed to announce that he would not die alone. His guide, like a real demon, answered him with a calm glance, full of power, and left him stretched out, taking care to keep his distance so as to escape his victim's despair. Finally, Monsieur de Montriveau found the strength for a last curse. The guide approached him, silenced him with a sign and a steady look, and said, "In spite of our warnings, you wanted to go where I am leading you, did you not? You reproach me for tricking you. If I had not done that, you would not have come this far. You want the truth, here it is. We still have another five hours' march, and we can no longer turn back. Search the depths of your heart, and if you do not have courage enough, here is my dagger." Surprised by this terrifying understanding of human suffering and strength, Monsieur de Montriveau would not be less than a barbarian, and drawing a new measure of courage from his pride as a European, he rose up to follow his guide. The five hours passed. Monsieur de Montriveau still saw nothing ahead and turned a failing eye toward his guide, but then the Nubian hoisted him onto his shoulders and showed him, a hundred paces away, a pool surrounded by greenery and an admirable forest, illuminated in the fires of the setting sun. They were now some distance from a huge granite ledge that hid this sublime landscape as if in a shroud. Armand felt reborn, and his guide, that giant of intelligence and courage, finished his labor of devotion by carrying him across the hot, polished paths scarcely traced on the granite. On one side he saw the hell of burning sand and on the other the earthly paradise of the most beautiful oasis in these deserts.

The duchess, already struck by the appearance of this romantic figure, was even more impressed when she learned that this was the Marquis de Montriveau whom she had dreamed of during the night. She had been with him in the burning desert sands, he had been her nightmare's companion: For such a woman, was this not a delicious foretaste of a new amusement in her life? Never was a man's character better reflected in his face, and no one could be more intriguing in his appearance alone. His head, large and square, was notable chiefly for his luxurious and abundant black hair, which framed his face in a way reminiscent of General Kléber. The resemblance continued in the vigor of his forehead, in the cut of his features, in the calm audacity of his eyes, and a kind of fiery vehemence expressed by his prominent features. He was short, with a broad chest, and muscular as a lion. There was something imposing, even despotic in his bearing, his movement, his slightest gesture—he projected an ineffable confidence in his strength. He seemed to know that nothing could oppose his will, perhaps because he wanted nothing but what was right. Nonetheless, like all truly strong people, his speech was soft, his manners simple, and he was naturally kind. Yet all these fine qualities seemed to disappear in grave circumstances when a man had to be implacable in his feelings, firm in his resolutions, terrible in his actions. A close observer could have seen a habitual movement at the corner of his mouth, something that betrayed his penchant for irony.

The Duchesse de Langeais, knowing the fleeting glory to be won by such a conquest, resolved in the brief time the Duchesse de Maufrigneuse took to introduce them to make Monsieur de Montriveau one of her lovers, set him above all others, attach him to her person, and use all her wiles to do so. This was a fantasy, a pure duchess's caprice, the sort used by Calderón or by Lope de Vega in *The Gardener's Dog*. She would not permit this man to belong to another woman, but she had no intention of belonging to him. The Duchesse de Langeais had been endowed by nature to play the coquette, and her education had perfected this endowment. Women envied her and men fell in love with her for good reason. Her every quality was meant to inspire love, to justify it, and to perpetuate it. Her sort of beauty, her manners, her speech, her bearing—all matched her talent for a natural coquetry that in a woman seems to be her consciousness of power. She was graceful and perhaps exaggerated her movements with too much complacency, the one affectation for which she might have been reproached. Everything about her was harmonious, from her slightest gesture, to her particular turns of phrase, to the deceptive innocence of her glance. Her most striking feature was her elegant nobility, which was not compromised by her very French vivacity. This incessantly changing manner was prodigiously attractive to men. She would be the most delicious mistress when removing her corset and the paraphernalia of her performance. Indeed, all the joys of love were surely budding in the freedom of her expressive looks, in the tender tones of her voice, in the grace of her words. All these gestures implied that within her there was a noble courtesan whom the duchess's religion tried in vain to deny.

You might be seated near her during a soiree and find her by turns gay and melancholy, and both moods would seem genuine. She knew how to be gracious or disdainful, impertinent or confiding. She seemed good and was. In her situation, nothing forced her to descend to meanness. But her mood was changeable, first pliable then wily, easily moved then so hard and dry it would break your heart. But to depict her accurately there would be no need to invoke all the extremes of a feminine nature. In short, she was what she wanted to be or to appear to be. Her face was slightly too long, but it had grace, something fine and thin that recalled the faces in medieval portraits. Her complexion was pale, slightly pink. Everything about her erred, as it were, by an excess of delicacy.

Monsieur de Montriveau was pleased to be introduced to the Duchesse de Langeais, who, following the habit of persons whose exquisite taste leads them to avoid banalities, made her welcome him without an avalanche of questions or compliments but with a sort of respectful grace that surely flattered a superior man, for superiority in a man assumes a bit of tact that allows women to understand all sorts of feelings. If the duchess showed any curiosity it was through her look; her manners conveyed any compliments; and she deployed that caressing speech and refined desire to please which she could display better than any of her rivals. Yet all her conversation was in some way merely the body of the letter; there should have been a postscript in which the chief thought was still to come. When, after half an hour of trivial chitchat whose accent and smiles alone gave value to the words, Monsieur de Montriveau was about to retire discreetly when the duchess retained him with an expressive gesture.

"Monsieur," she said to him, "I do not know whether the few moments in which I have had the pleasure of chatting with you have proved attractive enough to allow me to invite you to pay me a visit—I'm afraid that it may be selfish to wish to have you all to myself. If I should be so fortunate that it would please you to call, you would find me at home every evening until ten o'clock."

This invitation was offered in such a charming way that Monsieur de Montriveau could not refuse it. When he hurried back to the groups of men gathered at a distance from the women, several of his friends congratulated him, half seriously, half teasingly, on the extraordinary welcome extended to him by the Duchesse de Langeais. This difficult and brilliant conquest was decisively achieved, and its glory had been reserved for the artillery of the guard. It is easy to imagine the pleasantries, good and bad, which the topic provoked in one of those Parisian salons so eager for such amusement, where mockeries are so brief that everyone hastens to take full advantage while they are still fresh.

The general felt unwittingly flattered by these inane remarks. From his vantage point, his eyes were drawn to the duchess by a thousand vague reflections. And he could not help admitting to himself that of all the women whose beauty had captivated him, none had offered him a more delicious expression of faults and virtues, harmonies the most juvenile imagination could want in a French mistress. What man, in any rank of life, has not felt in his soul an indefinable pleasure in a woman he has chosen, even dreamed of as his own, who embodies the triple moral, physical, and social perfections that allow him to see in her the satisfaction of all his wishes? If this is not a cause of love, this flattering combination is surely one of its greatest inducements. Love would be an invalid, said a profound moralist of the last century, were it not for vanity. For men and for women there is surely a wealth of pleasure in the superiority of the beloved. Is it not a great deal, if not everything, to know that they will never bruise our self-regard? That our beloved is so noble that a contemptuous glance will never wound her? Rich enough to be surrounded by a radiance equal to the splendors in which even the ephemeral kings of finance wrap themselves? Intelligent enough never to be humiliated by a good joke, and beautiful enough to be the rival of all her sex? These are thoughts a man has in the blink of an eye. But if the woman who inspires them introduces him at the same time, in the future of his precocious passion, to the shifting delights of grace, the innocence of a virgin soul, the thousand folds of a coquette's dress, the perils of love—would these qualities fail to move the coldest man's heart?

This was indeed Monsieur de Montriveau's situation at the present moment with regard to the duchess, and his past life in some way explained this bizarre fact. Tossed as a youth into the hurricane of the Napoleonic Wars, he had lived his life on battlefields, and he knew about women only what a hurried traveler knows about a country as he goes from inn to inn. The marquis might have said of his own years what Voltaire used to say at eighty: He had thirty-seven follies to regret. At his age, he was as new to love as a young man who has just read *Faublas* in secret. He knew everything about women but nothing about love, and his virginity of feeling made his desires entirely new.

Just as Monsieur de Montriveau had been absorbed by the course of war and the events of his life, some men are absorbed by the labors to which poverty or ambition, art or science have condemned them, and they are familiar with this singular situation, although they rarely admit it. In Paris, all men are supposed to have been in love. No woman wants what another woman has rejected. In France, fear of being taken for a fool is the source of a general tendency to lie, since no Frenchman can be taken for a fool. At this moment, Monsieur de Montriveau was gripped both by violent desire, a desire accumulated in the desert heat, and by a movement of the heart whose burning grip he had not known before. As strong as he was violent, this man knew how to control his emotions, but even as he chatted about meaningless things, he retreated into himself and swore to possess this woman, for this was the only way he could enter into love. His desire became a vow made in the manner of the Arabs with whom he had lived, and for them, a vow is a contract with destiny. The success of the enterprise consecrated by their vow is crucial, and they count even their death as merely a means to that success. A younger man would have said, "I should certainly like to have the Duchesse de Langeais for my mistress!" or "Anyone loved by the Duchesse de Langeais will be a very lucky rascal!" But the general said to himself, "I will have Madame de Langeais for my mistress." When a man with a virginal heart, for whom love becomes a religion, takes such an idea into his head, he does not know that he has just set foot into hell.

Monsieur de Montriveau abruptly left the salon and returned home, consumed by the first fevers of love he had ever felt. At around middle age, if a man still retains the beliefs, the illusions, the frankness, the impetuousness of childhood, his first impulse is, as it were, to reach out his hand and grab what he desires. Then once he has gauged the nearly impossible distance he must cross, he is overcome by a sort of childish astonishment or impatience, which reinforces the value of the coveted object and causes him to tremble or weep. So the next day, after the stormiest reflections that had ever racked his soul, Armand de Montriveau discovered he was under the yoke of his senses, made even heavier by a true love. This woman, treated so cavalierly the evening before, had become by the following day the holiest, most dreaded of powers. From that time forward she was his world and his life. The memory of the slightest emotions she had stirred in him was now his greatest joy, and his deepest sorrows paled beside it. The most violent revolutions only trouble a man's interests while passion overturns his feelings. And for those who live more by feeling than by interest, for those who have more soul and blood than mind and lymph, a real love produces a total change of existence. With a single line, through a single reflection, Armand de Montriveau thus erased all his past life. After asking himself twenty times, like a child, "Will I go? Won't I go?," he dressed, went to the Hôtel de Langeais at around eight o'clock in the evening, and was admitted. He was to see the woman—no, not the woman, the idol he had seen the evening before, in the light, like a fresh and pure young girl dressed in gauze, lace, and veiling. He arrived impetuously to declare his love for her, as if he were firing the first cannon shot on the battlefield.

Poor novice! He found his ethereal sylph wrapped in a brown cashmere peignoir, cunningly frilled, languidly reclining on the divan in a dimly lit boudoir. Madame de Langeais did not even rise, she lifted only her head, her tousled hair held back in a veil. Then the duchess made a sign to him to take a seat, gesturing with her hand which, in the shadows produced by the trembling light of a single, distant candle, seemed to Montriveau's eyes as white as a hand made of marble. And with a voice as soft as the candlelight, she said to him, "If it had not been you, monsieur le marquis, if it had been a friend with whom I could be frank or someone indifferent to me who was only of slight interest, I would have sent you away. You see me suffering terribly."

Armand said to himself, "I will go."

"But," she went on, giving him a piercing glance, which the simple warrior attributed to the heat of fever, "I do not know whether it was a presentiment of your kind visit, for whose promptness I am only too conscious, but for a moment now I felt my head somewhat clear of its vapors."

"So I can stay," Montriveau said to her.

"Oh, I would be so sorry to see you leave. I was saying to myself only this morning that I must not have made the slightest impression on you, and that you had doubtless taken my invitation for one of those banal remarks Parisian women scatter at random. And I forgave your ingratitude in advance. A man who comes in from the deserts cannot be expected to know how exclusive we are in our friendships in the Faubourg."

These gracious, half-murmured words fell one by one, as if they were laden with the joyful feeling that seemed to dictate them. The duchess wanted to have all the benefits of her migraine, and her speculation was successful. The poor soldier was truly suffering from this lady's pretended suffering. Like Crillon hearing the story of Jesus Christ, he was ready to draw his sword against the vapors. Ah, how could a man dare to speak to this suffering woman of the love she inspired? Armand already understood that he was ridiculous to fire off his love point-blank at such a superior woman. He understood in a single thought all the delicacies of feeling and demands of the soul. To love—what is this but to know how to plead, to beg, to wait? Feeling such love, did he not need to prove it? He found his tongue paralyzed, frozen by the conventions of the noble Faubourg, by the majesty of the migraine, and by the shyness of true love. But no power in the world could veil the look in his eyes, which burst with warmth, the endless vastness of the desert—eyes as calm as those of panthers that rarely blinked. She adored this fixed look that bathed her in light and love.

"Madame la duchesse," he answered, "I fear I am clumsy in expressing my gratitude for your inspiring kindnesses. At this moment I wish for only one thing, the power to relieve your suffering."

"Allow me to take this off, I feel too warm now," she said, gracefully tossing aside the cushion that was covering her bare feet.

"Madame, in Asia your feet would be worth nearly ten thousand sequins."

"A traveler's compliment," she said, smiling.

This witty woman took pleasure in casting the rough Montriveau into a conversation full of silliness, commonplaces, and nonsense, as Prince Charles might have done in battle with Napoleon. She took mischievous amusement in seeing the extent of this budding passion displayed by the number of foolish words drawn from this novice, whom she led little by little into a hopeless maze where she wished to leave him ashamed of himself. So she began by mocking this man, though it pleased her to make him forget the passage of time. The length of a first visit is often a compliment, but Armand was not informed of this. The famous traveler was in this boudoir for an hour, chatting about everything, saying nothing, feeling that he was merely an instrument being played upon by this woman, when she rose, sat down again, put the veil she had worn on her head around her neck, leaned on her elbow, did him the honor of a complete cure, and rang for someone to light the candles in her boudoir. Her absolute inaction was followed by the most graceful movements. She turned toward Monsieur de Montriveau and told him, in response to a confidence she had just drawn from him and which seemed of vivid interest to her, "You want to make fun of me by trying to make me think that you have never loved before. This is the great pretense of men with us. We believe them. Out of pure politeness! Do we not know what to expect of it ourselves? Where is the man who has not fallen in love at least once in his life? But you like to deceive us, and we allow you to do so, poor fools that we are, because your deceptions are still homage paid to the superiority of our feelings, which are all purity."

These last words were spoken with a proud disdain that made this novice lover feel like a ball tossed to the bottom of a chasm, while the duchess was an angel soaring back to her private heaven.

"Good grief!" Armand de Montriveau exclaimed to himself. "How can I tell this wild creature that I love her?"

He had already told her twenty times, or rather the duchess had read it twenty times in his eyes and seen in the passion of this truly great man something to amuse her, something of interest to inject into her dull life, so she prepared with great cleverness to raise a certain number of fortifications around her for him to overcome before allowing him to enter her heart. As the plaything of her caprice, Montriveau would have to stay still while jumping from one difficulty to another, like one of those insects a child torments by making it jump from one finger to another, thinking that it is going forward while its mischievous executioner keeps it in place. Nonetheless, the duchess recognized with inexpressible happiness that this man of character was true to his word. Armand had, indeed, never loved. He was about to retreat, displeased with himself, still more displeased with her, but she was joyful to see him in a sulk, which she could dispel with a word, a glance, or a gesture.

"Will you come tomorrow evening?" she said to him. "I am going to the ball, but I will wait for you until ten o'clock."

The marquis spent most of the following day sitting at the window of his study, smoking an indeterminate number of cigars. In this way he passed the hours until it was time to dress and go to the Hôtel de Langeais. It would have been a great pity for one of those who knew the magnificent value of this man to see him become so small, so trembling, to see the thought that might encompass worlds shrunk to the proportions of the boudoir of a "*petite-maîtresse*." But he already felt so fallen in his happiness that to save his life, he would not have confided his love to any of his closest friends. Is there not always a touch of shame in the modesty a man feels when he loves, and perhaps in a woman a certain pride in his reduced standing? But for a host of motives of this kind, how shall we explain why women are nearly always the first to betray the secret of their love—a secret that perhaps bores them?

"Monsieur," said the valet, "madame la duchesse is not presentable, she is dressing and begs you to wait for her here."

Armand strolled around the salon, studying the taste reflected in the smallest details. He admired Madame de Langeais by admiring her things, which betrayed her habits before he could grasp in them her person and her ideas. After about an hour, the duchess emerged from her room without a sound. Montriveau turned, saw her walking toward him with the lightness of a shadow; he was shaken. She came to him, without saying in bourgeois fashion: "How do I look?" She was sure of herself, and her steady look conveyed: "I have embellished myself like this to please you."

No one but an old fairy godmother to some unheralded princess could have wrapped around this coquettish woman's neck the cloud of gauze whose bright folds floated to reveal the dazzling satin of her skin. The duchess was radiant. The pale blue of her gown, repeated in the flowers of her coiffure, seemed to lend body by the richness of its color to the fragile, ethereal forms. Gliding quickly toward Armand, she made the ends of her scarf, which had been hanging by her sides, float on the air, and the brave soldier could not then help but compare her to the pretty blue insects that hover above the water, among the flowers with which they seemed to mingle.

"I've made you wait," she said, in a voice that women know how to use for the man they want to please.

"I would wait patiently for an eternity if I were sure to find a goddess as beautiful as you. But to speak to you of your beauty is no longer a compliment; nothing but adoration can touch you. Therefore, let me only kiss your scarf."

"Oh, pooh!" she said, with a proud gesture. "I admire you enough to offer you my hand."

And she held out to him her still-moist hand to kiss. A woman's hand, when she emerges from her bath, has an ineffable soft freshness, a velvet smoothness that sends a tingle from the lips to the soul. And in a man in love, who is so sensual that love has filled his heart, this seemingly chaste kiss can stir formidable storms.

"Will you always give it to me like this?" the general humbly asked.

"Yes, but we shall stop here," she said, smiling.

She sat down and seemed very clumsy pulling on her gloves, wishing to slide the narrow, delicate leather the length of her fingers, and looking at the same time at Monsieur de Montriveau, who was admiring first the duchess, then the grace of her repeated gestures.

"Oh, that's quite right," she said. "You were punctual, I love punctuality. His Majesty says it is the courtesy of kings, but to my mind, I think that it is the most respectful of flatteries a man can show a woman. Now is it not? Tell me..."

Then she gave him another look to express a seductive friendship, finding him mute with happiness and quite happy from these nothings. Ah! The duchess understood to perfection the art of being a woman, she knew admirably how to raise a man in his own esteem as he humbled himself to her and to reward him with empty flatteries at every step he took in his descent to sentimental inanities.

"You will never forget to come at nine o'clock."

"No, but will you go to the ball every evening?"

"How do I know?" she answered, shrugging her shoulders with a childish gesture, as if to admit that she was utterly capricious and that a lover should take her as she was. "Besides," she went on, "what difference does it make to you? You shall be my escort."

"For this evening," he said, "it would be difficult. I am not properly dressed."

"It seems to me," she answered, looking at him proudly, "that if someone must suffer from your dress, I must. But you should know, Monsieur Explorer, that the man whose arm I accept is always above fashion, no one would dare to criticize him. I see that you do not know the world, and I like you the more for it."

And so she threw him into the pettiness of the world, attempting to initiate him into the vanities of a woman of fashion.

"If she wants to do something foolish for me," Armand said to himself, "I would certainly be a simpleton to prevent her. She surely loves me, and of course she does not despise the world more than I do myself. So let us go to the ball!"

The duchess surely thought that in seeing the general follow her to the ball in boots and a black cravat, no one would hesitate to believe he was passionately in love with her. Happy to see the queen of this elegant world wishing to compromise herself for him, the general's hope gave him wit. Sure to please, he displayed his ideas and feelings without the restraint that had deeply embarrassed him the evening before. This substantive, animated conversation was filled with those first confidences as sweet to speak as to hear. Was Madame de Langeais really seduced by his talk or had she devised this charming bit of coquetry? In any case, she looked mischievously at the clock when it struck midnight.

"Ah, you are making me miss the ball!" she said, expressing surprise and vexation that she had forgotten. Then she justified this exchange of pleasures by a smile that made Armand's heart leap. "I really had promised Madame de Beauséant," she added. "Everyone is expecting me."

"Well then, go."

"No—go on. I will stay. Your adventures in the Orient charm me. Tell me all about your life. I love to take part in the sufferings experienced by a man of courage, for I feel them, truly!" She played with her scarf, twisting it and tearing it by her impatient movements that seemed to speak of an inner discontent and deep feelings.

"We are worthless, we society women," she went on. "Ah, we are contemptible creatures, selfish and frivolous. We know only how to bore ourselves with amusements. Not one of us understands what part to play in life. In the old days in France, women were benevolent lights, they lived to comfort those who wept, to encourage great virtue, to reward artists and animate their lives with noble thoughts. If the world has become so petty, the fault is ours. You make me hate this world and the ball. No, I am not sacrificing much for you."

She finished destroying her scarf, like a child playing with a flower who ends by tearing off all its petals. She rolled it up and threw it away from her, so she could display her swan's neck.

She rang the bell. "I will not be going out," she said to her valet de chambre. Then she timidly turned her big blue eyes toward Armand, and by the fear they expressed he was meant to take this order for an admission, for a first and great favor. "You have surely had a difficult life," she said, after a pause full of thought and with the tenderness that women often have in their voice, if not in their heart.

"No," replied Armand. "Until today, I did not understand happiness."

"You know it now?" she said, looking up at him with a sly, hypocritical glance.

"For me, from now on happiness is to see you, to hear you . . . Until today I have only suffered, and now I understand that I can be unhappy—"

"Enough, enough," she said. "You must go, it is midnight, we must respect the conventions. I did not go to the ball and you were here. Let us not make people talk. Farewell. I do not know what I will say, but the migraine is a good friend and tells no lies."

"Is there to be a ball tomorrow?" he asked.

"You will grow used to it, I think. Very well, yes, we will go to the ball again tomorrow night."

Armand went home the happiest man in the world and came every evening to Madame de Langeais's at the hour reserved for him by a sort of tacit agreement. It would be tiresome and redundant for a multitude of young men who have such fine memories to follow this story step by step, like following the poem of these secret conversations that were advanced or retarded at a woman's whim— quarreling over words when feelings were too rampant or appealing to feelings when words no longer corresponded to her thought. So to mark this work in progress in the manner of Ulysses's Penelope, perhaps we would have to mark its material expressions of feeling.

For instance, a few days after the first meeting between the duchess and Armand de Montriveau, the assiduous general had won and kept the right to kiss his mistress's insatiable hands. Wherever Madame de Langeais went, Monsieur de Montriveau was inevitably seen to follow, so that certain persons jokingly called him "the duchess's orderly." Armand's position had already made him the object of envy, jealousy, and enmity. Madame de Langeais had attained her goal. The marquis was just one of her numerous admirers and helped her to humiliate those who bragged of being in her good graces by setting him publicly a step above the others.

"Decidedly," said Madame de Sérizy, "Monsieur de Montriveau is the man the duchess prefers."

Who does not know what it means, in Paris, to be preferred by a woman? Things were thus perfectly in order. The stories people were pleased to tell about the general made him so formidable that the clever young men quietly abdicated their claims on the duchess and remained in her circle only to exploit the importance it reflected on them, to make use of her name, of her person, to put themselves on a better footing with certain powerful persons of the second order, who would be delighted to take a lover away from Madame de Langeais. The duchess had a shrewd enough eye to spot these desertions and alliances, and she was too proud to be duped by them. And as Monsieur le Prince de Talleyrand, who was very fond of her, used to say, she knew how to take renewed revenge by striking these "morganatic" unions with a double-edged remark. Her disdainful mockery contributed more than a little to making her feared and thought to be excessively clever. In this way, she consolidated her reputation for virtue while amusing herself with the secrets of others and never letting them penetrate her own. Nonetheless, after two months of regular attendance, she had a sort of vague fear deep in her soul that Monsieur de Montriveau still understood nothing of the Faubourg Saint-Germain sort of coquetry and took Parisian mannerisms seriously.

"That man, my dear duchess," the old Vidame de Pamiers said to her, "is first cousin to the eagles. You will not tame him and he will carry you off to his aerie if you do not take care."

The day after the evening when the shrewd old nobleman had made this remark, which the duchess feared would be prophetic, she tried to make herself hateful, to appear hard, demanding, nervous, detestable to Armand, who disarmed her with his angelic sweetness. This woman was so unfamiliar with the generosity of great characters that she was penetrated with the gracious pleasantries by which her complaints were first met. She was looking for a quarrel and found proof of affection. Then she persisted.

"How could a man who idolizes you cause you displeasure?" Armand said to her.

"You do not displease me," she answered, suddenly becoming sweet and submissive. "But why do you want me to compromise myself? You must be only my *friend*. Don't you think so? I wish I could see that you have the instinct and delicacies of true friendship, in order to lose neither your esteem nor the pleasures I feel when I'm with you."

"To be only your *friend*?" cried Monsieur de Montriveau, whose mind shook with electric shocks at the sound of this terrible word. "On the faith of the sweet hours you grant me, I slumber and wake in your heart, and today, without any reason, you take pleasure in gratuitously killing the secret hopes that give me life. After making me promise such constancy and showing such horror for women who are all caprice, do you wish to tell me that like all Parisian women you have passions and no love? Then why have you asked me for my life and why have you accepted it?"

"I was wrong, my friend. Yes, a woman is wrong to let someone go to such lengths of abandon when she neither can nor should reward them."

"I understand, you have been merely a coquette, toying with me, and—"

"Coquette? I hate coquetry. To be a coquette, Armand, means to promise oneself to several men and to give oneself to none. To give oneself to everyone is to be a libertine. That is my understanding of our ways. But to be melancholy with humorists, gay with the frivolous, and politic with the ambitious; to listen to gossips with apparent admiration, to discuss war with soldiers, to be passionate about the good of the country with philanthropists, to grant each person his little dose of flattery—this seems to me as necessary as putting flowers in our hair, wearing diamonds, gloves, and clothes. Talk is the moral aspect of the toilette, it is put on and taken off with the plumed toque.

"Do you call this coquetry? But I have never treated you as I treat everyone else. With you, my friend, I am honest. I have not always shared your ideas, and when you have convinced me, after a discussion, have I not been happy about it? In short, I love you, but only as a religious and pure woman is allowed to love. I have thought about this. I am married, Armand. If the way that I live with Monsieur de Langeais leaves me free to give my heart, laws and conventions have deprived me of the right to give my person. A dishonored woman of any rank in life is an outcast, and I have yet to meet any man who has known what our sacrifice involves. Even more so, the break between Madame de Beauséant and Monsieur d'Ajuda, who, they say, is marrying Mademoiselle de Rochefide, has proven to me that these very sacrifices are almost always at the root of our abandonment.

"If you loved me sincerely you would stop seeing me for a time! As for me, I will lay aside all my vanity for you—is this not something? What do they say about a woman to whom no man is attached? Ah, she has no heart, no mind, no soul, above all no charm. Oh, the coquettes will not spare me; they will rob me of the very qualities that mortify them. If my reputation is still intact, what do I care if my rivals dispute my advantages? They will surely not inherit them. Come, my friend, give something to her who sacrifices so much for you! Do not come so often, I will not love you the less for it."

"Ah!" answered Armand, with the sharp irony of a wounded heart. "Love, so the scribblers say, feeds only on illusions! Nothing could be truer, I can see, so I must imagine that I am loved. But hold on—there are some thoughts, like some wounds, from which you do not recover. You were one of my last beliefs, and I now see that everything here is false."

She began to smile.

"Yes," Montriveau went on in a stricken voice, "your Catholic faith to which you would convert me is a lie that men concoct for themselves, hope is a lie at the cost of the future, pride is a lie between us all, pity, wisdom, terror are cunning lies. So my happiness will also be a lie. I must delude myself and be willing to give a gold louis for a silver ecu. If you can so easily dispense with my visits, if you admit me as neither your friend nor your lover, you do not love me! And I, poor fool, I tell myself this, I know it and yet I love."

"But heavens, my poor Armand, you are getting carried away."

"I am getting carried away?"

"Yes, you think that everything is in question because I ask you to be careful."

In her heart she was charmed by the anger that filled her lover's eyes. At this moment she was tormenting him, but she was judging him as well and noticed the slightest changes that passed over his features. If the general had been so unfortunate as to display his generosity unquestioningly, as sometimes happens to certain candid souls, he might have been banished forever, accused and convicted of not knowing how to love. Most women want to feel their morality violated. Is this not one of the ways they flatter themselves by surrendering only to force? But Armand was not sufficiently informed to see the trap the duchess had so cunningly set. Strong men who love have such childlike souls!

"If you wish only to preserve appearances," he said naïvely, "I am prepared to—"

"Only preserve appearances," she cried, interrupting him. "What ideas must you have of me! Have I given you the slightest right to think that I should be yours?"

"Oh, well then, what are we talking about?"

"Monsieur, you frighten me. No, pardon me—thank you," she went on in a cold tone of voice. "Thank you, Armand. You warn me in time of an imprudence that was certainly not deliberate, believe me, my friend. You know how to suffer, you say? I, too, I will know how to suffer. We will stop seeing each other. Then, when we have both learned to recover a measure of calm, well then, we will consult and devise a happiness approved by the world. I am young, Armand, and a man lacking in delicacy might make a woman of twenty-four commit many foolish and careless things. But you! You will be my friend, promise me."

"The woman of twenty-four," he answered, "knows how to manage."

He sat down on the divan in the boudoir and rested his head in his hands.

"Do you love me, madame?" he asked, raising his head and showing her a face full of resolution. "Speak clearly: yes or no."

The duchess was more horrified by this interrogation than she would have been by a threat of death, a vulgar trick that has frightened few women in the nineteenth century, seeing that men no longer carry swords at their side. But are there not the effects of eyebrows, eyelashes, narrowing looks, trembling lips that communicate the terror they so vividly and magnetically express?

"Ah!" she said. "If I were free, if—"

"Well! Then is it your husband who prevents us?" the general cried joyfully, pacing boldly around the boudoir. "My dear Antoinette, I possess a power more absolute than the autocrat of all the Russias. I am in collusion with Fate; socially speaking, I can make it move forward or back, as you do with a clock. In our political machine, you can direct Fate simply by knowing its inner workings. Before long you shall be free, and then you must remember your promise."

"Armand," she cried, "what do you mean? Good God, do you think that I could be the prize of a crime? Do you wish my death? Have you no religious beliefs? As for me, I fear God. If Monsieur de Langeais has given me the right to despise him, I do not wish him any harm."

Monsieur de Montriveau beat a tattoo mechanically with his fingers on the marble of the mantelpiece, content to look calmly at the duchess.

"My friend," she said, continuing, "respect him. He does not love me, he is not good to me, but I have obligations to him that must be fulfilled. What wouldn't I do to avoid the disasters with which you threaten him? . . . Listen," she continued after a pause, "I will no longer speak to you about separation, you will come here as in the past, I will always give you my forehead to kiss; if sometimes I refused you in the past, it was pure coquetry, truly. But let us understand each other," she said, seeing him come near. "You will allow me to increase the number of my suitors, receiving more of them in the morning than I used to do. I wish to be twice as frivolous, I want to treat you with apparent negligence, to feign a rupture. You will come a little less often, and then, after . . ."

With these words, she allowed herself to be held around the waist; Montriveau held her tightly and she seemed to feel the extreme pleasure most women feel at this pressure, which appears to promise all the pleasures of love. Then she meant to produce some confidence, for she stood up on her toes to bring her forehead to Armand's burning lips.

"From now on," replied Montriveau, "you will no longer speak to me of your husband: You should banish him from your thoughts."

Madame de Langeais remained silent.

"At least," she said, after a meaningful pause, "you will do everything I wish without grumbling, without sulking—say yes, my friend. Did you want to frighten me? Come, then, admit it...you are too good ever to imagine criminal thoughts. But might you not have secrets that I do not know? How can you master fate?"

"When you confirm the gift of the heart you have already given me, I am far too happy to know exactly how to answer you. I trust you, Antoinette, I will have no suspicions or false jealousies. But if chance should make you free, we are united—"

"Chance, Armand," she said, making one of those pretty turns of the head that seem so weighty yet are tossed off so lightly, like a singer playing with her voice. "Pure chance," she went on. "You must surely know that if something were to happen to Monsieur de Langeais through your fault, I would never be yours."

They parted, content with each other. The duchess had made a pact that allowed her to show the world by her words and actions that Monsieur de Montriveau was certainly not her lover. As for him, the cunning woman vowed to wear him out. She would grant him no favors but those surprising moments in these little battles that she would stop at her will. She knew so prettily how to revoke the following day the concessions she had granted the day before. She was so seriously determined to remain physically virtuous, that she saw no danger to herself in preliminaries perilous only to women deeply in love. After all, a duchess separated from her husband, a marriage long since hollow, offered no great sacrifice to love.

For his part, Montriveau was quite happy to obtain the vaguest of promises, sweeping aside objections that a wife might plead conjugal fidelity to refuse love, pleased with himself for having once more conquered further ground. And for some time he took unfair advantage of rights won with such difficulty. More childish than he had ever been, this man gave himself up to all the childishness that makes a first love the flower of life. He became a boy again, and he poured out his soul and all the thwarted powers that passion had given him on the hands of this woman, on her blond hair whose curls he kissed, on that shining forehead that seemed so pure to him. The duchess was flooded with love, subdued by the magnetic scents of such warmth, and she hesitated to start the quarrel that might separate them forever. She was more woman than she thought, this poor creature, trying to reconcile the demands of religion with the lively emotions of vanity, with the semblance of pleasure that makes a Parisian woman lose her footing.

Every Sunday she attended Mass, never missing a service; then in the evening, she would plunge into the intoxicating bliss of repressed desire. Armand and Madame de Langeais were like those Indian fakirs who are rewarded for their chastity by the temptations it offers them. Perhaps, too, the duchess had ended by resolving love into those fraternal caresses, which surely must have seemed innocent to the world but to which her bold thoughts lent extreme depravity. How else to explain the incomprehensible mystery of her perpetual fluctuations? Every morning she thought to shut her door to the Marquis de Montriveau, then every evening at the appointed hour she succumbed to his charms. After a feeble defense, she became less unkind; her conversation grew sweet, soothing. Lovers alone could carry on this way. The duchess displayed her most sparkling wit, her most captivating wiles. Then, when she had inflamed her lover's soul and senses, if he seized her, she indeed wished to let herself be broken and twisted by him, but she had her *nec plus ultra* of passion, and when it reached this point, she always grew angry if, submitting to his enthusiasm, he looked as though he might cross the line.

No woman dares to refuse love without some reason, nothing is more natural than to cede to it, so Madame de Langeais quickly surrounded herself with a second line of fortifications more difficult to breach than the first. She evoked the terrors of religion. Never had the most eloquent church father pleaded the cause of God better than she; never was the vengeance of the Almighty better justified than by the voice of the duchess. She used neither ecclesiastical phrases nor rhetorical amplifications. No, she had her own pathos. To Armand's most ardent supplication she replied with eyes full of tears, with a gesture laden with feelings; she stopped him short with an appeal for mercy. She would not hear one more word or she would succumb, and death would be preferable to a criminal happiness.

"Is it nothing, then, to disobey God?" she asked him, recovering a voice weakened by the inward struggles over which this pretty actress seemed to find it difficult to maintain temporary control. "I would willingly sacrifice everything to you—men, the whole world. But you are so selfish as to demand my entire future for a moment's pleasure. Come now, are you not happy?" she added, holding out her hand to him. And the careless dress in which she showed herself to him certainly offered consolations to her lover, who made the most of them.

If to keep a man whose ardent passion gave her unaccustomed emotions, or if out of weakness she let herself be ravished by a swift kiss, she feigned fear, blushed, and banished Armand from her sofa as soon as the sofa became dangerous to her. "Your pleasures are sins that I must expiate, Armand; they cost me penitence and remorse," she cried.

When Montriveau was two chairs away from that aristocratic skirt, he began to blaspheme and railed against God. The duchess grew angry then.

"But my friend," she said dryly, "I do not understand why you refuse to believe in God, for it is impossible to believe in men. Keep quiet, do not speak this way; you have too great a soul to espouse the nonsense of liberalism and its pretention to annihilate God."

The theological and political discussions acted like cold showers to calm Montriveau, who did not know how to return to the subject of love when the duchess made him angry, throwing him a thousand miles away from this boudoir in her theories of absolute monarchy, which she defended to perfection. Few woman dare to be democrats, for this would be in contradiction to their sentimental despotism. But often, too, the general shook out his mane, dropped politics, incapable of holding his heart and thought in contradiction, he would growl like a lion and lash his flanks as he leaped upon his prey, returning fiercely to his mistress with love. If this woman felt the prick of fancy exciting enough to compromise her, she knew how to escape from her boudoir: She would leave the air she had been breathing, thick with desire, and would come into her salon, sit down at the piano, sing the most delightful melodies by modern composers, and thus trick the sensual love that sometimes left her no mercy but which she had the strength to defeat. In these moments she was sublime in Armand's eyes. She did not pretend, she was true to her feeling, and the poor lover believed he was loved.

This selfish resistance gave her the appearance of a saint and a virtuous creature, and he resigned himself and spoke of platonic love, this general of the artillery! When she had played long enough with religion in her personal interest, Madame de Langeais played with it in Armand's. She wanted to bring him back to Christian feelings, so she brought out her edition of *Génie du Christianisme*, designed for the use of military personnel. Montriveau grew impatient with this, found his yoke too heavy. And then, out of a spirit of contradiction, she tried to knock God into his head to see if God might not rid her of this suitor, for the man's persistence was beginning to frighten her. In any case, she was glad to prolong any quarrel that seemed to keep the dispute on moral grounds indefinitely. The material struggle that followed was much more dangerous.

But if the opposition in the name of marriage laws represents the *époque civile* of this sentimental warfare, the current struggle constituted the *époque religieuse*, and like its predecessor, it would also have its crisis and then diminishing severity. One evening Armand happened to come quite early and found Monsieur l'Abbé Gondrand, the director of Madame de Langeais's conscience, ensconced in an armchair by the fireside, like a man digesting his dinner and the pretty sins of his penitent. At the sight of this fresh-faced, well-rested man with a calm forehead, an ascetic mouth, a maliciously inquisitive look, with a noble ecclesiastical bearing and already dressed in the episcopal purple, Montriveau's face grew unusually dark; he pronounced no greetings and remained silent. Apart from his love, the general was not lacking in tact; he guessed, therefore, by exchanging glances with the future bishop that this man was the real promoter of the obstacles in the way of the duchess's love for him. Let an ambitious priest dabble and interfere with the happiness of a man of Montriveau's temper? This thought boiled in his face, clenched his fists, and made him stand up, pace back and forth. Then, when he came back to his place intending to make a scene, a single look from the duchess was enough to calm him. Madame de Langeais, not at all embarrassed by her lover's gloomy silence, which would have unsettled any other woman, continued to converse very intelligently with Monsieur Gondrand about the necessity of re-establishing religion in its former splendor. She expressed better than the priest why the church should be a power at once temporal and spiritual, and regretted that the Chamber of Peers did not still have its Bishops' Bench, as did the House of Lords. Nonetheless, the abbé yielded his place to the general and took his leave, knowing that during Lent he would be allowed to take his revenge. The duchess scarcely rose to return her director's humble bow, so intrigued was she by Montriveau's attitude.

"What is the matter, my friend?"

"I cannot stomach that abbé of yours."

"Why did you not bring a book?" she said to him, unconcerned whether she was overheard or not by the abbé, who was just closing the door.

Montriveau stayed mute for a moment because the duchess accompanied this remark with a gesture that enforced its sheer impertinence.

"My dear Antoinette, I thank you for giving love precedence over the church, but for pity's sake, permit me to ask you a question."

"Ah! You are going to interrogate me. I am quite willing," she went on. "Are you not my friend? Certainly I can show you the bottom of my heart, and you will see only one image inside."

"Do you speak to that man of our love?"

"He is my confessor."

"Does he know that I love you?"

"Monsieur de Montriveau, you are not, I think, claiming permission to penetrate the secrets of my confession?"

"So this man knows about all our quarrels and my love for you—"

"A man, monsieur! Say God."

"God! God! I must be alone in your heart. But leave God in peace where He is, for the love of Him and of me. Madame, you will no longer go to confession or—"

"Or?" she said, smiling.

"Or I will not come back here again."

"Leave, Armand. Farewell, farewell forever…"

She rose and went into her boudoir without a single look at Montriveau, who remained standing, his hand resting on a chair. How long he stood this way he could not have said. Love has the unknown power to extend as well as to compress time. He opened the door of the boudoir and saw that it was dark. A weak voice grew stronger, saying bitterly, "I did not ring. Besides, why do you enter without an order? Suzette, leave me alone."

"Are you suffering?" exclaimed Montriveau.

"Stand up, monsieur, and leave the room at least for a moment," she said, ringing for the servant.

"Madame la duchesse is asking for some light," he said to the valet, who came into the boudoir and lit the candles.

When the two lovers were alone, Madame de Langeais remained reclining on her divan, speechless, immobile, absolutely as if Montriveau had not been there.

"Dearest," he said with a note of pain and sublime kindness, "I was wrong. I would not have you without religion."

"It is fortunate," she replied without looking at him, her voice hard, "that you recognize the necessity of conscience. I thank you in God's name."

Here the general, beaten down by the harshness of this woman who knew how to become a stranger or a sister to him at will, took a step toward the door in despair and was going to abandon her forever without saying a single word. He was suffering and the duchess was laughing inside over the suffering caused by a mental torture much crueler than the judicial torture of former times. But this man was not strong enough to leave. In every sort of crisis, a woman is somehow full of a certain quantity of words, and when she does not say them, she feels a sensation of something incomplete. Madame de Langeais, who had not finished speaking her mind, took another turn.

"We do not have the same convictions, General, I am pained to admit. It would be dreadful for a woman not to believe in a religion that allows us to love beyond the grave. I set Christian sentiments aside since you do not understand them. Let me speak to you only of expedience. Do you want to forbid a woman of the court *the Lord's table* when it is customary to take the sacrament at Easter? But you must do something for your party. The Liberals, whatever their preference, will not kill religious feeling. Religion will always be a political necessity. Would you take on the responsibility of governing a people who live by reason alone? Napoleon did not dare; he persecuted the ideologues. To prevent peoples from reasoning, you must impose feelings on them. Let us accept the Catholic religion with all its consequences. If we want France to go to Mass, should we not begin by going ourselves? Religion, Armand, is, you see, the bond uniting all conservative principles that enable the rich to live peacefully. Religion is intimately bound to property. It is certainly finer to lead people by moral ideas than by scaffolds, as in the time of the Terror, the only means that your detestable revolution had invented to instill obedience. The priest and the king—they are but you and me, they are my neighbor the princess. In short, they are all the interests of respectable people personified. So, my friend, be so good as to belong to your party, you who might become its Sulla if you had the slightest ambition. I myself am ignorant of politics, I reason through feeling; nonetheless I know enough to understand that society would be overturned if we put in question its basis at each moment—"

"If your court, if your government thinks this way, I pity you," said Montriveau. "The Restoration, madame, must tell itself—as Catherine de Médicis did when she believed the Battle of Dreux to be lost—'Very well; now we will go to hear the sermon'! Today, 1815 is your Battle of Dreux. Like the throne of that time, you have won in practice but lost in principle. Political Protestantism is victorious in people's minds. If you do not want to issue an Edict of Nantes or if after doing so you wish to revoke it, if one day you are accused and convicted of repudiating the Charter, which is merely a pledge to maintain revolutionary interests, the Revolution will rise again, terrible in its might, and will give you only a single blow. It will not be the Revolution that will leave France—it is the soil itself. Men will let themselves die, but not their interests... My God, what is France, the throne, legitimacy, the whole world to us? They are nonsense compared to my happiness. Reign or be overthrown, no matter. Where am I now?"

"My friend, you are in the boudoir of Madame la Duchesse de Langeais."

"No, no, no more duchess, no more Langeais, I am with my dear Antoinette!"

"Do you wish to do me the pleasure of staying where you are," she said, laughing as she pushed him away, but gently.

"Then you have never loved me," he said with a rage that shot like lightning from his eyes.

"No, my friend."

This "no" stood for a "yes."

"I am a great idiot," he replied, kissing the hand of this terrible queen, who became a woman once more.

"Antoinette," he went on, leaning his head on her feet, "you are too chastely tender to speak of our happiness to anyone in the world."

"Ah! You are a great fool," she said, standing up with a swift but graceful movement. And without adding a word, she ran into the salon.

"What is it now?" wondered the general, little knowing that the touch of his burning head had sent a jolt of electricity through her from head to foot.

Just as he arrived, furious, in the salon, a run of celestial chords was heard. The duchess was at her piano. Men of science or poetry, who can both understand and enjoy without harm to their pleasures, know that the alphabet and musical phrasing are the musician's intimate tools, just as wood or copper are tools of the orchestral performer. For them music exists apart at the basis of the double expression of this sensual language of souls. *Andiam, mio ben* can draw tears of joy or pitying laughter, depending on the singer. Often, here and somewhere in the world, a young girl expiring beneath the weight of an unknown punishment, a man whose soul vibrates beneath the pricks of passion, takes a musical theme and reaches to heaven, or they speak to each other through some sublime melody, a kind of lost poem. Just now the general was hearing one of those unknown poems, like the solitary plaint of some bird dying without a mate in a virgin forest.

"My God, what are you playing?" he said, his voice betraying his emotion.

"The prelude of a romance called, I believe, 'Fleuve du Tage.'"

"I did not know that a piano could produce such music," he replied.

"Ah, my friend," she said, looking at him for the first time like a woman in love, "neither do you know that I love you, that you make me suffer horribly, and that I must express my pain without making myself too clearly understood, otherwise I would be yours . . . But you see nothing."

"And you do not want to make me happy!"

"Armand, the next day I would die of sorrow."

The general left abruptly, but when he found himself in the street, he wiped away two tears that he had been strong enough to contain until then.

Religion lasted for three months. Once this term expired, the duchess grew bored with repeating the same thing and offered God, bound hand and foot, to her lover. Perhaps she feared that having spoken so forcefully of eternity, she would only perpetuate the general's love in this world and the next. For this woman's honor, we must believe she was a virgin, even in her heart, otherwise she would be too horrible. The youthful duchess was still far from that age when a man and a woman realize they are too close to the future to waste time arguing about their joys. She was certainly not on the verge of her first love but of its first sensual pleasures. For want of the experience to compare good to bad, for want of the pain that would have taught her the value of the treasures thrown at her feet, she dallied. Not knowing the dazzling delights of the sun, she was content to remain in the shadows. Armand, who was beginning to glimpse this bizarre situation, put his hope in the first language of nature. Every evening as he was leaving Madame de Langeais's residence, he thought that a woman didn't accept seven months' worth of a man's solicitations and the tender proofs of his love then yield to the superficial demands of a passion only to betray love in a moment, and he waited patiently for the season of sun, having no doubt that he would harvest the fruits in their ripeness. He had perfectly conceived the scruples of the married woman and her religious feelings. He even rejoiced in these battles. He took the duchess's dreadful coquetry for modesty, and he would not have wished her otherwise. So he loved to see her invent obstacles. Would he not triumph over them gradually? And every triumph would surely increase little by little the small sum of amorous intimacies long denied, then conceded with every sign of love. But he had sampled at such leisure the small progressive conquests timid lovers feed on that they had become mere habits to him. In the way of obstacles, he no longer had anything but his own terrors to overcome; he saw nothing left standing between him and his happiness but the caprices of this woman who allowed herself to be called "Antoinette." He then made up his mind to demand more, to demand all. Embarrassed like a young lover who dares not believe that his idol will stoop so low, he hesitated for a long time and experienced terrible pangs, those desires that were brought up short with an annihilating word, those resolves that died on the threshold of a door. He despised himself for a weakling, unable to say a word, and still he did not say it. Nonetheless, one evening his gloomy melancholy transformed into a fierce demand for his illegally legitimate rights. The duchess did not have to wait for her slave's request to guess his desire. Is a man's desire ever a secret? And do not all women have a deep knowledge of certain changes of countenance?

"What! You wish to stop being my friend?" she said, interrupting him at the first word and casting him looks embellished by a divine blush that suffused her diaphanous complexion like new blood. "To reward me for my generosity, you want to dishonor me. Think a little longer. As for me, I have thought a great deal; I always think about *us*. There is something called a woman's honesty which we must not lack any more than you should discard your honor. I do not know how to dissemble. If I am yours, I could no longer be Monsieur de Langeais's wife in any sense. You thus demand the sacrifice of my position, my rank, my life for a doubtful love that could scarcely wait patiently for seven months. What! You would already rob me of my right to dispose of myself freely. No, no, do not talk to me like this again. No, not another word. I do not want—I am unable—to hear you."

Madame de Langeais raised both hands to her hair to push back the bunches of curls from her warm forehead, and seemed very excited.

"You come to a weak creature with all your calculations made, telling yourself: 'She will talk to me about her husband for a while, then about God, then of love's inevitable consequences. But I will use and abuse the influence I have gained; I will make myself necessary, I will be able to count on the bonds of habit, the arrangements ratified by the public. And at last, when society will have ended by accepting our liaison, I will be this woman's master.' Be honest, these are your thoughts. Oh, you calculate and you talk of loving me! Indeed, you are amorous! I certainly believe that! You desire me and want me as your mistress, that's all. Well, no, *the Duchesse de Langeais* will not stoop so low. Let some naïve bourgeois women fall for your falsities; as for me, I never will. Nothing guarantees your love. You speak of my beauty; I could be ugly in six months, like my neighbor the dear princess. You are captivated by my wit, my grace; heavens, you would grow used to them, just as you would grow used to your pleasure. Have you not already grown used to the favors that I have been weak enough to grant you in the past few months? When one day I will be lost, you will give me no reason for your change beyond the final word: 'I have ceased to love you.' Rank, fortune, honor, and all that is the Duchesse de Langeais will be swallowed up in disappointed hope. I will have children who will bear witness to my shame, and . . ." But with an involuntary gesture of impatience, she went on, "I am too good to explain to you what you know better than I. Come! Let us remain as we are. I am only too fortunate that I am still able to break the bonds that you think so strong. Is there anything so heroic in coming to the Hôtel de Langeais to spend a few moments every evening with a woman whose babble amuses you, whom you treat like a plaything? But several young bucks come here just as regularly every afternoon between three and five o'clock. They, too, are very generous. I make fun of them; they put up rather calmly with my petulance, my impertinence, and make me laugh. Whereas you, to whom I grant the most precious treasures of my soul, you want to ruin me and cause me endless pain. Quiet then, enough, enough," she said, seeing him ready to speak, "you have neither heart nor soul nor delicacy. I know what you want me to say. Ah well, yes. I would rather seem to you a cold, insensitive woman, with no loyalty, even no heart, than to seem like an ordinary woman in the eyes of society, to be condemned to eternal damnation after being condemned to the claims of your pleasures, of which you will surely tire. Your selfish love is not worth so many sacrifices."

These words imperfectly represent those the duchess warbled with the rapid verbosity of a little canary. She could have gone on even longer; poor Armand answered this torrent of trilled notes with a silence full of horrible feelings. For the first time, he caught a glimpse of the coquetry of this woman and instinctively guessed that devoted love, mutual love, did not calculate, did not reason like this in a true woman. Then he experienced a kind of shame, remembering that he had involuntarily made the calculations, odious in content, for which he was reproached. Looking inside himself with an angelic good faith, he found only egotism in his words, in his ideas, in the responses he imagined but did not express. He stood self-convicted, and in his despair he yearned to fling himself out the window. His *ego* was killing him. What could he say, indeed, to a woman who does not believe in love? "Let me prove to you how much I love you." Always *me*. Montriveau did not know what the heroes of the boudoir always know—how to imitate the crude logician walking before the Pyrrhonists, who deny movement. This otherwise audacious man precisely lacked the audacity that never deserts lovers who know the formulas of feminine algebra. If so many women, and even the most virtuous, are prey to gentlemen adept at love—given a bad name by the populace— perhaps it is because they are great *provers*, and that in spite of its delicious emotional poetry, love wants a little more geometry than we think.

Now the Duchesse de Langeais and Montriveau were equally inexperienced in love. She knew a bit of theory, was ignorant of its practice, felt nothing, and reflected on it at length. Montriveau knew something of the practice, was ignorant of the theory, and felt too strongly to reflect on anything. Both of them thus endured the misery of this bizarre situation. In this supreme moment, his myriad thoughts could have been reduced to this: "Let yourself be possessed." A horribly egotistical line for a woman in whom these words bore no freight of memory and awakened no image. Nonetheless, he had to say something. Although her little phrases whipped up his blood like sharp, cold, bitter arrows shot one after another, Montriveau had to hide his rage so as not to lose everything by some extravagant remonstration.

"Madame la duchesse, I am in despair that God has invented no way for woman to confirm the gift of her heart save by adding the gift of her person. The high price that you attach to yours shows me that I must value it equally well. If you give me your soul and all your feelings, as you tell me you do, what does the rest matter? Besides, if my happiness is such a painful sacrifice to you, let us no longer speak of it. Only, you will forgive a man of good heart if he feels humiliated in seeing that he is taken for a spaniel."

The tone of this last line might perhaps have frightened other women; but when one of these skirt-wearers sets herself above all others and allows herself to be addressed as a divinity, no power on earth is as proud as she.

"Monsieur le marquis, I am in despair that God has not invented for man a nobler way of confirming the gift of his heart than the expression of such prodigiously vulgar desires. If in giving our person, we become slaves, a man makes no commitment by accepting us. Who will assure me that I will always be loved? The love I might constantly show to cement your attachment to me would be, perhaps, a reason to be abandoned. I do not want to become a second edition of Madame de Beauséant. Does anyone ever know what keeps you with us? Our constant coldness is the secret of the constant passion in some of you; others require untiring devotion, continual adoration; for some, gentleness; for others, despotism. No woman has yet been able with confidence to read your hearts."

There was a pause, then she changed her tone.

"In short, my friend, you cannot prevent a woman from trembling at this question: Will I always be loved? Hard as they may be, my words are dictated by the dread of losing you. My lord! It is not me speaking but reason, and how can it exist in someone as mad as I am? The truth is, I know nothing about it."

To hear this answer begun with the most searing irony and ending in the most melodious accents an ingenious woman can adopt to depict love—surely this is a moment's dash from martyrdom to heaven. Montriveau grew pale and, for the first time in his life, fell on his knees before a woman. He kissed the hem of the duchess's dress, her feet, her knees. But for the honor of the Faubourg Saint-Germain, it is necessary to respect the mysteries of its boudoirs, where many are willing to take all that love has to offer without any proof of love in return.

"Dear Antoinette," cried Montriveau, plunged into delirium at the duchess's complete surrender, while she believed she was being generous in allowing him to express his adoration. "Yes, you are right, I do not want you to harbor any doubts. I am trembling at this moment as well, should the angel of my life leave me, and I would like to invent indissoluble bonds between us."

"Ah!" she murmured quietly. "So I was right, then—"

"Let me finish," Armand broke in. "I am going to banish all your fears with a single word. Listen, if I were to abandon you, I would deserve a thousand deaths. Be everything to me and I will give you the right to kill me should I betray you. I will myself write a letter in which I will declare certain reasons that would force me to kill myself—in short, I will make my final arrangements. You will keep this letter, which would legitimize my death and could thereby avenge you without anything to fear from God or me."

"Do I need this letter? If I had lost your love, what would life be worth? If I wanted to kill you, would I not be ready to follow myself? No, I thank you for the idea, but I do not want this letter. Would I not think you were faithful to me out of fear, or that the danger of an infidelity would be an attraction for a man who thus surrenders his life? Armand, what I ask is the one difficult thing to do."

"And so, what is it you want?"

"Your obedience and my freedom."

"My God!" he cried. "I am like a child."

"A willful and very spoiled child," she said, caressing the thick hair of his head, which she kept on her knees. "Oh, yes, much more beloved than he thinks, and yet so disobedient. Why not remain like this? Why not sacrifice to me those desires that offend me? Why not accept what I can give if this is all that I can honestly confer? Are you not happy this way?"

"Oh, yes," he said, "I am happy when I have no more doubts. Antoinette, is it not true that in love, to doubt is to die?"

And suddenly he displayed what he was and what all men are when lit by the fire of eloquent, insinuating desire. After tasting the pleasures permitted, surely, by a secret and Jesuitical fiat, the duchess was touched by Armand's love and that cerebral excitement that habit had made as necessary to her as society, the ball, or the opera. Seeing herself adored by a man whose superiority and character inspired her with a certain fear, turning him into a child, playing with him as Poppaea played with Nero, many women, like the wives of Henry VIII, paid for this perilous happiness with all the blood in their veins. Ah well, a strange presentiment! In offering him her pretty, ash-blond hair in which he loved to run his fingers, feeling the hand of this truly great man pressing her, playing with the black curls of his mane in this boudoir where she reigned, the duchess said to herself, "This man is capable of killing me if he sees that I am toying with him."

Monsieur de Montriveau stayed until two o'clock in the morning with his mistress, who from this moment on no longer seemed to him a duchess or a Navarreins: Antoinette had in the end disguised herself as a woman. During this delightful evening, the sweetest preface that ever a Parisienne had invented for what society calls "a sin," the general was allowed to see her, in spite of the affectations of coyness, in all her young woman's beauty. He could think with some reason that so many capricious quarrels had been but veils clothing a heavenly soul, veils that had to be lifted one by one, like those that enveloped her adorable body. To him, the duchess was the most naïve, the most girlish of mistresses, and he chose her as his woman. He went away happy to have at last led her to give him such guarantees of love that it seemed impossible that he would not be henceforth her secret husband, a choice approved by God. With this thought in mind, and the candor of those who feel all the obligations of love while savoring its pleasures, Armand slowly returned home.

He went along the quays in order to see as much of the sky as possible; he wanted to find the firmament and nature expanded as his heart expanded. His lungs seemed to him to breathe in more air than they had the evening before. He questioned himself as he walked and vowed to love this woman so religiously that every day she would find an absolution for her social sins in her constant happiness. The sweet agitations of a full life! Men who have strength enough to steep their soul in a single emotion feel infinite joys in contemplating glimpses of an ardent lifetime, as certain monks could contemplate the divine light in their ecstasies. Love would be nothing without this belief in its permanence; it grows great through constancy. So it was that, wholly absorbed by his happiness, Montriveau understood passion.

"We belong to each other forever!"

For this man, such a thought was a talisman that fulfilled his life's wishes. He did not wonder whether the duchess would change, whether this love would endure; no, he had faith, one of the virtues without which there is no Christian future but which is perhaps still more necessary to societies. For the first time, he conceived life in terms of feelings, he who had yet lived only through action, the most extreme of human efforts, a soldier's quasi-corporal devotion.

The next day, Monsieur de Montriveau set out early for the Faubourg Saint-Germain. He had a meeting in a house neighboring the Hôtel de Langeais, where, when his affairs were settled, he went as if he were going home. The general was walking at the time with a man for whom he seemed to have a sort of aversion when he met him in the salons. This man was the Marquis de Ronquerolles, whose reputation became so great in the boudoirs of Paris. He was a man of wit, talent, especially courage, and set the tone for all the Parisian youth; a gallant man, whose success and experience were equally envied, and who lacked nether fortune nor birth, which add such luster to the qualities of fashionable men in Paris.

"Where are you going?" said Monsieur de Ronquerolles to Montriveau.

"To Madame de Langeais's."

"Ah, it is true, I forgot that you let yourself be caught in her web. You are wasting a love on her that you could better employ elsewhere. I could give you ten women who are worth a thousand times more than this titled courtesan, who does with her head what other, franker women do—"

"What are you saying, my dear fellow?" Armand interrupted Ronquerolles. "The duchess is an angel of innocence."

Ronquerolles began to laugh.

"Since you have brought it up, my dear fellow," he said, "I must enlighten you. Just a word; there's no harm in it between us. Does the duchess belong to you? In this case, I will have nothing to say. Come on, confide in me. It is a question of not wasting your time grafting your great soul onto an ungrateful stock when all your hopes of cultivation will come to nothing."

When Armand had naïvely made a general report on the state of the situation in which he enumerated the rights he had so painfully won, Ronquerolles burst into a peal of laughter so cruel that in another man it would have cost him his life. But to see how these two men were looking at each other and conversing at the corner of a wall, as far removed from others as if they might be in the middle of a desert, it was easy to assume that they were united in a boundless friendship and that no earthly cause could estrange them.

"My dear Armand, why have you not told me that you are confused by the duchess? I would have given you advice that would have helped you in this intrigue. First, you must know that women of our Faubourg love, like all other women, to bask in love, but they want to possess without being possessed. They have made a sort of bargain with nature. The laws of the parish have allowed them almost everything, save positive sin. The sweets this duchess of yours enjoys are venial sins, which she washes off in the waters of penitence. But if you had the impertinence to desire in all seriousness the great mortal sin to which you must naturally attach the highest importance, you would see with what utter disdain the door to the boudoir and to the house would be impetuously closed to you. The tender Antoinette would have forgotten everything between you, and you would be less than zero to her. Your kisses, my dear friend, would be wiped away with the indifference a woman feels toward the items of her toilette. The duchess would wash the love off her cheeks along with her rouge. We know women like this, the pure Parisienne.

"Have you ever noticed a shopgirl trotting daintily through the streets? Her head is as pretty as a picture: a delightful bonnet, pink cheeks, charming hairdo, lovely smile, and the rest is relatively neglected. Is this not an accurate portrait? That's the Parisienne for you—she knows that her head alone will be seen. And so she devotes all her care, finery, and vanity to her head. Well, your duchess is all head, she feels only through her head, she has a heart in her brain, a voice in her head, all fondness is felt through her head. We call this poor thing a courtesan of the intellect. You have been played with like a child. If you doubt it, you will have proof this evening, this morning, this instant. Go to her, try to demand, to insist imperiously what you have been refused. Even if you go about it like the late Monsieur de Richelieu, you will get nothing for your pains."

Armand was struck dumb.

"Has your desire reached the point of foolishness?"

"I want her at any cost," cried Montriveau desperately.

"Very well. Now look here. Be as implacable as she is herself. Try to humiliate her, to wound her vanity. Do not try to move her heart or her soul but the woman's nerves and temperament, for she is both nervous and lymphatic. If you can once awaken desire in her, you are saved. But let go of these romantic boyish notions of yours. Once you have her in your eagle's talons, if you yield a point or draw back, if you so much as twitch an eyelid, if she thinks that she can regain her domination of you, she will slip out of your clutches like a fish, and you will never catch her again. Be as pitiless as the law. Show no more charity than the executioner. Hit hard, then hit again. Strike and keep on striking as if you were giving her the lash. Duchesses are made of hard stuff, my dear Armand, there is a sort of feminine nature that is only softened by repeated blows. And as suffering develops a heart in women of that sort, so it is a work of charity not to spare the rod. You must persevere. Ah! When pain has thoroughly relaxed those nerves and softened the fibers that you take to be so pliant and yielding, when a shriveled heart has learned to expand and contract and to beat under this discipline, when the brain has capitulated—then, perhaps, passion may enter among the steel springs of this machinery that turns out tears and affectations and swoons and melting phrases. Then you shall see a most magnificent conflagration (always supposing that the chimney ignites). The steel feminine system will glow red-hot like iron in the forge; that kind of heat lasts longer than any other, and the glow may possibly turn to love.

"Still," he continued, "I have my doubts. And after all, is it worthwhile taking so much trouble with the duchess? Between ourselves, a man of my stamp should first take her in hand and break her in; I would make a charming woman of her; she is a thoroughbred. You two, left to yourselves, will never get beyond the A B C of love. But you are in love with her, and just now you might not perhaps share my views on this subject...A pleasant time to you, my children," added Ronquerolles, after a pause. Then with a laugh: "For myself I prefer easy beauties; they are tender, and at any rate, the natural woman appears in their love without any of your social seasonings. A woman who haggles over herself, my poor boy, and only means to inspire love—well, have her like an extra horse, for show. The match between the sofa and the confessional, black and white, queen and knight, conscientious scruples and pleasure is an uncommonly amusing game of chess. A man who's a bit of a rake, who knows the game, wins in three moves. Now if I undertook a woman of that sort, I should start with the deliberate purpose of..." His voice sank to a whisper over the last words in Armand's ear, and he left quickly, before there was time to reply.

As for Montriveau, he sprang at a bound across the courtyard of the Hôtel de Langeais and went unannounced upstairs, straight to the duchess's bedroom.

"This is unheard-of," she said, hastily wrapping her dressing gown around her. "Armand! This is abominable of you! Come, leave the room, I beg you. Just go out, and go at once. Wait for me in the drawing room. Come now!"

"Dear angel, has a plighted lover no privilege whatsoever?"

"But monsieur, it is in the worst possible taste for a plighted lover or a husband to break in like this on his wife."

He came to the duchess, took her in his arms, and held her tightly to him.

"Forgive me, my dear Antoinette, but a host of dreadful suspicions are tearing at my heart."

"Doubts? Never...never!"

"Suspicions all but justified. If you loved me, would you quarrel with me like this? Would you not be glad to see me? Would your heart fail to be moved? I, who am not a woman, feel a thrill deep inside at the mere sound of your voice. Often in a ballroom a longing has come over me to rush to your side and put my arms around your neck."

"Oh! If you suspect me so long as I am not ready to rush into your arms before the world, I shall be suspect all my life, I suppose. Why, Othello was a mere child compared with you!"

"Ah!" he cried despairingly. "You do not love me."

"Admit, at any rate, that at this moment you are not lovable."

"Then I must still find favor in your sight?"

"Oh, I should think so. Come," she added with an imperious air, "go out of the room, leave me. I am not like you; I wish always to find favor in your eyes."

Never did a woman better understand the art of mingling charm and insolence, charm doubling the effect. Would this not infuriate the coolest of men? At this moment, her eyes, the sound of her voice, her attitude bore witness to a kind of perfect freedom that a loving woman never feels in the presence of the man who alone makes her heart leap at the mere sight of him. Enlightened by Ronquerolles's advice, helped also by a sort of second sight that passion brings at moments to the least instructed—while fuller with the strong—he guessed the terrible truth betrayed by the duchess's nonchalance, and his heart swelled with a storm of rage, like a lake rising in flood.

"If you were telling the truth yesterday, be mine, my dear Antoinette," he cried, "I want—"

"First of all," she said, pushing him away forcefully and calmly when she saw him advancing, "do not compromise me. My chambermaid might overhear you. Respect me, I beg you. Your familiarity is all very well in my boudoir in the evening. But here, no. And what does this 'I want' mean? I want! No one has yet spoken to me like that. It seems to me quite ridiculous, perfectly ridiculous."

"You will not grant me anything on this point?"

"Ah! You call our freedom to dispose ourselves 'a point'—a point indeed. You will allow me to be entirely my own mistress on this point."

"And if, believing in your promises to me, I required it?"

"Ah! Then you would prove that I had been greatly in the wrong to make you the slightest promise, I would not be fool enough to keep it, and I would beg you to leave me in peace."

Montriveau blanched, about to throw himself on her; the duchess rang, her chambermaid appeared, and smiling with mocking grace the duchess told him, "Please be good enough to come back when I am ready to be seen."

Armand de Montriveau felt then the hardness of this cold and steely woman, crushing in her contempt. In a moment she had broken the bonds that held firm only for her lover. The duchess had read on Armand's brow the secret demands of this visit, and had judged that the moment had come to make this imperial soldier feel that duchesses could certainly lend themselves to love but did not give themselves to it, and that their conquest was more difficult to accomplish than the conquest of Europe.

"Madame," said Armand, "I have no time to wait. I am, as you yourself have said, a spoiled child. When I seriously resolve to have what we were just speaking about, I will have it."

"You will have it?" she said, with a haughtiness mingled with some surprise.

"I will have it."

"Ah! You would do me a great pleasure by 'resolving' to have it. For curiosity's sake, I would be charmed to know how you will go about it."

"I am delighted," replied Montriveau, laughing in a way that frightened the duchess, "to inject some interest in your life. Will you permit me to escort you to the ball this evening?"

"A thousand thanks, but Monsieur de Marsay has already asked, and I have promised."

Montriveau bowed gravely and withdrew.

"So Ronquerolles was right," he thought, "we are now going to play a game of chess."

From this moment on, he hid his emotions beneath complete composure. No man was strong enough to bear such changes, which make the soul swing quickly from the greatest sense of well-being to supreme misery. Had he glimpsed such happiness only to feel more intensely the emptiness of his former life? This was a terrible storm, but he knew how to suffer and endured the assault of his tumultuous thoughts the way a granite boulder endures the breakers of the angry sea.

"I had nothing to say. In her presence I lose my wits. She does not know how vile and contemptible she is. No one has dared to bring this creature face-to-face with herself. She has certainly toyed brilliantly with men, and I will avenge them all."

For the first time, perhaps, love and vengeance mingled in a man's heart so equally that Montriveau found it impossible to know whether he was carried away by vengeance or love. That very evening he was at the ball where the Duchesse de Langeais was supposed to be, and he was nearly desperate to touch her heart. He was tempted to attribute something demonic to this woman, who was gracious to him and full of agreeable smiles, surely because she had no wish to let society think that she had compromised herself with Monsieur de Montriveau. Coolness on both sides is a sign of love. But while the duchess was the same as ever and the marquis was sullen and morose, was it not plain to everyone that she had conceded nothing? Society knows how to read the unhappiness of rejected men and not to mistake it for the distance that certain women order their lovers to display with the hope of concealing a mutual love. And everyone mocked Montriveau, who had not consulted his minder and remained abstracted and uneasy. Monsieur de Ronquerolles would perhaps have prescribed some compromise with the duchess by responding to her false gestures of friendship with passionate demonstrations. But Armand de Montriveau left the ball filled with a horror of human nature, and still he could hardly believe in such utter perversity.

"If there is no executioner for such crimes," he said, as he looked up at the lit window of the ballroom where the most enchanting women in Paris were dancing, laughing, and chatting, "I will take you by the back of your neck, madame la duchesse, and make you feel an iron more biting than the blade of the place de Grève. Steel against steel—we shall see whose heart will be cut more deeply."

3. THE TRUE WOMAN

For a week or so, Madame de Langeais hoped to see the Marquis de Montriveau, but Armand was content to send his card to the Hôtel de Langeais each morning. And each time this card was brought to the duchess, she could not stop herself from trembling, struck by dark thoughts that were as yet somewhat vague, like a presentiment of unhappiness. Reading his name, sometimes she thought she felt this implacable man's hand in her hair, sometimes his name foretold vengeance, and her lively mind would surrender to atrocious imaginings. She had studied him too well not to fear him. Would she be assassinated? Would this bull-necked man eviscerate her by flinging her over his head? Trample her under his feet? When, where, how would he catch her? Would he make her suffer horribly, and what kind of suffering was he thinking to impose on her?

She repented. At certain hours, if he had come she would have thrown herself into his arms with complete abandon. Every evening, as she was falling asleep, she would see Montriveau's face from a different angle. Sometimes his bitter smile, sometimes the Jupiter-like contraction of his brows, his leonine look, or some haughty movement of his shoulders made him terrible to her. The next day, his card seemed covered with blood. She became agitated by this name more than she had been by the spirited, opinionated, demanding lover. Then her apprehensions grew greater in the silence, and she was forced to prepare herself alone for a hideous, unspeakable struggle. This soul, proud and hard, was more sensitive to the titillations of hatred than she had been formerly to the caresses of love. Ha! If the general could have seen his mistress at the moment when her brow was creased with lines as she was plunged into bitter thoughts, in the depths of that boudoir where he had tasted such joys, perhaps he might have had great hopes. Is pride not one of the human feelings that can engender only noble acts? Although Madame de Langeais kept her thoughts secret, we are allowed to suppose that Monsieur de Montriveau was no longer an object of indifference. Is it not an immense conquest for a man to be constantly in a woman's thoughts? He is bound to make progress one way or the other.

Put any feminine creature under the feet of a furious horse or another terrible beast, and she will naturally fall to her knees and await death. But if the beast is forgiving and does not kill her altogether, she will love the horse, the lion, the bull, she will speak of it at her ease. The duchess felt she was under the lion's feet: She trembled, but she did not hate him. These two people, so singularly posed face-to-face, met in society three times that week. Every time, in response to coquettish questions, the duchess received Armand's respectful bow and smiles tinged with such cruel irony that they confirmed all the apprehensions inspired that morning by his visiting card. Life is only what we make of it with our feelings; their feelings had hollowed out an abyss between them.

The Comtesse de Sérizy, sister of the Marquis de Ronquerolles, gave a great ball at the beginning of the week to which Madame de Langeais had promised to come. The first figure the duchess saw upon entering was that of Armand—this time Armand was waiting for her, at least she thought so. The two of them exchanged a look, and a cold sweat suddenly broke from all her pores. She had believed Montriveau capable of some unimaginable vengeance in proportion to their positions; this vengeance had been discovered, it was ready, it was boiling hot. The betrayed lover shot lightning bolts at her, his face radiant with exultant hatred. And the duchess had a doleful look, in spite of her determination to be cold and impertinent. She went to stand next to the Comtesse de Sérizy, who could not prevent herself from saying to her, "What is the matter, my dear Antointette? You look frightful."

"I will revive after a quadrille," she answered, giving her hand to a young man who had just appeared.

Madame de Langeais began to waltz with a kind of frenzy and abandon that made Montriveau scrutinize her even more intensely. He remained standing in front of the onlookers, who amused themselves watching the dancing couples. Each time his mistress passed him, his eyes plunged onto her turning head, like those of a tiger on his prey. Once the waltz was done, the duchess came to sit beside the countess, and the marquis never stopped watching her as he spoke with a stranger.

"Monsieur," he was saying to him, "one of the things that has struck me most on this journey..."

The duchess was all ears.

"...is the remark the guard at Westminster makes while showing you the ax used by a masked executioner, they say, to cut off the head of Charles I. The king apparently said these words to an inquisitive person and they are repeated in his memory."

"What did he say?" asked Madame de Sérizy.

"*Do not touch the ax*," answered Montriveau in a threatening tone of voice.

"In truth, monsieur le marquis," said the Duchesse de Langeais, "you are looking at my neck in such a melodramatic way as you repeat this old story, known to everyone who goes to London, that I seem to see an ax in your hand."

These last words were pronounced in laughter, although the duchess had broken out in a cold sweat.

"But circumstances have made this story quite new," he answered.

"How so? I beg you, for pity's sake, in what way?"

"In this way, madame: You have touched the ax," Montriveau said to her in a low voice.

"What a ravishing prophecy!" she replied smiling with affected grace. "And when is my head to fall?"

"I have no wish to see your pretty head fall, madame. I fear for you only some great misfortune. If you were shorn, would you feel no regrets for the charming golden hair you turn to such good effect—"

"There are men to whom women love to make these sacrifices, and often even to men who do not know how to make allowances for an outbreak of temper."

"Very well. And if some wag suddenly spoiled your beauty by some chemical process and made you look a hundred years old when we know you are only eighteen—"

"But, monsieur," she said, interrupting him, "the smallpox is our Waterloo. Afterward, we know who truly loves us."

"You would not regret this lovely face that—"

"Oh yes, very much, but less for my sake than for him who might have taken joy in it. However, if I were loved sincerely, well, what would beauty matter to me? What do you say, Clara?"

"This is a dangerous sort of speculation," replied Madame de Sérizy.

"Might one ask His Majesty the King of Sorcerers," Madame de Langeais went on, "when I committed the sin of touching the ax, since I have never gone to London?"

"*Non so*," he answered in Italian, with a burst of ironic laughter.

"And when will the punishment begin?"

Here Montriveau coldly pulled out his watch and checked the time with a truly terrifying conviction.

"Before this day is done, a horrible misfortune will befall you."

"I am not a child who is so easily frightened, or rather I am a child who does not know danger," said the duchess, "and goes on dancing fearlessly at the edge of the abyss."

"I am delighted, madame, to know you have such character," he replied, seeing her go to take her place in a quadrille.

In spite of her apparent disdain for Armand's dark predictions, the duchess was in the grip of very real terror. Her lover's presence filled her morally and almost physically with a sense of oppression that scarcely ceased when he left the ball. Nonetheless, after enjoying a moment's pleasure breathing more easily, she was surprised to feel regret for the emotions of fear, so avid is female nature for extreme sensations. This regret was not love, but it surely belonged to the feelings that precede it. Then, as if the duchess again felt the effect of Montriveau's presence, she remembered the air of conviction with which he had just looked at the clock and, suddenly gripped by a spasm of dread, she took her leave.

It was by then around midnight. One of her servants wrapped her pelisse around her and went ahead to call her carriage. Then, when she was seated inside, she fell into a rather natural daydream, provoked by Monsieur de Montriveau's prediction. Having arrived in her courtyard, she entered a vestibule almost identical to the one in her residence, but all of a sudden she did not recognize her staircase. The moment she turned around to call her people, several men quickly assailed her and threw a handkerchief over her mouth, tied her hands and feet, and carried her off. She cried for help.

"Madame, we have orders to kill you if you cry out," someone spoke in her ear.

The duchess's fear was so great that she could never explain to herself how or where she was transported. When she came to her senses, she found herself bound hand and foot with silken ropes, lying on the couch of a bachelor's quarters. She could not restrain a cry when she met the eyes of Armand de Montriveau, wrapped in his dressing gown as he sat calmly in an armchair smoking a cigar.

"Do not cry out, duchess," he said coldly, removing his cigar from his mouth. "I have a migraine. Besides, I am going to untie you. But listen carefully to what I have the honor to tell you." He delicately untied the knots that bound the duchess's feet. "What good would your cries do? No one can hear you. You are too well bred to make futile grimaces. If you should not keep quiet, if you should wish to fight me, I will bind you again, hand and foot. I think that, all things considered, you have enough self-respect to stay on that couch as if you were at home on yours, cold as ever, if you like ... You have made me shed many tears on this couch, tears that I hid from all eyes."

While Montriveau was speaking to her, the duchess cast around her a woman's furtive glance, a glance that can take everything in while appearing distracted. She liked this room that seemed so much like a monk's cell. The man's mind and soul hovered there. No decoration could change the gray paint on the blank walls. On the floor was a green rug. A black couch, a table covered with papers, two large armchairs, a dresser with an alarm clock as ornament, a very low bed with a red coverlet bordered in a black key design flung over it—the texture of these furnishings displayed the habits of a life reduced to its simplest expression. An Egyptian-style triple sconce on the mantel recalled the vastness of the deserts where this man had wandered so long. Beside the bed, its foot shaped like an enormous sphinx paw jutting from folds of cloth, was a door near the corner of the room, hidden by a green curtain with red-and-black fringes hanging from large rings circling a spear handle. The door through which the strangers had entered was similarly concealed, but its curtain was tied back from an ordinary rod. The duchess took a last look at the two curtains to compare them, and she perceived that the door next to the bed was open, and that a reddish light illuminating the other room flickered beneath the fringed borders. Naturally her curiosity was aroused by this somber light, which scarcely allowed her to distinguish the strange shapes that played there among the shadows. But at this moment she did not imagine that any danger to herself could come from that quarter and wanted to satisfy an increasingly ardent curiosity.

"Monsieur, is it indiscreet to ask what you mean to do with me?" she said, with impertinence and stinging mockery.

The duchess imagined an excessive love in Montriveau's words. Furthermore, surely a woman must be the object of a man's adoration for him to abduct her!

"Nothing at all, madame," he replied, gracefully puffing the last of his cigar. "You are here for a short while. First of all, I want to explain to you what you are, and what I am. I cannot put my thoughts into words when you are twisting on your divan in your boudoir. And when you are at home, you ring for your servant at the slightest thought that displeases you, you shout out loud and show your lover the door, as if he were the lowest of the low. Here my mind is free. Here no one can throw me out the door. Here you will be my victim for a few moments, and you will have the extreme goodwill to hear me out. Do not be afraid. I have not abducted you in order to insult you, to wrench from you by violence what I have not been able to merit, what you have not wished to grant me of your own free will. That would be beneath me. Perhaps you imagine rape; I, on the other hand, have no such idea."

Abruptly, he tossed his cigar into the fire.

"Madame, the smoke is no doubt unpleasant to you?"

Rising at once, he took a hot chafing dish from the hearth, burned perfumes and purified the air. The duchess's astonishment was equal only to her humiliation. She was in this man's power, and he did not wish to abuse his power. She saw those eyes, formerly blazing with love, now calm and steady as stars. She trembled. Then her dread of Armand was increased by one of those transfixing sensations like the agitations you feel in a nightmare, unable to move. Fear nailed her in place as she thought she saw the glow from behind the curtain intensify as from the work of a bellows. Suddenly the reflections, growing more vivid, illuminated three masked figures. This ghastly aspect vanished so suddenly that she took it for an optical illusion.

"Madame," Armand went on, regarding her with cold contempt, "a minute, a single minute is enough for me to reach you in every moment of your life, the only eternity I can touch. I am not God. Listen to me carefully," he said, pausing to give due weight to his words. "Love will always come at your bidding; you have a limitless power over men. But remember that one day you bade love come and it came pure and candid, as much as it can be on this earth; as respectful as it was violent; caressing as the love of a woman, or as that of a mother for her child; finally, so great that it was a kind of madness. You played with this love, and thus you have committed a crime. It is any woman's right to refuse a love she feels she cannot share. The man who loves without making himself loved cannot complain, nor has he any right to complain. But, madame la duchesse, to attract a poor man deprived of all affection by feigning love, giving him a glimpse of happiness at its fullest only to steal it from him, to snatch away his future felicity, to kill it not only today but for as long as his life lasts, poisoning all his hours and his thoughts—this is what I call a dreadful crime!"

"Monsieur—"

"I cannot yet allow you to answer me. Listen to me, then. Besides, I have rights over you, but I want only the rights of the judge over the criminal so as to awaken your conscience. If you had no more conscience, I would not blame you at all; but you are so young! I like to think that you must feel some life in your heart. While I believe you are depraved enough to commit a crime unpunished by law, I think you are not so degraded that you cannot comprehend the full meaning of my words. I continue."

At this moment, the duchess heard the hollow sound of a bellows; the strangers whom she had just glimpsed were no doubt using it to fan the fire clearly reflected on the curtain. But Montriveau's burning look forced her to stay still, her heart beating, her eyes staring in front of her. Whatever her curiosity, the fire of Montriveau's words interested her even more than the sound of this mysterious fire.

"Madame," he said, after a pause, "in Paris, when the executioner must lay hands on a poor murderer and place him on the block, where a murderer by law loses his head . . . You know, the newspapers forewarn rich and poor alike, telling the rich to remain calm and the poor to be watchful for their lives. Well, you who are religious, and even something of a bigot, go to say Mass for this man: You are part of the family, but you are of the elder branch. That branch can rest in peace, happy and carefree. Pushed by poverty or by anger, your brother the convict has only killed a man. And you! You have killed a man's happiness, the best part of his life, his most dearly held beliefs. Driven by misery or anger, your convict brother has quite naïvely lain in wait for his victim; he has killed him in spite of himself and in fear of the scaffold. But you . . . you have heaped up all the sins of weakness against an innocent strength; you have tamed the heart of your patient the better to devour it! You have lured him with caresses, you have left nothing undone that could lead him to imagine, dream, desire the delights of love. You have asked of him a thousand sacrifices in order to reject them all. Indeed, you have made him see the light before putting out his eyes.

"Admirable courage! Such villainy is a luxury beyond the ken of those bourgeois women whom you so despise. They know how to give themselves and forgive; they know how to love and suffer. They make us look small by the grandeur of their devotions. The higher we rise in society, we find as much filth as at the bottom, only it is hardened and gilded. Yes, to achieve perfect baseness you need a fine education, a great name, a pretty woman, a duchess. To fall as low as possible, you needed to be above it all. I express my thoughts poorly, I still suffer from too many wounds you inflicted; but do not imagine that I complain! No. My words are not the expression of any personal hope and contain no bitterness. Be assured, madame, I forgive you, and this forgiveness is so complete that you need not feel sorry that you've come here to find it against your will … But you might abuse other hearts as childlike as mine, and I must spare them that pain. You have thus inspired me with an idea for justice. Expiate your sin here on earth, perhaps God will forgive you—I certainly hope so—but He is implacable and will strike you."

At these words, the eyes of this woman—battered, torn—filled with tears.

"Why are you weeping? Stay true to your nature. You coldly contemplated the tortures of the heart you were breaking. Enough, madame, console yourself. I can suffer no more. Others will tell you that you have given them life. I, on the other hand, am delighted to tell you that you have given me nothingness. Perhaps you imagine that I haven't a minute to myself, that I live for my friends, and that from now on I will have to bear death's coldness and life's sorrows together? Do you really have such kindness in you? Perhaps you are like the tigers in the desert, who lick the wounds they have first inflicted?"

The duchess dissolved in tears.

"Spare yourself these tears, madame. If I believed in them, it would only put me on my guard. Is it merely one of your artful tricks or not? After all those you have used, how can one think there is any truth in you? Henceforth, you have no more power to move me. I have said all I have to say."

Madame de Langeais rose, moving with both a noble bearing and humility.

"You are right to treat me harshly," she said, holding out to this man a hand that he did not take. "Your words are still not harsh enough, and I deserve this punishment."

"*I* punish you, madame! But to punish someone is to love them, is it not? Do not expect anything from me that resembles an emotion. On behalf of my own cause, I might make myself both accuser and judge, pronounce your sentence and be your executioner. But for me the cruelest vengeance is to disdain any possible vengeance. Who knows! Perhaps I will be the minister of your pleasures. From now on, elegantly wearing the sad uniform society prescribes for criminals, perhaps you will be forced to have their integrity. And then you will love!"

The duchess listened with a submission that was no longer infused with calculated coquetry; she spoke only after an interlude of silence.

"Armand," she said, "it seems to me that by resisting love, I was obeying all the considerations of a woman's modesty, and I would not have expected such reproach from you. You have turned all my weaknesses against me and made them into crimes. How could you fail to understand that all the curiosities of love might have led me beyond my duties, and that the next day I would have been angry with myself, in despair that I had gone so far? Alas, there was as much good faith in my sins as in my remorse. My severity betrayed much more love than my concessions. And besides, what are you complaining about? The gift of my heart was not enough for you, you brutally demanded my person—"

"Brutally!" cried Monsieur de Montriveau. But he said to himself, "I am lost if I allow myself to take up this argument over words."

"Yes, you arrived at my house as if it were the house of one of those fallen women, showing no respect, none of the attentions of love. Had I not the right to think it over? Well, I have thought it over. The unseemliness of your conduct is excusable: Love is the main point—let me believe that and justify your behavior to myself. So, Armand, at the very moment this evening when you were predicting my unhappiness, *I* was thinking of our happiness. Yes, I had confidence in your proud and noble character—you've given me proof of that... and I was all yours," she added, leaning toward Montriveau's ear.

"Yes, I had some mysterious desire to make a man happy who has so violently suffered from adversity. Master for master, I wanted a great man. The loftier I felt, the less I wanted to settle for less. I had confidence in you and saw a life full of love while you were showing me death... Strength does not work without goodness. My friend, you are too strong to be wicked to a poor woman who loves you. If I was wrong, can I not be pardoned? Can I not set things right? Repentance is love's grace, I want to be full of grace to you. How could I, alone among women, fail to share those uncertainties, those fears, that timidity so natural when you are bound for life, and know how you men break such bonds so easily! Those bourgeois women, to whom you compare me, give themselves, but they struggle. Well, I have struggled, but here I am... My God! He isn't listening to me—" She broke off, twisting her hands and crying. "But I love you! I am yours!" She fell at Armand's knees. "Yours! Yours, my one and only master!"

"Madame," said Armand, trying to raise her, "Antoinette can no longer save the Duchesse de Langeais. I do not believe either one anymore. You give yourself today, perhaps you will refuse to give yourself tomorrow. No power on heaven or earth could guarantee the sweet constancy of your love. Love's pledges were in the past, and now there is no more past."

At this moment, a glimmer shone so brightly that the duchess could not help turning her head toward the curtain, and this time she saw distinctly three masked men.

"Armand," she said, "I would not like to misjudge you. What are those men doing there? What are you going to do to me?"

"Those men are as discreet as I will be myself on what will happen here," he said. "Think of them simply as my arms and my heart. One of them is a surgeon—"

"A surgeon," she said. "Armand, my friend, uncertainty is the cruelest form of suffering. Speak to me, then, tell me if you want to take my life. I will give it to you, you shall not take it."

"So you have not understood me?" replied Montriveau. "Did I not speak to you of justice?" he added coldly, taking a small steel object from the table. "I am going to put an end to your apprehensions, to explain what I have decided to do with you."

He showed her a cross of Lorraine at the end of a steel rod.

"Two of my friends are even now heating a cross like this one. We will apply it to your forehead, just there between your eyes, so that you shall not be able to hide it behind diamonds and avoid the questions of society. In short, your forehead will bear the brand of infamy your brother convicts wear on their shoulders. The pain involved is minor, but I was afraid of an attack of nerves or some resistance—"

"Of resistance?" she said, clapping her hands with joy. "No, no, I would have the whole world here to watch. Ah, my Armand, brand me quickly, brand your creature like some poor little thing you own. You were asking for pledges of my love, but here they are, all in one. Ah! I see only mercy and forgiveness, only eternal happiness in your vengeance...When you have marked a woman as yours this way, when you have a soul in bondage who will bear your red mark, well then, you can never abandon her, you will be mine forever. By isolating me on earth, you will be responsible for my happiness on pain of cowardice, and I will know your nobility, your greatness! But the woman in love is always branded by herself. Come, gentlemen, enter and brand me, brand the Duchesse de Langeais. Enter quickly, all of you, my forehead burns more than your iron."

Armand turned away quickly so as not to see the duchess on her knees, her heart throbbing. He spoke to them briefly and his three friends disappeared. Women used to salon life know the game of mirrors. So the duchess, intensely interested in reading Armand's heart, was all eyes, while Armand, unaware of his mirror, openly shed two tears before quickly wiping them away. The duchess's entire future lay in those two tears. When he turned back again to help her rise, he found Madame de Langeais already on her feet; she was sure that she was loved. And her heart must have throbbed hearing Montriveau tell her, with the firmness she knew so well how to take when she used to toy with him, "I spare you, madame. Believe me, this scene will be as if it had never taken place. But let us say farewell here. I like to think that you were sincere in your coquetries on your divan, and sincere in your emotional effusions here. Farewell. I no longer have faith. You would still torment me, you would always be a duchess. And . . . but farewell, we will never understand each other. Now, what would you like?" he said, assuming the air of a master of ceremonies. "To go home or to return to the ball at Madame de Sérizy's? I have done everything in my power to leave your reputation intact. Neither your servants nor the world can know anything of what has passed between us for the last quarter of an hour. Your servants believe you are at the ball—your carriage has not left Madame de Sérizy's courtyard, and likewise your brougham is in the courtyard of your own mansion. Where do you wish to be?"

"What do you think, Armand?"

"There is no more Armand, madame la duchesse. We are strangers to each other."

"Take me to the ball, then," she said, still curious to test Armand's power. "Throw back into the hell of society a creature who would suffer there, and who must continue to suffer if there is no happiness left for her. Oh, my friend, I still love you as your bourgeois women love. I would love to throw my arms around your neck at the ball, before everyone, if you asked me to. That dreadful society has not corrupted me. Go, I am young and I have just grown younger. Yes, I am a child, your child, you have just created me. Oh, do not banish me from my Eden!"

Armand shook his head.

"If I leave, at least let me take something with me, anything—this—to engrave this evening on my heart," she said, taking Armand's cap and wrapping it in her handkerchief, "No," she continued, "I am not part of that world of depraved women. You do not know it, and so you cannot appreciate me. Know this, then: Some give themselves for gold, others can be plied with gifts—all vile. Oh, I would like to be a simple bourgeois woman, a working girl, if you prefer a woman beneath you to a woman in whom devotion is bound up with high rank. But my Armand, I am one of those noble, great, chaste, pure women, and they are lovely. I would like to have all the noble virtues that I might sacrifice them all to you. Misfortune has made me a duchess; I would like to have been royalty so that I might make the greatest possible sacrifice to you. I would be a shopgirl to you and a queen to others."

He was listening while moistening his cigars.

"When you want to leave," he said, "let me know."

"But I would like to stay—"

"That is another matter!" he said.

"Come, that was badly done," she cried, seizing a cigar and devouring what Armand's lips had touched.

"Do you smoke?"

"Oh, what would I not do to please you?"

"Very well. Leave, madame."

"I will obey you," she said, weeping.

"You must be blindfolded so as not to get a glimpse of the way back."

"I am ready, Armand," she said, covering her eyes.

"Can you see?"

"No."

Noiselessly he knelt before her.

"Ah! I can hear you!" she cried, allowing a caressing gesture to escape, believing that this pretended harshness was over.

He leant as if to kiss her lips; she held up her face.

"You can see, madame."

"I am just a little curious."

"So you are deceiving me still?"

"Ah!" she said with the rage of great generosity scorned. "Take off this handkerchief and lead me, monsieur, I will not open my eyes."

Armand felt certain of her honesty in that cry. He led the duchess who, true to her word, kept herself nobly blind. But in taking her paternally by the hand to help her climb up, then descend, Montriveau studied the throbbing of this woman's heart so quickly invaded by a true love. Madame de Langeais, happy to be able to speak to him this way, took pleasure in telling him everything; but he remained inflexible, and when the duchess's hand felt for him, his remained mute. At last, after having traveled for some time together, Armand told her to come forward. She did so and perceived that he was preventing her dress from touching the walls of what must have been a narrow opening. Madame de Langeais was moved by this care, which betrayed still a little love for her; but this was Montriveau's way of bidding her farewell, for he left without a word. Feeling the warmth around her, the duchess opened her eyes. She saw that she was alone in front of the fireplace in the Countess de Sérizy's boudoir. Her first concern was to see to her disordered toilette; in a moment she had readjusted her dress and restored her charming coiffure.

"Well, my dear Antoinette, we have searched for you everywhere," said the countess, opening the door to the boudoir.

"I came in here to breathe," she said, "it is unbearably hot in the public rooms."

"We thought you had gone, but my brother Ronquerolles told me he had seen your servants waiting for you."

"I am worn out, my dear, let me rest here a moment."

The duchess sat down on her friend's divan.

"What's the matter with you? You're trembling all over."

The Marquis de Ronquerolles entered.

"I was afraid, madame la duchesse, that something had happened to you. I just saw your coachman looking as tipsy as the Swiss."

The duchess did not answer but looked at the fireplace, at the mirrors, trying to see some trace of her passage. Then she experienced an extraordinary sensation to see herself in the midst of the pleasures of the ball after the terrible scene that had just set her life on another course. She began to tremble violently.

"Monsieur de Montriveau's prediction this evening has shaken my nerves. Joking or not, I shall see if his London ax will haunt my sleep. Adieu then, my dear. Adieu, monsieur le marquis."

She went through the salons, where she was stopped by flatterers, who seemed to her pitiful. Small and humiliated as she was, she was the queen of this world, and she found it petty. Besides, what were these men compared to the one she truly loved, whose character had been temporarily belittled by her but was now perhaps exaggerated beyond all measure, once again taking on gigantic proportions? She could not stop herself from looking at her servant and those who had accompanied her, and seeing him fast asleep.

"You didn't leave here?" she asked him.

"No, madame."

Climbing into her carriage, she understood that her coachman was in such a drunken state that in other circumstances she would have been frightened. But the great crises in life deprive fear of its usual fodder. Moreover, she arrived home without incident, but she felt utterly transformed and prey to feelings surprisingly new. For her there was now but one man in the world, that is, henceforth she wished to be of some value only to him.

While the physiologists can promptly define love according to the laws of nature, the moralists are much more hesitant to explain it when they wish to consider love in its various social developments. Still, in spite of the heresies of the thousand sects that divide the Church of Love, there is one straight, deep line running clearly through all their doctrines, a line whose strict application explains the crisis in which, like nearly all women, the Duchesse de Langeais was plunged. She was not yet in love—she had a passion.

Love and passion are two different conditions of the soul that poets and men of the world, philosophers and fools alike, continually confuse. Love involves mutual feelings, a certainty of bliss that nothing can change, and a too-constant exchange of pleasures, a too-complete clinging of hearts—not excluding jealousy. Possession is then a means and not an end; infidelity causes suffering but no breach; the soul is neither more nor less ardent or aroused, it is incessantly happy. In short, desire extended by a divine breath from one end of time's vastness to the other tints us with the same color: Life is as blue as a pure sky. Passion is the presentiment of love and its infinitude to which all suffering souls aspire. Passion is a hope that will perhaps be dashed. Passion signifies both suffering and transition; passion ceases when hope is dead. Men and women can, without dishonor, conceive several passions; it is natural to leap toward happiness! But in life there is only one love. So all discussions of feelings, written or oral, can be summed up by these two questions: Is it a passion? Is it love?

Since love comes to life only with the intimate pleasures that perpetuate it, the duchess was suffering beneath passion's yoke, and by enduring its devouring agitations, involuntary calculations, fevered desires—in other words everything embodied by the word *passion*—she suffered. In the midst of her soul's troubles, she was buffeted by sudden gusts of vanity, self-regard, pride—all those varieties of egotism held together.

She had said to a man, "I love you, I am yours!" Could the Duchesse de Langeais have uttered these words in vain? She would either be loved or abdicate her social role. Feeling the solitude of her voluptuous bed where lust had not yet set its hot feet, she rolled about twisting and repeating, "I want to be loved!" And the faith she still had in herself gave her hope that she would yet succeed. The duchess was piqued, the vain Parisienne was humiliated, the true woman glimpsed happiness, and her imagination, avenger of time lost by nature, took delight in kindling in her the inextinguishable fires of pleasure. She almost attained the sensations of love, for gripped by the doubt that she was loved, she found happiness in telling herself, "I love him!" Society and love, she wanted to trample them underfoot. Montriveau was now her religion. She spent the following day in a state of moral stupor mingled with bodily agitations that nothing could express. She tore up as many letters as she had written and indulged in a thousand impossible speculations. At the hour when Montriveau used to come, she wanted to believe he would come and took pleasure in waiting for him. Her life was concentrated in her single sense of hearing. She sometimes closed her eyes and willed herself to listen across space. Then she wished she could erase all obstacles between her and her lover so as to reach that absolute silence that allows us to perceive noise at a vast distance. In this reverential silence, the ticking of her clock was hateful, a sinister gossip that she stopped. Midnight struck in the salon.

"My God!" she said to herself. "What happiness it would be to see him here. And yet he used to come here, led by desire. His voice filled this boudoir. And now, nothing!"

Remembering the scenes in which she had played the coquette and which had torn him from her, tears of despair ran freely down her cheeks.

"Madame la duchesse," said her ladies' maid, "does not perhaps know that it is two o'clock in the morning. I thought that madame was indisposed."

"Yes, I am going to bed. But remember, Suzette," said Madame de Langeais, wiping her tears, "never enter my boudoir without being ordered to do so, and I will not tell you a second time."

For a week, Madame de Langeais went to all the houses where she hoped to meet Monsieur de Montriveau. Contrary to her habits, she arrived early and left late; she no longer danced but played cards. Useless efforts! She could not manage to see Armand, whose name she no longer dared pronounce. One evening, however, in a desperate moment, she said to Madame de Sérizy, with as much nonchalance as it was possible for her summon, "So you have quarreled with Monsieur de Montriveau? I no longer see him at your house."

"He does not come here any more?" answered the countess, laughing. "He is not seen anywhere, for that matter. He is interested in some woman, no doubt."

"I thought," the duchess continued softly, "that the Marquis de Ronquerolles was one of his friends."

"I have never heard my brother say that he knew him."

Madame de Langeais did not reply. Then Madame de Sérizy thought that she could apply the whip with impunity to a discreet friendship that had long embittered her and continued the conversation.

"So you miss that melancholy personage. I have heard the most monstrous things about him: Wound him, and he never returns, never forgives. Love him, and he puts you in chains. To everything I have said about him, one of those that praise him to the skies would always answer, '*He knows how to love!*' They continually repeat to me: 'Montriveau will drop everything for a friend, he has a great soul.' Bah! Society does not demand great souls. Men of that character are better off at home, let them stay there, and let them leave us to our small pleasures. What do you say, Antoinette?"

Despite being a woman of the world, the duchess seemed agitated, but nonetheless she said with a facility that fooled her friend, "I am sorry to miss him. I took a great interest in him and wished him my sincere friendship. You may find me ridiculous, dear friend, but I love great souls. To give oneself to a fool is a clear admission, is it not, that one is governed wholly by the senses?"

Madame de Sérizy had never *distinguished* any but ordinary men and was loved at the moment by a handsome man, the Marquis d'Aiglemont.

The countess cut short her visit, you may be sure. Madame de Langeais, seeing a hope in Armand's absolute withdrawal, immediately wrote him a humble, sweet letter that ought to bring him back to her if he still loved her. The following day she had her personal valet carry the letter, and when he returned, she asked him if he had given it to Montriveau himself; his affirmation prompted her unrestrained gesture of joy. Armand was in Paris, he was staying at home alone, he was not going out into society! So she was loved. All day she waited for a reply, and the reply did not come. Amidst recurring crises caused by her impatience, Antoinette justified this tardiness to herself: Armand was preoccupied, the reply would come by post. But that evening she could no longer lie to herself. A dreadful day, a mingling of pleasing sufferings, of crushing palpitations, rapid heartbeats wasting her life-force. The next day she sent to Armand's for a reply.

"Monsieur le marquis sent word that he would call on madame la duchesse," announced Julien the valet.

She fled so as not to let her happiness show and fell on her couch to devour her first emotions.

"He is going to come!" This thought rent her soul. Indeed, woe unto those for whom waiting is not the most dreadful of tempests and the germination of the sweetest pleasures; they have nothing in them of that flame that awakens the images of things and doubles nature in binding us as much to the pure essence of objects as to their reality. What is waiting in love but the constant drawing upon unfailing hope, submission to the terrible scourge of passion, happy without the disenchantments of truth! Waiting is a constant emanation of force and desire. Is it not the equivalent in the human soul of the perfumed exhalations of certain flowers? We have left behind the gaudy and sterile colors of coreopsis or tulips and we turn repeatedly to breathe in the delicious thought of the orange blossom or the volkameria flower, which their countries have involuntarily compared to young brides-to-be, full of love, beautiful in their past and their future.

The duchess learned the pleasures of her new life by reeling with the flagellations of love; then, changing her sentiments, she found other destinations and a better sense of things. Rushing into her *cabinet de toilette*, she understood the careful adornment and the most fastidious bodily attentions when they are ordered by love and not by vanity; already these rituals of dressing helped her to bear the slow passage of time. Once her toilette was finished, she fell again into excessive agitations, into the nervous convulsions of that dreadful power that stirs up all ideas and that is perhaps only an illness whose sufferings we love. The duchess was ready at two o'clock in the afternoon. Monsieur de Montriveau had not yet arrived at eleven thirty in the evening. In order to explain the anguish of this woman, who could pass for a spoiled child of civilization, we would have to know how much poetry the heart can concentrate in one thought, how powerful a force the soul exhales at the sound of the bell, or how to estimate the life-force consumed by a carriage that rolls past and does not stop.

"Is he toying with me?" she said, listening to the stroke of midnight.

She grew pale, her teeth chattered, and she clapped her hands as she leapt across the boudoir, where formerly, she thought, he appeared without being called. But she resigned herself. Had she not made him turn pale and twinge under the sharp arrows of her irony? Madame de Langeais understood the horror of the fate of women who, deprived of man's means of action, must wait when they love. To take the first step toward her beloved is a fault that few men know how to forgive. Most of them see degradation in this celestial flattery; but Armand had a great soul and ought to count among the few men who know how to excuse such an excess of love by eternal devotion.

"Well then, I shall go," she said to herself, tossing sleepless in her bed. "I shall go to him, I shall not exhaust myself holding out a hand. An exceptional man sees in each step a woman takes toward him promises of love and constancy. Yes, angels must descend from the heavens to come to men, and I want to be an angel for him."

The next day she wrote one of those notes in which the minds of Paris's ten thousand Sévignés excel. However, knowing how to plead without abasing herself, flying with both wings spread without humbly trailing them, complaining without offending, rebelling gracefully, forgiving without compromising her personal dignity, saying everything and admitting nothing, one had to be the Duchesse de Langeais and raised by Madame la Princesse de Blamont-Chauvry to write this delicious note. Julien was, like all personal valets, the victim of love's advances and counter-advances.

"What did Monsieur de Montriveau reply?" she asked Julien as indifferently as she could, when he came to report on his mission.

"Monsieur le marquis begged me to say to madame la duchesse that it was all right."

Dreadful reaction of the soul on itself! To have this matter of the heart exposed before curious witnesses, and not to murmur, and to be forced into silence. One of those thousand sorrows of the rich!

For twenty-two days Madame de Langeais wrote to Monsieur de Montriveau without receiving a reply. She had finally let it be known that she was ill in order to excuse herself from her duties, whether to the princess to whom she was attached or to society. She received only her father, the Duc de Navarreins; her aunt the Princesse de Blamont-Chauvry; the old Vidame de Pamiers, her maternal great-uncle; and her husband's uncle the Duc de Grandlieu. These persons easily believed in Madame de Langeais's illness, finding her from day to day increasingly worn out, pale, and thin. The vague ardors of a real love, the irritations of wounded pride, the constant prick of the only contempt that could touch her, her yearnings toward perpetual pleasures perpetually desired and betrayed; finally all her forces were stimulated to no purpose and undermined her double nature. She was paying the arrears of her life of make-believe.

She went out at last to see a military review. Monsieur de Montriveau was sure to be there. For the duchess, seated on the balcony of the Tuileries with the royal family, it was one of those celebrations that linger in the soul's memory for a long time. She looked supremely beautiful in her languor, and all eyes paid homage to her with admiration. She exchanged several looks with Montriveau, whose presence only enhanced her beauty. The general marched nearly at her feet in all the splendor of that military uniform whose effect on the feminine imagination is avowed by even the most prudish women. For a woman so in love, who has not seen her lover in two months, this brief moment surely resembles that phase of our dreams when our view fleetingly embraces nature without horizons.

So it is that only women or young people can imagine the dumb, delirious hunger expressed by the eyes of the duchess. As for men, if during their youth they experienced in the paroxysm of their first passions these phenomena of nervous power, later they forget them so completely that they end by denying such luxuriant ecstasies, the only possible name for these magnificent intuitions. Religious ecstasy is the madness of thought disengaged from corporal bonds; while in the ecstasy of love, the forces of our two natures are mingled, united, and embraced. When a woman is prey to the frenzied tyrannies under which Madame de Langeais was forced to bend, definitive resolutions came so quick and fast that it is impossible to define them. Thoughts are born in this way, one from the other, and pass through the soul like clouds borne by the wind on a gray backdrop that veils the sun.

Henceforth, facts tell all. So here are the facts. The day after the review, Madame de Langeais sent her carriage with her livery to wait at the door of the Marquis de Montriveau from eight o'clock in the morning until three o'clock in the afternoon. Armand lived on rue de Seine, a few doors down from the Chamber of Peers, where he was to have a meeting that day. But long before the peers met at their palace, several persons glimpsed the duchess's carriage and livery. The Baron de Maulincour, a young officer disdained by Madame de Langeais and taken up by Madame de Sérizy, was the first to recognize her servants. He went on the spot to his mistress to tell her, sworn to secrecy, about this strange folly. Instantly the news was telegraphed to all the coteries of the Faubourg Saint-Germain, reaching the Élysée-Bourbon palace, becoming the news of the day, the subject of all conversations from noon to evening. Nearly all the women denied the fact, but in such a way that the report was confirmed, and the men believed it, showing the most indulgent interest in Madame de Langeais.

"That savage of a Montriveau has a heart of bronze, no doubt he insisted on this scandal," said some, casting the blame on Armand.

"Ah well," said others, "Madame de Langeais has committed the noblest form of imprudence! To renounce, for her lover, society, rank, fortune, and respect in the face of all Paris—that is as fine a coup d'état for a woman as the wig-maker's knife-wielding that so affected Canning in the assize court. Not one of the women who blame the duchess would make this kind of declaration worthy of the old regime. Madame de Langeais is a heroic woman to proclaim herself so frankly. Now she can love no one but Montriveau. There is surely some greatness in a woman who says, 'I have but one passion.'"

"But what is to become of society, monsieur, if you so honor vice without respect for virtue?" said the attorney general's wife, the Comtesse de Granville.

While the palace, the Faubourg, and the Chaussée d'Antin were discussing the decline of aristocratic virtue, while excited young men went galloping off to see the carriage on rue de Seine and confirm that the duchess really was at Monsieur de Monrriveau's, she lay with her heart beating fast in the depths of her own boudoir. Armand, who had not slept at home, was strolling in the Tuileries with Monsieur de Marsay. Meanwhile, the older members of Madame de

Langeais's family were calling on one another to arrange a meeting at her mansion to reprimand her and conceive a way of stopping the scandal caused by her conduct. At three o'clock, Monsieur le Duc de Navarreins, the Vidame de Pamiers, the old Princesse de Blamont-Chauvry, and the Duc de Grandlieu had gathered in Madame de Langeais's drawing room and were awaiting her. To them, as to several curious people, the servants had said that their mistress had gone out. The duchess had made no exceptions to her orders. But belonging to that aristocratic sphere documented in the *Gotha Almanac*, which is devoted yearly to its revolutions and hereditary pretensions, these four illustrious persons require a quick sketch to complete this social canvas.

The Princesse de Blamont-Chauvry was the most poetic among the female debris of the reign of Louis XV. In her lovely youth, it is said, she had done her part to win that monarch his appellation "the well-loved." All that remained of her former charms was a remarkably prominent and slender nose, curved like a scimitar and the chief ornament on a face reminiscent of an old white glove, then some crimped and powdered hair, high-heeled slippers, a cap with upright lace loops, black mittens, and diamond brooches. But to do her complete justice, we must add that she had such a lofty idea of her decrepitude that she wore low-cut evening dresses with long gloves and still painted her cheeks with Martin's classic rouge. A formidable amiability in her wrinkles, a blazing fire in her eyes, a profound dignity in her entire person, a triple-barbed wit on her tongue, an infallible memory in her head made this old woman a real power. The whole Cabinet des Chartes lined the pathways in her brain, and she knew the alliances of every noble house in Europe—princes, dukes, and counts—indeed the whereabouts of the last descendants of Charlemagne. No usurped title could escape the Princesse de Blamont-Chauvry.

Young men who wanted to be seen paid her constant homage. Her salon had authority in the Faubourg Saint-Germain. The words of this female Talleyrand were taken as final pronouncements. Certain persons came to her for advice on etiquette or customs, and to take lessons in good taste. Surely no old woman knew how to put her snuffbox back in her pocket the way she did, and in sitting and crossing her legs, she moved her skirt with a precision and grace that made the most elegant young women despair. Her voice had resided in her head during a third of her life, but she had not been able to prevent it from descending into the membranes of the nose, which made it strangely impressive. She still possessed a hundred and fifty thousand pounds of her great fortune, for Napoleon had generously returned her forests to her, so that as regards her person and possessions, she was a woman of considerable consequence.

This curious antique was seated in a low chair by the fireside, chatting with the Vidame de Pamiers, another contemporary ruin. This old lord, a former commander of the Order of Malta, was a big, tall, spare man, a whose neck was always so tightly compressed by his collar that his cheeks hung slightly over his cravat and kept his head high—an attitude full of self-importance in some men but justified in his case by a Voltarian wit. His wide prominent eyes seemed to see everything and had, in effect, seen everything. He put cotton in his ears. In short, his person altogether provided a perfect model of aristocratic lines, lines thin and delicate, supple and agreeable, which like those of a snake can bend at will, straighten up, become fluid or rigid.

The Duc de Navarreins was strolling up and down the salon with the Duc de Grandlieu. Both were fifty-five years of age, still healthy, corpulent and short, well fed, with slightly florid complexions, tired eyes, and already drooping lower lips. Without the exquisite tone of their language, without the affable polish of their manners, without their ease that could suddenly become impertinence, a superficial observer might have taken them for bankers. But any such mistake would have to be rectified by listening to their conversation, on guard with those they feared, dry or vapid with their equals, slyly manipulative with their inferiors whom courtiers or statesmen know how to tame by tactful words or to humiliate by an unexpected phrase. Such were the representatives of this great nobility determined to perish rather than submit, who deserved as much praise as blame, and will always be imperfectly judged until some poet comes along to tell how happy they were to obey the king in expiring under Richelieu's ax, and how they scorned the guillotine of '89 as a foul revenge.

These four persons were all distinguished by a reedy voice that was particularly in harmony with their ideas and bearing. Besides, the most perfect equality prevailed among them. The courtier's habit of hiding their emotions surely prevented any show of displeasure caused by their young relative's escapade.

And to prevent critics from condemning the beginning of the next scene as puerile, perhaps we might observe that Locke, finding himself in the company of English lords renowned for their wit, distinguished by their manners rather than by their political consistency, amused himself by jotting down their conversation in some private shorthand; when he read it back to them to see what they could make of it, they all burst out laughing. Truthfully, the clinking jargon that the upper class use in every country, washed in literary and philosophic ashes, yields very little gold. In every rank of society, save in some Parisian salons, the observer finds a same silliness distinguished only by the transparency or opacity of the varnish. Thus serious conversations are the social exception, and Boeotian stupidity is current coin in the various zones of the social world. In the higher regions they must of course talk more, yet they give little thought to it. To think is tiring, and the rich love to see life glide by without great effort. It is by comparing the content of pleasantries by rank, from the Paris street urchin to the peer of France, that the observer understands Monsieur de Talleyrand's remark that "Manner is everything," an elegant translation of that judicial axiom: "Form over content." In the eyes of the poet, the advantage will remain with the lower classes, who never fail to give a rough element of poetry to their thoughts. This observation will perhaps also clarify the inferiority of the salons, their vapidity, their lack of depth, and the disgust superior men feel engaging in the shoddy commerce of exchanging their ideas in this setting.

The duke suddenly stopped himself, as if he just had a brilliant idea, and said to his neighbor, "So you have sold Thornton?"

"No, he is ill. I am rather afraid of losing him, and I would feel bereft; he is an excellent hunter. Do you know how the Duchesse de Marigny is faring?"

"No, I did not go there this morning. I was going out to see her when you came to speak to me about Antoinette. But she was much worse yesterday, they had nearly given up hope, she has been given the sacraments."

"Her death will change your cousin's position."

"Not at all. She gave away her property in her lifetime, keeping only an annuity. She made over the Guébriant estate to her niece, Madame de Soulanges, subject to a yearly charge."

"It will be a great loss for society. She was a good woman. Her family will have one less person whose advice and experience carried weight. Between us it may be said, she was the head of the house. Her son, Marigny, is an amiable man; he has a sharp wit, he knows how to talk. He is pleasant, very pleasant—oh, when it comes to pleasant, he is certainly that. But...no sense of how to behave. Yes, it is extraordinary, he is very acute. The other day he was dining at the Cercle with all that rich set from the Chaussée d'Antin, and your uncle (who always goes there for his card game) saw him. Astonished to meet him there, he asks him if he is part of the Cercle. 'Yes, I do not go only into society now, I live among bankers.'"

"Do you know why?" said the marquis, giving the duke a thin smile.

"He is infatuated with a new bride, that little Madame Keller, the daughter of Gondreville, a woman thought to be very fashionable in that world."

"But Antoinette is not wasting her time, it seems," said the old vidame.

"The affection I feel for that little woman causes me to take up at the moment a singular pastime," replied the princess, pocketing her snuffbox.

"My dear aunt," said the duke, halting his step, "I am extremely vexed. It was only a man of Bonaparte's time who could ask such an inappropriate thing of a woman of fashion. Between us, Antoinette might have made a better choice."

"My dear," replied the princess, "the Montriveaus are an old family with powerful connections. They are related to all the highest nobility in Burgundy. If the Arschoot Rivaudoults, from the Dulmen branch of the family, should come to an end in Galicia, the Montriveaus would succeed to the Arschoot properties and titles. They inherit through their great-grandfather."

"Are you sure?"

"I know it better than Montriveau's father did; I used to see a good deal of him and I told him about it. Though a chevalier of several orders, he laughed; he was really an Encyclopedist. But his brother profited nicely from the relationship in the emigration. I have heard it said that his northern relations behaved impeccably toward him—"

"Yes, certainly. The Comte de Montriveau died in St. Petersburg where I met him," said the vidame. "He was a big man with an incredible passion for oysters."

"How many did he eat at a sitting?" asked the Duc de Grandlieu.

"Ten dozen every day."

"Without discomfort?"

"Not in the least."

"But that is extraordinary! This taste did not give him kidney stones, or gout, or any other complaint?"

"No, he was in perfect health and died accidentally."

"Accidentally! Nature had told him to eat oysters, they were probably necessary to him; for up to a certain point, our dominant tastes are the conditions of our existence."

"I am of your opinion," said the princess, smiling.

"Madame, you always construe things maliciously," said the marquis.

"I only want to make you understand that these things would be very badly construed by a young woman," she replied. She interrupted herself to say, "But my niece! What about my niece!"

"Dear aunt, I still refuse to believe that she could have gone to Monsieur de Montriveau's house."

"Nonsense!" replied the princess.

"What do you think, vidame?" asked the marquis.

"If the duchess were naïve, I would believe—"

"But a woman in love becomes naïve, my poor vidame. Are you getting old?"

"Well, what is to be done?"

"If my dear niece is wise," said the princess, "she will go to court this evening, since fortunately this is Monday, the day to be received there. You must see to it that we all rally around her and give the lie to this ridiculous rumor. There are a thousand ways of explaining things, and if the Marquis de Montriveau is a gallant man, he will participate in this effort. We shall make these children listen to reason."

"But it is difficult to change Monsieur de Montriveau's view of the matter. He is one of Bonaparte's pupils, and he has a position. Why, he is one of the great men of the day, he has an important command in the guard, where he is very useful. He does not have the slightest ambition. At the first word that might displease him, he would say to the king, 'Here is my resignation, leave me alone.' "

"What are his opinions, then?"

"Very disagreeable."

"Really," said the princess, sighing, "the king remains what he has always been, a Jacobin covered with the fleur-de-lis."

"Oh, not so bad," replied the vidame.

"No, I've known him a long time. The man who said to his wife the day of the first state dinner, showing her the court, 'These are our servants!' could be only a black-hearted scoundrel. I can see Monsieur, as he once was, in the king, the same as ever. The bad brother who voted so wrongly in his department of the Constituent Assembly surely conspired with the Liberals to let them discuss and argue. This philosophical cant will be just as dangerous for his younger brother as it was for him because I do not know if his successor will manage to pull out of the difficulties created by this large, small-minded man to amuse himself. Besides, he abhors his younger brother and would be happy to tell himself as he lies dying, 'He will not reign long.'"

"My aunt, he is the king, I have the honor to be in his service, and—"

"But my dear, does your charge strip you of your right to speak? You are from as good a noble house as the Bourbons. If the Guises had only possessed a little more resolution, His Majesty would be a poor lord today. It is time I left this world, for the nobility is dead. Yes, all is lost for you, my children," she said, looking at the vidame. "Should the town really be concerned with my niece's behavior? She was wrong, I do not approve of it, a useless scandal is a blunder. That is why I still have my doubts about this neglect of appearances, I raised her and I know that—"

At this moment the duchess come out of her boudoir. She had recognized her aunt's voice and heard her pronounce the name of Montriveau. She was in her morning gown, and when she appeared, Monsieur de Grandlieu, who was looking carelessly out the window, saw his daughter's carriage return without her.

"My dear girl," the duke said to her, holding her head and kissing her forehead, "you do not know what is going on, then?"

"What is happening that is so extraordinary, dear Father?"

"But all of Paris believes you are at Monsieur de Montriveau's."

"My dear Antoinette, you have not gone out, have you?" said the princess, holding out her hand, which the duchess kissed with respectful affection.

"No, dear Mother, I have not gone out. And," she said, turning to greet the vidame and the marquis, "I wanted all of Paris to think I was at Monsieur de Montriveau's."

The duke raised his hands heavenward, clapped them desperately, and crossed his arms. "Surely you know what will result from this mad escapade?"

The old princess silently straightened up on her heels and was looking at the duchess, who began to blush and lowered her eyes. Madame de Blamont-Chauvry gently drew her closer and said, "Let me kiss you, my little angel." Then she kissed her on the forehead very affectionately, squeezed her hand, and, smiling, continued: "We are no longer under the rule of the Valois, my dear girl. You have compromised your husband, your standing in society; however, we are going to make everything right."

"But my dear aunt, I do not want to make everything right. I want all of Paris to know or say that this morning I was at Monsieur de Montriveau's. Destroying this belief, false as it is, would hurt me, strange as it may seem."

"My girl, so you want to lose yourself and cause suffering to your family?"

"By sacrificing me to their interests, my father, my family have unintentionally condemned me to irreparable miseries. You can blame me for seeking alleviation, but you must surely sympathize with me."

"And you take such trouble to settle your daughters suitably!" murmured the Duc de Navarreins to the vidame.

"Dear girl," said the princess, shaking off grains of tobacco that had fallen on her dress, "be happy if you can. We are not talking about interfering with your happiness but about respecting convention. All of you here know that marriage is a defective institution tempered by love. But when you take a lover, is there any need to make your bed on the place du Carrousel? Come now, be reasonable and listen to us."

"I am listening."

"Madame la duchesse," said the Duc de Grandlieu, "if uncles were duty-bound to look after their nieces, they would have a position in the world; society would owe them honors, rewards, and a salary, just as it does the king's servants. So I did not come to talk about my nephew but about your interests. Let us perform a little calculation. If you persist in making a scandal, I know the lord and I have no great liking for him. Langeais is rather a miser and to hell with anyone else. He will want a separation from you. He will keep your fortune, leave you poor, and consequently you will be a nobody. The income of a hundred thousand pounds that you have just inherited from your maternal great-aunt will pay for the pleasures of his mistresses, and your hands will be tied, garroted by the law, obliged to say *amen* to these arrangements.

"Should Montriveau leave you! My Lord, dear niece, let us remain calm—a man will not abandon you, young and beautiful as you are. However, we have seen so many pretty women left neglected, even among the princesses, that you will allow me to imagine the nearly impossible—as I wish to believe. Well, what will happen to you without a husband? Take care of your husband just as you care for your beauty, which is after all a woman's insurance as much as a husband. I am assuming that you will always be happy and loved; I am not considering any unhappy event. This being so, fortunately or unfortunately, you may have children. What will you do about them? Make them Montriveaus? Well, they will never inherit their father's entire fortune. You will want to give them all you have; he will wish to do the same. My Lord, nothing is more natural. You will find the law against you. How many suits have we seen brought by the legitimate heirs against love children! I hear about it in every court of law in the world. Will you have recourse to some fideicommissum? If the person in whom you put your trust wrongs you, truly human justice will know nothing about it. But your children will be ruined.

"Choose carefully! See what a complex situation you are in. In any case your children will be necessarily sacrificed to the fantasies of your heart and deprived of their estate. Heavens, when they are small, they will be charming, but one day they will reproach you for having thought more about yourself than about them. We know all this, we old gentlemen. Children become men, and men are ungrateful. Have I not heard young de Horn in Germany saying after supper, 'If my mother had been an honest woman, I would be prince regent.' But this 'if'—we have spent our life hearing commoners say it, and it has brought about the revolution. When men can accuse neither their father nor their mother, they reproach God for their ill fate. In short, dear child, we are here to enlighten you. I will sum up what I have to say with a thought on which you ought to meditate: A woman must never allow her husband to be in the right."

"My uncle, so long as I did not love anyone, I calculated. Like you, I saw only interests then, where now I have nothing but feelings," said the duchess.

"But my dear girl, life is always quite simply a complication of interests and feelings," replied the vidame. "And to be happy, especially in your position, one must try to bring feelings in line with interests. Let a shopgirl love according to her fancy, that is understandable, but you have a fine fortune, a family, a title, a place at court, and you must not toss these things out the window. And what do we ask you to do to reconcile these matters? To maneuver the conventions deftly instead of violating them. Heavens, I will soon be eighty years old, I do not remember having encountered under the ancien régime a love that was worth the price you wish to pay for the love of this fortunate young man."

The duchess silenced the vidame with a look; and if Montriveau could have seen it, he would have forgiven everything.

"It would be very effective on the stage," said the Duc de Grandlieu, "and meaningless where your personal fortune, position, and independence are concerned. You are ungrateful, my dear niece. You will not find many families where the relatives are brave enough to offer the lessons of experience and make young, foolish minds listen to the language of reason. Renounce your salvation in two minutes, if it pleases you to damn yourself—fine! But think a bit longer when it is a matter of renouncing your income. I do not know a confessor who absolves poverty. I believe I have the right to speak to you this way, for if you are damned, I alone will be able to offer you asylum. I am nearly Langeais's uncle, and I alone will have the right to cross him."

"My daughter," said the Duc de Navarreins, in waking from a painful mediation, "since you are talking sentiment, let me remind you that a woman who bears your name owes herself to sentiments other than those that animate commoners. You want to give aid and comfort to the Liberals, those Robespierre Jesuits who claim to detest the nobility? There are certain things that a Navarreins cannot do without failing the whole house. You would not be the only one dishonored."

"Come, come!" said the princess. "Dishonor? Do not make such a fuss about an empty carriage, children, and leave me alone with Antoinette. All three of you will come and dine with me. I take responsibility for making a suitable arrangement. You men understand nothing, letting bitterness seep into your words, and I do not want to see you quarrel with my dear girl. Do me the pleasure of leaving."

The three gentlemen surely guessed the princess's intentions, and they bid their relations goodbye. Monsieur de Navarreins came to kiss his daughter on the forehead, saying, "Come now, dear child, be good. If you want, there is still time."

"Might we not find in the family some good fellow who would provoke a quarrel with this Montriveau?" said the vidame while descending the stairs.

"My precious one," said the princess once they were alone, gesturing to her to come and sit on a low chair beside her, "I know nothing more slandered in this world below than God and the eighteenth century, for in reviewing my youth, I do not recall a single duchess who trampled the proprieties underfoot as you have just done. Novelists and scribblers dishonored the reign of Louis XV, but do not believe them. The Du Barry woman, my dear, was just as worthy as the widow Scarron, and she was a better person. In my time, a woman knew how to keep her dignity in the midst of her gallantries. Indiscretions were the ruin of us, and the beginning of all misfortune.

"The philosophes, those men—the nobodies we admitted to our salons—had the indecency and the ingratitude to put a price on our benevolence, to make an inventory of our hearts, to condemn us all in detail, and to rant against the century. The people, who are not in a position to judge, saw the content but not the form. But in those days, my dearest, men and women were quite as remarkable as at any other period of the monarchy. Not one of your Werthers, none of your 'notables,' as they are called, not one of your men in yellow gloves whose trousers hide their spindly legs would cross Europe disguised as a peddler to shut himself up—at the risk of life and braving the Duke of Modena's daggers—in the daughter of the regent's *cabinet de toilette*. None of your little consumptives with tortoiseshell glasses would hide, like Lauzun, for six weeks in an armoire to a give his mistress courage while she gave birth. There was more passion in Monsieur de Jaucourt's little finger than in all your race of rivals who leave women to pursue their advantage! Can you find me pages today who would be cut in pieces and buried under the floorboards for one kiss on Königsmarck's mistress's gloved finger?

"Really, today it would seem that the roles have reversed, and women must devote themselves to men. These gentlemen are worth less and think more of themselves. Believe me, my dear, those adventures that have become public and are now used to revile our good Louis XV were kept secret at first. Without a pack of poetasters, scribblers, and moralists who spoke freely with our waiting women and wrote down their slanders, our era would have been portrayed in literature as a time in tune with convention. I justify the century and not its fringe. Perhaps a hundred women of quality were lost, but the wags counted a thousand, just as the gazetteers do when they reckon the dead of the defeated.

"Furthermore, I do not know what the Revolution and the Empire have to reproach us for: They were coarse, dull, licentious times. Fie! It is revolting. They were the fleshpots of French history…

"This preamble, my dear child," she continued after a pause, "is only my way of coming around to tell you that if Montriveau pleases you, you are quite free to love him at your ease, and as much as you can. I know from experience (unless you are locked up, but that is out of fashion today), that you will do as you please, and that is what I would have done at your age. Only, my precious girl, I would not abdicate the right to be mother of the future Ducs de Langeais. So mind appearances. The vidame is right, no man is worth a single sacrifice that we are fool enough to pay for their love. Put yourself in the position of power: If you should have the misfortune to repent of your situation, you will still be the wife of Monsieur de Langeais. When you are old, you will have the comfort of hearing Mass at court and not in a provincial convent.

"Therein lies the whole question. A single imprudence means an allowance, a wandering life at the mercy of your love; it means the pain caused by the insolence of women who are less worthy than you, precisely because they have been villainously clever. It is worth a hundred times more to go to Montriveau's every evening in a fiacre, disguised, than to send your carriage there in full daylight. You are a little fool, my dear child! Your carriage has flattered his vanity; your person would have conquered his heart. All that I have said is just and true, but I am not angry with you. You are two centuries behind with your false grandeur. Come along then, let us arrange your affairs, we will say that Montriveau has bribed your servants to satisfy his self-regard and to compromise you—"

"In the name of heaven, my aunt," cried the duchess, jumping up, "do not slander him."

"Oh, dear child," said the princess whose eyes were sparkling, "I would like to see you with illusions that would not be fatal to you, but all illusions must cease. You would soften me up if I were not so old. Come now, do not cause anyone grief, neither him nor us. I will take charge and satisfy everyone, but promise me not to permit yourself a single step from now on without consulting me. Tell me all, and perhaps I may steer you in the right direction."

"Dear aunt, I promise you—"

"To tell me everything."

"Yes, everything, everything that can be said."

"But, my darling, it is precisely what cannot be said that I want to know. Let us understand each other. Come now, let me put my dry old lips to your beautiful forehead. No, let me do it, I forbid you to kiss my old bones. Old people have a courtesy of their own . . . Come now, take me to my carriage," she said, after kissing her niece.

"Dear aunt, may I go to him in disguise?"

"But of course, this can always be denied," said the old woman.

Only this idea had clearly caught the duchess's attention in the sermon the princess had just delivered. When Madame de Blamont-Chauvry was seated in the corner of her carriage, Madame de Langeais bid her a gracious farewell and happily went back into her house.

"My person would have snared his heart. My aunt is right, a man surely cannot refuse a pretty woman when she knows how to offer herself."

That evening, in Madame la Duchesse de Berry's circle, the Duc de Navarreins, Monsieur de Pamiers, Monsieur de Marsay, Monsieur de Grandlieu, the Duc de Maufrigneuse triumphantly denied the offensive rumors that were circulating about the Duchesse de Langeais. So many officers and other people attested to having seen Montriveau walking in the Tuileries that morning that this silly story was attributed to chance, which takes everything on offer. And the following day, the reputation of the duchess, despite her parked carriage, became as clean and spotless as Mambrino's helmet after Sancho had polished it. Except, at two o'clock in the Bois de Boulogne, Monsieur de Ronquerolles, passing Montriveau in a deserted allée, said to him, smiling, "She is doing well, your duchess— go on, keep it up!" he added, giving a meaningful cut of his riding whip to his mare, who took off like a bullet.

Two days after her useless scandal, Madame de Langeais wrote to Monsieur de Montriveau a letter that remained unanswered like the others. This time she had taken measures and corrupted Auguste, Armand's personal valet. So that evening, at eight o'clock, she was led to Armand's, into a room quite different from the room where the secret scene had transpired. The duchess learned that the general would not return that night. Did he have two residences? The valet did not want to reply. Madame de Langeais had bought the key to this room and not the man's complete honesty. Left alone, she saw her fourteen letters resting on an old side table. They were uncreased and unopened. He had not read them. At this sight, she fell into an armchair and lost all consciousness for a moment. Upon waking, she saw Auguste, who was holding vinegar to her nose.

"A carriage, quickly," she said.

The carriage arrived and she went down to it with a convulsive quickness, returned home, went to bed, and barred her door. She stayed there for twenty-four hours, letting no one come near but her chambermaid, who brought her several cups of orange-leaf tisane.

Suzette heard her mistress moan once or twice and caught a glimpse of tears in her bright eyes, now circled with dark shadows.

Two days later, amid despairing sobs, she resolved on the path she would take. Madame de Langeais had a meeting with her business consultant and doubtless charged him with some preparations. Then she sent for the old Vidame de Pamiers. While waiting for the commander, she wrote to Monsieur de Montriveau. The vidame was punctual. He found his young cousin pale and worn but resigned. Never had her divine loveliness been more poetic than now in the weakness of her agony.

"My dear cousin," she said to the vidame, "your eighty years make you worthy of this meeting. Oh, do not smile, I beg of you, as a poor woman who is deeply unhappy. You are a gallant man, and I would like to believe that the adventures of your youth have inspired some indulgence for women."

"Not in the least," he said.

"Really!"

"Everything is in their favor," he replied.

"Ah well, you are one of the inner family circle; perhaps you will be the last relation, the last friend whose hand I will grasp, so I can ask you for a good turn. My dear vidame, do me a favor I would not know how to ask from my father, or from my uncle Grandlieu, or from any woman. You must understand me. I beg you to obey me and to forget that you have obeyed me, whatever may come of it. The matter is this: Take this letter to Monsieur de Montriveau, see him, show it to him, talk things over man to man, for between you there is an integrity of feelings that you forget with us, ask him if he would be willing to read my letter, not in your presence—men conceal certain emotions from each other. I authorize you to decide, and if you judge it necessary, to tell him that for me this is a matter of life or death. If he deigns—"

"*Deigns!*" repeated the vidame.

"If he deigns to read it," the duchess continued with dignity, "tell him one more thing. You will see him at five o'clock, he dines at home today at this time, I know. Well, by way of answer, he must come to see me. If three hours later, by eight o'clock, he has not left his house, it will all be settled. The Duchesse de Langeais will have vanished from the world. I shall not be dead, my dear, no, but no human power will find me on this earth. Come dine with me. At least I will have a friend to help me in my last agony. Yes, this evening, dear cousin, my life will be decided, and whatever happens to me, it can be only a searing ordeal. Go now, not a word. I will hear nothing, neither comments nor advice. Let us chat and laugh together," she said, holding out her hand, which he kissed. "Let us be like two old philosophers who know how to enjoy life until the moment of their death. I shall dress up, I will be enchanting for you. You will perhaps be the last man to see the Duchesse de Langeais."

The vidame bowed, took the letter, and went on his mission without a word. At five o'clock he returned and found his cousin dressed with great care, indeed enchanting. The salon was decorated with flowers as though for a party. The meal was exquisite. For this old man, the duchess displayed all the brilliance of her wit and looked more seductive than she had ever been. The commander at first wished to see all these preparations as a young woman's joke. But from time to time the false magic of his cousin's seductions paled. He detected a shudder caused by a kind of sudden dread, and at times she seemed to listen in silence. Then if he said to her "What is the matter?" she would answer, "Hush!"

At seven o'clock the duchess left the old fellow. She returned promptly, but dressed as her maid might have dressed for a journey. She took her companion's arm and rushed into a hackney coach. Toward quarter to eight they were both at the door of Monsieur de Montriveau.

During this time, Montriveau read and meditated on the following letter:

My friend, I spent several moments at your house, without your knowledge; I took back my letters. Oh, Armand, you cannot be indifferent toward me, and hatred displays itself otherwise. If you love me, stop this cruel game. You are killing me. Later you will be in despair, realizing how much you are loved. If I have misunderstood you, if you feel only aversion for me, which leads to contempt and disgust, then I give up all hope. A person never recovers from these feelings. This thought will bring consolations to my long suffering. You will have no regrets! Ah, my Armand, if I have caused you a single regret . . . No, I will not tell you what desolation I would feel. I would be still alive and could not be your wife. After giving myself to you entirely in my thoughts, to whom could I give myself? . . . to God. Yes, the eyes that you loved for a moment will see no man's face again, and may God's glory close them! I will hear no human voice after hearing yours, so sweet at first, so terrible yesterday, for I am always on the day after your vengeance. May the word of God then consume me! Between His anger and yours, my friend, I will be left with only tears and prayers.

Perhaps you will wonder why I am writing to you? Alas, do not deprive me of a last glimmer of hope, of one more sigh for a happy life before leaving it forever. I am in a dreadful situation. I have all the serenity the soul imbibes from making a great resolution, yet I still feel the last rumblings of the storm. When you went on that terrible adventure that so drew me to you, Armand, you were going from the desert to an oasis with a good guide leading you. Well, as for me, I am dragging myself from the oasis to the desert, and you are a pitiless guide. Nonetheless, you alone, my friend, can understand the melancholy of my parting looks at happiness, and you are the only man to whom I can moan without blushing. If you grant me my wish, I will be happy; if you are inexorable, I will expiate my wrongs. Indeed, is it not natural for a woman to want to remain clothed in the noblest sentiments in the memory of her beloved? Oh, my only dear, let your creature bury herself with the belief that you acknowledge her greatness. Your harshness has made me reflect, and since I love you dearly, I have found myself less guilty than you think I am. Listen, therefore, to my justification: I owe it to you. And you, who mean everything in the world to me, you owe me at least a moment of justice.

I have come to know, through my own anguish, how my coquetry made you suffer. But then I was utterly ignorant of love. You are party to the secret of these tortures, and you impose them on me. During the first eight months you granted me, you never roused any feeling of love in me. Why, my friend? I no more know how to tell you than I can explain to you why I love you now. Oh, to be sure, I was flattered to see that I was the object of your passionate pleas, of your fiery looks, but you left me cold and without desire. No, I was not a woman, I had no conception of the devotion or the happiness of our sex. Who was to blame? You would have despised me, would you not, had I given myself without being carried away? Perhaps this is our sex's experience of the sublime, to give oneself without receiving any pleasure; perhaps there is no merit in yielding to ardently desired bliss. Alas, my friend, I can tell you these thoughts came to me when I was playing the coquette, but I found you already so great that I did not want you to owe me to pity... What have I written here?

Ah, I have taken back all my letters, and I am throwing them in the fire! They are burning. You will never know what they confessed—love, passion, madness... I keep silent, Armand, I cease, I no longer wish to tell you anything of my feelings. If the prayers from my soul to yours have not been heard, as a woman I decline to owe your love to pity. It is my wish to be loved irresistibly or dropped without mercy. If you refuse to read this letter, it will be burned. If, having read it, you are not three hours later forever my only husband, I will have no shame knowing that it is in your hands: The pride of my despair will protect my memory from any insult and my end will be worthy of my love. As for you, when you see me no more on earth, though I shall still be alive, you will not think without a shudder of a woman who in three hours will no longer draw breath but to overwhelm you with her tenderness, a woman consumed by hopeless love, and faithful—not to shared pleasures but to unknown feelings.

The Duchesse de La Vallière wept for lost happiness, for her vanished power, while the Duchesse de Langeais will be happy in her weeping and will remain a power for you. Yes, you will regret me... I see clearly that I was not of this world, and I thank you for having made it clear to me.

Farewell, you will never touch my ax; yours was that of the executioner, mine is that of God; yours kills and mine saves. Your love was mortal, it knew how to bear neither disdain nor ridicule; mine can endure everything without weakening, it is eternally live. Oh, I feel a dark joy in crushing you, you who believed in your greatness, in humbling you by the calm and protective smile of weak angels who, in lying down at the feet of God, have the right and the power to watch over men in His name. You have had merely passing desires, while the poor nun will shed on you the light of her ardent prayers and cover you always with the wings of divine love.

I have a presentiment of your reply, Armand, and grant you a meeting... in heaven. Friend, there strength and weakness are equally admitted; both are bound to suffer. This thought soothes the anguish of my final ordeal. You see, I am so calm that I would fear I no longer loved you, if it were not for you that I am leaving this world.

Antoinette

"Dear vidame," said the duchess, arriving at Montriveau's house, "do me the grace of asking at the door if he is in."

The commander, obeying in the manner of the eighteenth century, disembarked from the carriage and returned to answer "yes" to his cousin's question, an answer that made her shiver. At this word, she took the commander, squeezed his hand, let him kiss her on both cheeks, and begged him to go at once without spying on her or trying to protect her.

"But the passersby?" he said.

"No one can fail to respect me," she replied.

This was the last word from the lady of fashion and the duchess. The commander went off. Madame de Langeais remained on the threshold, wrapped in her cloak, and waited for the clock to strike eight. The hour struck and all was still. This unhappy woman gave herself ten minutes, a quarter of an hour; indeed, she was inclined to see a new humiliation in this tardiness, and faith abandoned her. She could not help exclaiming, "Oh my God!" then left that deadly threshold. These were the first words of the Carmelite.

Montriveau was in a meeting with several friends; he hurried them to finish up, but his clock was slow and he left for the Langeais mansion only when the duchess, transported by cold rage, was fleeing on foot through the streets of Paris. She wept when she reached boulevard d'Enfer. There, for the last time, she looked at Paris, smoking, burning, covered with a reddish glow from its streetlights; then she mounted a cab for hire and left this city never to return. When the Marquis de Montriveau came to the Langeais mansion, he did not find his mistress there and thought she was toying with him. So he ran to the home of the vidame and was received there just as the good man was slipping into his dressing gown, thinking of his pretty cousin's happiness. Montriveau gave him a terrible look, a look that struck men and women alike as an electric shock.

"Monsieur, would you lend yourself to this cruel joke?" he cried. "I have come from Madame de Langeais's, and her servants say that she has left."

"A great disaster has happened, doubtless because of you," answered the vidame. "I left the duchess at your door—"

"At what time?"

"At quarter to eight."

"My best to you," said Montriveau, who quickly returned home to ask his porter if he had seen a lady at the door that evening.

"Yes, monsieur, a beautiful woman who seemed to be having a good deal of trouble. She was weeping like a Madeleine without making a sound and was holding herself as straight as a needle. At last she said 'Oh my God!' in a way that—begging your pardon—broke our hearts, my wife's and mine, who were there without being seen."

These few words made this hard man go pale. He wrote some lines to Monsieur de Ronquerolles, which he sent him on the spot, and went back to his apartment. Toward midnight, the Marquis de Ronquerolles arrived.

"What is it, my good friend?" he said, seeing the general.

Armand gave him the duchess's letter to read.

"Well?" asked Ronquerolles.

"She was at my door at eight o'clock, and at quarter past eight she disappeared. I have lost her, and I love her! Ah, if my life belonged to me, I would already have blown my brains out!"

"Now, now!" said Ronquerolles. "Calm down. Duchesses do not fly away like wagtails. She will not manage more than three leagues per hour; tomorrow we men shall do six.

"Oh, confound it!" he continued. "Madame de Langeais is not an ordinary woman. We will all be on horseback tomorrow. The police will tell us where she has gone. Whether she is on the road or hidden in Paris, we shall find her. Do we not have the telegraph to stop her without following her? You will be happy. But my dear brother, you have committed the sin that men of your energy are more or less guilty of committing. You judge other souls according to your own, and do not know where humanity breaks when you pull the cords too tight. Why did you not tell me sooner? I would have told you: Be there on time.

"Until tomorrow, then," he added, shaking Montriveau's hand while he remained silent. "Sleep if you can."

But the vast resources in which men of state, sovereigns, ministers, bankers, indeed all human power is socially invested, were deployed in vain. Neither Montriveau nor his friends could find a trace of the duchess. She had obviously taken refuge in a cloister. Montriveau resolved to search or have searched all the convents in the world. He must have the duchess, even if it cost him the life of an

THE DUCHESSE DE LANGEAIS · 409

entire city. To do justice to this extraordinary man, we must say that his passionate furor did not abate for a day and lasted five years.

Not until 1829 did the Duc de Navarreins learn by chance that his daughter had departed for Spain, as Julia Hopwood's chambermaid, and that she had left this lady in Cádiz. Lady Julia had no notion that Mademoiselle Caroline was the illustrious duchess whose disappearance was the talk of Parisian high society.

We may now understand the depth of the lovers' feelings when they found each other again at the grille of the Carmelite convent, in the presence of a mother superior. And the violence awakened in them both will doubtless explain the ending of this adventure.

4. GOD GIVES THE ENDING

In 1823 the Duc de Langeais died and his wife was free. Antoinette de Navarreins was living consumed by love on a ledge of the Mediterranean, but the pope could break the vows of Sister Theresa. The happiness bought by such love could blossom for the two lovers. These thoughts sent Montriveau flying from Cádiz to Marseille, from Marseille to Paris. Some months after his arrival in France, a merchant brig armed for war set sail from Marseille for Spain. The vessel had been chartered by several men of distinction, nearly all French, who were taken with a great passion for the East and wanted to travel to those lands. Montriveau's familiar knowledge of Eastern customs made him an invaluable traveling companion for these persons, who begged him to join them on their expedition and he agreed. The minister of war named him a lieutenant general and put him on the artillery committee to facilitate this pleasure party.

Twenty-four hours after its departure the brig stopped northwest of an island in sight of the Spanish coast. The vessel had been specially chosen for her shallow draft and light sail so that it might lie at anchor safely half a league away from the reefs that secure the island from approach in this direction. If fishing boats or the island's inhabitants perceived the brig in this anchorage, they could not imagine any reason for concern. Then it was easy to justify its presence. Before arriving in sight of the island, Montriveau hoisted the flag of the United States. The sailors hired for service on the vessel were Americans and spoke only English. One of Monsieur de Montriveau's companions took the men ashore in a longboat and made them so drunk at an inn in the little town that they could not talk. Then he let on that the brig was manned by treasure seekers, men known in the United States for their fanaticism and whose story had been recorded by one of the writers of that country. Thus the presence of the vessel among the reefs was sufficiently explained. The owners and passengers, said the self-styled boatswain, were searching for the remains of a galleon sunk in 1778, carrying treasure from Mexico. The innkeepers and authorities of the country asked no more questions.

Armand and his devoted friends, who backed him up in his difficult enterprise, thought at first that neither ruse nor strength could succeed in delivering or carrying off Sister Theresa from the side of the little coastal town. So by common agreement, these audacious men resolved to take the bull by the horns. They wanted to cut a path to the convent through the most inaccessible places and to conquer nature the way General Lamarque had conquered in the assault on Capri. In this instance, it seemed to Montriveau, who had been on that incredible expedition, the sheer granite blocks at the end of the island offered less purchase than those of Capri, and the nuns seemed to him more fearsome than Sir Hudson Lowe. Raising a hubbub in order to carry off the duchess seemed shameful to the men. They might as well lay siege to the town and the convent, leaving not a single witness to their victory, as pirates do. For them, this enterprise had therefore only two aspects: either a fire, an armed struggle that would frighten a Europe ignorant of the reason for the crime, or some mysterious aerial abduction that would persuade the nuns that the devil had paid them a visit. This last plan prevailed in the secret council held in Paris before the departure. Then everything had been foreseen for the success of an enterprise that offered these men, bored with the pleasures of Paris, a real caper.

An extremely light pirogue, manufactured in Marseille after a Malaysian model, allowed them to navigate the reefs to a spot where they could go no farther. Two cables of iron wire served as a bridge, such as the Chinese use, going from rock to rock. The reefs were bound together in this way by a system of cables and baskets that resembled those threads on which certain spiders move as they wrap a tree. This was instinctive work, which the Chinese—a people essentially given to imitation—were the first to copy, historically speaking. Neither the crests nor the caprices of the sea could displace these fragile constructions. The cables had enough play to offer the waves that curvature studied by an engineer, the late Cachin, the immortal creator of the harbor at Cherbourg. Against this cunningly devised line the angry sea was helpless; the law of that curve was a secret wrested from nature by the genius of observation, which accounts for nearly all human genius.

Monsieur de Montriveau's companions were all alone on this vessel. They were out of sight of every human eye. The most powerful telescopes manned on the top decks by sailors on passing ships could not have discovered the cables hidden in the reefs or the men hidden in the rocks. After eleven days of preparatory work, these thirteen human devils were able to reach the foot of the cliff, which rose thirty fathoms from the sea. This sheer rock of granite was as difficult for a man to climb as the polished contours of a plain porcelain vase would be for a mouse. Still, there was a cleft, a straight line of fissure where blocks of wood could be firmly wedged about a foot apart, into which these daring workers could nail iron crampons. These crampons, prepared in advance, held by a broad bracket on which they set a step made out of an extremely light plank of pine, and this plank was adapted to the notches of a mast as tall as the promontory and firmly planted in the rock at the shore. With ingenuity worthy of these men of action, one of them, a skillful mathematician, had calculated the angle from which the steps must gradually rise, like a fan, starting at the middle of the mast and reaching its upper end at the top of the rock. This method was repeated in reverse by the steps from below. This stairway, miraculously light and perfectly solid, cost twenty-two days of labor. A phosphorous light and the undertow of the waves would destroy all trace of it forever in a single night. No indiscretion, then, was possible, and no search for the violators of the convent could succeed.

The top of the rock formed a platform with sheer drops on all sides. The thirteen strangers, examining the terrain with telescopes from atop the masthead, were reassured that in spite of some difficulties they could easily reach the gardens of the convent where the trees were thick enough to offer certain shelter. There, no doubt, they would have to decide how to manage the nun's abduction. After such great efforts, they did not want to compromise the success of their enterprise by risking discovery and were obliged to wait until the last quarter of the moon had faded.

Montriveau slept on the rock for two nights, wrapped in his coat. The evensongs and matins filled him with inexpressible joy. He went up to the wall to be able to hear the music of the organ and made an effort to distinguish one voice among the mass of voices. But in spite of the silence, only the jumbled effects of the music reached his ears in the vast space. In those sweet harmonies defects of execution are lost; the pure thought of art alone reaches the soul without demanding efforts of attention or a strain on understanding. For Armand, overwhelming memories of love flowered again whole in this breath of music, in which he wanted to find airborne promises of happiness. The day following the last night, he climbed down before sunrise after several hours inert, with his eyes focused on the window of a cell without a grille. The grilles were not necessary above this abyss. A light shone there all night long. And that instinct of the heart—which is false as often as it is true—had cried to him, "She is there!"

"She is surely there, and tomorrow I will have her," he said to himself, mingling joyous thoughts with the slow tolling of a bell. Odd quirkiness of the heart! He loved even more passionately the nun withering in the yearnings of love, consumed by tears, fasting, and prayer vigils, the woman of twenty-nine tried and tested years, rather than the insouciant young girl, the sylphlike twenty-four-year-old. But men with strong souls have a penchant for sublime expressions that noble misery or impetuous movements of thought have engraved on the face of a woman.

Is the beauty of a sorrowful woman not the most affecting of all for men who feel in their hearts an inexhaustible treasure of consolations and tenderness for a creature so gracious in weakness and strong in feeling? The fresh-faced beauty, smooth-skinned with high coloring, the *pretty woman*, in short, is the popular attraction of ordinary people. Montriveau could not but love those faces in which love awakened amid the folds of sadness and the ruins of melancholy. Does a lover not call forth a new creature by his powerful desires, a young woman, throbbing with life, who breaks through an envelope beautiful for him alone, which the world sees as destroyed? In truth he possesses two women: one who presents herself to others as pale, discolored, sad; the other who dwells in his heart, unseen, an angel who understands life through feeling and appears in all her glory only for the celebrants of love. Before leaving his post, the general heard weak harmonies, sweet voices full of tenderness coming from this cell. Climbing down beneath the rock where his friends were waiting, he told them that never in his life had he felt such captivating bliss, and his few words bore the stamp of that discreet but communicative passion whose imposing expression men always respect.

The following evening, eleven devoted companions ascended in the darkness to the top of the rocks, each of them carrying a dagger, a provision of chocolate, and all the tools required by the thieves' trade. Reaching the surrounding wall, they breached it by means of ladders they had devised in the cemetery of the convent. Montriveau recognized the vaulted long gallery by which he had previously come to the parlor and the windows of that room. On the spot, his plan was made and adopted. Open a passage through the window of that parlor which lit up the section belonging to the Carmelites, penetrate the corridors, see if the names were inscribed on each cell, go to Sister Theresa's cell, surprise her as she slept, and carry her off, bound and gagged. All these aspects of the plan were easy for the men, who combined boldness with a convict's dexterity as well as knowledge peculiar to men of the world, and they were quite prepared to wield their daggers to buy silence.

The grille of the window was sawed apart in two hours. Three men stood guard outside and two others remained in the parlor. The rest were posted, barefoot, at even intervals through the cloister. Young Henri de Marsay, the most nimble man among them, out of caution disguised in a Carmelite's robe identical to the dress of the convent, led the way with Montriveau hidden behind him. The clock struck three just as the false nun and Montriveau reached the dormitory. They had quickly recognized the placement of the cells. Then, hearing no noise, they read with the aid of a dark lantern the names fortunately written on each door and accompanied by those mystic words, those portraits of saints male or female that each nun inscribed in the form of an epigraph for her new life and in which she revealed her last thought. Arriving at the cell of Sister Theresa, Montriveau read this inscription: SUB INVOCATIONE SANCTAE MATRIS THERESAE! The epigraph read: ADOREMUS IN AETER-NUM. Suddenly his companion put a hand on his shoulder and gestured toward the strong beam of light coming through a crack in the door, lighting up the tiles of the corridor. Just then, Monsieur de Ronquerolles joined them.

"All the nuns are at the church and are beginning the Mass for the Dead."

"I will stay here," said Montriveau. "Go back to the parlor and shut the door at the end of the passage."

He rushed into the cell, pushing past his disguised companion, who pulled the veil down over his face. They saw then, in the ante-chamber of the cell, the dead duchess, resting on the ground on her bed board, lit by two candles. Neither Montriveau nor de Marsay said a word or uttered a cry, but they looked at each other. Then the general made a gesture meaning, "Let us carry her off."

"Run," cried Ronquerolles, "the procession of nuns is coming, you will be caught!"

With the magical swiftness prompted by an extreme desire, the dead woman was borne into the parlor, passed through the window, and transported to the foot of the walls, just as the abbess, followed by the nuns, arrived to take the body of Sister Theresa. The sister charged with guarding the dead woman had been imprudent enough to ransack her room in search of secrets and was so busily occupied that she heard nothing; she came out horrified to find the body gone. Before the amazed women thought to conduct a search, the duchess had been lowered by cables down to the rocks, and Montriveau's companions had destroyed their work.

At nine o'clock in the morning, no trace was left of the stairway or the cable bridges; the body of Sister Theresa was on board as the vessel came to the port, collected the sailors, and disappeared into the morning. Montriveau remained alone in his cabin with Antoinette de Navarreins. For some hours it seemed as if her face was transfigured for him by that unearthly beauty that the calm of death gives to our mortal remains.

"Oh, that," said Ronquerolles to Montriveau, when the general reappeared on the deck, "that was a woman, now it is nothing. Let us tie a cannonball to each foot, throw her in the water, and think no more about it than we would about a book we read during childhood."

"Yes," said Montriveau, "for this is now nothing but a poem."

"That is sensible of you. From now on, have passions, but as for love, a man must know how to invest it wisely; only a woman's last love can satisfy a man's first."

Geneva, at Pré-Lévêque, January 26, 1834
Translated by Carol Cosman

ACKNOWLEDGMENTS

My thanks to the three translators who responded to the call for new versions of Balzac, a writer who speaks well in twentieth-century English when expertly made to do so.

My thanks as well to Meera Broome Seth, deft scholar who helped me annotate the stories where needed.

My thanks also to Sara Kramer, editor at New York Review Books and, especially, to Edwin Frank who believed in this project from the beginning and magisterially carried it through to completion.

NOTES

FACINO CANE

11   *provveditore:* A government official in the Venetian Republic.

ANOTHER STUDY OF WOMANKIND

19   *like the dolphin in the fable:* A reference to "The Monkey and the Dolphin," one of Jean de La Fontaine's *Fables* (IV.7).

20   *According to Sterne:* See *Tristram Shandy*, chapter CCCXXXI.

21   *Lord Dudley:* Henri de Marsay is in fact the natural son of Lord Dudley.

27   *a happy Clarissa:* Clarissa Harlowe is the tragic heroine of Samuel Richardson's epistolary novel *Clarissa*.

29   *La Malibran:* A famous singer who was a great success in Paris during the 1830s.

45   *Camille Maupin:* This is Mademoiselle des Touches's literary pseudonym.

46   *Agnès Sorel:* The longtime mistress of Charles VII, who considerably influenced him.

53   "Son'io!": "It's me!"

55   ULTIMAM COGITA: "Think of the end."

57   Il bondo cani: The pseudonym of the caliph who, while incognito, seduces women in *The Caliph of Baghdad*, an opéra comique by François-Adrien Boieldieu.

THE RED INN

73   *our great Carême:* A French chef famous for his gourmet cuisine.

74   *her education at the Gymnase:* A popular theater. Balzac is punning on the German Gymnasium (secondary school).

76   in anima vili: "On the base mind."

93   *imperial:* A card game similar to piquet.

100 *her father refused to acknowledge her ... She's very beautiful and very rich*: In Balzac's *Père Goriot*, we find Mademoiselle Taillefer disowned by her father and living in the Vauquer boardinghouse. However, upon her brother's death (arranged by the scheming Vautrin), she becomes one of the richest heiresses in Paris.

104 *Like virtue, there are different degrees to a crime:* Racine, *Phèdre* (act IV, scene 2).

105 *Doctrinaire Party:* The group of royalists who favored constitutional monarchy during the Bourbon Restoration.

108 *Jeanie Deans's father:* A character in Walter Scott's novel *The Heart of Midlothian*.

SARRASINE

111 *Madame Malibran, Madame Sontag, or Madame Fodor:* Well-known singers of the period.

112 *Antinous:* The beloved of the Roman emperor Hadrian, whose beauty was considered effeminate.

112 *Vespasian's axiom: Pecunia non olet* (Money has no smell).

116 Tancredi: An opera by Rossini which was a great success in Paris around the time "Sarrasine" was published.

121 "Addio, addio!": "Farewell, farewell!"

130 "Poverino!": "Poor fellow!"

133 al Bambino: To the child Jesus.

140 *Girodet's* Endymion: Balzac greatly admired this painting. He initially wrote that it was Girodet (rather than Vien) who copied Sarra-

sine's statue of Zambinella for the Lanty family. A look at the painting suggests its relevance to the theme of the story.

A PASSION IN THE DESERT

142 *Monsieur Martin's menagerie:* In 1819, the animal trainer Henri Martin became the first man to enter a tiger's cage. He also performed a pantomime with lions in 1831, around the time when wild animals were first introduced into the circus.

143 *the expedition undertaken in Upper Egypt:* After the French victory over the Mamluks at the Battle of the Pyramids in 1798, General Desaix received orders from Napoleon to pursue the Mamluk leader Murad Bey, who had fled to Upper Egypt.

148 *simarre:* A woman's long dress or robe.

ADIEU

159 *Article 304 of the Penal Code:* This article mandated the death penalty.

167 *the crossing of the Berezina:* While retreating from Russia, Napoleon's army was forced to make an impromptu crossing of the Berezina River in November 1812, which resulted in tens of thousands of casualties at the Battle of Berezina.

172 *pelisse:* A women's fur-lined coat.

Z. MARCAS

203 *We watched all these developments like theater:* Balzac's narrator in *La Duchesse de Langeais* denounces the insular and static nature of the ruling class of the prior regime.

208 *Dressing up like the Coachman of Longjumeau:* A costume made fashionable by Adolphe Adam's 1836 opéra comique, *The Coachman of Longjumeau.*

210 *Toussaint Louverture:* Toussaint Louverture led the slave rebellion in the French colony of Saint-Domingue (present-day Haiti). Once

slavery was abolished in Saint-Domingue, Louverture allied himself with Napoleon and the French but was ultimately betrayed.

210 *Napoleon, on his rock, babbled like a magpie:* During his exile on the island of Saint Helena, Napoleon dictated to his aide Las Cases his voluminous memoirs, *Le Mémorial de Sainte-Hélène.*

210 *Morey, that Cuauhtémoc of the Montagne Sainte-Geneviève:* Pierre Morey, one of the conspirators in an 1835 plot to assassinate King Louis-Philippe, and Cuauhtémoc, the last Aztec emperor, are both believed to have evinced a stoic resolve while being executed.

211 *He had Berryer's qualities of warmth ... Monsieur Thiers's finesse and skill:* Antoine Pierre Berryer was a lawyer and ardent Legitimist (a conservative royalist who refused to recognize the July Monarchy and favored the Bourbon line over the Orléans); Adolphe Thiers was a politician and liberal adversary of the July Monarchy.

211 *the triumph of the Orléans branch over the elder Bourbon branch:* The July Revolution saw the abdication of King Charles X of the House of Bourbon and the rise to the throne of Louis-Philippe of the cadet Orléans line.

212 *Like a new Bonaparte, he sought his Barras; like Colbert, he hoped to find a Mazarin:* As the commander of the Army of the Interior during the Revolution, Paul Barras appointed Napoleon as his second-in-command in 1795. When Barras became a leader of the Directory, Napoleon replaced him as the commander. Cardinal Mazarin left the management of his personal fortune to Jean-Baptiste Colbert, who eventually succeeded him as minister of finances to Louis XIV.

212 *the requirements of the election law:* In response to the demands made by liberal reformers, in 1831 the French government enacted a law that lessened the monetary requirements for voting eligibility. These measures, however, only allowed the bourgeoisie, not the common people, to gain enfranchisement.

212 *All Richard III wanted was a horse:* An allusion to Shakespeare's *Richard III* (act V, scene 4).

212 *the antipodes of the Luxembourg Palace:* The Luxembourg Palace was the site of the Chamber of Peers, a legislative assembly similar to the modern senate.

214 *Pozzo di Borgo had lived in that condition for a period:* Pozzo di Borgo was a Corsican politician and diplomat who, while negotiating Russia's peace agreement with Austria, was able to escape Napoleon's call for his extradition as a French subject by fleeing Vienna and abstaining from official political activity for a year. Here Balzac alludes to this period, in which Pozzo di Borgo was probably plotting his attack against Napoleon.

216 *Carrel is dead:* Armand Carrel was a journalist who helped to found the daily newspaper *Le National* in 1830. After the July Revolution, Carrel alone managed the paper, which became the primary voice of the opposition. He died in a duel with Émile de Girardin, the founder of the conservative daily *La Presse.*

216 *he hasn't a palace, a stronghold of royal favor, like Metternich; nor like Villèle the sheltering roof of a reliable majority:* Klemens von Metternich was a German prince and influential statesman; Jean-Baptiste de Villèle, a long-serving prime minister, was a leader of the Ultra-Royalists during the Bourbon Restoration.

216 *August 1830:* In the aftermath of the July Revolution, many observed that the new members of Louis-Philippe's administration differed little from those of the Bourbon Restoration.

220 *Emperor Diocletian to the unknown martyr:* Thousands of Christians were martyred under the reign of the Roman emperor Diocletian.

223 *Charles fell silent:* The narrator is revealed to be Charles Rabourdin, son of the protagonist of another Balzac novel, *Les Employés.*

224 *It is too late:* This was allegedly the response that a liberal deputy pronounced to one of Charles X's ministers when he declared that the king would order the annulment of the July Ordinances (which notably limited freedom of the press and appointed reactionary councillors of state).

GOBSECK

226 *she behaved so very badly toward her father:* In Balzac's *Père Goriot,* Madame de Restaud, née Goriot, is ashamed of her father, who has sacrificed everything for his daughters. When he lies dying, she arrives too late to say farewell to him.

227 *the indemnification law restored further enormous sums to her:* Under the reign of Charles X, the Law of Indemnity of 1825 restored to nobles their estates, which had been seized during the Revolution.

229 *Like Fontenelle, he was sparing with his vital energies:* Fontenelle lived to be nearly a hundred years old.

230 *name was Gobseck:* the name in French sounds like Gobe-sec, "gulp dry"

231 *He had known Monsieur de Lally . . . :* Some of the names that follow are of historical figures, while others are fictional.

240 *the* Monsieur Dimanche *scene:* Molière, *Dom Juan* (act IV, scene 3).

249 *the Counts de Horn, the Fouquier-Tinvilles, the Coignards:* The Comte de Horn assassinated Gustav III, the King of Sweden; Fouquier-Tinville was a notorious public prosecutor during the Reign of Terror in the French Revolution; Coignard was an escaped convict who assumed the false title Comte de Sainte-Hélène.

278 *the new Haitian government:* The unification of Haiti and Santo Domingo (present-day Dominican Republic) occurred in 1822 and lasted until 1844.

279 *The Torpedo:* Gobseck's great-grandniece, Esther Gobseck, appears in Balzac's *Splendeurs et misères des courtisanes*. She commits suicide only hours before she would have inherited Gobseck's fortune.

281 *"Who will all these riches go to?":* See previous note. In *Splendeurs et misères des courtisanes*, after Esther's suicide, Gobseck's fortune goes to her lover Lucien de Rubempré. However, he is prevented from marrying the rich Clotilde de Grandlieu when her father finds out the true source of his fortune. Suspected of being connected to Esther's death, Lucien is arrested and ends up committing suicide. Gobseck's fortune then passes to Lucien's relatives and eventually to Vautrin, the criminal mastermind behind Lucien's provisory rise to social prominence.

THE DUCHESSE DE LANGEAIS

285 *the French expedition to Spain:* This expedition took place in 1823.

287 *his* Moses: Rossini's *Moses in Egypt*, which premiered in 1818.

287 *Theater Favart:* A venue at the Paris Opéra-Comique.

288 *"Fleuve du Tage":* Benoît Pollet's song "The River Tagus," which was popular in the 1820s.

289 *alcalde:* The mayor or magistrate of a Spanish town.

293 *The visitor:* A clergyman whose duty is to inspect convents.

296 *a robe whose color has become proverbial:* Pale brown.

305 *knight banneret:* A medieval knight entitled to carry a rectangular banner and lead a military troupe.

305 *Fuggers:* A powerful dynasty of German bankers in the sixteenth century.

307 *its defeat in 1830:* The July Revolution saw the end of the Bourbon Restoration and of the sovereign power of the nobility.

309 *the marriage of Monsieur de Talleyrand:* Talleyrand married an English adventuress.

309 *Madame's:* The title of the Duchesse de Berry.

313 *the uprising of the Hundred Days:* Napoleon escaped from exile on the island of Elba and marched on Paris with an army of men, in a campaign that lasted from March until June, 1815, ending with his defeat at the Battle of Waterloo. Shortly after Waterloo, Louis XVIII returned to power, initiating the second Bourbon Restoration.

315 *Chevalier de Folard:* A French soldier and military writer of the eighteenth century.

318 *Joubert's side at Novi:* At the Battle of Novi in August 1799, the French, led by Barthélemy-Catherine Joubert, were defeated by Austrian and Russian forces. Joubert was killed in the conflict.

318 *the Fontainebleau disaster:* The 1814 Treaty of Fontainebleau stipulated Napoleon's abdication and exile to Elba.

324 The Gardener's Dog: A play by Lope de Vega which illustrates the proverbial theme of the dog in the manger.

327 Faublas: A libertine novel of the late eighteenth century by Louvet de Couvray (the novel's full title is *Les Amours du chevalier de Faublas*).

330 *Crillon hearing the story of Jesus Christ:* Apparently, upon hearing a sermon on the Passion, the sixteenth-century military officer Crillon drew his sword and cried, "Where were you, Crillon?"

337 *"morganatic" unions:* A marriage between a member of the royalty or nobility and an individual of inferior social rank, whose children do not inherit the former's titles and privileges.

338 *the break between Madame de Beauséant and Monsieur d'Ajuda, who, they say, is marrying Mademoiselle de Rochefide:* This story line is depicted in Balzac's *Père Goriot* and continues in *La Femme abandonnée.*

343 nec plus ultra: "Nothing further beyond."

345 Génie du Christianisme: In 1802, Chateaubriand wrote this defense of Christianity in response to attacks made on the faith during the French Revolution.

348 *Sulla:* A prominent Roman statesman who famously marched on Rome, initiating a civil war. He became dictator before abdicating power shortly before his death.

348 *the Battle of Dreux:* A 1562 battle in which the Catholics defeated the Huguenots.

350 Andiam, mio ben: A phrase from the duet "Là ci darem la mano" in Mozart's *Don Giovanni.*

354 *Pyrrhonists:* The disciples of Pyrrho of Elis, an ancient Greek skeptic philosopher.

356 *as Poppaea played with Nero:* Poppaea was the second wife of the Roman emperor Nero. It was widely believed among ancient historians that Nero murdered Poppaea.

364 *place de Grève:* A site of public executions and torture.

368 "Non so": "I don't know."

385 *Paris's ten thousand Sévignés:* The Marquise de Sévigné was a seventeenth-century writer, best known for the letters she wrote to her daughter.

387 *the wigmaker's knife-wielding that so affected Canning in the assize court:* An obscure allusion to the career of the British statesman George Canning.

390 *until some poet comes along to tell:* Alfred de Vigny, in his historical novel *Cinq-Mars.*

390 *Boeotian stupidity:* An allusion to the ancient Greek region of Boeotia.

393 *Monsieur, as he once was... The bad brother who voted so wrongly...
   This philosophical cant will be just as dangerous for his younger brother*:
   The current monarch, "the bad brother," was Louis XVIII. He was
   formerly known as "Monsieur" (the title given to the eldest brother of
   the reigning king) when Louis XVI was on the throne. Charles X was
   the youngest of the three brothers.

396 fideicommissum: In a legal will, a gift that is bequeathed to an intermediary, with the intention that he or she will give it to a third person,
   the desired recipient of the bequest.

396 *young de Horn:* The Count de Horn conspired to assassinate Gustav
   III, the King of Sweden.

398 *The Du Barry woman... the widow Scarron*: Once a courtesan, Madame Du Barry became Louis XV's last official mistress. Madame
   Scarron was widowed prior to coming to court and eventually became
   Louis XIV's second wife (he gave her the title of Marquise de Main-
   tenon).

398 *Not one of your Werthers:* The Romantic hero of Goethe's *The Sorrows
   of Young Werther.*

399 *braving the Duke de Modena's daggers:* After marrying the Duke de
   Modena against her wishes, the daughter of the Regent for Louis XV,
   Charlotte-Aglaé d'Orléans, was visited by her former lover the Duc de
   Richelieu.

399 *Monsieur de Jaucourt's little finger:* Surprised by the return of his mistress's husband, the Marquis de Jaucourt hid himself in a cabinet. Jaucourt's finger was crushed in the door, but he did not cry out.

399 *Königsmarck's mistress:* Philip Christoph von Königsmarck was murdered shortly after attempting to elope with his mistress, the wife of
   the elector of Hanover. It was rumored that Königsmarck's body was
   buried under the floorboards.

401 *Mambrino's helmet:* In Cervantes's novel, Don Quixote takes a bar-
   ber's bowl to be the Moorish king Mambrino's golden helmet and
   wears it on his head, believing it will render him invincible.

406 *Duchesse de La Vallière:* Louis XIV's first mistress, who became a Carmelite nun.

410 *the way General Lamarque had conquered in the assault on Capri:* General Lamarque led a surprise attack on the British (commanded by Sir Hudson Lowe—see the next note), who occupied Capri at the time.

410 *Sir Hudson Lowe:* The British general and governor of Saint Helena when Napoleon was exiled on the island. Lowe was criticized for his severe treatment of Napoleon.

414 SUB INVOCATIONE SANCTAE MATRIS THERESAE!*:* Under the invocation of the holy mother Theresa!

414 ADOREMUS IN AETERNUM*:* Let us adore [her] for eternity.

TITLES IN SERIES

For a complete list of titles, visit www.nyrb.com or write to:
Catalog Requests, NYRB, 435 Hudson Street, New York, NY 10014

J.R. ACKERLEY Hindoo Holiday*
J.R. ACKERLEY My Dog Tulip*
J.R. ACKERLEY My Father and Myself*
J.R. ACKERLEY We Think the World of You*
HENRY ADAMS The Jeffersonian Transformation
RENATA ADLER Pitch Dark*
RENATA ADLER Speedboat*
CÉLESTE ALBARET Monsieur Proust
DANTE ALIGHIERI The Inferno
DANTE ALIGHIERI The New Life
KINGSLEY AMIS The Alteration*
KINGSLEY AMIS Girl, 20*
KINGSLEY AMIS The Green Man*
KINGSLEY AMIS Lucky Jim*
KINGSLEY AMIS The Old Devils*
KINGSLEY AMIS One Fat Englishman*
WILLIAM ATTAWAY Blood on the Forge
W.H. AUDEN (EDITOR) The Living Thoughts of Kierkegaard
W.H. AUDEN W.H. Auden's Book of Light Verse
ERICH AUERBACH Dante: Poet of the Secular World
DOROTHY BAKER Cassandra at the Wedding*
DOROTHY BAKER Young Man with a Horn*
J.A. BAKER The Peregrine
S. JOSEPHINE BAKER Fighting for Life*
HONORÉ DE BALZAC The Human Comedy: Selected Stories*
HONORÉ DE BALZAC The Unknown Masterpiece *and* Gambara*
MAX BEERBOHM Seven Men
STEPHEN BENATAR Wish Her Safe at Home*
FRANS G. BENGTSSON The Long Ships*
ALEXANDER BERKMAN Prison Memoirs of an Anarchist
GEORGES BERNANOS Mouchette
ADOLFO BIOY CASARES Asleep in the Sun
ADOLFO BIOY CASARES The Invention of Morel
CAROLINE BLACKWOOD Corrigan*
CAROLINE BLACKWOOD Great Granny Webster*
NICOLAS BOUVIER The Way of the World
MALCOLM BRALY On the Yard*
MILLEN BRAND The Outward Room*
SIR THOMAS BROWNE Religio Medici and Urne-Buriall*
JOHN HORNE BURNS The Gallery
ROBERT BURTON The Anatomy of Melancholy
CAMARA LAYE The Radiance of the King
GIROLAMO CARDANO The Book of My Life
DON CARPENTER Hard Rain Falling*
J.L. CARR A Month in the Country*
BLAISE CENDRARS Moravagine
EILEEN CHANG Love in a Fallen City

* *Also available as an electronic book.*

TAYEB SALIH Season of Migration to the North
TAYEB SALIH The Wedding of Zein*
JEAN-PAUL SARTRE We Have Only This Life to Live: Selected Essays. 1939–1975
GERSHOM SCHOLEM Walter Benjamin: The Story of a Friendship*
DANIEL PAUL SCHREBER Memoirs of My Nervous Illness
JAMES SCHUYLER Alfred and Guinevere
JAMES SCHUYLER What's for Dinner?*
SIMONE SCHWARZ-BART The Bridge of Beyond*
LEONARDO SCIASCIA The Day of the Owl
LEONARDO SCIASCIA Equal Danger
LEONARDO SCIASCIA The Moro Affair
LEONARDO SCIASCIA To Each His Own
LEONARDO SCIASCIA The Wine-Dark Sea
VICTOR SEGALEN René Leys*
ANNA SEGHERS Transit*
PHILIPE-PAUL DE SÉGUR Defeat: Napoleon's Russian Campaign
GILBERT SELDES The Stammering Century*
VICTOR SERGE The Case of Comrade Tulayev*
VICTOR SERGE Conquered City*
VICTOR SERGE Memoirs of a Revolutionary
VICTOR SERGE Unforgiving Years
SHCHEDRIN The Golovlyov Family
ROBERT SHECKLEY The Store of the Worlds: The Stories of Robert Sheckley*
GEORGES SIMENON Act of Passion*
GEORGES SIMENON Dirty Snow*
GEORGES SIMENON The Engagement
GEORGES SIMENON Monsieur Monde Vanishes*
GEORGES SIMENON Pedigree*
GEORGES SIMENON Red Lights
GEORGES SIMENON The Strangers in the House
GEORGES SIMENON Three Bedrooms in Manhattan*
GEORGES SIMENON Tropic Moon*
GEORGES SIMENON The Widow*
CHARLES SIMIC Dime-Store Alchemy: The Art of Joseph Cornell
MAY SINCLAIR Mary Olivier: A Life*
TESS SLESINGER The Unpossessed: A Novel of the Thirties*
VLADIMIR SOROKIN Ice Trilogy*
VLADIMIR SOROKIN The Queue
NATSUME SŌSEKI The Gate*
DAVID STACTON The Judges of the Secret Court*
JEAN STAFFORD The Mountain Lion
CHRISTINA STEAD Letty Fox: Her Luck
GEORGE R. STEWART Names on the Land
STENDHAL The Life of Henry Brulard
ADALBERT STIFTER Rock Crystal
THEODOR STORM The Rider on the White Horse
JEAN STROUSE Alice James: A Biography*
HOWARD STURGIS Belchamber
ITALO SVEVO As a Man Grows Older
HARVEY SWADOS Nights in the Gardens of Brooklyn
A.J.A. SYMONS The Quest for Corvo
ELIZABETH TAYLOR Angel*